THE
ANDY McNAB
DOSSIER

CONFIDENTIAL

www.andymcnab.co.uk

ANDY McNAB

⮕ In 1984 he was 'badged' as a member of 22 SAS Regiment.

⮕ Over the course of the next nine years he was at the centre of covert operations on five continents.

⮕ During the first Gulf War he commanded Bravo Two Zero, a patrol that, in the words of his commanding officer, 'will remain in regimental history for ever'.

⮕ Awarded both the Distinguished Conduct Medal (DCM) and Military Medal (MM) during his military career.

⮕ McNab was the British Army's most highly decorated serving soldier when he finally left the SAS in February 1993.

⮕ He is a patron of the *Help for Heroes* campaign.

⮕ He is now the author of seventeen bestselling thrillers, as well as three Quick Read novels, *The Grey Man*, *Last Night Another Soldier* and *Today Everything Changes*. He has also edited *Spoken from the Front*, an oral history of the conflict in Afghanistan.

50 p

BRAVO TWO ZERO

In January 1991, eight members of the SAS regiment, under the command of Sergeant Andy McNab, embarked upon a top secret mission in Iraq to infiltrate them deep behind enemy lines. Their call sign: 'Bravo Two Zero'.

IMMEDIATE ACTION

The no-holds-barred account of an extraordinary life, from the day McNab as a baby was found in a carrier bag on the steps of Guy's Hospital to the day he went to fight in the Gulf War. As a delinquent youth he kicked against society. As a young soldier he waged war against the IRA in the streets and fields of South Armagh.

SEVEN TROOP

Andy McNab's gripping story of the time he served in the company of a remarkable band of brothers. The things they saw and did during that time would take them all to breaking point – and some beyond – in the years that followed. He who dares doesn't always win . . .

Nick Stone titles

Nick Stone, ex-SAS trooper, now gun-for-hire working on deniable ops for the British government, is the perfect man for the dirtiest of jobs, doing whatever it takes by whatever means necessary…

REMOTE CONTROL
⊕ Dateline: Washington DC, USA

Stone is drawn into the bloody killing of an ex-SAS officer and his family and soon finds himself on the run with the one survivor who can identify the killer – a seven-year-old girl.

'Proceeds with a testosterone surge' *Daily Telegraph*

CRISIS FOUR
⊕ Dateline: North Carolina, USA

In the backwoods of the American South, Stone has to keep alive the beautiful young woman who holds the key to unlock a chilling conspiracy that will threaten world peace.

'When it comes to thrills, he's Forsyth class' *Mail on Sunday*

FIREWALL
⊕ Dateline: Finland

The kidnapping of a Russian Mafia warlord takes Stone into the heart of the global espionage world and into conflict with some of the most dangerous killers around.

'Other thriller writers do their research, but McNab has actually been there' *Sunday Times*

LAST LIGHT
⊕ Dateline: Panama

Stone finds himself at the centre of a lethal conspiracy involving ruthless Colombian mercenaries, the US government and Chinese big business. It's an uncomfortable place to be . . .

'A heart thumping read' *Mail on Sunday*

LIBERATION DAY
⊕ Dateline: Cannes, France

Behind its glamorous exterior, the city's seething underworld is the battleground for a very dirty drugs war and Stone must reach deep within himself to fight it on their terms.

'McNab's great asset is that the heart of his fiction is non-fiction' *Sunday Times*

DARK WINTER
⊕ Dateline: Malaysia

A straightforward action on behalf of the War on Terror turns into a race to escape his past for Stone if he is to save himself and those closest to him.

'Addictive . . . Packed with wild action and revealing tradecraft' *Daily Telegraph*

DEEP BLACK
⊕ Dateline: Bosnia

All too late Stone realizes that he is being used as bait to lure into the open a man whom the darker forces of the West will stop at nothing to destroy.

'One of the UK's top thriller writers' *Daily Express*

AGGRESSOR
⊕ **Dateline: Georgia, former Soviet Union**

A longstanding debt of friendship to an SAS comrade takes Stone on a journey where he will have to risk everything to repay what he owes, even his life . . .

'A terrific novelist' *Mail on Sunday*

RECOIL
⊕ **Dateline: The Congo, Africa**

What starts out as a personal quest for a missing woman quickly becomes a headlong rush from his own past for Stone.

'Stunning . . . A first class action thriller' *Sun*

CROSSFIRE
⊕ **Dateline: Kabul**

Nick Stone enters the modern day wild west that is Afghanistan in search of a kidnapped reporter.

'Authentic to the core . . . McNab at his electrifying best' *Daily Express*

BRUTE FORCE
⊕ **Dateline: Tripoli**

An undercover operation is about to have deadly long term consequences . . .

'Violent and gripping, this is classic McNab' *News of the World*

EXIT WOUND
⊕ Dateline: Dubai

Nick Stone embarks on a quest to track down the killer of two ex-SAS comrades.

'Could hardly be more topical . . . all the elements of a McNab novel are here' *Mail on Sunday*

ZERO HOUR
⊕ Dateline: Amsterdam

A code that will jam every item of military hardware from Kabul to Washington. A terrorist group who nearly have it in their hands. And a soldier who wants to go down fighting . . .

'Like his creator, the ex-SAS soldier turned uber-agent is unstoppable' *Daily Mirror*

DEAD CENTRE
⊕ Dateline: Somalia

A Russian oligarch's young son is the Somalian pirates' latest kidnap victim. His desperate father contacts the only man with the know-how, the means and the guts to get his boy back. At any cost . . .

'Sometimes only the rollercoaster ride of an action-packed thriller hits the spot. No one delivers them as professionally or as plentifully as SAS soldier turned author McNab' *Guardian*

Andy McNab and Kym Jordan's new series of novels traces the inter-woven stories of one platoon's experience of warfare in the twenty-first century. Packed with the searing danger and high-octane excitement of modern combat, it also explores the impact of its aftershocks upon the soldiers themselves, and upon those who love them. It will take you straight into the heat of battle and the hearts of those who are burned by it.

WAR TORN

Two tours of Iraq under his belt, Sergeant Dave Henley has seen something of how modern battles are fought. But nothing can prepare him for the posting to Forward Operating Base Senzhiri, Helmand Province, Afghanistan. This is a warzone like even he's never seen before.

'Andy McNab's books get better and better. *War Torn* brilliantly portrays the lives of a platoon embarking on a tour of duty in Helmand province' *Daily Express*

BATTLE LINES

Coming back from war is never easy, as Sergeant Dave Henley's platoon discovers all too quickly when they return from Afghanistan – to find that home can be an equally searing battlefield. When they are summoned to Helmand once more, to protect the US team assigned to destroy the opium crop, it is almost a relief to the soldiers. But now Dave's team must learn new skills to survive, while their loved ones in England find their lives can be ripped apart by prejudice, corrosive anger, harsh mis-understanding and ugly rumour.

Meet Andy McNab's explosive new creation, **Sergeant Tom Buckingham**:

RED NOTICE

Deep beneath the English Channel, a small army of Russian terrorists has seized control of the Eurostar to Paris, taken four hundred hostages at gunpoint – and declared war on a government that has more than its own fair share of secrets to keep. One man stands in their way. An off-duty SAS soldier is hiding somewhere inside the train. Alone and injured, he's the only chance the passengers and crew have of getting out alive.

ANDY McNAB
& KYM JORDAN
BATTLE LINES

CORGI BOOKS

TRANSWORLD PUBLISHERS
61–63 Uxbridge Road, London W5 5SA
A Random House Group Company
www.transworldbooks.co.uk

BATTLE LINES
A CORGI BOOK: 9780552161435
9780552168991

First published in Great Britain
in 2012 by Bantam Press
an imprint of Transworld Publishers
Corgi edition published 2013

Addresses for Random House Group Ltd companies outside the UK
can be found at: www.randomhouse.co.uk
The Random House Group Ltd Reg. No. 954009

The Random House Group Limited supports The Forest Stewardship
Council® (FSC®), the leading international forest-certification
organisation. Our books carrying the FSC label are printed on
FSC®-certified paper. FSC is the only forest-certification scheme
supported by the leading environmental organisations, including
Greenpeace. Our paper procurement policy can be found at
www.randomhouse.co.uk/environment

Typeset in 10.75/13pt Palatino by Falcon Oast Graphic Art Ltd.
Printed and bound by CPI Group (UK) Ltd, Croydon, CR0 4YY.

2 4 6 8 10 9 7 5 3 1

BATTLE LINES

Prologue

They lay motionless on the cave's rocky ledge, straining to hear in the extreme darkness. Dave wasn't sure if that deafening thud was his own heart or the combined hearts of all four of them, thumping in unison against the rock.

Sure enough, there were voices. At first it sounded like just a couple of men. Good. With the element of surprise on their side they could deal with a couple. But then more voices joined the others, calling from outside. They were climbing the steep ridge, silenced by the gradient until they reached the cave.

Then he heard a dog bark. Shit! Another dog snapped back at it and the barking that followed reassured him that these animals were not following a scent. They were arguing over essentials like food and resting places. Dave felt the hairs on the back of his neck stand up when he realized that the men were coming up to the cave to stay here. For the rest of the night, perhaps. Maybe for longer.

His heart ached. They had come so far. In their lives. And on their journey tonight. Was this as far as they were destined to travel? For a few moments he allowed himself to give in to despair. It was as black and cold and rocky as the cave itself, only despair had a much smaller exit.

A few moments later, voices entered the cave. He did not hear anyone strike a match but a hand held up a tiny flame. By its light Dave saw dark faces, moistened with sweat, eyes bright. He could not count how many. The hand holding the match stretched out so that the light flickered around the cave walls. Dave did not breathe. He shut his eyes as the light neared his face. The other lads all had their heads down and were pretty well undetectable unless someone happened to climb up here. In which case, they were dead. Because he had time to see an AK47 thrown carelessly across a shoulder before the light blinked out.

So these men were not wandering camel-keepers or local goat-herders who had scrambled up here for the night to rest. They were Taliban. They perceived no danger. They made no attempt to drop their voices. They called to each other and one man shouted at the dogs to get outside. Dave thought the whole cave must stink of terror, the terror of four silent, trapped British soldiers. But the insurgents chatted amiably among themselves, oblivious to their presence.

1

You could hear the clock tick. The freezing night was silent. There was not a gust of wind or the sound of a distant motor. The darkness out there seemed to crouch, motionless, like an animal waiting to pounce on its prey.

Dave heard someone flinging open the door and a moment later a blast of icy air hit him. He didn't turn around. He focused. Steadily, quietly, he reached out.

The beer glass stung his hand it was so cold, cold enough to have been sitting in the snow. He lifted it, gulped and swallowed. Shit. It scratched his throat it was so icy. He put the glass down heavily in disgust. He had been looking forward to a quiet pint slipping down easily and instead the beer was half-frozen. He glared at the barman's back.

Someone was standing next to him now.

'Bloody hell, Sarge, the missus has got a strop on tonight.' Simon Curtis, corporal of 3 Section in Dave's platoon, was trying to attract the barman's attention.

'Are you talking about my missus or yours, Si?'

Curtis's face was red, as though he was still arguing with his wife.

'If there was yelling over at yours I wouldn't have

heard it. On account of all the yelling over at mine.'

The door opened again.

'Fucking hell!' said a voice.

'Evening, Jonas,' Dave said.

'My bird's giving me so much shit I'm not putting up with it,' said Lance Corporal Danny Jones from 2 Section. 'I mean, I'm just not fucking having it. All I did was pay the car tax. And she's: I already did it! Who do you think you are? And I'm like: Duh, I'm the bloke who owns the car. And she's: Don't you come back here thinking you're going to tell me what to do! And I haven't told her what to do, I've just tried to pay the fucking car tax and I'm—'

'Spare us the details, Jonas,' said Dave, catching the barman's eye by glowering at him, 'and I'll buy you a pint. We've heard it all before.'

'Not from me you haven't, Sarge. Me and my bird don't do a lot of arguing.'

'From you, from me, from everyone.'

The door slammed behind them.

'Dave!'

This time Dave turned around in surprise. Corporal Sol Kasanita from 1 Section seldom came to the pub. Dave looked at Sol's wide, dark face carefully. You had to know the Fijian well to know when he was ruffled and right now he was angry or upset or both.

'Anything up with Adi?' Dave asked cautiously.

'Adi and me don't ever fight, not ever, and guess what? Tonight she shouted at me!'

'Never had a cross word until tonight?' asked Si Curtis sceptically. 'Not ever?'

'Listen, we get annoyed with each other sometimes and she goes sort of cold on me but *shouting*? If anybody shouts in my house it's me.'

'Don't suppose you'll have a pint?' Dave asked him. 'In the circumstances?' He knew that Sol sometimes did drink with the other Fijians at the camp, but Sol had never yet shared a pint with him.

'Nah, it's orange and lemonade for me.'

'Ice?' demanded the barman.

'Ice, no way, I just slipped on some of that outside. It's enough to make you fantasize about Helmand.'

'Yeah,' agreed a few voices nostalgically.

'The way the sweat used to run down your back all the time, I sort of miss it,' said Danny Jones.

'Run faster in the morning, Jonas, and you'll sweat more,' Dave told him.

More men arrived. Everybody was moaning. After another pint Gerry McKinley and Andy Kirk of 2 Section were admitting to a group of mates that Christmas with the family hadn't been much fun.

'You forget,' said Gerry McKinley, 'when you're in a hot FOB dreaming of a white Christmas with your kids opening presents around the tree, you forget that they start at four in the morning and your fucking mother-in-law's around the tree too.'

By the time Rifleman Adam Bacon walked in, the pub was heaving with men who had escaped from home. He paused to stare at the crowds and then saw Dave at the bar.

'Hello, Streaky,' said Dave. 'My round, what are you having? I thought you were in Wolverhampton.'

Streaky avoided his eye. 'Came back, Sarge.'

Dave looked at him closely and saw that the dark face had closed in on itself.

'It's just my little brothers are in my bedroom now and . . . well, everything round my manor's a bit different, see, since I went away.'

They joined the others and Sol, who was Streaky's section commander, greeted him warmly. 'So you came back early. That proves the barracks is your home now.'

Sol and Dave both caught the look of sadness which flickered rapidly across Bacon's face before it disappeared behind his pint.

'Fighting out in theatre can change you,' said Dave. 'So sometimes lads don't always fit straight back in when they go home.'

'Yeah,' said Streaky. They waited for him to say more but he just looked down at his pint. Finally he asked: 'Where's Mal and Angry tonight then?'

'I saw them going back into barracks,' Sol told him.

Streaky said: 'They can't have run out of money this early in the month.'

'They left when they realized that this place is full of men getting away from the missus tonight,' said Dave.

Streaky continued to look around.

'Everyone here married except me?'

'Soon we'll all be fucking divorced,' said Jonas.

'Too right,' agreed Si Curtis.

'Yeah,' McKinley and Kirk said grimly.

'Lads, this is normal,' Dave told them. 'The more often you go away the more you get used to it. There's banners and flags and hugs and tears when the coach pulls in. And a few weeks later they're ripping us apart.'

'They're all weeping at the medals parade . . .' Sol began.

'And screaming at us before we've got the fucking things mounted,' Jonas finished.

Dave nodded. 'That's the way it always is. There's usually a bit of truce for the holidays and Christmas, then the yelling starts again. Lasts around three months as a rule.'

'Well, if she thinks she can manage without me, let her try!' muttered Jonas. 'I don't mind moving back into barracks.'

'This is no time to make decisions like that,' Dave told him.

'I've been to the supermarket three fucking times in two days for Rose and every time I get back I've spent a fortune and she still yells at me,' said Gerry McKinley. 'And the supermarket's mad this time of year, it's like an FOB under fire.'

'Forward Operating Base Tesco,' agreed Sol.

'Three fucking times,' muttered Gerry again. 'In two days. Then I get home with almost nothing left in my wallet and the mother-in-law's there talking to Rose about some nursery school which costs an arm and a leg.'

'I've heard about that place,' said Dave uncomfortably. That was how tonight's row with Jenny had started: when she announced that she was going to look at some posh, expensive nursery school for Vicky.

'I keep telling Tiff there's one in camp. Why are they all suddenly saying they want to drive miles and pay a fortune somewhere else?' demanded Si.

'Bloody ridiculous,' agreed Andy Kirk. 'We get paid a bit extra for going out to theatre and they want to blow it on some nursery school.'

'Have you seen what that place wants for a deposit?' asked Gerry. 'Let alone the fees.'

Si shook his head. 'It all leads to one thing: no sex. I mean it. You think about sex all the time you're away and then you come back and after a while you're shouting at each other and what's the outcome? No fucking sex.'

'Welcome back to reality,' said Sol.

'Yeah, well maybe we don't like this reality,' said Gerry McKinley.

'Being in theatre,' added Andy Kirk. 'That's the best reality.'

Many heads nodded in agreement.

Dave sipped his beer. Now that the pub was busy its temperature had risen a little. He felt the velvety liquid slip down his throat.

'They're adjusting; we're adjusting,' he said evenly. 'Just go with the flow.'

'So have you had a row with Jenny, then?' asked Sol.

Mid-swallow, the beer turned thin and cold and scratchy.

'Well . . . yes,' Dave admitted. 'Because Jenny's heard about this new nursery. And we're both sleep-deprived because the baby's had a cold. And . . .'

'And,' said Sol, 'it's nicer at the pub tonight.'

'Fucking right it is,' Gerry McKinley said. Everyone agreed and took another swig of beer.

Dave looked around at their faces. The same features as in Afghanistan but back here their expressions were different. They stood in the pub looking discontented, their eyes dull, their backs rounded. They'd been home only a few months and in that time they had changed. Most had put on weight; a few had developed beer paunches. And they had all lost the lean, alert look of front-line soldiers.

Jenny Henley was still livid with Dave when she sat down at the computer and began to look for a job. Leanne and Rose were coming over but she had a few minutes before they arrived. If the baby didn't wake up again.

She couldn't exactly remember all the words she and

Dave had hurled at each other tonight but it had started when Jenny said she wanted to see the new nursery school everyone was talking about. Dave thought it cost too much. Jenny said the staff at the camp nursery school weren't interested in the children and didn't supervise them properly. Dave said Vicky had to learn to stick up for herself some time and why spend all that money to take her out of the camp and away from her friends? From there they had argued about money in general, reverting to familiar firing positions. Jenny said that Dave could earn a lot more outside the army and he said didn't she know there was a recession and if she thought there were so many jobs out there why didn't she get one herself?

And wasn't it then that he'd said it? Said that thing? Said that she was turning out just like her mother? *The bastard*.

Her fingers clattered across the keys. She found the jobs website of the local newspaper. Jenny had been working at a travel agency when she met Dave. But in the time it had taken to have two children travel agents had all but evaporated, so there was no point looking for that sort of job again. She needed something part-time which would bring in enough cash to make a good nursery school for Vicky affordable. As for baby Jaime, she would pay someone nice to take her for a few hours a week: maybe Adi.

Jenny scanned *JobsJobsJobs: General*. There were a surprising number advertised. But they all seemed to start with questions to which the answer was no. *Could fostering be your next challenge? Are you a campaigner? Do you have experience of fund-raising? Are you a carer with a car and the right attitude? Can you work nights? Are you ready to get on in sales? Do you have a degree in Hotel*

Management? Are you a nurse who'd like to get back into nursing? Always wanted to work with children?

She tried *JobsJobsJobs: Administrative and Office.* Most were full-time but there was one vacancy for a part-time medical receptionist. *Presentable appearance, pleasant manner, ability to work under pressure and good typing skills required.* She decided to apply and then found she had to submit a curriculum vitae electronically. She had been taught how to write a CV at school but that seemed a long time ago. And what would she write now? 'As a mother of two I have highly developed coping skills. My nappy-changing is second to none. All army wives, especially those who are married to front-line soldiers, have daily experience of stress management.'

She widened her search. *Nanny needed for busy, cheerful family . . . Trainee negotiator for estate agency, must work weekends . . . Assistant required for popular city bakery.* That one sounded OK. *No early mornings, training given, uniform provided. Must have experience dealing with the public and an enthusiasm for home-cooked, quality produce.* She closed her eyes and imagined the smell of fresh bread. The bakery was a nice one in the city with fancy breads and continental cakes covered in fruit. It was the sort of place you went if you wanted to buy a treat. It would be full of smiling people buying cakes for happy occasions.

She noticed the closing date. Tomorrow. *Applications in writing.* She would have to do it quickly and drive it over to Market Street.

She wrote:

My last job involved helping clients choose the right holiday destination. Whether people sat

down for an hour or just put their head around
the door, I enjoyed establishing the kind of
relationships which encourage customer loyalty.
Finally, I enjoy cooking myself and have a passion
for good food which I like to share.

She was so engrossed that she hardly heard the quiet
tap at the door. Leanne Buckle and Rose McKinley
stood there grinning and holding a bottle of white wine.

They greeted each other in quiet voices. Everybody in
this street spoke quietly after about seven in the evening
because every house had small children. Dave and
Jenny's bitter row earlier had been conducted entirely
in whispers.

'You didn't need to bring a bottle, I've got one in the
fridge,' said Jenny.

Leanne stepped inside and small, thin Rose behind
her was completely eclipsed by her vast frame.

'So we drink two!' Her whisper was loud. Everything
about Leanne was loud. 'We're celebrating!'

'What are we celebrating?' asked Jenny. They
followed her to the kitchen and plonked themselves
down at the small table as she reached for glasses.

Leanne looked mysterious.

'I've got some news,' she said. 'I'll tell you when I'm
wrapped around the outside of a glass of vino.'

'Did Steve mind staying with the boys?' asked Jenny.

Leanne grimaced. 'I didn't ask him if he minded.'

'My mum came over to look after the kids,' said Rose.
'Gerry's at the pub with Dave and the lads.'

Jenny rolled her eyes. 'I'm sure they meet up there to
moan about their wives.'

'Bastards,' said Leanne. 'They're all bastards.'

Jenny thought about Dave. She knew he wasn't a

bastard. Her fury had drained away now, leaving her exhausted, as if she had spent the evening running instead of arguing. How could they both have been so angry? Dave had stood right here in the kitchen, his hands on his hips, the features which she loved and had longed to see all the time he was away contorted with the effort of containing his anger to a whisper.

She was still holding the bottle of wine. Leanne took it gently from her and poured it.

'Get this down you, Jenn,' she said.

'Come on!' said Rose. 'Before that baby screams.'

They clinked glasses. Jenny's felt cold in her hand. She sipped the wine and found it pleasantly sharp. It smelled of fruit. Suddenly she thought of summer, of sitting out in the back garden with Dave while Vicky played contentedly on the lawn in the evening sunshine before bed. But not last summer. Because last summer he had been in Afghanistan. While she had been giving birth to Jaime.

'This is nice!' she said, picking up the bottle. Dave had started to develop a liking for wine in the last year or two and she had bought him a book about it for Christmas. Then, while he was away in theatre, she'd read it herself. She studied the label now. 'I think it's a good one.'

'It's out of that case of booze the platoon commander gave us.'

'Gordon Weeks?'

'Yep. Steve hardly knew the bloke.' Steve had been casevaced home at the start of the last tour. 'People keep giving us things because of Steve's leg. He only has to go into the pub and everyone buys him a pint.'

'Does he get legless?' Rose asked. Jenny gave a dutiful guffaw. Leanne frowned and topped up her glass.

'Yeah, well,' she said. 'Excuse me if I don't laugh but

there probably isn't a legless joke left on earth which I haven't heard.'

'Sorry, Leanne.' Rose flushed. She had a small, round face with skin which reddened so easily to the colour of her hair that it seemed transparent.

'Come on then, Leanne,' Jenny said. 'Tell us your news.'

Lance Corporal Billy Finn was in a pub with old photos and horse brasses on the wall which could have been anywhere but happened to be near Kempton Park. He looked around. Nothing interesting about the place. Nothing interesting about the people. Old men. Few women.

On the TV at the end of the bar was today's horse racing from Kempton. It was the two thirty all over again. A mate had given Finn an insider's tip and it had seemed worth driving to Kempton to enjoy the sight of his 25 to 1 punt romping home first. Over the day the odds with the course bookies had shortened and he had felt more and more confident.

The race had begun and the horse had leaped into the lead and then stayed a nose ahead of the field. It was a good jumper and, watching it sail over the hurdles, Finn experienced that soaring feeling he loved, a surge of joy which could turn a grey, cold day into summer and the chapped, red faces of the race-goers beautiful. His heart lifted and beat faster to a new rhythm of its own. His horse would be first past the post and then everything else would be right with the world too. Because when one thing went well, the rest fell into place . . .

'They're showing the two thirty from Kempton!' said an old man at the bar standing next to him. 'Just you watch number three, Asbo Boy!'

On the screen, Finn's horse was again leaping out of

27

the starting stalls and leading the field by a nose, its mane and tail flying. Finn allowed his spirits to soar briefly once more even though he knew what would happen next.

There it was, number three, a big, dull thug, more elephant than horse, lumbering up on the inside. There was another, a bay, close behind it. Finn blinked slowly and, when he opened his eyes, number three was loping past his horse and the bay was just about to. Behind them the sky was leaden and the faces of the punters pinched and cold.

'Gooo on!' roared the old man at the screen as Asbo Boy passed the winning post.

'Have any money on that?' asked Finn.

'Yep, a tenner!' announced the old man proudly.

'On Asbo Boy? At sixty-six to one?' demanded Finn in disbelief.

'I saw him in the paddock and I said to myself: That's the one. I reckon I've got an eye for a good horse.'

Finn glanced at the man, who was probably over a hundred years old and wore such thick glasses that he could hardly see his pint, let alone a good horse.

Finn sighed. After Asbo Boy and the bay had pushed his horse into third place, the rest of the afternoon had been predictable. Loser after loser. Finn had been glad to get into his new car – well, second-hand new – and zoom away from the racecourse. But then he had felt an itch in his throat which said he needed a pint.

The old man at the bar was still smiling. 'Sixty-six to one!' he repeated happily.

'It's a great feeling,' said Finn. 'When your horse overtakes the field.'

'Yeah. There's nothing else sets your heart beating like that by the time you get to my age.'

Finn drank his pint thoughtfully. Afghanistan made your heart beat a lot faster than any race could. Fighting in theatre was real excitement. Racing was just pretend excitement because it didn't really matter who won. You could make it matter by having a bet. But in Afghanistan you realized that racing wasn't real. There, your heart beat every time you got out of a wagon into the hot, harsh terrain, knowing the enemy might be anywhere and your life could depend on your eyes and your wits and your speed with a rifle. The races were a poor substitute for that. Everything at home in England was flat and dull in comparison. Suddenly, surprisingly, piercingly, Finn felt a longing to go back.

Rifleman Mal Bilaal sat in the barracks under the No Smoking sign and made a roll-up. Rifleman Angus McCall, propped up against a bed, watched him.

'You going home for the weekend, Angry?' asked Mal.

'Nah. It's not long since I saw my mum. And too fucking soon since I seen my dad.'

'What about your mates, then?'

'My old mates are nothing but a bunch of tossers,' spat Angus. 'All the time I've been slotting the Taliban for real they haven't done nothing but hang around in the same old places and play CoD. And when I try telling them what it's really like out there, they don't want to know. Tossers.'

It didn't take much to turn Angry from brooding to apoplectic. Mal passed him a roll-up and then started on his own. He said: 'My mum and dad are talking about coming down again.'

Mal's family had travelled all the way from Manchester to see him a couple of weeks ago. Angus had been

29

shocked when they walked in because Mal drank and got off with fit girls in clubs just like any normal person. But when Angus saw his family he had to admit to himself that Mal wasn't normal. Because he was a Muslim.

His dad was brown-skinned and smiling. A couple of Mal's sisters, one in particular, were downright fit. But his mum! She dressed like the civilians in Afghanistan. She didn't actually wear a sheet thing all over her face but she had a scarf across her hair. And when she spoke she sounded like she'd only just got off the boat. It had taken all Angus's concentration to understand what she was saying. He'd nodded and grinned while she held his big hand somehow inside her tiny one, talking to him until Mal dragged her off. Despite the clothes and scarf, the woman had shown him a lot of respect. Angus tried to imagine his own mother greeting one of his mates so warmly. Impossible. And impossible to imagine his dad looking at Angus with the same pride and affection Mr Bilaal showed his son.

'Your mum's really nice,' Angus said now to Mal. Mal lay back and blew a thin line of smoke from the skinny roll-up.

'I'm fucking worried about her. It's driving me crazy that there's people in Wythenshawe out to get my mum.'

Angus laughed. 'Out to get your mum? *Get?* Your *mum?*'

Mal nodded. His face was beginning to narrow with anger. His eyes widened; his voice was raised.

'And my dad and all of them. Because there's some people in Wythenshawe don't agree with me fighting my Muslim brothers out in Afghanistan. And you know how they show it? They've put petrol and flames through her letterbox. Proper fucked up the carpet, and she likes to keep it nice.'

Angry breathed out noisily. 'Whooooar. They could kill your mum and dad doing that.'

Mal's voice grew louder. 'Shit, man, you don't know how I worry about it. And there's my brothers' taxis: someone tried to torch them. That's everything they've got, their living, all gone up in smoke! And my sisters are walking down the street and there's blokes who come up to them and spit right at them. At my sisters. And they ain't done nothing wrong. I'll tell you. I want to go up there to Wythenshawe and I want to sort these people out. I just want to fight them till they stop. Or till one of us dies.' His hands closed into fists and his knuckles whitened.

'Fucking hell,' said Angus. 'I never seen you so upset, mate.'

'Well, it's all because I'm in the army, right? So it's my fault. My mum and my dad and all my brothers and sisters, they all got trouble because of me.'

Angus's fury was easily triggered on his friends' behalf and now his face was reddening.

'Shit! Shit, go up there, Mal! Sort it!'

'I can't—'

'These bastards are bothering your whole family! Don't let them get away with it! You've got to go up there and see them off!'

Faced with Angus's fury, Mal seemed to deflate and his own anger became smaller.

'They've asked me not to, Angry. They say I'll just cause more trouble. That's why they come down here.'

'You've got to sort it, mate.'

'I was thinking of it at the end of the tour when the first letterbox fire happened but Sarge said to me, he says: No, listen to your family. They don't want you up there making things worse.'

31

'Did your mum tell the police?'

'Yeah. And the police don't do nothing. Community relations or some crap reason.'

'Fucking hell.'

Mal hung his head and drummed his fingers on the top of a tin of lager. 'If there was some way I could kill him, I would,' he said miserably. 'I mean it. I want to kill him.'

'Kill who?' demanded Angus. 'Is it just one bloke doing these things?'

'There's more than one but I know who the main man is. It's my friend Aamir.'

'Your friend! A fucking friend's torching your mum's hallway!'

'Well, he used to be my friend. All through primary school. Then we went to the Quran study centre every week and he used to be round at ours all the time; my mum treated him like her own son. Then we got old enough to discover girls. Man, I knew what I wanted. And I wasn't going to get it at the mosque so—'

'Where does he work, then, this Aamir?' Angus was impatient.

'Big furniture warehouse shop by the motorway, the last I heard.'

'What's the name of this warehouse?'

Mal thought. 'Dunno. World in Your Lounge. Lounge in Your World. Something like that. My mum went there once but she said their chairs was too pricey unless they was on special offer.'

Angus chewed the roll-up, his eyes half shut. Mal looked closely at him.

'So . . . why're you asking?'

2

Dave was thinking that if he stayed at the pub late with the lads then by the time he got home Jenny would be asleep and he would find the bedroom dark and her back turned silently towards him and their stupid row would hang around in the air all day tomorrow. He decided to finish his pint and then slither home along the icy streets to make his peace.

But before he could gulp it down, the atmosphere in the pub changed suddenly. All movement stopped.

'Shhhhh!' people were hissing.

Then someone roared: 'Quiet!'

Even the pool game paused so that every neck could wind around towards the big screen on the wall. Usually it showed sports but now there was a news programme. The pub fell completely silent as everyone watched men in desert camouflage jumping into wagons and screaming out of a base somewhere in Afghanistan. Every man in the room recognized, the way he recognized his oldest friend, the Hesco, the wheels turning in hot dust, the contained, focused energy visible on the faces of the soldiers who were leaving base to confront an enemy. Watching them,

Dave could almost feel the Osprey on his back.

'. . . Prime Minister has given an undertaking to the American President to supply temporary reinforcement from the UK to help tackle the problem. The UK hasn't yet committed on numbers but it is expected that further troops will be arriving in Helmand within the next few weeks. Meanwhile, despite American efforts, the Taliban is increasing its hold on the area.'

Dave glanced around. All eyes were fixed on the screen. Every man suddenly looked sharp and alert.

'The reason is clear to see . . .' announced the journalist. The picture flickered and suddenly they were in the Green Zone, flying low over huge, irrigated fields.

'Poppies. Afghanistan is the world's biggest poppy producer and the resin from these plants will find its way on to the world's streets, particularly those of Europe and America, as heroin. There is no other crop Afghan farmers can produce which will give them a return like this one, even though growing it is illegal and the risks are high.'

Poppy flowers, blazing red, a few white, filled the screen as though it was on fire.

'Despite attempts to sabotage it, the indications are that this year's poppy harvest in Helmand Province will be a bumper one. And that means bumper profits not just for the farmer but for the Taliban, who rely on it for much of their funding. No wonder, then, that the American President sees the war on poppies as a double war – against the illegal drugs industry and against the insurgents.

'Britain does not take part in the poppy-eradication programme. But while America does so, the Prime Minister has pledged further support by temporarily increasing troop numbers.'

The screen flickered to the next story. A new report suggested that British teenagers were leaving school with a low reading age and a grave-faced journalist stood outside a school gate to discuss this with a head teacher. The soldiers did not move, not even to drink. They remained silent, watching the screen as though hanging on the head teacher's every word. But not one of them was listening to her. They were all rooted to the spot by the same amazing thought.

'I'm going to get a job!' announced Leanne excitedly.

'Oh! What kind of job?' asked Jenny. She didn't want to ruin Leanne's news by saying that she was looking for a job too.

'Anything. My favourite is one at the garden centre. I applied for it last week. And the company which makes ammo over by the helicopter base is taking shift workers . . .' She took an enormous gulp of wine. 'Because I've made a decision. I don't have to stay at home and get yelled at by Steve all the time. I can make my own money and spend it how I like. Got any crisps, Jenn?'

Jenny rummaged in a cupboard. At the back she found a bag of spicy tortilla chips and threw them over to Leanne.

'What about the boys?' asked Rose. 'Will you send them to nursery?'

'Nah, not if you mean that new place everyone's drooling over. The Magic Cottage. Called that because they magic so much money out of your account into theirs.' Leanne opened the chips and stuffed some into her mouth. 'There's the camp nursery and I'll pay Adi to take them as well and Steve's not going off on training like he used to so he might be able to help.'

'Have you told him?' asked Jenny.

Leanne shook her head.

'Nah. I'm going to get a job first and then he won't have much choice.'

'But Steve's not staying in Stores,' Rose said. 'He's telling everyone he's going back into 1 Platoon.'

'They'll never let him with one leg,' said Leanne. She glanced down at her own hand, full of chips, powdery with spices, as if it belonged to someone else. 'Eat some, girls!' she cried. 'Save me from myself.'

She relinquished the bag only long enough for Rose to dip into it once. Then she grabbed it back again.

'They might be stale,' said Jenny apologetically. Leanne did not hear her.

'Steve's driving me crazy. He's always angry about something and mostly he's angry with the army for not putting him back in the platoon with the other lads. I mean, he's fucking good with his prosthetic leg, and he's probably fitter than most of them. But they're not going to let a P3 go and fight.'

Rose and Jenny looked at each other.

'Our boys probably won't be fighting again,' said Jenny. 'They've only just come back so they're not supposed to go out there for another two years. And by that time it'll all have wound down in Afghanistan.'

Leanne was munching chips non-stop. Her hand was on a continuous loop between the bag and her mouth. 'Yeah, well, they're all hoping they'll go back, aren't they? And they're soon on spearhead.'

Rose and Jenny looked at each other again. It was one of the most bruising aspects of the men's return: that within a few weeks they were restless to go back.

'Spearhead doesn't mean a thing,' said Rose. 'No one ever gets called back out when they're on spearhead.'

'It's only used for emergencies,' Jenny said.

36

'But the army's really stretched these days,' Leanne insisted. 'Steve reckons there's a possibility the boys'll go back into theatre. And he thinks he's going with them, the idiot.'

Jenny shook her head. She knew that companies which had just returned from theatre were given a break and then held on standby to fly back out while they were still a fit, fighting unit. But they were seldom called and she preferred to think the impossible wouldn't happen.

Rose leaned forward. Her red hair was loosely plaited this evening and the plait flopped forward too. Her face was pink. She spoke in a low, confessional voice.

'There's some days I wish they bloody well would go back.' She looked shocked at her own words but Leanne nodded encouragingly. 'I mean, Gerry's been horrible since he got home. Nothing's good enough. He goes to Tesco for ten minutes and then complains about it for the next three hours. He wears me out. Everything's more difficult when he's around. I'd rather just get on and do things for myself now.'

'Yeah, Steve's a complete shit nearly all the time these days,' said Leanne. 'That's why I want out of the house.' She poured more wine. 'And if they tell him he can go back to the front line, that's fine by me.'

'You always said you wouldn't let him!' exclaimed Jenny, remembering the couple's fierce rows when he first returned from hospital.

'Well, now I have to live with him, I'm more than happy for him to go back into theatre.'

Jenny said: 'You don't mean that. You've already for-gotten what it's like when they're away. I wake up every day and know Dave could be coming back in a body bag. Before I even open my eyes I think: Is this the day I'll get bad news?'

There was a silence.

'Jenny, we can't afford to do that,' said Rose. 'Or we'd all go mad.'

'We *are* all going mad!'

'Nah! When they get home is when we go mad,' said Leanne.

Jenny felt herself reddening now. 'We just hide how we feel when they're away. We get on with our lives and keep cheerful and chatter to our men on thesatellite phone when they ring. But all the time we're scared. We're so scared we can hardly look at Agnieszka when we pass her in the car. Because we don't want to be reminded of what we're really feeling.'

At the very mention of Agnieszka's name Jenny felt the atmosphere in the room change subtly. The women had been listening to her words with reluctant recognition but now Rose leaned back, her plait flopping over her shoulder, and Leanne's face seemed to grow larger as she pressed her chins into her neck with disapproval.

'No one ever sees Agnieszka,' said Rose stiffly.

Jenny persisted: 'Just driving past her house reminds me. Just glimpsing her door, or her car, or Luke's buggy left in front . . .'

'She's a bitch,' said Leanne. 'I don't want to see her.'

Agnieszka was Jamie Dermott's widow. Her body all angles, movements swift, head down, she was sometimes spotted at the supermarket early in the morning. Otherwise, she had become invisible. How did she manage this in camp, where everyone watched everyone else all the time? Was it because she reminded people that some husbands don't come back?

'Does Dave visit her?' asked Rose.

'Tried to. But she wouldn't let him in.'

'Typical,' said Leanne, tutting.

'So we sat down and wrote her a letter. Dave knocked and gave it to her by hand.'

Leanne looked surprised. 'She answered the door?'

'Yeah and she took it but she still wouldn't let him in.'

'What did it say?'

'All about how Jamie died in a really brave way . . .' Jenny swallowed. 'And how it matters a lot that we named the baby after him . . .' She felt hot suddenly, as though she was going to cry. She had helped Dave with the letter and even he had fought tears as they worked on it. That was the first time, the only time, Dave had tried to tell her what Afghanistan had been like. And for a few moments she had understood. Briefly, she had experienced it: the heat; the hostility of the terrain; the sullen silence of the people; the fear; the knowledge that a formidable enemy was always there but never seen. An enemy which was fast, merciless and focused on killing someone she loved.

Rose and Leanne watched her closely. Rose swallowed. 'But Jamie was killed by an RPG. So he must have died really quickly . . . ?'

'Not quickly enough,' whispered Jenny. And she took a big, big gulp of wine, throwing back her head so that the others couldn't see her face.

Leanne said: 'The rumour is that Agnieszka's moving back to Poland with her compensation. One hundred and fifty grand. That sort of money'll go a long way there.'

'But what about Jamie's parents?' asked Rose. 'They'll want to know their grandson.'

'Well, Luke's never going to be like Jamie, is he?

There's something wrong with that kid and as far as Jamie's mum and dad are concerned, it's because Luke's mum is a slag from Poland.'

Jenny blinked at Leanne.

'I'm not saying anyone's told them about that other bloke,' added Leanne quickly. 'I'm just saying that they saw her for what she was right from the start.'

Jenny said: 'We don't know for a fact that Agnieszka was playing around.'

'Why are you trying to protect her?' demanded Leanne. She got up and opened the second bottle, which was waiting in the fridge. Jenny looked at Leanne's face, redder, rounder and, now, angrier. And Rose's cheeks looked like bright red apples too, as though something was making her furious or embarrassed or both. That's how everyone at the camp seemed to feel about Agnieszka. Maybe it was just as well that the Polish girl had decided not to talk to anyone; it had deprived many people of the opportunity to show that they were ignoring her.

Leanne said: 'She was cheating on her husband while he lay dying, the slag. And no one loved a woman more than Jamie loved her!'

Rose nodded agreement while Leanne finished the tortilla chips and scrunched up the bag in one hand. When she opened her fingers it crackled back to its original shape.

Jenny heard the bitterness in Leanne's voice. She thought of the way Steve shouted at his wife these days, as though some of his love for her had been blown away with his leg. She remembered how she and Dave had snarled at each other in angry whispers tonight and how the house had rattled as he slammed the door. Gerry and Rose evidently weren't getting on and even

Adi had looked tearful earlier as she pushed the kids through the snow to the playground. And Adi and Sol were a close, loving couple. It was Afghanistan which had done this to them all, as though the fighting hadn't ended in that faraway, foreign place but had come home with their men.

Angus and Mal did some gaming and had some more beer. Angus was quiet. Then suddenly he said: 'I've got it all worked out, mate.'

Mal waited, watching as Angus's enormous cheeks narrowed when he pulled on the roll-up. Then he breathed out smoke but he still did not speak.

'What have you worked out, Angry?' Mal prompted.

'How we're going to deal with your little problem up in Wythenshawe.'

Mal cleared his throat.

'I told you. They've asked me not to do anything and I'm into respecting my parents so . . .'

'. . . so you won't be doing nothing,' said Angus.

Mal looked at him and waited while Angus drew on the cigarette again. At last Angry said: 'You won't be doing nothing. 'Cos I'll be doing it.'

'Eh?'

'Just listen to it, Mal. There's some new sprogs starting and they won't know nothing. I wait until one's on duty in the guardroom. And then I check a sniper rifle out for cleaning. He won't know any better. I get up to Wythenshawe, locate the target and do a quick job, and no one guesses there's a bloke sharpshooting a kilometre from the target.'

Mal stared at him in silence.

'Well, don't you want that bastard Aamir dead?' said Angus.

'Yeah. But—'

'They'll think he's had a fit or something like that geezer in 3 Platoon last week. So they call an ambulance. Sirens, blue lights. An hour later three doctors are scratching their heads over him before they take him down to the hospital morgue. They finally find the wound and they call the police and the police are still wondering where to start on this one when I'm back in barracks and the weapon's hanging in the guardroom.'

There was a long silence.

'Shit,' said Mal. His face was darkening. 'Angry, you can't do that.'

'Why not? You said you'd go up there and fight him if you could, right? You said you'd like to kill him, right?'

Silence. Then: 'But I—'

'Mal, don't go chicken on me, I've thought it all out.'

'I'm not chicken. But it won't work.'

'Why?'

'Well, first because you can't get a clear fucking one-kilometre shot at World in your Lounge even if the target's right outside, because there's going to be too many cars and people and shops and things in the way.'

Angus frowned. 'Well, I don't have to be so far from the target.'

'And the next thing is that they'll call the police as soon as they see the blood. It won't take three doctors in white coats half a day to work that one out.'

'Yeah, but there'll be confusion and mayhem and by the time they're looking for a man with a weapon, I'll be far away and getting farther every fucking minute.'

'You'll be inching down the motorway in a traffic jam at one mile per hour. You can only check weapons out of the guardroom for six hours. Fuck it, Angry, it can take more than six hours just to get up the M6 sometimes, let alone back again.'

'That's why we need a new sprog on duty. We tell him I've forgotten to clean the weapon and I'm out for a run and he has to cover for me until I can get it back. And new sprogs can't argue with us.'

'No! It still won't work!' Mal was breathless. His skin colour had changed again and now was several shades whiter than usual. 'If they find the round then they can identify you.'

Angus shook his head. 'No fucking way!'

'It's true! Every round tells a story. That monkey woman who was out at FOB Senzhiri told me that. She's investigated a shitload of deaths and they get ballistics guys in who work out which weapon it was fired from. The barrel of your weapon marks the round. That's how they ID them.'

Angry knitted his brows together.

'Hmmm. Well, we could throw the weapon in the river and then say it got nicked.'

'No, no, no! Because if they traced the round to the weapon and it had been checked out for cleaning, they'd link you to me and me to Aamir . . . Fuck! Shit! Angry, it's a crazy idea!'

He saw his friend's face fall.

'Although,' Mal added, 'it's brilliant. And only like . . .' He faltered. 'Only . . . like . . . a really good friend would offer to do that for someone. But it's too fucking risky. You could spend the rest of your life in jail. A really good friend wouldn't let you take that risk.'

'Listen, mate,' said Angus. 'This Aamir bloke could kill your brother and your mum and dad. If I get the plan right, he's out of the way, your family's safe, and no one knows who sorted it. The plan's basically sound, it just needs a few modifications.'

Mal started to protest again but at that moment someone came in. Streaky Bacon stood in the doorway, grinning at them broadly.

'Man, where did you come from?' they asked.

'Got a train, got a bus, walked up here from the village, nearly got my dick frozen off so I stopped at the pub.'

'Have a tin, mate!' Angus reached under his bed for a lager and then handed another to Mal. Streaky threw down his kit and sat on Angus's bed. He opened the can and took a long swig in one swift, fluid movement.

'Binman due back soon?' Mal asked. Rifleman Jack Binns was Streaky's closest mate.

'Nah, he's sunning himself on some beach with his bird.'

'Didn't think you were here for another week either,' said Mal. 'Bust up with your girl?'

They watched the smile fade from Streaky's face. 'Well, she's not exactly how I remember. Wolverhampton's changed since I went away. My bredren are still my bredren but ... they're different, too.'

'Maybe they're the same and you're different,' suggested Mal.

'They've got, like, really into crack. My girl's buying it and selling it, even, and she never used to do that. So I'm thinking that she's doing this thing maybe just so she can get more of it. And then I'm asking myself: What else is she buying and selling for crack?'

For a brief moment Streaky's features twisted themselves into a rapid caricature of pain and confusion.

'You do crack, too, Streaky?' Mal asked.

Streaky nodded.

'A bit with my girl when I first get home but I'll be honest, that crack don't do a lot for me.'

Angus said: 'I just do booze, me.'

'I like a bit of weed, though,' said Mal.

'Well, yeah,' Streaky said, 'but weed's not a drug, it's a way of life where I come from. Even my mum likes a nice weed tea.'

Angus said: 'My mum likes whisky and ginger.'

Mal said: 'My mum's a good Muslim. She likes PG Tips and she prays five times a day, and mostly she's praying that I don't go back to Afghanistan.'

Streaky's eyes widened and he looked from Mal to Angus and back again. 'You two not been watching the TV tonight?' he asked.

They shook their heads.

'You don't know, then? About the troop reinforcements?'

'What reinforcements?'

Streaky said: 'We're on spearhead next month. Right?'

Angus and Mal waited and froze. They couldn't nod. They couldn't even blink.

'Well, the Prime Minister's promised the President of America to send a load more extra troops because there's some big fighting on now. To do with the poppies.'

'More troops? To Afghanistan?' muttered Mal.

'And we're on spearhead?' murmured Angus.

'You got it, dudes.' Streaky smiled happily. 'It could be us.'

Billy Finn was about to get in his car and drive away from Surrey when the old man offered to buy him a pint.

45

'What are you having, lad? It's not every day I have a winner at sixty-six to one,' he cackled.

It took a while to order because two blonde women had just walked up to the bar. They were probably race-goers; they didn't belong in the place. Finny watched them with interest. Middle-aged, probably married to well-off men. But not too old to be attractive.

'Evening, ladies,' he said charmingly. 'Had a good day at the races?'

They muttered something polite.

'I had a terrible day, didn't pick a single winner.' He knew he sounded smooth. The women would never guess he had been born in a caravan.

One of the women, the prettier of the two, was looking sympathetic. 'Neither did I,' she said.

'Did you see the two thirty?' asked Finn. 'Wish I'd had a fiver on Asbo Boy. And guess what, my friend here did!'

Now the women looked impressed. The old man grinned toothlessly.

'I've got an eye for a good horse,' he boasted.

'Well done,' said one of the women. 'Asbo Boy just powered his way through the field.'

'Wasn't he sixty-six to one?' asked the other and the old man nodded in reply.

The barman delivered the women's drinks.

'That's why I insist on paying for your drinks,' said the old man gallantly, just as Finn had intended him to. Now the women would have to talk to them.

'How long have you been interested in racing?' he asked.

'My ex-husband had a stake in a racehorse,' the prettier one replied. 'When we divorced I decided I could do without the husband but not without the horses!' She laughed and the other woman joined in; she wore a lot of make-up, but she had a hard face and could not hide it. Finny felt his fingers itch. These were wealthy, betting women.

'You don't look old enough to be married, let alone divorced,' the man said, still grinning, still gallant.

'Maybe the lady was a child bride,' suggested Finn.

Bull's-eye. The woman reddened and smiled and looked pleased. 'I'm no spring chicken,' she said.

'I know exactly how old you are,' Finn told her. His heart was thumping now. The conversation had gone his way even faster than he had hoped.

'How?' asked the woman. She had a nice smile.

'It's a special gift of mine,' Finn said.

'What, telling women their age?' demanded the old man. 'I hope you're better at that than you are picking a horse.'

'I'm seldom wrong,' Finn told the pretty woman, just as he had heard his grandfather say to many pretty women many times. 'A tenner says I can tell your age spot on.' He turned to the hard-faced woman: 'And another tenner says I can tell yours.'

Billy Finn's grandfather worked for a fair and sometimes, as a child, Finn had travelled with him. If his grandfather was short of money he set up a stall and bet women he could guess their age. If he got it wrong he paid up willingly, but he seldom did.

Finny could never understand why so many women played the game. Were they all so desperate for a fiver? Then his grandfather explained that mostly they played because they hoped he would underestimate their age.

He had handed on his tricks to Finn, and whenever Finn needed money, this was a reliable way of obtaining it. But today he didn't need money. After a bad day at the races, he just wanted the thrill of winning some-thing. And now here was the thrill, here was the heartbeat. He recognized it from Helmand Province.

'Let's get this straight. You'll guess our ages and you'll pay up if you're wrong. We pay up if you're right,' said the hard-faced woman.

'That's about it,' said Finn.

'But how do you know we'll tell the truth?'

'I'm trusting you.'

There was a pause.

'Go on then, guess my age,' said the hard one, and Finn could tell that his grandfather was right; this woman wanted him to underestimate.

He stared hard at her, pretending to study her closely, acting as if this was difficult. When in fact he had already looked at her neck and around her eyes.

After making a show of considering, he decided to flatter her. He said: 'You only look thirty. But you're thirty-eight.'

The woman's face flashed surprise and anger at the same time and with such intensity that he knew he was right. He could feel his face twisting itself into a smile. He tried to repress the grin but it just twisted right out again like a trout from a net.

'Am I correct?' he asked the woman politely.

She rolled her eyes and reached for her purse. Finn had been unaware that the whole bar was watching, but now they burst into applause. Finn enjoyed being a showman and he took a bow.

'Me next,' said the prettier woman.

The bar fell silent again. Everyone watched him. Finny really did scrutinize this woman, because he wasn't sure. When he looked at her carefully she seemed very like the other woman, but less worn: he realized for the first time that they must be sisters. The other one had been out there fighting her corner for years; this was the sister who had stayed at home.

Tension grew as he stared at her. The woman's eyes and neck were giving him different messages. She watched him with a half-smile. He became aware, out of the corner of his eye, that her sister was watching with the same half-smile. There was something about these two that they weren't saying . . .

'You're not just sisters, you're twins. So you're thirty-eight too,' he heard himself say, before he had time to think about it.

The expression on the women's faces told him he was right again. Finn felt relief well up inside him and escape as a broad smile. Because his luck had changed. He had lost every bet at the races but now he was winning again. His luck had wheeled around in a sudden, tight circle like the roller coaster where he had sold tickets as a lad.

The bar broke into spontaneous applause, the pretty twin gave him ten pounds and a sweet smile and he decided to use it to buy them both a drink.

He was doing so when he felt his phone ring in his pocket. It was a message.

Get ready you son of a gun looks like we're fucking out there again! Yes, that's right lol lol lol

Angus McCall. What was he on about now? If he had to guess, Finn would have thought Angry was trying to tell him they were going back to the FOB in Helmand. He felt his heart thud for a moment. Then common sense got the better of him. Nah. Probably Angry was just texting meaningless, drunken shit.

As he waited for the barman, Finn's phone rang again, a call this time. He didn't bother to check who the caller was. It would be Angus, raving incoherently. But he answered it anyway, not liking to admit his longing to hear a familiar voice, even Angry's.

'Is that Billy Finn?'

It was someone loud and male, but it wasn't Angus. Finn was cautious.

'Maybe it is. Maybe it isn't.'

'Doncha know who's calling you, Billy Boy? And you're the guy who saved my life!'

It was Martyn! Martyn Robertson! A few months ago the oilman had been one of the most famous faces in the world, flashing up behind newsreaders everywhere. Then, he had been held hostage by the Taliban and with the clock ticking towards his execution, his rescue had been widely credited to the SAS. Luckily Martyn knew whom he really had to thank.

'I recognized you the moment I heard your voice, Martyn. Are you calling from Texas?'

'Right now I'm in Texas but soon I'll be in London staying at the Dorrr-chester Hotel. And you and me and your boys are going to have a wild time. I know I owe you my life and I'm going to show how I grateful I am. I want you to come to London with Dave and Angry and Mal and Streaky and . . . all of you. The whole section, the whole platoon, all the boys who were out at Senzhiri with me. I'll be calling your commanding officer and arranging it.'

Amazing how luck worked. You changed one thing and everything changed. Women smiled, you started winning bets, you suddenly got invited to parties at the Dorchester. Maybe England wasn't so dull after all.

As he delivered some more drinks to the twins, Finn remembered Angry's mad text. For a minute there he had believed that they were actually going back to

Afghanistan and the thought had made his heart leap. Now that would be a real change in his luck. But Angry was probably just trying to tell him about the party in London.

3

When Dave got home he closed the door very quietly behind him and stood in the still hallway feeling the house's warmth. Nothing moved. It was the opposite of the chain reaction he had started as he left the house: noisy slam, Jenny's yell of annoyance, the baby's cry from upstairs.

The place was in darkness but Jenny had left on an outside light and the hall light. Which might mean she had forgiven him. A bit. Because Jenny's anger was pure mortar. Over the wall, bang, splat and then silence. No complicated, heat-seeking, carefully targeted, slow-burn weaponry for Jenn. Contact and out.

He stumbled into the kitchen. There were two empty wine bottles on the table, three empty glasses and a lot of crumbs. The crumbs looked like spicy tortilla. He opened the bin. Hmmm. Congratulations, Detective Sergeant Henley, on your investigative work. There is, indeed, a big empty bag of spicy tortilla chips in the bin. And since Jenny is keeping a close eye on her weight and refusing to snack or even drink much, the large empty bag and quantity of alcohol consumed indicate the presence here earlier of one Leanne Buckle plus some other mate. Theory confirmed, Detective, by Steve Buckle's absence from the pub tonight. Because he must have been at home babysitting.

Still congratulating himself on a superb forensic analysis, he shed his outer layers, trod too heavily up the stairs and tripped over the last one on to the landing, swearing loudly. His words were met by the sudden wail of baby Jaime, as if she had just been waiting for another excuse to start crying. He went into the girls' room and fumbled around for the cot. Not hard to find, just follow your ears and inside the cot you will find, Detective, a small, hot, noise-emitting baby.

He picked up Jaime and her wails grew louder.

'Shhhh, shhhh,' he instructed her gently. 'You'll wake your sister and she'll start crying. Then she'll wake your mother. And then the safest thing I can do is go straight back to Afghanistan until it's all quiet again.'

He said that just in case Jenny was listening. He made going back to Afghanistan immediately into a joke of an idea. He made it sound absurd. Even though he knew now that it wasn't.

Sure enough, a voice rang out from the darkness over Jaime's roars.

'Put that baby down. You're drunk!'

He knew at once that she wasn't angry. She hadn't even been asleep. She had been waiting for him to come home.

'I'm not. Anyway, you and Leanne and someone else got through a lot of wine tonight.'

He was swinging Jaime back and forth and the intervals between each wail were getting longer.

'Who was here with you and Leanne?' he asked.

'Matt Damon.'

'Oh yeah?'

'Leanne bumped into him in Marks and Spencer's.' This was a fantasy of Leanne's, which she had publicized widely. 'She asked him over for a quick drink. He couldn't stay long, though.'

He looked at her and through the dark was sure she smiled.

'Go back to bed,' he said.

'No.'

'I'm on stag. So you can leave Jaime to me and sleep safely.'

'Don't shoot her, Sergeant, she's a civilian.'

'That's never stopped me before. Do you know how many small, helpless Afghan children I've mortared just in case they grow up to be insurgents?'

'Whole nurseries full. They said so on *Panorama*.'

'Must be true then.'

'Come to bed, Dave.'

He looked down. He could see in the dark now. Jaime had stopped crying and was blinking up at him, wide-eyed. In the little bed along one wall, Vicky slept soundly, her face angelic. His wife, his two daughters, their home. He had built this family, he held it together, the safety and happiness and welfare of these people he loved were in his hands. It was too easy to get dragged down in the day-to-day and forget how much they mattered, and at this moment they mattered so much it made his heart ache. Shit. Maybe he was drunk.

Carefully, very carefully, as though she was an un-exploded bomb, he laid the baby back in her cot. She watched his face. He watched hers. He leaned over the cot. She closed her eyes. He did not move. Her eyes remained shut. After a minute he turned and walked silently from the room. He paused, waiting for her to start yelling. There was silence.

Jenny was already back in bed. He shut the door quietly, tore his clothes off and left them lying all over the floor in a way he would not have tolerated in his platoon. He slid into bed next to her and put his arms around her. She was warm and soft and she smelled nice.

'Sorry,' he whispered into her ear. 'I'm stupid. Whatever I said, I was wrong. 'Specially the bit about your mother.'

'I'm sorry too,' she whispered back. 'And don't ever, ever say that again.'

'I won't ever say it because it's not true.'

'Dave, I only had to think about Agnieszka and what she's lost and how lucky I am to have you here with me . . .' He held her tighter. She turned to him. 'Thank God they aren't sending you back to that horrible country any time soon.'

Dave swallowed. Should he tell her now? Before she heard the rumours which would be flying around the camp tomorrow? He decided that Afghanistan was the place to be a hero and home was the place to be a coward.

He said: 'Yeah. Thank God for that.'

Binman stretched out in the sand. The Afghan sun was scorching his face, his desert camouflage was soaked with sweat and deep in his leg was a dull, throbbing pain.

'Oh fuck, oh fuck,' he moaned.

'All right?' asked someone. Female. Must be a medic.

'Rifleman Jack Binns 23379917,' he muttered mechanically before she could ask him.

'Wake up, Jacko!'

Binns opened his eyes with an effort. He looked

around. Alison. Beach umbrellas. Bodies with no clothes on, not because the clothes had been blown off them but to saturate the skin with sun. He stared anxiously at the people lying closest. All body parts in place. He listened. The crash of sea on sand. No mortars.

'Oh Alison, I thought I was in . . .'

'I know where you thought you were.' Her voice was gentle as usual. But it was flat. And somewhere, buried under the flatness, like a landmine, was her anger. He knew Alison was getting sick of it. She was fed up with the way he woke up yelling in the night or just sat there nodding while she was talking to him, far away inside his head.

'The umbrella fell on you, that's all.'

She tried to dig it back into the sand, the wind tugging against it. Her muscles were negligible, small, jutting things like little elbows which were no match for a huge, wind-filled beach umbrella. Her body was white and slim and vulnerable. He had thought about this body of hers so often lying in his cot at the forward operating base, longed for it, and now he was here with her, on the beach, he felt a strange detachment. As if he was still back in Helmand and she was on a Moroccan beach with some other bloke.

She turned an angry face back to him.

'Well, sitting there watching isn't going to help much, is it?' she snapped and he leaped up and grabbed the umbrella and shoved it in the ground for her.

They both settled back down in the sand. The silence between them was filled by the slapping of the waves.

Her words and her tone echoed in his ears. She had never been so sharp before. He wanted to talk to her, to tell her how good the sound of water was when you'd come from a dry, dry place where you were always thirsty, no matter how much time you spent chewing on your Camelbak, because your mouth was always coated with sand and it wasn't nice beach sand but more like dust. He would try to explain all that right now, this minute. He turned to her.

'Alison . . .'

'Yes?'

Still sharp. The yes that means no. It was her building society voice. She worked in the local branch of a building society in Dorset and old folks shuffled up to her all day and hollered through the glass that they'd saved fifteen pounds in ten-pence pieces. Alison's e-blueys moaned a lot about the customers and he had loved to lie on his cot at the FOB and read about her small world and hear her complaints. It was all so insignificant that it had been a sort of comfort. He should have realized that none of it was insignificant to Alison. Her life was composed of all those little things: demanding customers, a nosy boss, a lost umbrella; they all mattered to her. Maybe they used to matter to him. But they didn't any more.

'What?' she demanded without opening her eyes. He knew she was reluctant to hear about Afghanistan. She had wanted him to come back the same Jack Binns who went away, the one she had met working in Curry's before he joined up. She didn't really want to know what had happened in between.

Her voice softened. 'Jacko, why don't you talk to me?'

'Sometimes I start to say things. But I don't get the feeling you want to hear them.'

Alison rearranged herself in the sand. She washed her hands with gel. She was always doing that. She looked clean, as if she washed a lot, and on this holiday together, their first, Binman had learned that she did

57

indeed wash a lot. He wondered how she would manage in a dirty old FOB like Senzhiri where you could only shower once every three days at the most.

'Of course I want to hear,' she said awkwardly. 'You can tell me anything you like.'

And suddenly it seemed vital that he did tell her. He had to make her understand. Before they got back to Dorset and she went into the building society and they settled with their families again, he had to tell her.

'There was this minefield, see,' he began. 'Been there for years and years because the Russians left it behind and the locals didn't go near it so you couldn't tell just by looking at it. We thought it was a clearing in the woods. Everyone did. And 2 Section started crossing it. And then a bloke got his leg blown off and they thought the enemy was watching from the trees, chucking mortar. So they started firing back and then there was another explosion. And they realized no one was mortaring them. It was a minefield. And they were on it. But they couldn't move. And someone had to get to the casualties. And I got chosen.'

Alison was sitting up now. She was pointing to the sun-tan lotion. He picked it up and passed it to her and she began to apply it. After a moment she asked: 'So what happened in this minefield, then?' Her tone was casual, so casual it was almost resentful. The question was dutiful. She didn't really want to know the answer.

Binman shrugged. 'Nothing much. I had to get the casualties off, that's all. I had to crawl on my belly across the ground sort of feeling it and blowing on it.' The rough, red Afghan soil chafed his fingers again and its dust billowed into his eyes. 'In case there were more landmines. Then when we had a clear path, we carried the wounded men off.'

Alison nodded. 'Oh, right,' she said. 'So did you find any mines?'

'Yeah, a few.' They were no more than a discoloration of the soil, a clumping, a solidity, an irregularity. Try to find out more and your curiosity killed you. So you had to guess, you almost had to smell them. Your fingers developed a new sensitivity to the soil structure. Your whole body was a raw nerve; you were skinless as you progressed, millimetre by millimetre, sweating under the cruel sun. And all the time you could see your mate lying there ahead of you with his leg blown off, blood pooling, flies gathering, probably dying.

Binns said: 'If I thought there was a landmine I just had to go round it. That's all.'

'Oh. Sounds scary.'

Scary. The most massive experience of his life, so inflated that it seemed to take up years and years instead of only a few hours, had just been neatly packaged like a piece of meat in the supermarket. To help you forget that it comes from a cow.

'Did they die?'

'No. They lived. They're doing all right, considering.'

'Oh, that's good.' If the biggest, most focused task of your life had been to save your mates' lives, then their survival was fucking marvellous, so marvellous that there weren't words for the joy you felt when you saw them again at the medals parade.

Alison finished with the sun cream and lay down again. Jack Binns did not look at her. He had seen her face and it looked white beneath her newly acquired tan. They were on holiday but it was nothing but a strain for both of them: he not talking and she not listening. He reached out and took her hand and it felt limp in his. She did not respond to his squeeze. She said nothing.

Between the crash of waves he became aware that his mobile phone was beeping. He dived into Alison's beach bag to retrieve it as if he was expecting something really important instead of another dirty joke from Angus.

It was from Streaky Bacon, Binman's best mate.

Hey dude you not going to believe it but looks like we're going back because of spare head. Yes. Back there and soon. See you in barracks.

Jack Binns squinted at the text and then held the phone in the thin shade of the umbrella and read it again. Then again. Back there? Not *there*? He felt something lurch inside his body as if he'd been in a deep slumber and just woken up. His skin was suddenly electric; his legs and arms surged with a new blood supply.

He glanced over at Alison. She lay still with her eyes closed. He shoved the phone back in the bag. But he remained upright and alert, his body taut as he stared out to sea.

4

It was a relief for the men to gather together again to start work. A relief because the unstructured days of holiday and small demands of daily life had been harder to readjust to than most admitted. A relief because being busy stopped you thinking. And a relief to see their mates again because only their mates understood what had happened to them in Afghanistan.

The camp was buzzing with rumours that they were about to be sent back to theatre on spearhead. Martyn Robertson's party would no longer be a celebration of successes on their last tour but, if the rumours were right that they were leaving imminently, would turn into a farewell party.

Women discussed their dresses and lads without partners worried about whom to take to the Dorchester.

'Your sister's pretty, Mal . . .' said Streaky in barracks the night before they went back into training, glancing at a picture Mal kept by his bed.

'No way are you taking my sister to the party.' Mal reached out and put the family photo face down.

'Anyone else got a sister?' asked Streaky, looking

around the barracks hopefully, as if there might be one hiding under a bed.

'Streaks, Mal's sister's a Muslim so she's not going to be interested in a man called Bacon. You better let me take her,' said Angus, picking up the photo and gazing at it.

'I wouldn't let my sister near you either,' Mal told him.

'C'mon, mate. I wouldn't try anything. She'd be like my official partner for the evening.'

Mal sighed. 'Don't you know what she's wearing in that picture?'

'Is that some sort of Muslim mosque clothes?'

'No, Angry, she's wearing the stuff you wear when you get a degree. At a university. That's called graduation. Which means my sister is clever, the brains of the family. Which means she's not going to be interested in soldiers like you, especially since she's six years older.'

'I like an older woman. Has she got a boyfriend?'

'Nah. She used to go out with that bastard Aamir's big brother for a bit. But not for long, not when my dad found out.'

Angus leaned forward and spoke quietly. 'She won't be too upset when Aamir dies, then?' he muttered, glancing around to make sure no one passing down the corridor had heard.

Mal opened his eyes wide and watched Angus's immense face while he continued in an undertone: 'I've got it all worked out now. I've revised my plan.'

Mal pretended not to know what Angus was talking about. Angry nudged him.

'In Wythenshawe. Your little problem, Mal boy.'

'I'm not letting you do nothing in Wythenshaw to

Aamir,' said Mal. 'Or we'll be out in Afghanistan and you'll be in prison back here.'

'Nah, it can't go wrong this time. I'll nick a TA rifle when they're out on the Plain doing training. I'll use it and then I'll sell it straight on to the black market. So even if it marks the round which kills Aamir and they trace it back to that rifle, they'll reckon it got nicked and sold on to someone who slotted him.'

'They won't fucking reckon anything, Angry, when they're doing a murder investigation.'

It was dinnertime in the barracks now.

'Scoff,' the other lads said to each other. 'C'mon, scoff.' They trailed off down the corridor in ones and twos until only Mal and Angry remained. And, on the next bed, Jack Binns. He lay with his headphones on and his eyes open.

'Oy, Binman, SCOFF,' roared Angry at him, assuming he hadn't heard the call to food over his music. Binman sat up and took off his headphones but he did not follow the others out of the room. He waited until the last foot-fall had died away and then he turned to Angus.

'What the fuck are you two talking about?' he demanded.

Angus's features thickened.

'Mind your own fucking business. We thought you was into your music over there.'

'What are you planning, Angry?'

Mal and Angus exchanged looks.

'Why do you hate this Aamir bloke so much?' Binns persisted.

'Shhhhhh!' said Angus. He spoke in a low voice. 'He's firebombing Mal's mum and torching his brother's taxis. Just because Mal's been fighting in Afghanistan.'

63

Binman's small face knitted itself into an expression of concern and confusion.

'That's fucking awful. But I mean ... well, you should tell the police.'

'They've told the police! And the police don't do nothing!' said Angus too loudly. He looked anxiously around and ducked his head as if there was a sniper somewhere in the barracks.

'You're not really planning on ... ?'

'Listen, Binman, this Aamir could kill Mal's mum and dad with his firebombs. Someone's got to sort him out but Mal's promised his family he won't do nothing!'

Binman looked at Mal, who was sitting up now, cross-legged, on his bed. He untangled his ankles from his knees.

'I can't let you do it, mate. It would be the end of your army career. The end of your fucking life, practically, if they caught you.'

Binman added: 'It's not right, Angry! You can't just go round killing people!'

Angry's face bulged and reddened. 'Why is it right in Afghanistan and wrong back here? Bloody funda-mentalists cause trouble here, cause trouble there, it's the same thing.'

'I thought there was a UN resolution or something about Afghanistan. There's no fucking UN resolution about Wythenshawe!' Binman was reddening too, now.

Angus swelled up with fury. 'Listen, what do we do out in Afghanistan? We protect the locals from crazies who attack them so it's not even safe for them to stay at home. Well, why would we do that for a bunch of Afghans and not for people in Wythenshawe?'

Mal protested: 'But it could make things worse for my family if I—'

'*You*'re not doing nothing, mate. That's the point. *You* are running around with the other lads all day hundreds of miles away so everyone knows there's no way you've been to fucking Wythenshawe.'

'Shit!' said Binman. His tone was one of resignation. With a faint undertone of admiration. Angus was quick to detect the admiration.

'Reckon I've devised the perfect crime,' he said.

'I don't want you to do it for me,' Mal told him. 'I don't want you to take the risk.'

'No risk. And it's not even a crime, not really. It's a rescue. See, Martyn Robertson was a hostage so we rescued him. Well, Aamir and his mates are keeping your family hostage in Wythenshawe: you said your mum's too scared to go out most of the time. So, I'm going to rescue them. Simple.'

Binman and Mal looked at each other in silence. Finally Binman said: 'So you're planning to nick a TA sniper rifle?'

'Yeah, that won't be hard if they're out training.'

'Well, I bet there won't be any TA training out on the Plain before we leave for Afghanistan,' said Binman. 'So you won't be able to commit your perfect crime.'

Angry grinned broadly.

'I'm going to find out, lads.'

There were a few changes in 1 Platoon. New soldiers were expected to replace those who had been moved or lost. But there was no word, yet, about a platoon commander to replace Gordon Weeks, who had been sent from 1 Platoon to JTAC to train as a forward air controller.

'Any chance of getting him back if we do go into theatre?' Dave asked Sergeant Major Kila hopefully.

'Nope,' said Kila. 'I've already tried that one.'

'So we could be going back on to the front line with another new officer,' said Dave, who had spent much of the last tour knocking Gordon Weeks into shape.

'They'll make sure you get someone good in the circumstances. Don't worry,' Kila assured him.

'When? We should be training with the new commander now.'

Kila held two tattooed hands up to his great bald head. 'I know, I know, I've said all this to the major. I think the new bloke's due soon.'

They had a kit inspection and immediately afterwards Billy Finn, who never failed to ask a question, looked at Dave. 'Anyone new starting, Sarge?'

'Don't know about the new platoon commander. But you've got two lads arriving in 1 Section today,' Dave told him.

This news was followed by a silence from 1 Section, which, at the end of the last tour, had already been one man short when Jamie Dermott had died. Dave caught himself thinking that whoever the new sprogs were, they could never replace Jamie. And he knew the lads were all thinking the same thing.

'Is Steve Buckle coming back, Sarge?' Si Curtis from 3 Section was a friend of Steve's and Dave guessed that Steve had probably put him up to asking this.

'I know he wants to, Si, because he tells me every day. But I'd be very surprised if they let a bloke with one leg back into the platoon.'

Steve Buckle never gave up lobbying. At first Dave had been patient. Then, as Steve had become more insistent, he had begun to feel irritated.

'It's not a game, mate. Having a man on one leg could risk everyone's lives.'

'I'm as fit as the other lads and fitter than some!'

'Argue with the medics, argue with the major, but for Chrissake stop arguing with me because there's nothing I can do!' Dave said at last.

'You can put in a word for me! You could think about how to persuade them.'

'All right. I'll think about it.'

Sometimes he found himself avoiding Steve and his demands, but today it was impossible because the big man with the metal leg had arrived from Stores with boxes and boxes full of kit. They were training on Salisbury Plain with 2 and 3 Platoons, using some of the new, improved equipment. And specifically they had been asked to try out the next phase of the new pelvic-protection system before it was trialled in theatre.

They gathered on the tarmac by the vehicles, stamping on the ground to keep warm, and Sergeant Major Kila climbed on to the back of a wagon to talk to them.

'You should already be wearing the mine-protection underpants. Now try the overpants,' said Sergeant Major Kila, holding up some bulky triangles of camouflage which Steve was handing out. 'Basically, these are going to stop the British Army from losing its balls. I'm sure we all agree that we don't mind looking a bit silly for such a worthy cause.'

'They're not silly, sir,' said Sergeant Liam Barnes of 3 Platoon, standing at the front by the wagon, arms folded, with the other sergeants. 'Superman wears his underpants over his trousers.'

Kila swung his large frame towards Liam Barnes. 'That's right, Sergeant, so show us how a superhero should look.'

Barnes took a step back and then, realizing the kit

Kila had sent sailing through the air was aimed at him, caught it neatly.

'Watch closely, men,' Kila advised. 'Sergeant Barnes will now demonstrate how to put on the new codpiece, er, I mean pelvic girdle. Come up here, Liam.'

Barnes, reddening, leaped into the back of the wagon and stood turning the girdle this way and that.

While he fiddled with the Velcro straps, Kila said: 'The manufacturers are asking for feedback, so get ready to tell them the truth, the whole truth and nothing but the truth. For sensible, constructive comments they've got some fucking good prizes: tickets to concerts and shit like that.'

Dave was watching Liam Barnes. He could see exactly which way round the girdle should go and he was sure that this was because he had changed so many nappies in the last few weeks. The so-called pelvic girdle was nothing but a big, thick nappy in camouflage.

He stepped forward and helped Liam with the girdle. They both kept straight faces as Sergeant Barnes strapped himself in it to howls of derision. Men hummed strip-show music loudly.

'Not feeling silly, I hope, Superman?' demanded Kila when the noise had died down.

'I'll feel a lot less silly when everyone else is wearing them too,' said Liam, red-faced.

Men were grabbing the girdles from Steve now and putting them on their heads like bonnets and across their chests like bras.

'The British Army knows its men and has ordered three sizes. Large, extra large and ginormous,' Kila roared over the noise. 'I've told them not to bother supplying my lads with codpieces that are anything less than ginormous.'

They climbed into the wagons carrying their kit and weapons, looking around at each other's faces, bright and sharp. It felt like going out on patrol in Afghanistan. They were doing the job they loved, the job they were skilled at. And it was a lot easier than strapping angry toddlers into the back of the car and storming FOB Tesco.

Steve was standing nearby, watching the men getting into the wagons, his face long. He was holding a pile of empty boxes. As the men drove off they could see him from the back of the truck. He cut a dark, forlorn figure.

'Poor fucking bastard, he'd give his right arm to get in the wagon with us,' said Mal.

'He thinks he can do anything. But he can't,' said Finn.

Sol raised his eyebrows: 'Well, he can run fast on that leg.'

'Yeah, he overtook me the other day when I was running through camp,' said Bacon.

The others jeered. 'Streaky, anyone could overtake you.'

Finn said: 'Steve's trying to persuade everyone to let him back into the front line but it would be a fucking disaster. We'd all be carrying him. Risking our lives for him. I mean, I like him. But not that much.'

The others agreed. As the truck neared the guard-house, Steve's figure got smaller and smaller until he was no longer visible.

But, driving towards the Plain, Dave could not shake off the image of Steve's large frame standing, watching them go. The loneliness of the man. He used to be a mate; now he was a problem. The lads had tried to include him when they first got back but gradually, without really thinking about it, they realized that he had stopped being one of them. Wounded soldiers, thought Dave, lived in a no-man's-land. They could never be real soldiers again but, with their prosthetic limbs, the public could never see them as anything else. And that gave him an idea.

Dave reached for his mobile and pressed Steve's number.

A gruff voice answered. 'Yeah?'

'You know I promised to think about how to get you back out to Bastion with us? *If* we go back?'

Steve's voice changed. The same word but spoken louder now, charged with hope.

'Yeah?'

'I've had a sort of idea. Don't get too excited. It's probably going to lead nowhere . . .'

'What! What?'

'I can't talk now, mate. Don't know what time we'll get in from training but I'll try to drop round at yours tonight to discuss it.'

'Shit, Dave!'

'*Don't* get too excited.' Now what had he done? Well, even if it led nowhere, at the very least Steve would be happy for a day or two while they worked on it. 'I'll see you later.'

'Right! I'll get some beer in!'

Dave heard the old Steve again, strong, confident but not overbearing. He was in there somewhere. It was just a question of cracking this new, angry shell and pulling him out.

The training ground was wet and cold. However miserable the weather was in camp, you could be sure it would be more miserable out here. They reached the place they were to pretend was an Afghan compound today and, as they broke into sections, Kila appeared with a small group of men in new uniforms. They looked nervous and awkward. The new sprogs.

The sergeant major distributed the newcomers to the various sections, consulting a list. He reached 1 Section, 1 Platoon last of all when only two men remained with him. One was small and baby-faced. The other was exceptionally tall and thin. Kila was over six feet but this man towered over him.

'Think he swallowed a bottle of growth hormone?' Mal muttered to Angry who, until now, had been the big man of 1 Section.

Angry gave the newcomer a scathing look. 'He's tall but he's puny.'

'Yeah, looks so long and skinny he could snap in two,' agreed Binman, who was the smallest in the section.

'I'd like to be that big,' said Bacon. 'I tell you, no one in Wolverhampton would ever mess with me if I looked like him.'

'What about the other one? Think they've started recruiting twelve-year-olds?' asked Mal.

'Maybe his mum gave him up for adoption and the army took him,' suggested Finn.

'Shhhhh,' Sol hissed as Kila approached.

'This is Richard Hemmings, known to his mates as Tiny,' said Kila. The tall man nodded shyly at 1 Section. Sol held out his hand.

'I'm Sol Kasanita, your section commander. Dave Henley's sergeant of 1 Platoon. He'll be over in a minute.'

'And this is George Swindon,' said Kila, pushing the other man forward.

'Slindon, sir. Not Swindon,' the lad corrected him.

'Sorry, Slindon,' said Kila. 'At least I didn't call you Milton Keynes.'

The lads in 1 Section all introduced themselves. Tiny Hemmings was clearly making an effort to remember their names, repeating them to himself.

'Don't worry,' said Sol kindly. 'You'll learn them soon enough.'

'How tall are you?' Finny asked Tiny Hemmings.

'How old are you?' Binman asked George Slindon.

'Six foot seven and a half,' Tiny replied promptly.

'Nineteen,' said Slindon. 'Even if I look fifteen.'

In answer to their next question, Tiny said he came from London.

'You talk a bit posh,' said Finny suspiciously. 'What part of London are you from?'

'Sort of Chelsea,' said Tiny.

'You sound like an officer, man,' Bacon told him.

'Well I'm not,' said Tiny defensively. 'I've just finished at Catterick, not Sandhurst.'

'Jamie Dermott sounded like an officer and he was the best fucking rifleman in Afghanistan,' said Mal. The others murmured their agreement.

'I've already heard about Jamie Dermott,' said Tiny politely. 'I'll bet you miss him. No one can step into his shoes.'

'Yeah,' said the lads quietly. You had to hand it to this lanky bloke, he said the right thing. A few of them felt sorry for Tiny and Slindon because they had such a tough act to follow.

They asked Slindon where he came from but he did not reply. His mobile was ringing and he had turned his back on them to answer it.

'Probably his mum making sure he's wearing a warm

vest,' muttered Mal. 'Nineteen, my foot. That bloke can't be a day over twelve.'

Sol said: 'That's enough. Welcome, Tiny, welcome . . . er . . .' He looked around for Slindon, who was still on the phone. 'Right, now let's move. It's important to get Tiny and Slindon working as part of the section. They haven't been in theatre with us and we have to share our knowledge with them. Because if we do go back to Afghanistan, we all have to work as one unit.'

5

Jenny didn't know whether to be shocked or angry or upset about the rumours that the men were returning to theatre on spearhead. At first she and Dave didn't talk about it. She knew he was waiting for her to say something. She didn't. She stayed quiet, hoping spearhead would just go away. Even though, wherever she went, from the camp nursery to the dry cleaner's to the supermarket, the rumours were in overdrive.

'Have you got a dress yet for Martyn Robertson's party?' Dave kept asking.

And Jenny wanted to say: You may not be here for the party. It might be cancelled because you're flying back to theatre. That was the rumour at nursery.

She said: 'Well, I've got that blue one. It should do.'

Dave shook his head. 'Nope. You'll need a new dress for the Dorchester Hotel.'

'But I'll probably never wear it again.'

'There'll be other parties. Please. Whatever it costs. I want to take my beautiful wife in a beautiful dress.'

Then Leanne had announced that she and Jenny were going shopping. They were at Adi's house and the living room was vibrating with small children.

'But—' began Jenny.

'But nothing, Jenny Henley. The men have got this one worked out between them. Not this Saturday because it's my mum's birthday and we're going up to see her. But next Saturday. The men are looking after the kids and we're spending the day in retail therapy, my girl.'

'Are you buying something to wear at the party?' asked Adi.

'Yeah, wanna come?'

'I'm making my dress,' said Adi shyly. 'I just hope the party isn't cancelled.'

'No way! So the boys get shipped out to Afghanistan. We can still make whoopee at the Dorchester without them!'

Jenny got up to go.

'I'd better make a move. I want to stop at Agnieszka Dermott's on the way home to say goodbye.'

As usual, at the mention of Agnieszka's name the temperature dropped a few degrees.

'I didn't phone. But I put a farewell card through her door,' Adi admitted.

'What's taken them so long to come and pick the Polish slag up?' demanded Leanne, her voice harsh.

Battered old cars and a van had arrived from Poland. The drivers did not park outside Agnieszka's house but around the side roads at the fringes of the camp as if they did not want people to know that they were there, or why. All the same, everyone guessed.

Adi gently removed Jenny's car keys from a small child's mouth and disentangled one twin's hand from the other's hair. 'Well, I think there was a delay because the compensation for Jamie's death only just came through.' Adi always knew everything.

'She's a rich bitch now,' said Leanne.

Jenny picked up the baby, the other Jaime. She said quietly: 'Money won't bring Jamie back.'

'She didn't want him back!' Leanne retorted. 'All that money for a bloke she was ditching anyway!'

Jenny did not ring Agnieszka's bell because the door was open, the lights were on and people were moving in and out of the house with furniture and bags and boxes, loading them into a couple of small Polish vans which had pulled up at the kerb. She intercepted Agnieszka as she appeared carrying a transparent bag full of Luke's toys.

'You must be going back to Poland,' said Jenny.

Agnieszka surveyed her coldly. Jenny had always thought her beautiful but the Polish girl had avoided her for such a long time that Jenny had no idea how thin she had become. Her cheeks were too gaunt, her blue eyes too large, too sunken now. Jenny recognized the face of widowhood.

'I leave tonight. I take boat.'

'Agnieszka, I wanted to say goodbye.'

'Thank you, Jenny. Goodbye to you also.' The words were spoken without feeling. Jenny was stung by this.

'We used to be friends. And I've never blamed you for anything. A lot of people around here have judged you. But not me.' She looked down for a moment. 'It's been really hard for you, Agnieszka. I've tried to understand what you've been through.'

Agnieszka raised her finely plucked eyebrows.

'So what you think you understand, then? Understand how it is to lose husband? No, Jenny, you don't understand nothing.'

She was probably right. Jenny didn't want to

understand that. She said: 'I hope you recover from your loss in Poland and go on to have a calm, quiet, happy life, Agnieszka. I really hope all the bad things are over for you now. Good luck to little Luke too. You know our address. If you decide to keep in touch, we'll be more than happy.'

For a moment Agnieszka seemed to soften. Behind her a woman passing with a pile of cushions for the van muttered something in Polish but Agnieszka ignored her.

'Thank you, Jenny. You nicer to me than anyone else here. But you can't understand. I don't know if I keep touch or not.'

'We'll never forget you. And we'll never forget Jamie,' Jenny said, putting her arms around the Polish girl. Agnieszka felt so thin and brittle that she might break. She did not return the hug. 'And I'll never forget how kind you were to me when you visited the hospital just when I was having the baby. Thanks for that.'

They pulled away and for a moment the two women looked at each other in the dark, the dim light from the hallway falling softly across their faces.

'Well, good luck,' said Jenny, turning abruptly. She was fighting tears. Why? She had never been close to Agnieszka and since Jamie's death the Pole had barely spoken to her. Why did this young widow and her isolation touch her so deeply?

'Good luck, Jenny,' Agnieszka called after her, animation in her voice at last. But Jenny found that her throat was too tight to produce a cheery farewell. She turned around and waved instead. Agnieszka, her tall, thin figure framed by darkness in the soft pool of light, waved back. Jenny knew she would never see her again. It was as though someone else had died.

When she got home, both the children were asleep in the buggy and Dave was there, still in uniform. He did not ask her where she had been. He helped her with the buggy and picked up Jaime quietly without waking her. Before he turned to take the baby upstairs, Jenny saw his face clearly. Quiet, serious and a little sad. She knew what it meant.

'You're going,' she stated flatly, all emotion drained from her voice. 'You're going back into theatre.'

He looked at her.

'We deploy in less than three weeks,' he said. His voice was flat too.

They continued to stare into each other's eyes over the children in the darkness, the sound of the TV chatting meaninglessly to itself from the living room, a studio audience laughing softly. Jenny felt tears sting her. She turned away.

At the Buckles' house, Leanne was pinned down on the sofa.

'I just don't know what that shit letter's trying to tell me!' Steve Buckle roared. He was pacing the small living room, pirouetting on his prosthetic leg every time he reached the end.

Leanne waved the letter. 'It says that—'

A toy pinged against her shin. Whenever Steve passed a toy on the floor he kicked it vigorously in Leanne's direction. This was the third time he had scored a direct hit and now she heaved up her legs and lay down on the sofa, pulling some cushions in front of her for protection. Just in case Steve decided to throw the toys as well as kick them.

'I know what it says. But they haven't told me no yet! They haven't actually said no!' He aimed another toy at her. It skidded ferociously across the floor. He was a large man who was dark-haired and dark-eyed anyway but when she glanced up at his face she thought it looked as if a storm had hit it.

'Steve, they've said you're a P3. And everyone knows that a P3 can't fight in the front line.'

'Don't tell me I can't do things! I know I can fight like I used to. I'm as fit as I've ever been.'

'I'm not telling you anything. It's the army,' she said soothingly, because the boys were upstairs in bed and supposed to be asleep. Although a few telltale bumps overhead had told her they weren't.

'Listen, what the army needs to understand is that I'm as good as the other lads. I overtake some of them when I'm out running.'

Leanne had seen Steve overtaking people early in the morning. They would be jogging along, thinking their own morning thoughts, oblivious to the fact that they were targeted as hot competition by a runner coming up behind them. Steve would charge past, a blur of sweat, metal and muscle. Sometimes he would shout things. Not a cheerful good morning, either, more like triumph or even abuse. He shouted it in a jokey way but he was not jokey enough and the runners he overtook looked startled and perplexed because they hadn't realized they were in a race.

This Steve was a caricature of his old self, the man she had married, a soldier who was full of life and laughter. He thought if he became a soldier again he could get his old self back. But he couldn't. Because that man was gone for ever.

Leanne tried not to look sad. She knew how much it annoyed him. Luckily he hadn't seen her face; he was too busy searching for more toys to kick around. The twins were into little cars and there were always a few to stumble over around the sofa and at the edges of the room.

'I'm fucking going!' he roared loudly. A small, anxious face suddenly peered around the door.

'What are you doing down here?' Leanne demanded.

A little boy scuttled out like a mouse, grabbed a tiny metal ambulance which was perilously close to his father's foot and, head down, scuttled rapidly back. As if they wouldn't notice him if he didn't look at them.

'You're supposed to be in bed,' said Leanne sternly. Small feet could be heard scampering up the stairs. A rescue mission. Ethan had been rescuing the ambulance from his scary dad. The thought made her even sadder. Upstairs there was silence now.

Leanne said: 'Well, I hope you get what you want, Steve.' Her voice was so quiet that he halted suddenly and looked at her. When he replied his voice was quieter too.

'I will, Lee. Because Dave Henley's got an idea.'

Leanne raised her eyebrows.

'An idea which means you'll go back into his platoon?' Her voice was deepened by scepticism.

'I dunno what the idea is. I'm waiting for them to get back from training and he'll tell me.'

'They're back. I saw Danny Jones going home when I looked out half an hour ago.'

'Shit!' Steve leaped for the phone as if she had given him an electric shock. Leanne sat, unmoving, on the sofa, hearing Steve's end of the conversation, guessing what Dave was saying. That he'd just got home, that he was helping with the kids, that he was eating a meal, that Jenny . . .

'All right, all right, I'll see you in an hour!' said

Steve, after failing to persuade Dave to come sooner.

He paced the living room waiting for Dave's arrival, kicking toys, moaning about the P3 letter, occasionally shouting at Leanne. When she got up to clear the kitchen he did not follow her. She could hear his footsteps, the prosthetic leg noticeably heavier than his own, clumping back and forth, back and forth. She wondered if there was a more horrible sound in the world.

When Dave finally tapped at the door, Steve put his head inside the kitchen.

'Leave us alone to talk! We don't want you in there!' he snapped at her.

Dave knew, as soon as Steve answered the door, that he had returned to a state of anger and hopelessness. His face was shadowed, his mouth discontented and Dave was barely inside the hallway before Steve shoved the letter at him.

Dave followed him into the living room and sat down. Steve remained standing, watching as he read. The promised beer did not materialize. He could hear Leanne moving around upstairs but she did not appear.

'This is just one of the standard letters they send,' Dave said. 'It's computer-generated. No one's sat in an office saying: Oh we must send that Rifleman Buckle a letter telling him he's a P3.'

'Leanne told me that.' Steve was pacing the room. He found another toy, one which had ricocheted back when he kicked it last time, and took a swing at it.

'Steady on, mate.' Dave caught the small metal car neatly. 'Kicking your kids' toys into touch isn't going to help, is it?'

'What's your idea? Whatever it is, it can't work, not now I've had the letter.'

Dave eyed Steve with alarm. He looked dangerous, as if he could hit someone. It crossed his mind that he might sometimes hit Leanne. Or the kids. But Leanne wouldn't take that lying down. She'd march into the street and shout at him where everyone could see her, or she'd go to Welfare or the doctor, or at least she'd tell Jenny. Wouldn't she?

'Didn't you mention something about beer?' Dave asked mildly.

Steve started.

'Oh, yeah, beer!' He looked in too much of a hurry for Dave's idea to think about beer but Dave sat back and crossed his legs and tried to look relaxed, like a man who was expecting a beer to arrive any minute. Even though he felt far from relaxed.

Steve went into the kitchen. Dave could hear him banging the cupboard doors open and shut. Eventually he appeared with a couple of bottles.

'Well, sit down!' Dave told him when Steve showed every sign of hovering right in front of him.

Steve sat and this seemed to calm him. He stretched out his prosthetic leg on a coffee table which was so well rubbed you could see that the leg lay there often. He took a first sip of beer and then another and Dave thought he was relaxing a bit. Before talking about work, Dave made a point of discussing the beer with him, which was made by a small local brewery. It was expensive and Dave only bought it as an occasional treat. Steve just about managed to hold a normal conversation, although he was still agitated.

Finally Dave said quietly: 'I can't stay long because I should be at home with Jenny. She's upset.'

'Oh yeah?' Steve wasn't interested.

'It was confirmed today. We're going back.'

Steve leaned forward. 'Fucking hell.'

'Probably only for a month or two. While the Americans are busy annihilating the poppy crop they need a bit of extra support.'

'When do you leave?'

'Three weeks.'

Steve groaned. 'I'll never be able to persuade them to let me go that quickly.'

'Wait,' said Dave. 'Now listen. You did an interview with the local paper, didn't you?'

Steve leaned back again. 'Yeah, but the stupid bitch got my age wrong and spelt Leanne's name wrong and—'

'The point is, a lot of people read that and found it moving. You and Leanne were honest about how it felt to lose a leg in battle and how it had affected your lives.'

Steve looked interested. Just a bit.

'Yeaaaah?'

'And didn't the MoD tell you it was a good interview?'

'Yeaaaah . . .'

'Maybe there's some way you could go back out to do some PR? To show that, despite losing a leg, you're back in Bastion, that you're still fit and able to serve . . .'

'In the front line!'

'Steve, I don't know about the front line.' Not the front line. Not when it endangered the lives of the rest of the platoon. 'Let's just start with Camp Bastion. You'd have to go out with Stores and do your job and do it seriously. But they're always flying journalists in. You could do pictures and interviews. It's good PR for the army to show that wounded soldiers are still useful soldiers.'

Steve looked thoughtful.

'Hmmm. And once I've proved myself, maybe they'll let me out of camp. If I'm still a fighting soldier, that's even better PR.'

'Look, it's just an idea. I can't guarantee it'll even get you to Bastion, mate. But maybe it's worth a try.'

Steve's enthusiasm was mounting.

'You bet it's worth a fucking try!'

'We'll start by talking to Iain Kila. And then get back to whoever OKed that interview at the MoD and talk to them about it.'

'Let's do it, mate! You'll back me up, won't you?'

'Of course.'

Steve leaped over to the sofa where Dave was sprawling and seized his hand, shaking it vigorously.

'Shit, Dave, that's one helluvan idea. And I thought you didn't care. I mean, lately it's seemed like you're trying to get rid of me all the time. And now you've come up with this! And you'll back me!'

'Don't expect too—'

'You're a real friend. If you ever need me, mate, I'll be there for you. I promise.'

Dave disentangled his hand.

'Don't get too excited, Steve. It may not work.'

But Steve was unstoppable.

'I'm going to make it fucking work!' he announced loudly.

'Shhhh,' said Dave, 'you'll wake your kids.'

Too late. Steve was roaring up the stairs: 'Leanne! Leanne! You'll never believe it, come here, woman! Dave's had one helluvan idea. It's going to get me out to Bastion with the boys!'

6

Tiny Hemmings was proving a success in 1 Section. He got on with the other lads, took the taunts about being too new and too tall on the chin and tried hard during training. George Slindon was another matter. Dave had gripped him more than once because he wasn't ready for kit inspection, didn't have the right kit or listened to his iPod during an exercise instead of PRR.

They were training daily on Salisbury Plain by going back to basic drills with newer equipment. But now that the lads were nearly all seasoned veterans who had been under fire for real, pretend fire in Wiltshire could never be the same. It was times like this that Dave missed Jamie Dermott. He'd always set an example of serious, focused, professional soldiering, even in training. Jamie Dermott. A man who appeared frequently and suddenly inside Dave's head. Unfortunately it was usually the dying Jamie, his body bloody, chunks missing from it, his head lolling, his eyes unfocused.

Sergeant Major Kila thought the men were doing well. He strolled over to Dave. 'Usually when soldiers get back from a tour, you can't wake them up. This lot are sharp because they know they're going out there again.'

'Sharp but sloppy,' said Dave. 'Because they think they've seen it all before.'

'Maybe knowing their balls are safe in the new codpiece helps,' said Iain Kila.

'How much longer will we be trialling that bit of kit?'

'Just until the end of the week.'

'The lads take it off before we get back to camp because everyone who sees them starts taking the piss.'

'No one's going to be taking the piss in theatre if it keeps men's tackle safe.'

They watched in silence as 1 Section, 1 Platoon, pepperpotted forward on a grenade exercise. They were leopard crawling, stomachs down, their knees and elbows sliding through the Salisbury Plain mud. Slindon was the grenade launcher. To his right, about five metres away, stood Binns, covering him with a rifle, and behind was Finn in a yellow safety vest. Further back stood the instructor.

'Why does the sight of Slindon with a grenade in his hand fill me with horror?' muttered Dave. 'He looks as if he's in a fucking egg and spoon race.'

'Now give the lad a chance,' said Kila amiably.

'The other men in his section are getting tired of giving him chances,' said Dave. 'I don't even need to grip him now because everyone else does.'

'He's just out of training! Your men should show some patience.'

They watched as Slindon approached the target, a battered brick structure which was supposed to double as an Afghan mud compound. He got into the right position to post the grenade and shouted a warning as he pulled his arm back to throw.

'All correct so far!' said Kila to Dave. He spoke too soon. The grenade left Slindon's hand but instead of hurtling beyond the wall it tumbled to the ground, bouncing a few feet in front of Slindon.

'Check fire!' roared a voice, too late. Binman had already fired the SA80.

Finn darted forward. He moved with such speed that Dave's eyes were a fraction of a second behind him. He saw the grenade bounce, heard the yell and then watched Finn's yellow vest leaping on to Slindon, dragging him back into the trench.

'Fuuuuuuuuck!' said Kila as the grenade exploded on the wrong side of the wall, a jagged white flash which lit up the dull day.

Kila and Dave ran forward. Finn was lying on top of Slindon in the trench. Binns had not got to the trench but he had been far enough away to remain upright and, apparently, unharmed. The others were already on their feet, shouting at Slindon. The instructor was waving his clipboard around. As Dave and Kila reached them, they saw Finn lifting Slindon up by his webbing so that he could punch his face.

'Fucking, fucking, fucking dickhead!' he roared. Dave was in time to stop Finn hitting Slindon. But he allowed the lance corporal one blow before he shouted: 'OK, Finny, that's enough.'

Sol held Finn's arm, which was lining up for another punch. Finn, like any other man in the platoon, was powerless when solid Sol held him. But he could still shout.

'You fucking dickhead, you nearly got yourself killed!'

'Wasn't worth living just to get killed by you instead,' said Slindon reasonably. 'Stop hitting me, mate.'

'What happened?' demanded Kila. 'Why didn't you throw it?'

'I did throw it but it got caught on my webbing just when it left my hand.' Slindon's cheek was already swelling where Finn had punched him.

'When it comes to killing British soldiers, we try to leave that one to the Taliban,' Kila told him.

'It's thanks to Billy Finn that you're alive!' Sol said.

'You are so quick, mate.' Hemmings looked at Finny with admiration. 'You were on to it before I even realized what had happened.'

'Finny's fucking fast and if he wasn't Slindon would be dead,' said Mal.

'So why haven't you thanked him for saving your worthless life?' Angus asked Slindon.

Slindon said: 'Thanks, Billy Finn.'

'I didn't mean to save you, Slindon, because you are a fucking load of shit.' Finny's face was still lean with fury. Sol had not judged it safe to release his punching arm yet. 'If I'd given myself time to think, I wouldn't have fucking saved you!'

While the rest of the section hurled abuse at Slindon and the instructor started a muttered discussion with Kila, Dave walked over to Binns, who was still standing motionless with his SA80.

'You all right, Binman?' asked Dave.

'Yeah,' said Binns, not reassuringly.

'Bit startled?'

'Yeah.' Binman's eyes were wide with shock. 'Slindon nearly banjoed himself there, Sarge.'

'He nearly banjoed you too, Binman.'

'Yeah.'

'You going to puke?' It had started to rain, a thin, dismal drizzle. Binman's face had been a deathly white but now it looked grey like the rain.

'Probably, Sarge.'

'Get back to the wagons and we'll have a brew.' It was no use telling Binman to man up. However bad he felt, he kept going. He turned and stumbled off, mechanically following orders. Dave watched him go. Of all the men in the platoon, Binman would find a near miss like this hardest to take and hardest to forget. He was a sensitive kid. That was what made him so good on the minefield. But when Kila had suggested that Binns specialize in counter-IED work, Dave had shaken his head. He wasn't sure Binns had the mental stamina to live with the risk, pressure and tension of dismantling landmines day after day.

'Brew,' Dave yelled across the Plain and men started to filter back towards the wagons. Sol let go of Finn and made him promise to stay clear of Slindon.

'I'll stay clear, don't worry, I don't want a grenade up my arse,' said Finn grimly. Slindon was not a tall lad but he seemed to have more arm and leg than he could keep under control. He climbed awkwardly out of the trench and stood staring at the spot where the explosion had taken place. Then he looked around the empty Plain, scratching at his groin-protection system.

Dave turned his back and fell in beside Kila: 'Slindon's fucking useless. I don't know how we've ended up with him.'

'He's a kid just out of training,' said Kila protectively. 'Of course he's going to look like an amateur when he's working with a platoon of fucking hard men who're not long back from Helmand.'

'His reports from Catterick were nothing special.'

'He's just taking a bit of time to settle in. He'll be ready to go out to Helmand in a few weeks, you'll see.'

Dave thought to himself that it was doubly hard he

had been given this clown to knock into shape because a good soldier like Jamie Dermott had died.

Back at the wagons, the whole platoon had their hands wrapped around mugs of hot tea and 1 Section was telling the other two sections about Slindon and the grenade.

'Fucking hell,' Si Curtis, corporal of 3 Section, said to Sol, 'I'm glad he got allocated to you.'

'Yeah, but we got Tiny Hemmings too and he's good,' said Sol.

'You're only as strong as your weakest link,' Si reminded him.

Sol grinned. 'I'll sort him out. Binns and Bacon came after the last tour started and they manned up fast enough.'

Kila gathered everyone around and asked: 'What do you think of the groin protection, then, lads?'

'I feel like a dickhead,' said Bacon.

'You are a dickhead,' said Mal.

'Fuck off,' said Streaky. 'You need a smaller codpiece. You're not filling yours up.'

The colour had come back into Binns's face. Dave wondered if he had sneaked off to be sick behind the wagons. The lad was grinning now. 'Take it back and ask for extra small,' Binns advised his mate Streaky.

'Well, your codpiece makes you look like one of them dancing gits in *Strictly*,' Angus told Binns. He was a whole head taller than Binman. 'And I mean the women.'

Si Curtis said: 'Show us your pirouette, Binman.'

Binman did not but Kirk and McKinley from 2 Section attempted the tango while O'Sullivan mimed burlesque.

Kila rolled his eyes. 'That's enough, lads. I had all this

crap from other platoons yesterday. The question the manufacturers want answered is: Does it make your balls feel safer? Hemmings, I bet you can give me a sensible answer.'

Tiny reddened. 'I've got nothing to compare it to, sir. I've never been operational without the codpiece.'

'Well, I can give you a sensible answer, sir,' said Slindon. Everyone stared at him. Dave raised his eyebrows. In the short time he had been with the platoon, Slindon had not earned a reputation for sensible answers.

'No,' said Slindon.

'No what?' demanded the sergeant major.

'No, sir. It doesn't make my balls feel any safer.'

Everyone continued to stare at him and Slindon looked back at them defensively.

'Well, it doesn't,' he insisted but the other men in his section were already shouting.

'Stop throwing grenades at your balls and that'll help!'

'It won't save a fuckwit who tries to blow *himself* up, Slindon!'

'It's to stop the *enemy* getting your balls. It's not for *blue on blue* balls . . .'

'Hmmmm,' said Finny. 'Blue Balls Slindon. There's a good name for you.'

'No, it's not,' said Slindon.

But Finn was considering carefully, as if deciding who would win the four thirty at Cheltenham. 'Yeah, that's it, that's your new name, mate. Blue Balls Slindon.'

'What's wrong with my old name?' asked Slindon.

'Blue Balls?' muttered the lads. 'Good one, Finny. Blue Balls Slindon.'

Slindon responded by getting out his iPod and sticking his headphones into his ears. He wandered off with his tea, unhearing, while the lads continued to criticize him.

'He'll just get himself into trouble in Afghanistan.'

'And if Blue Balls gets into trouble, chances are we do too.'

'Steve would be better on one leg than fucking Blue Balls Slindon on two!'

'Let's keep Tiny Hemmings and send Slindon back to the shop and get our money back.'

Kila raised a hand and they were immediately silent.

'Slindon's new, he's learning and he hasn't had the benefit of your experience,' Kila told them. 'No one's injured, thank God. Now just give the kid a chance.'

Kila was a hard man who didn't suffer fools gladly, so why the soft spot for an idiot like Slindon? Dave wondered if he knew Kila well enough to ask whether Slindon was his secret love child. He decided he didn't.

A Land Rover was approaching them. You could see it coming from a long way off because the Plain was so flat. There were deep ruts left by other vehicles and the Land Rover crossed them like a boat plunging over brown waves of mud.

It finally pulled up nearby and Major Willingham's adjutant, Captain Thorp, jumped out. So did another man. The lads shifted their mugs of tea into their left hands and saluted with their right.

Kila approached the Land Rover. 'Sir!'

Dave was looking hard at the newcomers. He knew Captain Thorp, of course. It was the other man who interested him. Could this be the new platoon commander at last? He decided after a moment that was impossible. Anyone who was arriving to take charge of his first platoon would be looking at his men with keen interest. The small, square, unsmiling officer barely glanced at them.

'This is Second Lieutenant Chalfont-Price,' said the adjutant.

The second lieutenant stared over their heads expressionlessly.

The adjutant smiled. 'Let me introduce you to the new commander of 1 Platoon.'

7

Jenny had not told Dave that she was going to see the new nursery this morning. They had barely discussed it since that horrible row when they had shouted at each other about money.

She dropped Vicky off at the camp nursery and then drove the five miles to the Magic Cottage. It was situated in the grounds of a big house, up a private road and surrounded by fields and woods. The building itself was a converted barn of timber, brick and flint and one wall was solid glass so that the children could look out on to a green world.

'The other day we watched a fox trotting past and last week we saw an owl in the daytime!' said the teacher as she showed Jenny around. 'Of course, the animals vanish when we go outside. And we do spend a lot of time outside. We think it's healthier for the children, even if it's cold, as long as they're wearing the right clothes. That's our play area.'

Jenny watched a small group of children climbing on beautiful wooden equipment. Two staff joined in, talking to some, holding the hands of others. The children were laughing together. Inside, there was a lot of light and more wooden toys and art equipment. The atmosphere was one of quiet industry. All the children seemed calm and happy. Jenny wanted to sign up Vicky then and there.

As she left, the teacher warned her: 'We only opened three months ago but we're almost full already. If you're really interested, you'd better move fast.'

'I will,' Jenny assured her. She strapped Jaime into the car and threw the bundle of literature she had been given on to the front seat. When she reached the camp nursery she was twenty minutes early and Jaime was fast asleep. She reached for the information pack.

The more she read the more she wanted Vicky to go there. Until she saw the page headed Schedule of Fees. There was a hefty and non-returnable deposit which added up, with other deposits, to about eight hundred pounds. Eight hundred pounds! There was no way Dave would agree to that. Because if one child went there, Jaime would have to go as soon as she was old enough, and that would be sixteen hundred in deposits alone. Then there were the fees, which were substantially higher than camp nursery fees.

Other mothers were gathering now. It was the usual scrum until the automatic gates swung open, when mothers surged forward, a tide of coats, hats and scarves, into the play area. But the nursery doors were still firmly shut.

The mothers regrouped, talking and laughing together. Adi Kasanita was at the centre as usual; you could hear her laugh ringing over everyone else's. Jenny sneaked to the window and looked in.

A circle of children sat around one staff member who was reading to them. Another circle was at the play-dough bench but the children were throwing the play dough instead of modelling with it. Behind them boys were running wildly around, a teacher shouting at them over her shoulder to stop. Other staff members were busy clearing up pots of glue and small, brightly coloured pieces of paper. Where was Vicky?

Then Jenny's heart stopped. A throng of children, Leanne's boys among them, had been colouring an enormous picture on the floor but they were finishing now and were hurling crayons. Specifically, they were hurling them at one child. Vicky. Who sat hunched in the middle of the group as if she could not make herself small enough, her face pinched with misery, clutching at her hair in a strange, cowed gesture which seemed to bring her comfort.

Jenny's heartache was rapidly annexed by fury. She banged on the window. A couple of the mothers outside paused in their chatter to stare at her. But no one inside heard over the commotion.

As soon as the doors opened, Jenny found Vicky standing by her coat hook waiting anxiously. She wasn't howling, but tears fell silently down her small, pink cheeks.

'Darling, I saw them!' cried Jenny, scooping her up despite the fact that she was already holding Jaime. 'Why didn't you tell a grown-up?'

Vicky clung to her mother, sobbing. Jenny cuddled her and looked around for Shona, who was in charge of the nursery. She was locked in conversation with another mother.

'Right. We'll get your things and as soon as Shona's free we'll talk to her about what happened. Mummy is very angry,' said Jenny, letting go of Vicky in time to swing Jaime out of Tiff Curtis's way.

'Sorry,' said Tiff, grabbing her daughter's scarf. 'Didn't see you were carrying the baby.'

Leanne arrived, steaming through the crowd of mothers to the twins' coat hooks.

'I'm late, I'm late! Where's those boys? Causing havoc as usual?'

She was right. Ethan and Joel were currently shelling the play house with pretend mortar.

'STOP THAT AND COME HERE!' roared Leanne. The boys looked up at her briefly and then mortared the Quiet Corner.

Jenny wanted to tell Leanne angrily that the last bombardment had been aimed at Vicky but Leanne did not pause for breath.

'Guess what, Jenn, guess what, Rose. Tiff! Adi! Just guess.'

The mothers did not stop gathering their children and putting on their coats and gloves but their focus was now on Leanne.

'You got the job at the garden centre?' suggested Rose.

'Nah, I was shit at the interview.'

'What then?' asked Tiff Curtis.

'Steve's going to Afghanistan with everyone else!'

For a moment Jenny forgot her fury with the nursery and that her small daughter was crying.

'To Afghanistan? On spearhead?'

Leanne grinned widely. 'Yup!'

'Not . . . not with 1 Platoon?' asked Rose.

'No, he's a storesman. Until he sneaks out to the front line, that is.'

'He's going to be fighting!' said Jenny in amazement.

'Well, not officially. But you know Steve. He won't let them keep him in Bastion.'

'But a P3 can't go to Afghanistan at all, let alone out of Bastion!'

Dave had told Jenny that. He had said that no matter how good Steve was on his metal leg, it wasn't safe out of Bastion for him or the other lads who would have to support him.

'Yeah, well, that's my Steve! He doesn't care two hoots about your P3s!'

Jenny glanced at Rose in time to catch the concern on her face before the other woman looked away, saying loyally: 'I'm pleased if you're pleased, Lee.'

Leanne must be the only wife in camp who was delighted that her husband was going back into theatre, Jenny thought. Leanne, who seemed to read her mind, blushed.

'Well, I know I used to be against it but I am pleased, girls, because it's what he wants more than anything else. And I don't think he's going to settle until he's done it.'

'How did he persuade them?' asked Jenny.

'It was all thanks to Dave!'

Jenny stared at her.

'Dave?'

'It was his idea!'

Jenny was incredulous. 'For Steve to fight with the platoon?'

'Sort of. After that woman from the local paper came and wrote the article about him. Dave said he should go to the MoD press office about doing more interviews and publicity and promotion and stuff . . .'

'So what's he promoting?'

'He's showing people how losing a leg doesn't stop you living and doing your job. They're going to take pictures of him at Bastion and he has to do interviews when journalists visit . . . Major Willingham wasn't too keen, but they overruled him.'

There was no time to talk further. The room was thinning now and Jenny could feel Vicky's tiny hand clutching more tightly at her leg. Shona, across the room, was free. She was picking crayons up. Rose rustled out of the door, Tiff took her daughter and Leanne neatly grabbed one of her twins by the scruff of the neck as he ran past her.

'See you later!' the mothers called to each other as Jenny marched across the room to Shona.

'Don't slip on the crayons. They're all over the floor,' warned Shona. She was a relaxed and smiling Australian whom Jenny had liked until she had started to notice how badly supervised the nursery was.

'They're all over the floor because a bunch of kids were throwing them at Vicky!' said Jenny, her own words generating a new surge of anger.

Shona stood up. She did not look concerned.

'Is that what Vicky told you, Jenny? I don't think it's true.'

'She didn't tell me anything. I saw them through the window.'

Shona looked pained. 'Well, Vicky can sometimes antagonize the other children.'

'Antagonize them! They were antagonizing *her*!' exclaimed Jenny.

'She's a lively child who's beginning to learn how to develop relationships but she does have issues with some of the boys.'

'Issues! With boys! She's *three*!'

'She needs to assert herself more,' said Shona, shaking her head. 'Vicky tends to burst into tears before they've even done anything.'

99

'Just because you didn't see them, it doesn't mean they didn't do it,' Jenny retorted.

Shona's face was serious. 'Well, Jenny, I think we need to look at why Vicky cries so easily. Maybe we should ask ourselves if perhaps that's how she gets attention at home? Or maybe we should look at whether we're incentivizing her to cry in some other way.'

Jenny's anger was checked. It was all her fault. She was a bad mother. The other kids were picking on Vicky because her own mother had turned the little girl into a pathetic, sobbing victim. And didn't Dave always tell her not to mollycoddle the child?

'You see, Jenny,' said Shona, smiling kindly because Jenny's discomfort was obvious, 'everything a child does here at the nursery is a reflection of her home life. We can pick up the pieces but you mothers have to work on the fundamentals at home.'

That did it. Afterwards Jenny thought the expression 'pick up the pieces' had been the trigger, as if Vicky experienced anger or violence or neglect at home when all she got was love. But it might have been Shona's patronizing tone. Jenny knew then and there that Vicky was not coming back to this nursery. So there was no point shouting. There was no point telling Shona that she should stop blaming mothers when their children were unhappy in her badly run nursery.

The last child was being wrapped inside a coat, hat and scarf. In a moment everyone apart from the staff members would be gone and several already had their coats on. One was jangling her car keys loudly in her pocket. Jaime squirmed in Jenny's arms and began to gather her body up the way she did before she cried.

'I'll give that one some thought, Shona,' said Jenny

carefully. 'I can see you're all in a hurry to get home. But after what I saw today I have to tell you that I'm finding another nursery for Vicky.'

Shona's face contracted. Her eyes narrowed.

'I'm sorry you feel like that. We got a ninety-two per cent approval rating from parents in our last survey.'

Jaime was crying now and Jenny was forced to shout to make herself heard: 'Well, when I see kids bullying my daughter and no one stopping them, you can put me in the other eight per cent.'

The staff stared at her in hostile silence as she helped Vicky with her coat, her arm aching from holding Jaime. No one moved to assist her. She could feel that her face was flushed. Vicky's was swollen from crying and Jaime was wailing miserably. Jenny did not look at anyone or say goodbye as she left the nursery.

Outside, the shock of the cool air stopped Jaime's tears and she opened her big eyes wide. Jenny paused for breath. Shit. She felt the first twinge of regret, the way she usually did after a row with Dave. Had she been hasty withdrawing Vicky before she had found anywhere else for her to go? Although she had, of course, found somewhere else. Unfortunately, the Magic Cottage cost an arm and a leg and Dave would never agree to it.

Jenny decided, as she lifted the children up to the car and strapped them into their seats, that she would not tell him what had happened today until she could also tell him that she had found a job which would help pay for the new nursery. She had made several applications and had received one very encouraging acknowledgement, from the Market Street Bakery. Maybe she would even have a job by the time he went away.

8

At the arrival of the new Platoon Commander, Dave called the men over and they straightened up and stretched and yawned and stood around him in a ragged circle, most still holding their mugs. Dave tried to see them through the eyes of the new, young officer. They did not look impressive. They looked ally. And slapdash. Particularly since Slindon's ear was now clamped to his mobile. Dave tried glaring at him but Slindon did not meet his eye.

It crossed Dave's mind that he had been too easy on his platoon. Since they were back recently from theatre with their battle skills still sharp and shortly to return there, it had seemed unnecessary to jump down their throats right now about every little thing. He hoped this new commander, Something-Price, would understand this. And he hoped the man would notice the lads' affable and shy grins of welcome.

Captain Thorp said: 'There were not just one or two men here who showed distinguished service in theatre recently; the exceptional contribution of the entire platoon has been widely recognized. They played an extremely important role in the Special Forces release of the American hostage Martyn Robertson. They also sustained a number of casualties in an old Soviet mine-field and it is entirely due to the bravery, fast thinking and painstaking work of their colleagues that the casualty list wasn't longer . . .'

The lads shuffled their feet and looked at the ground and exchanged embarrassed looks. Even Dave felt himself reddening a little. The adjutant introduced Dave next.

'You'll be safe in the hands of one of our finest sergeants, Second Lieutenant.'

'And,' said Chalfont-Price quickly, 'he will be safe in mine. Pleased to meet you.' He spoke in a clipped accent, his eyes barely meeting Dave's, his mouth scarcely moving. Dave felt a flash of irritation. Who was in whose hands around here and how could you be pleased to meet someone if you didn't even look at them?

He made sure his voice remained warm and even. 'Welcome to the platoon, sir. We're all looking forward to working with you. If you've noticed we're wearing superhero underpants on the outside of our combats, I should explain that we're trying out the new anti-mine pelvic girdles.'

At this some of the men obligingly turned and gyrated their hips, while others pointed helpfully at the girdles or struck mannequin poses. Captain Thorp and the sergeant major laughed out loud. Only the new officer remained unsmiling.

'Sergeant, when exactly are we deploying?' he demanded grimly.

Dave gave him the date, although it was hard to believe he didn't already know it.

'So,' said Second Lieutenant Chalfont-Price, 'at this

stage, so close to redeployment, I'd have expected things to look a bit less ally, Sergeant.' The men shuffled and straightened sheepishly but Chalfont-Price did not stop. 'I'm seeing men with dirty boots and uniforms askew, I'm seeing body belts hanging loose, I'm seeing a man on the phone, I'm seeing some weapons which look as if they need a good clean . . .'

Dave stared at him, too shocked to reply. Kila's face, topped by his great, bald dome, was frozen in surprise. Captain Thorp's mouth was open.

Dave wanted to say: Fuck off. Even if the commander was right – and he probably was – this was no way to greet your men for the first time. But hadn't Kila just said (about Slindon, whose mobile Dave would like to smash to the ground now, since it was *still* clamped to his ear) that any man joining the war-torn platoon at this stage would look like an amateur? The new commander was simply another new boy who didn't know how to behave. And it would be Dave's job to show him.

'Well . . .' he said politely. 'I have relaxed a bit over the small things for this brief period between tours.'

Chalfont-Price interrupted him. 'We might as well start as we mean to go on. You'll soon discover that I believe the secret of a sound fighting unit *is* the small things.'

Everyone listened to the short, square officer. The men were still now, their eyes wide. Even Slindon had sensed that something was up and had put away his phone.

'If we get the small things right, we'll get the bigger things right too. That's my philosophy. So just let me see the men looking like this again and I'll be down on you like a ton of bricks, Sergeant, because sloppy presentation nearly always means sloppy fighting, in my experience.'

There was a long silence. Dave suppressed an urge to punch him. At the very least, he wanted to ask this arrogant young man just what experience he was referring to. There had apparently been a delay in replacing Gordon Weeks after his departure for JTAC because his successor hadn't finished his post-Sandhurst training at Brecon. So this self-important twat had no experience at all beyond training.

Captain Thorp broke the silence. 'Well, Dave,' he said, with forced cheerfulness, 'it seems it's time to tighten that vice-like grip for which you're so well known. Now then, there's a lot of paperwork waiting for your new commander but tomorrow he'll be joining you out here in training.'

The two officers returned to the Land Rover. Dave bristled as he caught a fragment of Chalfont-Price's words: '. . . have to get behind the sergeant to knock them into shape . . .'

The platoon watched in silence as the Land Rover roared back across the furrows of mud. Then they erupted, their voices incredulous. Kila came over to Dave.

'Fucking hell,' he said, scratching his bald head vigorously, his face surprised, as if he had just discovered hair there.

'Fucking hell,' echoed Dave. 'Just out of Sandhurst and telling us about *his* experience when *we've* come back from theatre!'

'He's a bit up himself,' admitted Kila.

'Up himself! If I met him in the pub, after a few pints I'd want to punch him. Is he going to speak to me like that in theatre?'

'You'll be good mates when you've all spent a few weeks training together.' Kila didn't sound convincing. 'He's just trying to impress you.'

'He hasn't impressed me.'

'He's probably a different bloke when you get to know him.'

But Dave could feel anger pumping around his body like an intruder in his blood vessels. The more he thought about the new commander, the angrier he felt. 'He didn't say a word to his men!'

'The army doesn't need people to be nice. In theatre it needs them to be hard. And it's not easy to look hard when you're as small as he is.'

'Self-important bastard,' Dave muttered. 'What's his name again?'

'Chalfont-Price.'

'Chalfont-Prick.'

Kila pointed. 'He was standing over on that mound, look. I reckon that's why he didn't come any closer, because he's a head shorter than most of his men. Even Binns has got a few inches on him.'

'Yeah, well, being four foot nothing shouldn't have stopped him looking at his men or speaking to them.'

'He looked at them. He just looked a bit too closely.'

Gordon Weeks had been easy to work with because he admitted all his faults, recognized how much he could pick up from his sergeant and learned fast. Whenever he tried to give orders they went pear-shaped but, all the same, he made sure he had a personal relationship with every lad in the platoon. It was hard to imagine this distant, unsmiling, dissatisfied young man doing that.

'All he did was criticize.'

'All right,' conceded Sergeant Major Kila. 'So the

bloke's tried to show he's hard and he's made a twat of himself. Now he's got a lot of ground to make up. It's your job to help him.'

Dave knew the sergeant major was right. He went over to the men, who fell silent as he approached. He could guess the kind of things they had been saying.

Angus asked loudly: 'Is it true he only left Sandhurst yesterday, Sarge?' His face was red with indignation.

'And the week before that he was in short trousers at fucking Eton,' Dave heard someone else say, probably Finn.

Dave made an immense effort.

'It doesn't matter when he left Sandhurst or where he went to school. What he said was right. We do look ally. Wearing these fucking pant things doesn't help. But tomorrow I want everyone looking their best. That includes you, Fife, Kirk, O'Sullivan, Slindon, Bilaal, Jonas . . .' He looked around. Well, why name names when every last man could improve? 'You all looked fantastic for the medals parade. That's the standard tomorrow. We've made a bad first impression and we'll have to work fucking hard to change it.'

'What about the bad first impression he made on us?' It was Lance Corporal Billy Finn again, the man with an answer to everything. 'I mean he's going to have to work fucking hard to change that.'

Dave tried not to look as though he agreed with Finn. Which he did.

'OK, back to work. Slindon, do you know what you're doing now? Slindon? *Slindon!*' Slindon was staring into the middle distance, eyes glazed.

'Christ,' said Dave. 'What's up with him?' Recently there had been a lad in 3 Platoon whose expression had been similarly glazed just before he had an epileptic fit.

'Blue Balls!' hollered Sol in Slindon's ear. The lanky lad started and tugged at the earphones which were hidden inside his helmet.

'I'm talking to you. And you're listening to your fucking iPod!' Dave roared.

'Sorry, Sarge, I thought we was still having a brew.' Slindon began winding the earphones carefully.

Dave looked at Sol in disbelief.

'He nearly killed himself and others. Has he listened to his safety talk?'

Sol nodded. 'He won't do that again, will you, Blue Balls?'

Slindon was concentrating so hard on winding his earphones that he didn't hear.

'SLINDON!'

The lad jumped. Even Sol, always patient, invariably smiling, looked pained.

'Sorry, Sarge,' Slindon said nervously.

Dave and Sol exchanged glances. Would this lad ever be ready for Afghanistan? They were deploying in ten days.

That evening, when the children were asleep and Dave and Jenny had sat down in the kitchen together with a brew instead of tackling the pile of washing up, Dave said: 'I wanted to punch a bloke today.'

'That's funny, I wanted to punch a woman today. Shona at the nursery . . .' She stopped, and Dave thought she was bracing herself to tell him something. But instead she said: 'Who did you want to punch?'

'Our new platoon commander.'

'He's arrived!'

'He can go back where he came from as far as I'm concerned.'

She looked at him uncertainly.

'He's a twat,' said Dave.

He told her what had happened and then wished he hadn't. Her face clouded with concern. He found himself downplaying the way the new officer had behaved but it was too late. She was biting her lip, always a bad sign.

'It'll probably be all right,' he said unconvincingly. 'When he's settled in.'

But Jenny had taken on that white, worried look.

'So you're going back into theatre with a man who sounds like a complete idiot in charge. It's just not safe.'

Dave made a superhuman effort and managed to shrug.

'We'll see what he's made of when we're training in Brecon next week. I expect we'll come back the best of friends. We'll probably be getting Martyn Robertson to invite him to the Dorchester with everyone else.'

Jenny knew Dave well enough to recognize this as sheer bravado. She just looked at him, chewing her lip. He tried to cheer her up.

'Don't forget that tomorrow morning you're going to shop until you drop with Leanne. And don't bother to come home without a party dress in a big, posh bag.'

She nodded, but he could see that not even the prospect of a Saturday morning of retail therapy would allay her concern.

Angus McCall strolled around the retail park in a scarf and thick hoody trying to look like a respectable shopper who was bundled up against the weather. He went to Homeware House and strolled through Accessories and Wall Art. Then into a big carpet shop. He did his best to avoid any assistants bounding up and wagging their tails: 'Can I help you, sir?' He didn't want anyone remembering his face.

He went upstairs towards the Berber Loop Pile area. There were a few windows here. He pretended to examine the carpets while peering out. Yes. World in Your Lounge had parking all around and was at an angle to the carpet shop and the motorway. The windows gave him a good side view; he could even see part of the back of the shop.

He went down the stairs and crossed the car park to the front entrance of World in Your Lounge.

No one who worked here seemed to care much about how the goods were displayed. Angus walked through about two kilometres of armchairs and another kilometre of coffee tables and everything was higgledy-piggledy.

Each time he passed a member of staff, Angus looked at their name badge. Because there weren't many assistants, it was easy to pick out Aamir. He worked in sofas. Since he would be unable to identify Angus when he was dead, Angus had decided that it was safe to talk to him.

''Scuse me, mate, can you give me a hand?'

'Sure,' said Aamir. He looked like a little shit, a weasel of a bloke with sticking-out ears, and, thought Angus, a coward who would cheek you and then run away rather than face the consequences.

Aamir listened to him as he asked: 'I've got this girl-friend who's really allergic. I only want a sofa with, like, natural fibres.'

He had read this problem in the homes section of a free magazine and it had sounded like a good one.

Aamir nodded as if he'd heard it before. He had very deep brown eyes and a surprisingly deep voice. He said: 'Well, you can check on that by looking at the labels. They're usually under the seating. Some of them say one hundred per cent natural. Depends how allergic she is. If it's just the covering you're worried about, you can have anything covered in a natural fabric.'

He stooped down to show Angus where the labels were and Angus silently hated the back of his head. He smelled of cigarettes, though, which was good, because it meant there was only one place for him to go during a break.

'OK, mate, thanks a lot.' He spent the next half-hour examining sofa labels, half watching Aamir as he wandered through the three-seaters for one customer and then the two-seaters for another. It was obvious when Aamir was taking his break because another staff member tapped his watch and Aamir nodded and disappeared.

Angus was quick. He went straight to the car park, crossed it and back to the carpet shop. Upstairs and over to Berber Loop Pile.

Through the windows he saw Aamir was having a smoke with two mates by the side door, huddled up because of the cold. Shit, if Angus had a rifle with him now and the window had been open . . .

'Can I help you, sir?'

Angus jumped. But he was ready. He had nicked a small piece of fabric earlier from Homeware House and he produced it now. 'What colour carpet goes with this?'

The man examined it. 'Well, sir, it's a question of choosing what kind of carpet you want and after that we can match the colour.'

Angus knew it was essential to be such a boring, ordinary customer that the man would not remember him. He tried to escape but the man led him to the back of the store to see some cheaper carpets and here was another window. This gave Angus some useful information. About five hundred metres, maybe more, down the motorway, was a footbridge which might allow a clear sight of the World in Your Lounge side door.

As soon as he escaped from the assistant, his pockets stuffed with leaflets and brochures, he walked smartly to the motorway bridge. It was cold as charity in Wythenshawe and the wind whistled down the motorway breaking the speed limit. The footbridge certainly gave him a great view and a clear shot at Aamir during his smoking break. But it was too exposed. In the time it took him to take aim and fire, about fifty cars would see him. However, from here something else was visible. A small building at the back of Homeware House. Now if he could get behind that, he would be invisible.

He walked to the building, which was evidently an ancient warehouse. He was now trying to look like a man who desperately needed to pee. He slipped behind the building and did not stop for more than fifteen seconds because in that time he could see everything he needed to. A clear sight on the side door of World in Your Lounge. And there were no security cameras here. Perfect.

Leanne pulled her large face into a tragic shape, mouth, eyes and maybe even ears drooping downwards.

She handed the assistant back a mountain of clothes and hangers. 'You look fantastic in anything and I look fucking awful in everything.'

'This dress costs so much it would look fantastic on anyone.' Jenny passed it firmly to the assistant.

'No good?'

'Bloody good!' insisted Leanne. 'Go on, buy it, Jenn.'

'I can't, Leanne. I just can't spend that much.'

The assistant grinned sharkishly. 'It's a classic style that will last and last. Classics are a great investment.'

'I don't need it to last. I'm a sergeant's wife and I happen to be going to a gig at the Dorchester. But guess what, I mostly spend my time up to my elbows in nappies and I'm probably not going to the Dorchester again, ever.'

Leanne put her hand on her hip and gave the assistant a conspiratorial look.

'C'mon, Jenn. Dave told you to do some serious spending today. That money he gets for being in theatre was earned by you, too. You earned it worrying about him and coping alone and having a baby by caesarean all by yourself.'

The assistant looked scandalized.

'All by yourself? You had a baby all by yourself!'

'No,' said Jenny. 'There were doctors everywhere, a million nurses, a whole roomful of paediatricians . . . What my friend means is that my husband couldn't be there.'

'Well, in my opinion, then,' said the assistant, 'he owes you this.'

Jenny paused, looking at the green dress which hung from the assistant's arm. It was almost sleeveless and tiny green beads were sewn into its fabric. When she had slipped it over her head it had come to life, falling immediately into place, somehow draping itself across her body in a subtle, sexy way. She knew Dave would love it.

'I can't. Not when I think of all the other things we should do with the money.'

Leanne grimaced. 'You're not still going on about that nursery!'

Jenny blushed.

'OK,' Leanne told the assistant. 'Put it by. And I'll work on her.'

'Will an hour be enough?' asked the woman. 'It's a gorgeous dress and there are a lot of people shopping today.'

'Hold it back until one o'clock,' Leanne instructed, sweeping out of the shop.

'I can't afford it, so don't bother,' said Jenny quietly to the assistant as she went, with a quick, sad glance at the dress.

'I'll hold it until one,' the woman said firmly. 'If your husband's told you to treat yourself, you should go ahead and do it.'

Jenny found Leanne standing outside, phone against her ear, shouting into the shopping mall. The crowds parted around her like water.

'Yes, I did. Oh wow! That's fantastic! What time did you say? I'll write it down. No I won't, I haven't got a pen.' Her face was reddening. 'Er, I'll remember it. Ten o'clock. And what day did you say? Tuesday, OK! Thank you, thank you very much!'

Jenny waited.

'Go into the caff, Jenn,' Leanne said. 'I have to ring Steve. I'll explain in a minute.'

Jenny went into the café with glass walls that ran along the street edge so you could watch people. She ordered them coffees. She knew Leanne liked frothy cappuccinos with chocolate on top served in immense cups which were as wide as her face. She watched Leanne through the window: chatting, her face animated. Then she watched as Leanne made another call. From the exasperated look on Leanne's face as she gave her news, Jenny guessed she was speaking to her mother. Then she felt her own phone buzz in her pocket.

'Hello, this is Raj Lerner from the Market Street Bakery. You applied for a job as an assistant here?'

Jenny felt her heart miss a beat.

'Oh yes! Yes, I did!'

'Well, Mrs Henley, we'd like to interview you for the job. We had seventy-two applications and we've drawn up a shortlist of just three people to interview, and you're one of them!'

Jenny was so surprised that she could hardly speak.

'Would you be available next week?'

'Certainly!'

'We'd like to invite you on Tuesday. You'll have a chance to meet us and ask any questions. We'll be choosing the person who we think will fit into our team best.'

'Right. That sounds good. What time?'

'Eleven, please.'

'Tuesday at eleven. I'll be there.'

While he gave her directions to the bakery's office she was thinking: Tuesday at eleven ... Hadn't she just heard Leanne sound similarly delighted and then similarly grateful when someone phoned to give her an appointment at ten on Tuesday? She felt her excitement drain away as if the tide was going out. She glanced up and saw that Leanne was entering the café now.

Flustered, she thanked Raj Lerner as Leanne advanced towards her, squeezing her large body between nearby tables.

'OK, we'll see you Tuesday,' he said just as Leanne plonked herself down and the coffees arrived.

'Oh God, do I deserve this!' Leanne smiled at her cappuccino. 'I am so bloody clever!'

Jenny forced a smile. 'What have you done?'

'I've only got myself into the final bloody three for a job interview, that's all!' Leanne raised her enormous cup high as if toasting Jenny with it.

This was the moment to say it. This was the moment to add, in a quiet, modest voice: 'Actually, so have I!' Instead Jenny heard her voice exclaim, with insincere surprise: 'That's fantastic! And you're down to the final three! That's amazing, Lee!'

'It's amazing because they had seventy-two applications!' chortled Leanne.

'Knock 'em dead, Lee. When is it?'

'Tuesday at ten! What will they ask me?'

'Well, it depends what the job is?' Jenny's voice was a question. As if she didn't know what the job was.

'Part-time assistant in that amazing bakery in Market Street which smells really nice all the way down the street. Never bought anything there, though. It's full of fancy breads which cost a fortune and they do these cakes . . . mmmmmm.'

'Oh yes. I know the one.' Jenny had walked past it at least five times since she had applied, staring through the windows, wondering how they made such spectacular cakes, sniffing the sweet, yeasty air which leaped out every time anyone opened the door.

'It's only about fifteen hours a week but you have to get on with people and make the customers like you. And get the change right. Shit like that. I hope I can do it, Jenn.'

'Of course you can. You'll make the customers love you.'

Leanne looked doubtful for a moment. Her face

116

shrank a little. 'What will they ask me at the interview?'

'Just make sure you tell them how much you enjoy helping people and how you'd like to establish the kind of relationships which encourage customer loyalty . . .'

'Shit, you're good! Will you write that down for me? And what do I say if they ask why I want to work in a bakery?'

Jenny knew the answer but she paused and looked thoughtful for a moment. 'How about telling them you're looking for a chance to share your passion for good food?'

'Jenny! You are a genius! How do you think of this stuff?'

Jenny tried to look modest.

'I can't believe it.' Leanne took an enormous gulp of coffee. 'I've got to do well at the interview. I was so nervous at the garden centre interview that I screwed up completely. But, I mean, if I can just get this job it'll make a big difference. I'll have some money and a life of my own . . .'

'What about the boys now Steve's going away?'

Leanne grinned. 'Sorted. Adi's going to take them. I'll have to pay her, of course. But not too much . . .' Leanne looked at Jenny closely. 'I thought of asking you. But you've got enough on your hands.'

'Yeah, Adi would be better, especially since I'm thinking of getting a job myself.'

'Good! What sort of thing are you after?'

'I don't know, I haven't started looking yet,' lied Jenny.

'Listen, I'm going to need something smart for the interview . . . you're never going to buy that green dress, are you?'

'Nope,' said Jenny firmly.

117

'So will you come with me to the outsize shop?'

'Where is it?'

'St Mark's Street.'

'Oh Lee, that's miles.'

'Yeah, but they have clothes which look OK on me. And they might have a dress for the party too.'

Jenny smiled. 'All right.'

While Leanne was in the outsize shop fitting room trying on an endless succession of clothes, she would phone back Raj Lerner from the Market Street Bakery and tell him she was withdrawing her application for the job. She still had not told Dave about her row at the camp nursery. She had been pinning her hopes on the bakery. But there was no way she wanted to compete with Leanne.

They finished their coffee and made their way across town to St Mark's Street. She did not glance back at the shop where the assistant was unnecessarily holding the green dress for her.

9

A lot of the lads complained when they were sent to Brecon on training since the following week they were leaving for Afghanistan. Finally it was announced that the training had been cut from seven days down to three.

'We'll just have to fit a lot in,' said Kila grimly. 'Or we won't be back in time for the party in London on Saturday.'

It seemed to Mal and Binman that Angus must have forgotten all about his plans to go to Wythenshawe. There had been no TA activity on the Plain, so he had not been able to steal a weapon. And he had been home last weekend and returned relaxed without mentioning Aamir.

'The thing about Angry is he just won't fucking listen,' muttered Mal as they lined up for a final kit inspection in the cold, grudging light of a February morning. 'But he's the sort of bloke who'd do anything for a mate.'

'The thing about Angry is he's mad,' said Binman. 'He's been slotting Taliban fighters called Aamir for so long that he gets back to Britain and he thinks it's all right to carry on slotting people called Aamir.'

'Well, he can start banjoing Terry Taliban next week,' said Mal. 'So that should keep him happy.'

Dave had finished with 3 Section and was approaching the 1 Section line-up. And so was Steve Buckle. He was here from Stores as usual, on the pretext that he was delivering something to someone. He stood tall, the structure of his metal leg on display. Kila and Dave had agreed to tolerate his continued and unnecessary presence because Major Willingham said it helped his rehabilitation. Dave just hoped Steve wouldn't hang around at kit inspection when they got to Bastion.

'Something missing, mate, something very important missing,' Steve informed Slindon. Seeing someone was speaking to him, Slindon tugged at his earphones.

'What's that?'

'Round your neck.'

'What?'

'What should you be wearing around your neck?'

By now Sol was bridling.

'Thanks, Steve,' he said. 'I'm section commander, so I'll deal with Blue Balls Slindon.'

But Steve, a towering, metallic presence, did not move. 'You should have your dog tag on, mate, Dave'll go spare if he catches you without your ID.'

'Thanks, Steve,' said Sol through gritted teeth as Slindon dived for his day sack, glancing around anxiously for Dave.

'We'll miss you like hell, Steve, when we get to Bastion and you're in some little office on the other side of the runway where you can't tell us what to do,' said Billy Finn sarcastically.

'We'll see, pal, if they manage to keep me in my little office!' Steve replied.

'He used to be our mate,' murmured Angus as Dave approached and Steve strolled off to annoy 2 Section. 'How did he turn into such a pain in the arse?'

'He changed after he got blown up,' said Finn.

'He was always a bit that way. Bossy and bigging himself up.'

'Yeah, but he could laugh at himself too.'

'They shouldn't let him go to Bastion,' Angry said.

'He'll be all right in Stores. But he's kidding himself if he thinks they'll let him fight.'

They fell silent as Dave's eagle eye ran over their kit and stopped when it reached Slindon, who had just finished putting his dog tag on.

'SLINDON! Where's your water?'

'It's raining in Brecon, Sarge,' explained Slindon. 'I saw it on the weather forecast.'

'Yeah. So what?'

'Well, if I get thirsty I could just open my mouth.'

The men burst out laughing. Dave held his head in disbelief.

Slindon sounded less sure of himself now: 'See, water weighs a lot, Sarge . . .'

Dave took a deep breath. 'There's an enemy ambush, you're under heavy fire, and you're standing there with your head tipped back and your mouth open *because you're thirsty . . .*' He illustrated the stance to loud laughter.

Sol said: 'Blue Balls, it rains on the Brecon Beacons but it doesn't rain a lot in Afghanistan.'

'Yeah,' said Slindon, 'but today we're heading for Brecon.'

Dave was still speechless.

Sol said slowly: 'The whole point of training is that

we prepare ourselves for what lies ahead. And what lies ahead is a dry, dusty country.'

Dave recovered. 'Blue Balls, I'm not arguing about it. Just get a fucking Camelbak, get some water in it and some more in your day sack. You keep your mouth shut and you wind your neck in or you won't stay alive long when we get to Afghanistan.'

The sun shone weakly as they loaded up the wagons. But by the time they rolled out of the camp, the winter morning had clouded over again. They had all seen the weather forecast. Rain. Turning to snow.

Dave was at the front of the second wagon. The new platoon commander had established that he always liked to sit at the front of the convoy by rudely telling Dave to move on the first morning they had worked together. Dave had bitten his tongue. Even this morning there had been a disagreement between them over who was picking up supplies and when. Dave had argued and Chalfont-Price had simply overruled him. The officer had ordered Finny to drive to Donnington halfway through training to get the supplies and Angus had immediately offered to go with him.

'There. Sorted,' snapped Chalfont-Price. 'Your analysis of the situation simply wasted time, Sergeant.'

Dave wished he could think of a smart retort but the best retorts seldom occurred to him within two hours, often not until the next day and sometimes not for a month. Although a put-down wouldn't help. The more he argued with the new boss, the worse relations would get. He knew that. And he knew that a sergeant and commander who can't work together are dangerous in theatre. He would have to try harder with Chalfont-Price.

His fury was overtaken by melancholy as they moved

122

off. They drove past the sentries and climbed the hill. The fields were sown in neat rows and below them were the houses of the camp, also in neat rows. He wondered if Jenny happened to be at a window watching them go. She had woken this morning with that sad going-away face he recognized too well. He had held her close and said: 'It's only for three days, love.' But they both knew that next week he would leave for a lot longer.

The men travelled quietly in the truck. As they passed from England into Wales the silence became pervasive. This was another arrival and the next arrival would be at Camp Bastion, Helmand. It might be hard living outside on the bleak Welsh mountains for a few days but at least they were safe here. The enemy were targets which popped up as if in a game, without ever firing back effectively. There were no roadside bombs. No one really died. Training was nothing more than a rehearsal. But it was a rehearsal for a grim reality. Reminded of this, some of the men began to ask themselves just why they had wanted so much to return to Afghanistan.

They got very wet tabbing across the hills to the RV in the rain. Now they were supposed to be resting before a night extraction exercise but the temperature had dropped dramatically. Most of the men felt too cold and wet to sleep. They lay in a hedge watching afternoon turn to evening.

Mal and Angus were huddling under their ponchos when Angus said quietly: 'By the way, mate . . .'

Mal knew at once, from Angry's careful tone, just what he was going to talk about. He braced himself.

'I couldn't get my hands on a TA sniper rifle.'

Mal felt relief spread all over him, as though someone had just switched on a heater.

Angry continued: 'But I won't need one. I've come up with a new plan to sort out your little problem up north.'

The relief ebbed away. Mal slid further down inside his maggot. His teeth began to chatter.

'Angry, mate, there's nothing you can do before deployment. There isn't time.'

'Oh yes there is. I've got time and I always keep my word.' Angus leaned forward and his voice hissed through the cold air. 'Now listen, you were right that there's no way I can get a clear sight on the target at one kilometre.'

Mal realized he was frozen. He had already been very cold but this was worse.

'How do you know that?' he demanded anxiously.

'Last weekend . . .'

'You went home last weekend!'

'Nah. I said I was going home. But I didn't.'

There was a long pause while Mal felt the impact of his words. They hurt his head, as though Angus had hit him there.

'Shit! Shit, Angry. You never went to Wythenshawe!'

'Don't worry, I didn't visit your mum. Would have been too dangerous. I just went to recce the place.'

'Fuck!'

'It's a bloody big shop Aamir works in, World in Your Lounge. And most of the furniture's crap. I agree with your mum, it's overpriced crap.'

'You went up to Wythenshawe to where Aamir works!'

'To World in Your Lounge, yeah. It's mostly cheap imports. They probably pay some Indian a fucking fiver for a sofa and then sell it for five hundred. Anyway, I saw Aamir. Smallish bloke, stocky, deep voice, with sticking-out ears, right?'

Mal gulped. 'His ears do stick out. Sort of,' he whispered.

'I got a good look at him. Then I recced the side door, which is where the target goes outside for a smoke. The best line of fire I could get would be from the motorway bridge. But that's a no-no.'

Mal said nothing. He had been turned to ice.

'The thing is, I can do the job with an SA80. I'm good for four hundred metres with it. I reckon there's one place I can fire from, around the back of this old ware-house place in the next car park. It's less than two hundred metres.'

'But they'll identify your round and find—'

'Nah. I've checked. The army's got fucking thousands of rifle barrels everywhere. There's no way they can identify the weapon from the round if I use an SA80.'

Mal still could not speak. He couldn't even swallow.

'I've got it all sorted, mate. I just needed to make sure I'm on the supplies run up to Donnington and guess what, I'm going with Finny. Easy. It's near enough to Wythenshawe and I've told Billy Finn I've got a hot chick up there I have to see before we deploy. He's going to wait at the NAAFI in Donnington chatting up birds until I get back. Then we're down the motorway and back to Brecon before you can say sniper. While the police are questioning every bloke in Manchester. Sweet, innit?'

Mal closed his eyes. Angus was insane. He was plotting to kill a civilian. Mal wanted to tell someone, to confide in Dave, even ask his mum for help. But God knew what would happen to Angry if he did. He decided that during the night exercise he would find a way to talk to Binman. And they'd make their own plan to stop Angry. He thought some more. The plan would probably have to involve Finny.

Jenny yawned and decided that she was too tired to carry out her daily trawl through the internet for jobs or even to check her email. She just wanted to go to bed, although it wasn't ten o'clock yet.

The bedroom felt cold and empty without Dave. He had been home just a few months and when he had first arrived it seemed to her that he filled every available space in the house – and some that weren't available – with his presence or his noise. But now that she was used to him again, his absence felt acute, as if he was a whole crowd of people who had suddenly disappeared.

She remembered how, that morning, she had paused at the window on the stairs as usual. From here you could look up the hill that swelled beyond the camp. It was always changing colour. Brown in the autumn. Green stripes in winter. The lines broadened in spring to a bright swathe of green. Then in the summer the whole hillside was magnificent in gold. But it wasn't summer now. It was winter and the land was a chalky brown dotted with the green pinstripes of some half-hearted crop. It was intersected by the road out of the camp and at that moment a convoy was crawling along it.

She had watched the vehicles snaking up the hillside and wondered which one Dave was in and whether he looked back at the camp, at their street, at their house.

As she climbed into bed now she felt something hard, with corners, dig into her side. She turned on the light and pulled back the bedclothes. An envelope. Her name was written across it in Dave's big writing.

She smiled and tore it open. She didn't care what was inside. It was from Dave and he had planned the note and hidden it so she would find it when he was gone, and she loved him for that.

Left you a small present. Because you are so beautiful. It's not medicine and it's not wine, it's in between. BTW, I love you.

She smiled more broadly. When they had first lived together he had left her something to find every time he went away. But that was the sort of game you gradually forgot to play when you married and had kids. Until now.

Jenny reread the clue. What was in between medicine and wine? Vinegar, maybe? Why would Dave give her vinegar? She threw on her dressing gown and went downstairs to the kitchen. She opened cupboards. Nothing unusual. She thought hard. Brandy! Some people used it as medicine. She went to the cupboard where they kept wine and beer and, maybe at Christmas, brandy. It was empty now except for two cans of beer.

She read the clue again.

It's not medicine . . .

Well, it was worth looking in the bathroom anyway. She hunted through the wall cabinet. Nothing. She went back to the kitchen. It had to be in the kitchen or the bathroom. No, wait. The treasure was *between* the medicine and the wine. It must be in the hallway.

She started an inch-by-inch search, including behind the radiator and under the phone. She ran her fingers along the edges of the stair carpet, around the top of the lamps on the landing, behind pictures. Nothing. It didn't help that she had no idea what she was looking for. But, since Dave's presents were often jewellery, she suspected it was a very small box.

Finally she gave up. She checked the doors were

locked one last time. Through the back door, she saw snow falling. She wondered if it was snowing in Wales. She dialled Dave's number. A mechanical voice, not his, informed her that he was unavailable and invited her to leave a message.

'I love you. Good night,' she said quietly. He would know that she had found the clue.

She went back up to bed and read the clue again before she turned out the light. She planned to lie thinking about it for a while, but within a few moments had drifted off to sleep.

10

When Dave tried to wake the platoon at 2200 hours, he found almost no one asleep. And no one who wanted to emerge from their maggot.

'My balls have frozen off.'

'Get moving! You're lucky it hasn't snowed.'

'It's too fucking cold to snow.'

'Get up, get ready, get on with it, lads!'

Some more trainers arrived, jumping energetically from their warm Land Rovers to join the men who had gathered around Second Lieutenant Chalfont-Price, stamping their feet, while he gave orders.

'This is an emergency night evacuation exercise and there is no GPS and strictly no mobile phones. I repeat, leave your mobile phone behind with your kit. Anyone caught with one will have me to answer to. Now, order of march is 3 Section, 2 Section, 1 Section. I'll be at the front, map-reading. Sergeant Henley at the back will round up stragglers. We hit a checkpoint every forty-five minutes to an hour and if we don't hang around we'll be back in bed at 0230 hours. Synchronize watches . . .'

Chalfont-Price was the opposite of their last platoon

commander, thought Dave. Gordon Weeks would not have been able to give such a clear set of orders. But everyone had liked him, he had known and cared for his men and he always performed well under fire. He wondered how Chalfont-Price would do in his first real battle. You could never tell until you got to theatre.

The men took their positions and plunged off into the night. The ground was frozen hard now and their boots sounded as though they were clanging on iron. Occasionally people slipped, a thud followed by swearing. Dave saw Angus tumble to the ground. About ten minutes later, the signaller did a comedy fall, arms and legs flailing, almost righted himself, and then was pulled over backwards by his Bergen. He lay winded for a few moments.

'All right, Goater?' Dave asked him.

'Yeah. Help me up, Sarge.'

Dave pulled at the signaller until he was on his feet and his antenna was pointing the right way and they set off again.

The moon was so bright that under trees it threw shadow branches with sharp edges. The commander set the pace and it was fast. Soon everyone felt warmer. Their breath could be seen above their heads in ghostly clouds. Each man's thoughts became lulled by the rhythm of his walk. Even Dave allowed his mind to wander in the silence. They swung into a gloomy wood, barely penetrated by moonlight.

Dave wondered if Jenny was in bed and whether she had found the clue. He doubted she had solved it yet; it was a good one. He smiled to himself, imagining her wandering over the house, her face puzzled, thinking hard, the clue in her hand. He was a lucky man, to have a woman like Jenny. He thought that often, but never when he was actually at home with her. Shit. That probably meant he was a fucking awful husband. Why didn't he ever say it?

They had emerged from the wood, crossed some fields and entered another wood, ancient this time, because they kept stumbling over big tree roots, before it occurred to Dave that they should have passed the first checkpoint by now.

He radioed to Second Lieutenant Chalfont-Price to halt at the front and there was no reply.

'Charlie One One to Charlie One Zero . . .'

Nothing. He tapped his radio, a sound which was usually ear-numbing, but he heard nothing. The light wasn't even on. Fantastic. The fucking radios weren't working.

He sent word up to the boss to go firm. He wanted to look at the map and give the signaller a chance to sort out comms. Chalfont-Price was invisible in the dark woods but it was easy to imagine his response, how he would stop short, angrily and impatiently.

The file came to a halt and, as Dave walked forward looking at the map, men hanging around him lighting cigarettes and opening flasks, he became aware of the sound of one pair of boots stomping towards him.

Chalfont-Price paused to question the signaller about the radios. The signaller, frantically juggling batteries, gave a harassed reply. Dave did not look up. He studied the map for long enough to be convinced that they had tabbed too far east. They should be among trees now, Chalfont-Prick was right about that. But not these trees.

'Just what are you doing, Sergeant?'

'Where are we, sir?' asked Dave.

The officer's voice was a few degrees lower than the freezing air temperature.

'Sergeant, who's supposed to be map-reading. You? Or me?'

'You, sir, but I'd be negligent if I didn't keep an eye on the map myself.'

'You have halted the whole platoon unnecessarily. I can assure you that I am fully aware of the route.'

'No harm in checking it.'

'I repeat. I am fully aware of the route.'

Dave took a deep breath. 'When do you think we'll be passing Checkpoint 1, sir?'

'Within the next ten minutes. I thought we'd get there sooner but I hadn't anticipated that the back of the file would be so slow.'

Dave felt the thump inside him of blood pumped rapidly around his body by anger. It boomed in his ears.

'There's nothing slow about the back of the march, sir. Everyone's keeping up.'

'No, Sergeant, they are not. Men keep falling at the back and I frequently have to slow down. Sometimes I feel as though the platoon is being torn in two directions: back by you and forward by me.'

This was untrue and the officer must know it. Why would any officer make stupid, snide comments about his sergeant? Was he trying to divert attention from a mistake of his own? Maybe Chalfont-Prick wasn't as confident of his map-reading as he pretended.

Dave made an immense effort. 'Right, sir. I apologize for that. I'll see to it that you don't have to slow down again.'

'Let's get going,' snapped the commander. 'And no more interruptions, please.'

Dave knew he had to tell the man that they were nowhere near Checkpoint 1. Saying nothing and letting him get completely lost would not help the platoon on a cold night. The trouble was that the pompous young git couldn't stand Dave correcting him. Not in front of the men, anyway.

'Sir,' said Dave, gesturing to a clearing, 'let's go over there and have a quick chat.'

'Chat? *Chat?* Sergeant, we are in freezing woodland in the middle of the night! This is neither the time nor place for one of your "chats".' He sounded as though Dave had suggested a bit of ballroom dancing or a quick game of snooker. A few men smothered laughter. Most watched tensely, though, sensing that an ugly row was brewing.

'I thought you might not want to discuss this in front of the men,' said Dave, his voice taut.

'At this moment in time, there is nothing we need to discuss, in front of the men or otherwise.'

The frosty woodland which enveloped them was still. There was no breath of wind. The men did not move either. Even the smokers did not raise the cigarettes to their lips.

Into the silence, Dave said: 'We're lost, sir.'

'I beg your pardon.' The commander's voice was threatening.

Dave said: 'We've missed the checkpoint because we've tabbed too far east.'

The silence got a lot louder.

'Sergeant. I have studied the route. I have studied the map. Please do not presume to give me advice.'

'Sir, I think we're in Hanging Woods. You may be confusing this with Gaunt Woods.'

'I am not confusing anything.'

'If you look at the map, sir . . .'

'I do look at the map, Sergeant. That's my job. Now you do your job and get the fucking radios sorted. That's enough of this nonsense.'

The officer turned and plunged back into the gloom of the woods.

'Sarge,' said the signaller when he could be sure the boss had gone, 'I've got a problem.'

'You don't say, Goater.'

'You know when I fell over . . . ?'

Dave nodded.

'I must've fallen on the spare battery.'

Dave looked at him. 'We've only got one radio?'

The signaller did not reply. He just looked miserable.

'And what's up with the battery? It's supposed to last eight hours.'

'I thought I put in a fresh one, Sarge . . . so either it's knackered. Or I didn't charge it properly.'

'Well, let's not go into that now, Goater. Are you sure the one in your Bergen won't work?'

'Yeah. See, with two batteries I thought I'd have sixteen hours. That's more than enough coverage for this exercise and I'm already carrying a lot of kit, see.'

'Yeah, I see,' said Dave gravely. 'I see we've got no fucking comms.'

Goater looked at the ground. 'Sorry, Sarge.'

'Good thing it's only training,' said Dave.

'It wouldn't happen if we were operational.'

'Wouldn't it, Goater?'

'We'd never be out in the middle of nowhere without comms in theatre, Sarge. Not ever.'

The thought was a chilling one. 'I hope you're right,' Dave said.

Si Curtis had pulled his men in behind the boss. Corporal Aaron Baker had shouted 2 Section into line. Sol did not need to speak to 1 Section, because they had already fallen in neatly at the back of the file and now

Dave slipped in behind them at the end of the march. Billy Finn dropped back.

'Shit, Sarge!' he hissed. 'Have we lost comms?'

'Yup.'

'How far out of our way are we?'

'You heard the boss. We're right on course.'

'Did you make a mistake, then?'

'Seems I must have done.' Dave's voice was wooden. He was beginning to doubt himself. The commander was so confident of his map-reading skills that Dave feared he might have to apologize to the man. One thing was sure, he thought grimly: he wouldn't be offering any further help.

They did not pass the checkpoint in ten minutes, fifteen minutes or thirty. They were crossing open fields now and men pulled alongside each other and began to chatter in concerned undertones as they walked. The boss tabbed on at speed and without looking back. Dave had to admit that the man had stamina. He just hoped that everyone else had enough stamina to keep up because it was going to be a long night.

After another hour, when they should have passed Checkpoint 2 and be well on the way to Checkpoint 3, Chalfont-Price stopped. Dave was relieved to see him get his map out. Danny Jones sidled up to Dave. 'Go on, Sarge, take a look at the map and give him a bit of help or we'll be out all fucking night.'

Dave raised his eyebrows but did not make a move towards his map.

Streaky Bacon from 1 Section looked miserable. 'Oh man, just try to put us straight, Sarge.'

Dave said: 'I already did. About six kilometres ago.'

'If he won't listen to you, maybe I should try to

help him?' said Sol. 'He can only bite my head off.'

'What about us?' suggested Andy Kirk and Gerry McKinley.

'Too late. Looks like he's already found someone.'

The men watched as the officer beckoned 2 Section's corporal, Aaron Baker.

'Oh no!' muttered Sol. Everyone liked Aaron but his map-reading skills were notorious. Once, during a night exercise on Salisbury Plain, he had ended up with all his men huddled by the London-bound carriageway of the M4. He was usually saved by GPS or the two men in his section who were outstanding with a map, Andy and Gerry.

Aaron Baker pored obligingly over the map with the officer now. He was talking and nodding his head. Dave could not hear what he was saying but it was probably rubbish. It wasn't that Aaron had no sense of direction. He had a sense of direction which was at least 180 degrees out.

Gerry McKinley and Andy Kirk hung around looking frustrated and awkward.

'If we're a bit lost now, we'll be fucking lost when Aaron's finished,' said Kirk.

'Maybe the checkpoint's on the M4. He can usually get us to the M4,' said McKinley hopefully.

'Go on, then,' Dave told them as the debate between the boss and Aaron Baker went on and on. 'You'd better offer.'

He watched Gerry McKinley approach the officer gingerly, Kirk behind him, as though he was a big dog which might snap. After a brief pause the riflemen retreated rapidly. So the dog had snapped.

'Well, now we're well and truly fucked,' said Finn, 'if Aaron Baker's finding our way home.'

'Could end up in Essex or Scotland or anywhere really,' agreed Mal.

'Why do we have to go so fucking fast? If we slowed down we might not get lost or need to go so far,' said Bacon.

'I'm knackered,' said Slindon.

'I'm hot,' said Binman.

'I'm hungry,' said Hemmings. 'I ate all my rations before we even started.'

'Have a fag, Big Man,' Angry told him, handing him a roll-up.

'No thanks, I hate fags.'

'If you have one you can go for longer without food.'

'Did someone say food?' asked Danny Jones. 'I am so fucking hungry. Give us some of your nuts, Sully.'

O'Sullivan's mouth froze mid-crunch and he shook his head and pulled his bag of peanuts protectively inside his webbing.

'Keep your hands off my peanuts.'

'It's painful listening to you chewing,' said Jonas. 'Sounds like a zoo.'

'Should have thought of that before you sold me your rations, mate,' said O'Sullivan cheerfully. He loved peanuts and had bought up everyone's rations before they had left Wiltshire.

'I've got a bit of scoff,' said Mal.

'Yeah, me too. I'll share it if you lot pay me back later, OK?' said Bacon.

As the discussions continued between Aaron and the boss, Dave finally decided that he should look at the map himself. The platoon commander had insulted him by ignoring his advice and asking a corporal instead. But almost thirty men were lost in the cold, with snow forecast. He should be ready to put things right if that twat Chalfont-Prick actually asked for help.

It took him a few minutes to work out what had happened. They had followed a strange and tortuous route. They'd moved off east, which was correct, but they had gone too far and then veered south-east. The swing had continued until they were going due south. And then south-west. After that, due west. Then ... Shit! They had been going around in a massive and ragged circle. However, he could also see that there was a road nearby which they could move along quickly and which would cut through all their mistakes and bring them to Checkpoint 4. True, they would have missed out all the earlier checkpoints and would be in trouble for that, but by now the training staff manning them would have given up and gone back to camp for a beer anyway, and at least the platoon would be on course and not too far behind time.

Suddenly there was a roar. The commander had looked up from his map.

'Just what do you think these men are doing, Sergeant?'

You could ask them yourself, thought Dave. Except that would mean talking to them.

Dave looked around at the men. Some were sitting on a wooden fence, others were on the ground, most were passing flasks or food around.

'We've been tabbing hard across country, sir, and now they're thirsty and hungry.'

'This is a night extraction exercise, not a picnic! Get them back on their feet and ready to go within three minutes.'

Dave said carefully: 'Are you confident of the route now, sir?'

Chalfont-Price threw him a contemptuous look.

'Corporal Baker has been very helpful and we'll shortly be arriving at Checkpoint 2. We've bypassed the first RV but that's not too much of a problem.'

Dave looked down at his map. There was no way they were within an hour, or even two, of Checkpoint 2.

'Sir—'

'Sergeant, get these men moving now. Corporal Baker and I have established our position.'

'We are nowhere near Checkpoint 2, sir.'

The small man inflated with anger, like a balloon which would soon be so full of air it would float away. 'Sergeant Henley. We know what we are doing and we have no time to waste *chatting* about it. Now sort out these men.'

Dave told the men to get back into file. They moved slowly. It took them a while to put away their food and drink and Chalfont-Price shouted twice at Dave to get the men to hurry up.

Just before the platoon commander moved off, Dave decided to swallow his pride and offer help one more time.

'Sir, if you look at the map—'

But the officer was already walking away. He either did not listen or did not hear. Dave knew it was his job to make the young man hear. He knew that if this situation arose in theatre they could all die. He should run after Chalfont-Price's retreating back and insist on showing him their position on the map. And if the officer had apologized or given some small indication that Dave had been right earlier, Dave would have done it. But Chalfont-Prick was an arrogant shit. So, thought Dave, fuck him.

11

Jenny woke up in the night. She didn't look at the clock; she looked at her mobile, to check she hadn't slept through a call from Dave. That was her waking routine when Dave was away and she had slipped back into it without even thinking about it because his absence was beginning to feel more normal than his presence these days.

No missed call; 1 a.m.

She gathered the covers more tightly around her and closed her eyes. Dave would be awake now; he had said that the platoon was on some kind of night exercise. He was probably loving it, especially if the snow had reached Wales. There was nothing Dave enjoyed more than stomping across a dark landscape, and the wilder the terrain and the weather the better.

Snuffle, sob, wail from the next room. So that was what had woken her. She waited, to see if Jaime would go back to sleep.

The crying stopped for a moment and then started again. Her body heavy, she dragged herself from the bed. She picked Jaime up out of her cot and the baby closed her eyes at once. In the other bed, Vicky slept soundly. Jenny wandered downstairs with Jaime, waiting for her to fall back to sleep.

She pulled back the curtain and looked up the road. The window emitted cold. She rested her cheek against its hard, freezing surface. Outside, under the street lamps, she could see snow was still falling, and more heavily now. It had settled and the children would be excited to wake up to a white world in the morning.

All the way down the street the houses were dark. It made you feel like the only person awake in the camp, in Wiltshire, in England, in the world. Then, suddenly, a light went on over at the Buckles. Leanne? Jenny thought of ringing her: occasionally, if the men were away, the women rang each other in the middle of the night if they saw a light on. Then she remembered that Steve had not gone to Brecon and he might be up tonight, clattering around on his metal leg. She didn't want to talk to him at one in the morning. Sometimes he was too much these days and she didn't want to talk to him at all. She thought Dave was crazy for helping him go back to Afghanistan.

She sat down at the computer. She had forgotten to switch it off so, Jaime asleep in one arm, typing with the other hand, she opened her email.

There was a message from the Appointments Agency. She remembered she had applied for a job with them. Which one? Was it the part-time hotel receptionist? Or the waitress for the busy deli? No, it was that other, strange ad which had asked for typing, simple accounting, organizational abilities and a helpful manner without saying exactly what the job was.

She was invited to an interview. She remembered that the ad had contained a phrase she loved: *Hours to suit*. That might mean that the hours would be arranged to suit her, although more likely it meant to suit the employer.

The interview was next Monday. Just when Dave was leaving for Afghanistan. But he would leave first thing in the morning and the interview was in the afternoon. She would ask Adi to take the children. She would need a bit of time to get herself looking smart. She glanced at the address again. Tinnington. She knew it was a village on the edge of the Plain; she had seen signs to it and would check the route before Monday. The interview was at Tinnington House. It was probably one of those country houses which had been taken over by IT companies and was full of dust and electrical leads. Did she want to work in IT? Did she care if it was hours to suit?

She switched off the computer and carried Jaime upstairs, laying her carefully back down in her cot. She decided not to tell Dave about the interview. Although he had told her to earn some money if she wanted Vicky at the new nursery, he had not seemed enthusiastic when she told him she was applying for jobs. She didn't want another row just when he was due to leave for theatre. It was better to wait and tell him if and when she was offered something.

Dave had noticed how the stars were disappearing and the temperature was rising. He couldn't see the clouds but he knew they must be there. He hoped they weren't snow clouds. Then he felt the first flakes land on his nose, like tiny whispers of cold breath. He heard a small buzz pass through the line of men as they noticed. But the commander still did not pause.

They tabbed on as the snow thickened. The flakes were so large and soft at first that they were unthreatening. They touched the ground and instantly disappeared.

But gradually they turned small and hard and the world became white.

Sol dropped back and walked alongside Dave.

'Are we still going the wrong way?'

'Yeah.'

'Some of the men are flagging a bit. Tiny's big but he's not bulky and he's not used to carrying kit around. Binman's never good over a distance.'

'It's not just 1 Section,' said Dave. 'Fife nearly didn't come to Brecon because he got some sort of a stomach bug and he's struggling. And look at Gayle. He got a foot injury on Salisbury Plain and now he's leaning on Senibua.'

The snow intensified the moon's light so that it was easy to see Gayle up ahead, his large frame walking unevenly. The top half of his body was leaning heavily to one side and each step looked an effort.

'The boss is beasting us,' said Sol. 'We don't need this just before a tour.'

Suddenly there was a shout ahead and the file came to an abrupt halt. From the noise it seemed someone had fallen over. Tiny Hemmings and Gayle sat down gratefully in the snow. Their faces glistened with sweat.

Gerry McKinley said to Gayle: 'You OK, mate?'

Gayle nodded but remained silent.

Dave pushed up past the men to the commotion at the front. The platoon commander and the 3 Section medic were leaning over Corporal Si Curtis.

'Shit, Si, what have you done?' demanded Dave.

'I've fucked up, Sarge.'

Si's face was distorted with pain and he was making no attempt to move. From his expression alone Dave was prepared to bet a bone was broken. Chalfont-Price was leaning over Si's left ankle and when he looked up his face confirmed the diagnosis without him saying a word.

'How did you do it?'

'I tripped over a rock and my other foot went down a hole and I sort of fell this way and . . .' Si breathed out pain and swallowed his words.

Dave studied the ankle. It was so misshapen that he knew this was a bad break. They were far from camp or base, it was snowing, the men were tired, too tired to carry a casualty far, and they had no radios just when they needed an air evacuation. He relived in a fraction of a second the entire night's events and saw his own foolishness. He had allowed the rudeness and arrogance of the young platoon commander to override the men's welfare. He should have stood up to the idiot hours ago. And now this was the result.

Si Curtis was saying something about Afghanistan and having to be all right for deployment but Dave ignored him. He ignored Chalfont-Price too, who was hanging over Si asking if he could keep walking by leaning on someone.

'Everyone over here!' Dave roared. Most of the men had already gathered around but now they formed one large group.

'We need to get Curtis out.' He was unfolding the map as he spoke. It was rapidly covered in snowflakes. 'Which means we need some comms. Which means that someone here has to be brave in the face of danger, only the danger's not the Taliban. It's me.'

They all stared at him. They waited while he studied the map.

'OK. I know, because I know you, that at least one man here will have disobeyed orders tonight and brought his mobile phone. He'll either have it because he forgot to take it out of his kit or because he couldn't be bothered to or because he wanted to use it. I don't care what the reason is. Right now, I don't give a shit. I'm offering an amnesty. Produce your phone if you have one and I promise no reprisals.'

There was a deathly silence.

'Come on, I know I'm scary but let's put Si Curtis first.'

The silence continued.

'No penalty, nothing written down, no one outside this platoon will know. Will the guy who disobeyed orders just get his fucking phone out now.'

There was a slow shuffling at the back. That would be 1 Section. Dave felt mild surprise, but then he remembered Blue Balls Slindon. It had to be him. It just had to be. But to Dave's astonishment Jack Binns stepped forward.

'Here you are, Sarge.'

Dave raised his eyebrows in surprise.

'You, Binns, I never would have thought it!'

'See, I was just—' Binman's face was a fire red.

'Don't bother to explain.' Dave grabbed the phone. 'The fact is you're man enough to admit it.'

'Well done, Binman,' said a few voices.

'Let's hope it's not the end of your fucking career,' said a few more.

Dave knew that the chances of finding a signal here were slim. But he knew where they were and it wasn't nearly so far from civilization as most of the men assumed. When he switched on the phone there was one bar of signal. Thank God.

He dialled Iain Kila. After a few rings it was picked up. The voice which answered had the uncertainty of someone who does not recognize the number.

'Yes?'

'It's Dave Henley, sir.'

There was a pause.

'Where the *fuck* are you?'

'We need to casevac someone out. Broken ankle. I'm going to give you our grid ref now.'

A small murmur went around the company when Dave rattled off their exact coordinates to the sergeant major.

'So Sarge knew all along where we were!'

'Why didn't he fucking tell us, then!'

'Because the boss wouldn't listen.'

'This is fucking nuts! It's more nuts than O'Sullivan's nuts.'

Dave ignored them and he did not look at the platoon commander's face. In fact, he had forgotten that the boss was there at all.

He gave Si Curtis's details and added: 'Iain, I'm leaving Max Gayle to care for the wounded. He's got a dodgy ankle himself. He'll have this mobile phone. I'm taking everyone else on.'

'On where? You haven't even got to fucking Checkpoint 1 yet!'

'We're near Checkpoint 5.'

'Listen, the checkpoints packed up hours ago and went on the piss. Just get back here now.'

'I estimate we're about an hour away.'

'I hope you've got a fucking good explanation for this.'

'Fucking good,' said Dave grimly.

He handed the phone to Gayle, who had limped up from the back on hearing his name. He looked better for the brief rest and relieved not to be tabbing on. While the medic was busy around Si Curtis, Dave turned to Chalfont-Price. He expected to find the man looking humbled or embarrassed in some way. He even hoped for an apology. But the man blinked back at him, lizard-like, his face expressionless.

'Right.' Dave moved closer to show him the map. 'We are here.'

Chalfont-Price studied Dave's finger. 'No, I think we are here.' He was pointing at a position miles away. But he did not sound quite so sure of himself now.

Dave sighed. 'Sir, it's time you listened to me. If you'd listened before this never would have happened. We're here. And the camp's there. Now will you lead the men back or will I?'

The boss grimaced and shook some snow off his head. 'I will. Of course.'

Progress to the camp was slow because, although the snow had stopped, in places it was deep. A new wind had carried it into drifts and occasionally the men found themselves plunged into unexpected valleys of snow. Behind the boss there were a few snowball fights but most of the men were too tired to play. They arrived back at the camp just over an hour later. The group of trainers who had been waiting for them had the wagon engines running to keep warm.

'OK, everyone sort out their kit now and get in a wagon,' Dave instructed. The men fetched their things and climbed in the back of the vehicles gratefully and wordlessly.

Kila positioned himself in front of Dave and Chalfont-Price. 'What the fuck happened?'

Dave remained silent. So did the boss.

'Well?' Kila looked directly at the officer.

'The platoon couldn't agree on its map-reading,' Chalfont-Price said through tight lips as he turned to climb into a cab. Implying that in some way he had been open to discussion, even persuasion. Dave wanted to punch the man.

Left alone with Dave, Kila turned to him, his face still a question mark.

'What news on Curtis?' asked Dave quickly.

'Helicopter had a bit of bother with the weather but it got him to hospital. They'll operate later.'

'Operate?'

'It's a bad fracture.' Kila's hands were still on his hips. 'And Gayle wasn't in a good way either. They've kept him in overnight.'

The men were all on board now.

'OK,' said the sergeant major to Dave. 'You're travelling down with me now, Dave, and I want to know what the fuck happened.'

In the warmth at the front of the truck Dave just wanted to go to sleep but he knew he had to tell the sergeant major the whole story. Kila listened in silence as the driver tugged the steering wheel to right and left while the wagon slithered along the icy tracks.

When Dave had finished he sighed.

'Who was the fucker who had the mobile phone?'

'Doesn't matter. I declared an amnesty.'

Kila raised his eyebrows but didn't pursue the question.

'I'll hear what Chalfont-Price has to say.'

'Well, he's not going to tell you that he's a pompous, arrogant little twat, but that's the truth,' said Dave. 'Can't Gordon Weeks come back for this tour?'

'You know he can't.' Kila sighed and wrinkled his brow. The truck skidded for fifty metres downhill, the driver grimacing, his arms tense. The light was still dim but it was the cold, precise light of dawn instead of the moon's glow.

'Now probably isn't the time to talk about this,' said Kila at last, 'but the fact is, Dave, you aren't handling your platoon commander too well. He's not the only one who has to clean up his act. So do you. Or your men are going to be in the shit when we get to Afghanistan.'

12

That morning, Adi came over with her brood. The Kasanita kids were always polite and well behaved, but in a small house they were overwhelming through sheer force of numbers. Jenny hid butter beans and the children raced everywhere looking for them, putting them into paper cups and then pouring the contents on to the living-room floor to count who had the most. At the centre was Adi, who shrieked and laughed and sometimes slipped butter beans into the cups of the smaller children.

'Again! Again!' yelled the children.

'We'll have a break for some lunch,' Jenny said, turning on the TV before she went into the kitchen. Adi positioned herself in the kitchen doorway so that she could watch the children and talk to Jenny at the same time.

'Sol says it's stopped snowing in Wales,' she reported.

'That's good,' said Jenny absently, pretending to be busy cutting slices of cake to hide the fact that she didn't even know it had started snowing in Wales. Because, as usual, Dave had failed to phone. But somehow Adi seemed to guess.

'They were on an exercise which went wrong and they spent all night tabbing in a snowstorm,' she explained. 'And then Si Curtis broke his ankle and had to be casevaced out.'

'Oh no!'

'I doubt Dave's had a chance to call you . . .'

Jenny concentrated hard on cutting the cake.

'. . . because he's been too busy rearranging 3 Section. They can't go out to Afghanistan without a section commander.'

Jenny knew Adi was creating excuses for Dave. She was trying to make things better, smoothing rough surfaces over as usual. Adi's favourite phrase was 'Blessed are the peacemakers'. Which was a strange phrase for a soldier's wife but it was the right one for Adi, who brought good humour wherever she went.

'Why did the night exercise go wrong?' Jenny asked.

There was a pause.

'Some kind of argument over the map-reading, I think,' said Adi carefully.

Now Jenny looked up.

'Argument between . . .' She searched Adi's face and knew the truth at once. '. . . between Dave and someone?'

Adi nodded and her grave look helped Jenny guess the truth.

'Dave and the new platoon commander?'

'Well, darling, I don't know the whole story.'

Jenny wanted to defend Dave but she knew it was only too likely that he had rowed with the new boss.

Adi was watching her. She smiled, as usual. 'Sol doesn't like the new officer either. No one does. Apparently he doesn't talk to his men or show any interest in them.'

But Sol, Jenny knew, would make an effort to get on with Chalfont-Price. Because he was the boss, because he was new, because he was young and foolish and needed to be knocked into shape. Dave was always so patient and generous with the new young officers. Why not this one?

The children were flooding into the kitchen now. There wasn't room for them all but they crowded in anyway and a young Kasanita dropped her blackcurrant squash on the floor. While everyone snatched pieces of pizza or helped clear it up, Adi stole out to plant the butter beans.

As the children rushed out again with their paper cups to find them, crumbs and blackcurrant rings around their mouths, Adi said to Jenny: 'I was planting a butter bean by your computer keyboard and I saw something you've printed off. I shouldn't have looked. But it was lying on the top . . .'

'Oh wow, Vicky, you've found three already!' Jenny said enthusiastically as Vicky tottered towards her proudly with a rattling cup.

'Are you really looking for a job?' asked Adi.

'If I can find one. You've probably heard about the row I had with Shona at the nursery . . .'

'Everyone's heard, darling. You can't walk out on the camp nursery without the whole world knowing.'

'Well, I'd like to earn enough to send Vicks to that new nursery school.'

'So you won't need any childcare then?'

Jenny found herself colouring.

'Oh Adi, yes I will. That job you saw printed out, I've got an interview for it next week . . . and even if Vicks goes to the new nursery while I work, Jaime's too young.'

'And can I help you? I'm looking after Leanne's

152

boys for her, you know, when she starts at the bakery.'

'I'd love you to take the girls. I'd pay you, of course . . .'

'It would be a nice way for me to earn a little bit and help you at the same time. So think about it, Jenny. And let me look after them when you go for your interview.'

'Thanks, Adi . . . I haven't actually told anyone yet. I mean, not even Dave. I wasn't going to say anything. Unless I get the job.'

Adi pressed her finger to her lips and made her eyes big.

'Your secrets are safe with me.'

Vicky returned and tugged her mother off to find butter beans.

'Look along the bookshelves, look very carefully!' Jenny told her. Vicky stood on the sofa and her fingers crept along the line of books. Jenny liked these shelves. It wasn't only that they had been her father's and that her father had actually made them himself. She liked the colourful spines of the books and the way they reminded her not just of the worlds inside them but where she had been when she read them. And she loved to pull a children's book out on a wintry afternoon and snuggle down with Vicky looking at the pictures.

Vicky's fingers found a butter bean on top of the vast *Family Guide to Medical Matters: Making Sure the Worst Never Happens!* Right next to it was *Emergencies in the Home and How to Prevent Them*, hiding another butter bean. Both books were presents from Jenny's mother, Trish, a doomsayer who liked to read out loud some of the hideous scenarios described.

Jaime was awake now, so Jenny carried her in one arm while she showed Vicky how to make her tiny fingers walk along the shelves.

'Little legs!' cried Vicky, walking the little legs past a book on fashion to *Understanding Wine, Wines of Europe* and *Wines of the New World* and then the cookery books, where she found a small nest of butter beans.

'Three! You've found three more!' Jenny told her as she dropped them into Vicky's cup. She could hear the Kasanita children rampaging up the stairs. Adi was chasing behind them, yelling: 'Now then, just calm down!'

Vicky continued to walk her fingers along the shelf but Jenny was suddenly distracted. Medicine and wine. Hadn't Dave's clue said there was a present somewhere between medicine and wine?

She ran her eye across the books again and saw *Fashion For You! Look a Million Dollars!* She realized she had never seen this book before and in the same moment noticed that the jacket was only photocopied and roughly coloured with a kid's felt tip. She pulled it from the shelf and it was immediately obvious that this wasn't a book at all but a slim box which had been covered to look like a book.

Billy Finn was watching the cloud formations over the white hills as he had a quiet cigarette outside a hut. There hadn't been so much snow down here at the base but the tops were covered in icing sugar and above them the clouds were forming into billowing towers and massive white hill forts.

'I bet that's more snow coming,' said Mal Bilaal.

Finn was surprised to find Mal standing next to him. He drew on his cigarette. 'Nah, they're not snow clouds.'

'You still going on the supplies run up to Donnington?' asked another voice and Finn saw that Jack Binns was standing on his other side.

Suspicious now, he took a step back and turned around so that he could face them.

'Why? You two got a bird up there? So's Angry.'

He saw them both flinch at this.

'Listen, I can't take the whole fucking platoon just because they're needing a shag.'

Mal and Binman looked miserably beyond him at the spectacular view. Finn's back was turned on the hills now but he could see the strange cloud formations reflected in miniature in the pupils of their eyes.

'We don't want to go to Donnington. We just think you should go without Angry,' said Binman at last in a small, squeaky voice.

'Why?'

Neither of them replied. Their faces drooped miserably.

'Some reason he shouldn't see this bird?'

Mal and Binman exchanged glances.

'Well . . . yeah,' said Mal at last. 'We need to stop him seeing her.'

Finn waited but no one explained.

'Let me guess. She's married and her old man's going to shoot him?'

He saw Mal and Binman look at each other again.

'Well . . .' said Mal awkwardly.

'You're not a million miles from the truth there,' said Binman.

Finn looked thoughtful. His eyes darted in his lean face and behind them his brain was busy. 'No, this is Angry we're talking about. More likely he's going to shoot her old man.'

'Now you're very close,' admitted Mal.

'So don't do no more guessing, Finny,' pleaded

Binman. 'Just trust us. He shouldn't go and pick up supplies with you.'

'You don't want to tell me?'

'No,' they said together.

'I'll probably find out sooner or later. Because Billy Finn knows.'

Their eyes said they wanted to tell him. But their mouths remained firmly closed. The three of them watched in silence as Dave appeared, crossing the base. He was going towards the command post where Major Willingham stayed for the exercise. At the wooden door, the sergeant major was waiting. When Dave arrived Kila went inside with him and the door shut behind them.

As soon as they were gone, Finn sighed.

'All right,' he said. 'I'm trusting you two. If you say there's some good reason to stop Angry McCall, I'll sort it out. Just leave it to Finny.'

'So you're telling me that you tried to point out to Second Lieutenant Chalfont-Price once, twice, three times that he was going the wrong way? On three separate occasions?' said Major Willingham.

They were standing in the commanding officer's hut. It was sparse but there was a tiny old two-bar electric heater glowing in the corner. After the Welsh hillside, its thin heat made the place feel tropical. Major Willingham's face was red. Either with the heat. Or perhaps, Dave thought, because he was annoyed.

Dave said: 'I stopped the platoon and asked him about three times to check the map and he said he didn't need to. Finally I told him outright that we were in the wrong place . . .'

'Did you tell him in front of the men?' asked Sergeant Major Kila.

'I tried to take him off to one side, sir, but he . . . he didn't find that idea very acceptable. So I had to say it in front of everyone.'

'And his response was . . . ?' demanded the major.

'He was so sure of himself that. . . well, he made me think maybe I was wrong.'

'Surely not, Sergeant! You have years of map-reading under your belt and St John Chalfont-Price is a very new officer.'

So that was how you pronounced Chalfont-Prick's ridiculous first name, thought Dave, who had seen it written down and wondered at it. Did his mates call him Saint? Well, here was the answer. They called him Sinjun. And how daft was that?

'Surely,' the major was saying, 'you knew that poor Sinjun Chalfont-Price had made a mistake through inexperience and it was your job to put him right?'

What was 'poor' about the twat?

'Sir, I tried. The platoon commander wouldn't listen.'

'So here he was, completely lost with a platoon of men behind him. And no one helped him!'

'He asked one of the corporals to look at the map with him.'

'You let a corporal map-read with him! When you were standing right there!'

'He *asked* a corporal. When I was standing right there.'

'Which one?'

'Aaron Baker, sir.'

Kila groaned.

The major turned to Iain Kila. 'Is Corporal Baker noted for his map-reading skills?'

Kila shook his head. 'He's fucking useless, actually, sir.'

'Unbelievable! You let your platoon commander ask the wrong man and follow the wrong advice. Because, Sergeant, he had put your nose out of joint by failing to listen earlier. For your own petty reasons you were prepared to see him lead the whole platoon over the hills in a snowstorm, completely lost. The result is that one good corporal has a badly broken ankle and will no longer be able to go into theatre. And, frankly, you're lucky that was the only injury.'

Dave swallowed. He thought he deserved a reprimand, but maybe not this much of a reprimand. And he thought the major should be even tougher on Chalfont-Prick.

The major continued: 'Well, I shudder to think what would have happened if you had been in theatre.'

'I never would have let it happen in theatre,' said Dave. 'But this is training and if I couldn't train him by explaining, I decided I had to let him learn the hard way.'

'You didn't like the way he spoke to you. That was why you decided to let him learn the hard way, and your whole platoon suffered for it. I understand that your men showed sheer incredulity when you phoned the sergeant major and coolly gave him your exact coordinates.'

'To be frank, sir, I wanted the boss to learn what can happen if an officer ignores his sergeant's advice.'

'I could get Corporal Kasanita in here to tell us how he saw Second Lieutenant Chalfont-Price behaving towards Dave,' suggested Iain Kila. 'He'd be a very reliable witness.'

'That's not necessary. I will personally have a word with St John and explain that he must take advice when it's offered . . .' The major stopped, suddenly, and sighed. 'Well, Dave . . .' His tone was changing. Dave watched the commanding officer's face. The man did not meet his eye. 'There's something I hadn't planned to tell you. But I think that now I must.'

The major's voice was low. He leaned back in his chair, staring at the ceiling.

'St John Chalfont-Price is the nephew of Lord Goodwich of Brough. You may be aware that the Government's current defence review is being conducted under the guidance of Lord Goodwich and he will be the author of the final report, which is expected at the end of this year. I need hardly tell you the importance of this report to all three armed services and, of course, we are particularly concerned about the army. When St John Chalfont-Price, who is very close to his uncle, entered Sandhurst, there was jubilation. It was generally believed that he might have some influence, however indirect, over his uncle's view of the army. We were honoured, therefore, when he was placed in our regiment.'

The major stopped looking at the ceiling now and instead fixed his eyes directly on Dave.

'I chose you, Sergeant Henley, to be his first sergeant. I chose you for your many qualities, qualities which I felt demonstrated everything the army stands for. I wanted young St John to talk to his uncle about his experiences. You have a great ability to support and train the new officers who command your platoon. Everyone knows you worked wonders with Gordon Weeks. I hoped that you would do the same for St John Chalfont-Price. I felt that, if you could succeed, the army as a whole might benefit.'

He stopped talking. Dave and the major stared at each other.

'No pressure then, Dave!' said Iain Kila cheerfully.

'Did you know this all along?' asked Dave, turning to him.

The sergeant major grinned. 'Yup!'

Dave remembered the Land Rover crossing Salisbury Plain and the first time Chalfont-Price had addressed the men so badly and how Kila had defended him.

Dave looked at Major Willingham again. He felt miserable and happy at the same time. Happy because his platoon had been chosen. Miserable because it had been chosen for Chalfont-Prick.

'Seems I've screwed up, sir,' he said at last.

The major looked gloomy.

'We've got to try to retrieve the situation without compromising on any of our high standards. It's a question of how well he's managed from now on.'

'With respect, sir, I don't want the safety of the platoon endangered because we're trying to impress his uncle.'

'All right, Dave, you don't have to say that. We don't want anyone coming back in a body bag: not St John, not anyone. We'll be doing our best to support the situation but it's essential you develop a strong working relationship with him. I have thought about moving him to another platoon . . .'

Good idea. Hand Chalfont-Prick over to some other poor bastard, Dave thought.

'But . . .' continued the major, 'the best solution is you, Dave.'

Dave's heart stopped thumping and sank an inch as the major gave him a winning smile: 'You have *got* to find a way to deal with him.'

13

Jenny was suddenly surrounded by children peering at the box which looked like a book. As though they had all sensed at the same moment that something was up, they had gathered around her, even the ones who just a moment ago had been galloping up the stairs.

'What's that?' demanded the eldest Kasanita child, reaching out to touch the box in Jenny's hands.

'I've been on a bit of a treasure hunt myself,' confessed Jenny, hoisting Jaime higher on her hip and staring at the box.

The children pushed closer against her.

'So what's this, Jenn?' asked Adi.

'Well, Dave hid a present for me to find while he was away. With a clue. Which I couldn't solve . . . and I think I've just cracked it.'

Adi's eyes filled with tears. 'Oh Jenny Henley, you are married to a lovely, lovely man!' she said. Jenny looked at her in surprise.

'Well, how many other men in this camp do you think leave presents hidden for their wives?' demanded Adi, sniffing.

'What was the clue?' asked the eldest Kasanita boy, a tall, sweet-faced child.

'He said it was between the medicine and the wine. So I was looking in the kitchen and the bathroom . . .'

'Ha, he meant the books on medicine and the books on wine! Clever!' shrieked Adi. She was capable of crying and laughing in rapid succession and even at the same time. 'He made it look just like a book! That Dave of yours is so clever!'

'Open it!' yelled all the children, including Vicky. On Jenny's hip, Jaime, sensing the excitement, raised her arms and waved them like a conductor.

Hoping that the box did not contain skimpy underwear, as Dave's boxes occasionally did, Jenny gently prised the lid open. It was almost impossible to complete this manoeuvre with only one hand and the eldest Kasanita boy helped her, pulling it open to reveal something which looked dangerously like underwear. Except that it wasn't. Jenny reached into the box and pulled out a piece of fabric: green and beaded and made of the softest silk which had been easily folded to the size of a book but now fell out into the shape of a dress.

The children and Adi let out a communal sigh of wonder. Jenny felt tears pricking behind her eyes. Adi was right. She was married to a lovely, lovely man.

'Oh Jenny,' breathed Adi. 'It's beautiful!'

There was a card, which Jenny read quickly and put into her pocket. That at least would remain private.

'It's for the party in London,' she explained.

'Oh, put it on now so that we can see you!'

Adi had taken the dress and was holding it as though it was made of the finest gossamer which could easily split.

'No, not now!'

But all the Kasanita children and Adi and Vicky and even, in her way, Jaime too, shouted: 'Please! Please! Try it on!'

So she handed Jaime to Adi and went upstairs and once again the dress slipped over her hips and came to life.

The children exclaimed when they saw her and Adi's eyes began to water again.

'Mummy is a beautiful princess!' Vicky announced proudly.

'I'm not thinking about what Dave paid,' Jenny told Adi. 'I saw this when I was out shopping with Leanne and I wouldn't buy it because it cost so much. Leanne must have told Dave about it . . .'

'I'm phoning her now to tell her to get right over here!' yelled Adi and before Jenny could stop her she was tapping on her mobile. Within a few minutes Leanne was there with the twins, smiling knowingly.

'Looks even bloody better than it did in the shop, Jenn,' she said, adding a mechanical 'Sorry, Adi!' at the end of the sentence. Everyone else tried not to swear in front of Adi, who was a devout Christian, but Leanne just swore and apologized.

Ethan, staring, asked: 'Why is she wearing that funny clothes?'

Leanne told him: 'That's the kind of clothes ladies wear to parties when they're tall and slim like Jenny Henley.'

'But when did Dave buy it?' Jenny asked.

'I rang him almost as soon as we got out of the shop. Remember, the assistant put it aside for us and then I dragged you all the way across town to the outsize shop? That was so we wouldn't bump into Dave when he was buying it.'

'Oh!' said Jenny. 'I've been tricked!'

Leanne looked pleased with herself. 'I didn't tell a soul! Not a soul, not even Steve! Ring Dave and tell him you've found it!'

Adi glanced at her watch. 'No, not now.'

'Why, what's happening in Brecon?' asked Leanne.

'Dave's got a meeting with the major.'

'How do you know *everything*?'

Adi just looked mysterious. Suddenly Jenny felt silly, standing in her glamorous dress in the untidy living room with mothers in ordinary clothes and children counting butter beans all over the floor.

'Is Dave in trouble?' she asked cautiously.

It seemed even Leanne knew the answer.

'He let the new platoon commander get lost and march them all over bloody Wales, sorry, Adi, in the middle of the night when Dave knew the way all along. And then Si Curtis in 3 Section broke an ankle and had to be casevaced out. And Gayle too.'

Jenny did not know what to say. She just knew she wanted to get out of the green dress, endangered by the sticky fingers of the smallest children, who wanted to touch the beads. She realized how she had taken Dave's popularity for granted. Evidently people were criticizing him now, and it made her feel unsure of herself. She wanted to defend him but wasn't sure how to – since Dave hadn't phoned to tell her what had happened.

'No, Leanne, you've got that wrong, I think,' Adi was saying. 'Dave tried to tell the platoon commander and he wouldn't listen.'

As she went up the stairs, Jenny heard Leanne reply: 'Well, according to Steve, some people are saying he didn't try hard enough.'

'Sol said—'

164

Jenny paused on the stairs.

'Listen, they're wrong but that's what they're saying. Steve got so furious with one bloke who was going round saying Dave's in trouble that he nearly started a fight.'

'Steve's a good mate of Dave's, isn't he?'

'Dave got Steve back out to Bastion and as far as Steve's concerned, he walks on water and he's ready to kill anyone who says a word against him . . .'

Jenny closed the bedroom door. She slipped the dress off and, hanging in the wardrobe, it turned once again into a beautiful shred of beaded fabric, lifeless without her body to animate it. She sighed and went downstairs.

'No one's asked me about my job interview,' said Leanne.

Adi and Jenny stared at her.

'Oh, it was today! What happened?'

Leanne's face broke into a wide smile.

'Girls! You are talking to the new assistant at the Market Street Bakery!'

She erupted into an ungainly dance routine, grabbing the nearest child to partner her.

'Well done, Lee,' said Jenny, beaming at her friend.

'How many applicants for the job did I say there were, Jenn?' Leanne was still dancing, although breathless. 'Was it about two hundred?'

Jenny smiled. 'Not far off two hundred.'

'I told them I wanted to develop customer relationships to ensure customer loyalty!' Leanne said. 'How good did that sound?'

'Brilliant,' Jenny assured her.

'And I said that it's important to me to share my passion for good food!'

'Also brilliant,' said Adi.

'I'll have to learn to pronounce the names of all that fancy bread. Ci-a-batta. Fo-cac-cia. Bacon But-ty. God, I hope I get the change right.'

'When do you start?' asked Adi.

'Next Tuesday at nine. It would have been Monday but Steve's going that day and they were very understanding. Can I leave the boys at eight so I can get myself ready?'

'Of course, darling. They can have breakfast with us if you like.'

'This is the beginning of the new me! I'll have some money all of my own and I'm going to get my hair done for the party anyway. Then I'm going to start losing weight. Steve'll get back from Afghanistan and he won't recognize me!'

'What you doing?' demanded Angry. He had pitched up by the Land Rovers to go to Donnington to find Finny crouched down beside one, his fingers dirty.

'Just been having a look at these tyres,' said Finn. 'Does this one look flat to you?'

'No.' Angry climbed into the Land Rover. 'C'mon, let's get going.'

Finn glanced behind and saw Angry's rifle. He remembered the conversation with Mal and Binman and how uncomfortable they had looked when he had joked that Angus might want to shoot someone. And he had only been joking.

'OK, she's been on night exercise with some other company but she's filled up and she's ready to go.' Finn turned the key.

Angry said nothing. They set off. Finn, who had spent much of his life on the road, looked contentedly at the way the hills swelled up to the distant horizon and the clouds seemed like a continuation of the landscape. The vehicle veered occasionally because he was staring at the view, or because he was reaching for his cigarettes.

'For Chrissake!' growled Angus every time Finn took his eyes off the road. Finn handed him a cigarette and Angus did not thank him, just smoked it moodily and threw the butt out of the window with unnecessary violence. His face was haggard. His expression was grim. Yes, thought Finn, Angus McCall was a big angry bear today. There was certainly something on his mind. Finn had been planning to fish around until he found out what Mal and Binman were so worried about but now he thought he wouldn't. He decided just to let things happen.

After about forty-five minutes, the Land Rover began to splutter. Angry looked alarmed.

'What the fuck's up?'

Finn shrugged. 'These old Land Rovers keep going no matter what.'

The Land Rover stopped as he spoke.

'Shit! Shit!' shouted Angry.

Finn was calm. 'Chill, big man. These are simple machines and Billy Finn is a master mechanic.'

'Well, get on with it!'

Finn stopped and put his head on one side. 'Why are you so keen to get to Donnington?' he asked. Angus looked away from him. Traffic whizzed past them and each car rocked the Land Rover as though they were at sea. 'What's so fantastic about this bird that you've *got* to see her?'

'Just get on with it!'

Finn opened the bonnet and peered at the tubes and plugs which were hidden inside. Angus came to look as well.

167

'Smells oily,' he said.

Finn got a rag and tested the dipstick, turning it this way and that way in the light.

'Hmmm . . .'

Angus erupted. 'Don't tell me she's got no fucking oil!'

Finny turned on the Land Rover and it spluttered reluctantly into life. Then died again.

'Ah.' Finny pulled up the dashboard cover.

'Ah fucking WHAT?' roared Angus. 'What does "ah" mean?'

'Ah, the oil light's been on but I couldn't see it because I didn't take the flap up off the dashboard . . .'

'What! The oil light's been on all this time?' Angus sounded desperate.

'It was covered up. For night manoeuvres.'

'Well, why the fuck didn't you take it off?' roared Angry.

Finn raised his eyebrows.

'Why the fuck do you always carry your medipouch on your left hip?' he asked calmly, going back to the bonnet and sticking a hand into the Land Rover's greasy innards. His words halted Angry.

'I don't,' Angus said at last.

'You do. Should be in your Osprey by your right hip, mate. Now there's a little mistake which could cost you your life.'

Angus was silenced again.

'Hmmmm. Oil everywhere here,' reported Finny. 'Something's leaking.'

'What?'

'Could be anything. I'll have to call base . . .' Finny was reaching for his phone.

'But if all we need is more oil . . .' Angus looked

around desperately. The hills were lower here and the landscape softer but they were in the middle of nowhere. The next petrol station was probably miles away.

'We can't just pour in more oil or it'll all leak out again five miles down the road,' said Finny, switching his attention to whoever had answered his call. Angus watched his face as he spoke.

'OK, mate. All right. Yeah, not a problem. OK. Yup.'

'Well?' demanded Angus breathlessly.

'It's going to take them a few hours to get to us.'

'A few hours!'

'That's what he said. Maybe three. So let's get some kip while we wait. After last night, we both need it. In fact, I'd say, looking at you, that Angus McCall is more in need of a kip than a shag.'

Angus's face was so shadowy he seemed to have black eyes. His jaw hung. His brow furrowed. His cheeks sagged.

'Course,' Finn continued cheerfully, 'you might still have time to get to your bird, depending on where she lives.'

Angry was looking at his watch.

'We won't get to Donnington until nearly five o'clock! That's too late! Now I'll never do it before we leave for theatre!'

Finn settled back in the driver's seat and closed his eyes.

'Do what?' He sounded uninterested.

Angus did not answer the question. Instead he shouted: 'Oh shit! Oh fuck! Why didn't you pull back the cover and look at the oil light?'

Finn ignored him, as though he was already asleep. Angus reached across and grabbed him by the collar.

'You lazy shit, do you know what you've done? It's nothing to you, is it, waiting here for three hours? But it's really, really, really fucked me!'

Finny opened his eyes halfway. They were angry slits in his face. He said, hissing through his teeth: 'Get off me, mate, or you'll regret it.'

Slowly, Angus released his collar.

'Sorry you can't see your bird,' said Finn, his voice returning to normal. 'She must be one hell of a woman. But you're here to train. Shagging's nice if you can get it but training comes first. Now shuddup so I can sleep.'

'We're just sitting here by the side of the fucking road. For three hours. We're not training, we're not shagging, we're not doing *nothing*! And I had *things* I wanted to *do*.'

Finny closed his eyes again. Angry's plans, whatever they were, had been completely scuppered by a loosened sump nut. His last thought, before he went to sleep, was that Mal and Binman owed him a pint for this. No, make that pints.

14

The Dorchester Hotel was lit up as though it was still Christmas and outside in Park Lane a thousand tiny lights twinkled in every tree and snow glistened on the ground.

'Oh, the girls would love this!' exclaimed Jenny as they approached. She sounded like a little girl herself, excited at the evening ahead, delighted with the hotel, the lights, the big cars pulling up, pleased to be in London. Dave put his arm around her. Her heels made that important going-to-a-party click clack on the pavement; she smelled lovely and looked gorgeous. But inside his arm, her body tensed. Despite her excitement, she was furious – because Martyn Robertson's party had turned into a farewell party and Dave was going away, back to the front line. Again.

'Jenn, stop with the bad mood now,' he said. 'Let's try to enjoy it.'

'It's not a mood. I'm angry and I can't help it.'

Every time he went there was a short spell of fury. Until the morning of his departure, when it all dissolved into tears.

'You've been nice to everyone today. Except me.'

They were staying with Dave's mother and stepfather so he could say goodbye to them too. Amazingly, this afternoon, Dave's father had appeared from nowhere. It was too much to hope that the old drunk had actually remembered Dave was staying or that he was leaving to fight on Monday. He just arrived on Dave's mother's doorstep from time to time and today happened to be one of those days. He had taken obvious delight in Dave and his family, was given a meal and some cans of beer and finally had stumbled happily off into the London streets.

'I don't know why you put up with it!' Jenny had said to Dave's stepfather.

'Because my Suzy's worth it,' he replied, grinning. Jenny grinned back at him.

'Dave was lucky his mum met you,' she told him.

Suzy and Frank took pictures of them in their smart clothes and Vicky kissed them goodbye at least fifty times ('Mind your fingers on my beads, darling!') and then they all stood at the door waving as Dave and Jenny climbed into the taxi like royals.

And then, all the way to the Dorchester, Jenny had been monosyllabic with anger.

'Listen,' he said as they approached the entrance and a liveried doorman held it open for them. 'Let's have a truce tonight and you can be angry again tomorrow. Deal?'

The bright lights and marble floors of the hotel lobby glittered ahead of her.

'Deal,' she said.

A few minutes later, coats left behind, champagne glasses in their hands, they walked into another world. Cameras flashed; people talked and laughed and smiled; music played; waiters shimmied rapidly around the standing groups with trays of champagne. There were

plenty of faces they knew, but here, away from the everyday, their features glowed. In this other world, colours
were more vivid; talk was more animated, people more
beautiful.

Jenny wanted to ask Dave: 'How can they all look so
happy? When they all know what happens on
Monday?'

But when she turned to him she saw that he looked
happy too and remained silent.

Martyn Robertson was greeting the men of 1 Platoon
like his long-lost sons as they entered the room. Press
photographers and TV news teams filmed the famous
hostage reuniting with his rescuers while Martyn kept
assuring them these men were heroes.

As the lads of 1 Section passed down the line-up,
Angus was met by a pretty girl reporter. She asked
breathlessly: 'Are you in the SAS?'

'Certainly am,' said Angus. 'Want to go to bed with
me?'

'Don't waste your time with an unranked junior
member of the team,' Finn intervened. 'I'm a second in
command and I'd be happy to show you my shooting
skills.'

'Second in command!' she whispered, wide-eyed. 'Of
the SAS?'

Finn said nothing but raised an enigmatic eyebrow.

'This is the man,' said Mal, 'who actually found the
hostage. Hidden in a doghouse.'

'Oh! I must ask my producer if I can interview you!'

'You can interview me all night long in my room,' said
Billy Finn. 'But not in front of the camera. It's in my
Special Forces contract.'

She begged Finn for an interview but all he would

say was: 'Thanks to my Special Forces training, I'm able to guess your age with the accuracy of a top marksman. If I'm right, will you dance with me later?'

The woman looked surprised.

'You're twenty-seven,' he told her. She looked even more surprised.

Mal left Finn impressing the woman and targeted another camera crew. He approached a young woman encumbered with a clipboard.

'Do they give you the shit jobs, gorgeous? The army gives me shit jobs, too. We should get together and discuss it.'

She glowered at him. 'I'm the producer. Actually.'

'Well, there's a few things I could produce which would impress you. So why don't we talk about it?'

'Because you're standing in the way. My cameraman is trying to get a headshot of the hostage and then . . . Look, can you get the black guy over there for me?'

Mal blinked.

'Streaky Bacon? You want my mate Streaky instead of me?'

'Can you get him standing next to the hostage for a two-shot?'

'Why? Because he's black?'

The woman hesitated. For a moment she looked embarrassed. He took ruthless advantage of her discomposure.

'You've got beautiful eyes. 'Specially when you blush.'

She turned the beautiful eyes on him and, as though seeing him for the first time, they narrowed.

'So where are you from?' she demanded.

'Wythenshawe.'

'I mean, what is your ethnic origin?'

'Well ... my folks came here from Yemen.' He was beginning to feel misgivings. Now he had her attention, he wasn't sure he wanted it.

'So you must be a Muslim!' she said excitedly.

OK, she was attractive, but not attractive enough for the way things were going.

He said coldly: 'Yes, sister. So what if I'm a Muslim?'

'That's very interesting! Would you mind just—'

Mal thought of everyone in Wythenshawe switching on the news and seeing him. His brothers' taxis would get an extra torching, his mum and dad would hear the hiss and clunk of another firebomb through the letter-box. And if that happened, Angry wouldn't go to Afghanistan and forget all about Aamir when he got back, as Mal was hoping. Angry would return to the UK and head straight for Wythenshawe with his rifle.

'Nope,' he told the woman.

She flashed her beautiful eyes. 'A lot of our viewers probably don't realize how many Muslims there are in the British Army. They think Muslims are the people we're fighting against. An interview with you could do a lot to improve community relations, so if you could just stand over there with the hostage, Melanie will—'

'Hey, gorgeous, I'm a Muslim too!' said Angus. 'Interview me!'

'Yeah, interview him,' said Mal. He managed to melt back into the crowd. When, from a safe distance, he turned around, he could see the producer still scanning the room for him while the camera advanced on a surprised Streaky, who had been shoved by Martyn's side.

Steve and Leanne had been invited to the party, although Steve had been casevaced out of theatre long before the hostage rescue.

'Good to meet you at last, Steve,' said Martyn, grasping his hand. 'The guys never stopped talking about you.'

'You met my leg, though,' said Steve.

'Oh sure, everyone knew it was lurking in the freezer.'

They were joined by two other casualties of the tour, Ben Broom and Ryan Connor. Only Steve had chosen to wear an obviously prosthetic leg, a streamlined network of gleaming metal which invited stares. Leanne watched the reactions to it, how people meeting him could look neither at the leg nor into his eyes.

'I think Steve enjoys showing that leg off!' said Adi in her ear. The press had been told that the hostage was meeting injured soldiers and Leanne was shrinking into the background now, trying to make herself small, as the cameras whirred and flashed. She avoided having her photo taken at all costs these days. She knew she was obese: Steve reminded her almost every day. But it was truly awful when she saw herself.

'He sort of enjoys watching how people react,' Leanne whispered back.

'They try hard not to look at it,' said Adi, sipping her orange juice.

'Anything's better than pity. And Steve likes making people squirm. He's a sadist.'

Adi gave Leanne a searching look before glancing around for Sol, who was deep in conversation with a journalist.

Meanwhile, Steve had spotted Dave and beckoned him over.

'This is the man who understood that I'm still useful to the British Army!' he cried, slapping Dave on the back. 'I owe him everything.'

Martyn hugged Dave emotionally.

'Shit, Sergeant Dave, I know how much I have to thank you for. And now I know what you went through out there, too, losing Jamie Dermott. He was a great solider.'

Dave had tugged Jenny behind him. Seeing her, the old oilman grabbed her hand, looked at her, and then embraced her too.

'Dave, you son of. You didn't tell me you had such a beautiful girl back home!' he said.

The cameras took advantage of the opportunity to snap the hostage with a photogenic woman and the room lit up with flashes again.

Leanne and Adi looked at each other.

'She's going to be on the front page of *The* fucking *Times*, sorry, Adi,' said Leanne.

Adi appeared not to notice the swearing.

'Good. She looks lovely. That dress is fantastic.'

'You look lovely too,' said Leanne. 'All those bright colours. I can't believe you made it yourself.'

'I've unpicked every seam at least twice, darling.'

'Want to know something, Adi?' Leanne gulped back her champagne and in one deft movement exchanged it for a full glass on a passing tray. 'By the time Steve gets back, I'm going to look shit hot too. He won't recognize me. And if I happen to bump into Matt Damon in M&S, he won't be able to resist me.'

'You're fine as you are, girl,' said Adi. 'Red, white and blue was a great idea.'

But Leanne shook her head.

'Are you kidding? If that had been me up there with the boys those cameras wouldn't have flashed. I look like a flag in a washing machine. When it's on spin cycle. Correction, I look like the whole fucking washing machine. Sorry, Adi.'

Adi laughed. They were joined by Si Curtis, his leg in plaster, and Tiff and the McKinleys and the Kirks.

Tiff Curtis said: 'Don't we all look amazing?'

'Yeah,' said Si Curtis. 'Every hairdresser in Wiltshire can afford a holiday this year.'

Rose McKinley said: 'I want to remember this for the rest of my life. I'm glad they're taking photos.'

A rustle of anticipation passed around the room when an elderly woman of ample frame, in an ill-fitting long dress, appeared.

Angus said: 'It's Emily!'

Mal grinned. 'The sex bomb! Exploding at the Dorchester!'

'Look, Martyn,' said Finny. 'Your mate Emmers is here.'

'Oh shit,' said the oilman, the creases in his face suddenly deepening. 'I had to invite her but I didn't think she'd come.'

'Fair dos, Mart. Emmers was fucking miserable when you were kidnapped,' said Finny.

Martyn rolled his eyes. 'Only because of the ransom. Probably earmarked the money for her research.'

But the two geologists greeted each other warmly.

'Who on earth is that?' Jenny asked Dave.

'The best geophysical brain in England,' Dave said. 'Clever. But no common sense.'

'She looks like a funny old stick.'

'You could put it that way. She spent the whole tour telling us our safety precautions were completely unnecessary. Until Martyn was kidnapped.'

Dave had been waiting to see whether Gordon Weeks arrived with Asma, the interpreter he had fallen for at FOB Senzhiri. Privately Dave had not predicted the relationship would last but here they were, Weeks looking taller and more handsome and confident than Dave remembered him, with Asma on his arm.

'She's pretty,' said Jenny.

'I didn't think they'd still be an item.'

'Why? They look really good together.'

'She's from Hackney and he's from some posh farmhouse in Hampshire.'

'Well, good luck to them,' said Jenny.

'I didn't think Iain Kila and Jean would last either, but they're both here.'

'Jean looks a bit too sensible for Iain.'

'Iain Kila wasn't born in the normal way, he was hewn. Hewn from a block of solid Aberdeen granite.'

'How many times has he been married?'

'Three, at least.'

They watched the sergeant major talking animatedly to the trim, blonde Jean. Jenny said: 'He's the sort who falls for people big time and then he gets bored with the day-to-day. But just look at his face, it goes all soft when he talks to her.'

When the meal was over, Martyn made a speech which embarrassed Dave so much that he was unable to remember a word of it afterwards. There was a moving tribute to Jamie Dermott, followed by a minute's silence. Finally there was warm applause for the wounded: Steve and the two other lads injured by landmines.

After the meal, Gordon Weeks caught up with Dave and Kila and told them about his new job.

'It's good but I wish I was going back into theatre with you,' he said.

'So do I,' Dave told him.

'I tried to persuade them. They said I'd already been replaced.'

179

'Yeah,' said Dave unenthusiastically. 'You have.'

Weeks looked at him quizzically. 'I thought your new platoon commander might be here tonight. Even though he wasn't in theatre with Martyn, I thought he might be invited.'

Dave remained pointedly silent. Weeks looked at Iain, who said nothing.

Asma, forthright as ever, said: 'I've heard he's a right git.'

'That's an understatement,' Jenny told her.

The men shuffled their feet and looked grateful when the dance music started. Dave pulled Jenny towards him and murmured in her ear: 'Want to have a slow dance with me?'

'No.'

'Aw, c'mon. You won't get another chance for a few months.'

'Good. I'm looking forward to all that slow dancing I'll be doing with other blokes once you're out of the way.'

'Oh Jenn, stop being angry with me. You promised a truce,' he said, tugging her towards the dance floor.

'I want to kill you,' said Jenny as he put his arms around her.

'You don't mean that.'

'I do. You and all the other men here who look so happy tonight. You're going away to do what you enjoy. And leaving us alone.'

'Shuddup and dance.'

Word rapidly spread through the hotel that most of the large and noisy party was shortly to return to Afghanistan. Complete strangers shook their hands and bought them drinks; a few sat down in any empty chairs they could find to ask about their experiences. But not all the other guests were friendly.

'I didn't come here to listen to people boasting about the state-licensed murder of Afghan civilians,' said one man loudly as Streaky and Binman described a firefight in graphic detail to a hushed group. He and his wife were tall, lean, tanned and expensively dressed.

'We aren't politicians. We didn't ask to go there,' Finny said to their retreating backs. 'We're soldiers doing what our country asks.'

The couple did not break their stride.

'Hey, they left before they had a chance to hear my Dorchester rap!' said Streaky.

'Go, man, give us your rap!' shouted the lads.

'Well, I haven't really finished—'

'Go, Streaky!'

'I'll beat box,' said Binman, leaping on to a chair.

Alison, who had not left his side all evening, looked shocked.

'Jack, I think you should get down.'

But Streaky had already begun. People stopped talking and listened, and as he reached the last few lines there was an outbreak of applause:

'*. . . the invitation to this evening said Dress to Impress,*
Smile, ladies, we're alive, don't get us depressed.
Things here are all so good, sorry that we've got to go,
But there's still a couple other things the Taliban need to
*   know.'*

'Very good,' said Alison primly to Binman as he sat down. 'I had no idea you could make all those noises.'

'I learned at Catterick,' said Binns, still out of breath.

'He's got a lot of talents, this boy, that you probably don't know about,' Finny told her.

'Like puking,' said Angus.

Alison looked at Binman closely. 'You're different with your mates,' she said.

'Different from what?'

'Different from how you are back in Dorset.'

Binman's face shone. He was staring around at the lads leaning on tables talking loudly, the light bouncing on to the glasses in their hands and then bouncing off, muted by the colours of their drinks, amber and red and white. He was looking at his mates, their faces young, their eyes full of hope, their bodies strong and ready for whatever lay ahead.

Nearby Angus, Mal, Streaky and a group of girls from the oil company were raucously laying some sort of bet with Finny, something to do with guessing how old the girls were. Then the band struck up again, and men and women catapulted towards the dance floor. The sergeant major shuffled around all wrapped up with that blonde monkey woman he'd met at FOB Sin City. And there was the boss being extremely intimate with the look-don't-touch interpreter from Sin City. Sarge and his missus were entwined, dancing and looking into each other's eyes, which was surprising for a married couple. With considerable awkwardness and at arm's length, Martyn was dancing with Emily. And Binman could see Jonas and Mrs Jonas and Andy Kirk and his wife, while O'Sullivan was already on intimate terms with an oil-company woman.

The couples rearranged themselves and now Binns saw Gerry McKinley and his missus, her long red hair, which had been piled on her head, beginning to escape its clasp. Sol and Adi were pivoting slowly under pale lights, murmuring to each other while they danced. Steve and his fat wife were energetically proving to everyone that three legs were as good as four, while Si and Tiff Curtis, shifting their weight awkwardly around his plaster, hadn't yet mastered that art. Tiny Hemmings, the new sprog, who had been invited even though he had only just joined the platoon, was trying to dance with a woman who wasn't much higher than his waist. The other new sprog, Slindon, was clasping some woman, probably from the oil company, a lot closer than she wanted him to.

Alison was right. They were all of them different people when they were out of uniform, when their tight fighting unit suddenly broke up into a series of domestic circumstances.

'Shit, Alison,' Binman heard himself say suddenly. 'It might never be this good again.'

She flicked back her neat hair and stared at him.

'It's lovely, Jack. But it's just a party.'

'I don't mean now. I mean the last tour. It was amazing. Everything that happened was sort of intense. When I was out there, I just lived it. I wasn't thinking that I'd remember it for the rest of my life. But I will. Every day was exciting. Every day was real. Every day was intense. Maybe nothing's ever going to be that good again.'

Alison looked at him with incomprehension. But Streaky Bacon had overheard him and understood. 'Binman, I know what you're feeling. But just you remember something, dude. We're going back there, man. We're going back on fucking Monday! And we don't know what's going to happen but it might be just as mad as the last tour. So stay cool, Binman, we're getting back on the roller coaster for another ride.'

183

15

The morning A company left for Afghanistan was a grey and leaden Monday. There was no snow any more to make the camp seem brighter and disguise the dirty gutters and prettify the rows of dull army housing. In front gardens just a few shapeless, half-melted snowmen remained.

Dave opened his eyes early, before the alarm went off, and Jenny rolled over in bed to face him, as though she had been waiting for him to wake. It was dark but somehow he could still see her sad going-away face.

'It's not for long,' he said softly.

She curled her body up against him.

'It might be.'

'The MoD says it'll probably be two months.'

'That could mean six.'

'I'm not spending more than two months in Afghanistan with Chalfont-Prick or I'll be shooting him instead of the Taliban.'

'Maybe you'll like him when you get to know him.'

Dave snorted. 'He only gets to know the other officers. Stands around laughing with them, goes to the mess for a drink with them. He never has anything to do with his men, and that includes me.'

'Maybe he's scared of you and the lads.'

'Nah, he's just up himself.'

'That's really dangerous.'

'You think he's so far up himself he could do some internal damage?'

'No, idiot. He's dangerous in theatre. Not working closely with you and the boys.'

'Yup. That is dangerous.'

'Try and like him. Otherwise I'll worry.'

'You'll worry anyway.'

'I'll worry more if I know you're a human IED waiting to explode in the face of the boss.'

'I won't explode.'

'You will, Dave. I know you. I know how you put up with things and keep it all in. Then, out of the blue, you just erupt.'

'Erupting's not professional. Not in theatre. I wouldn't do it.'

Jenny rolled on to her back and studied the ceiling, her face anxious.

'Please try to get along with him. Please. For me.'

He put his arms around her.

'OK. For you.'

'And ring me more often. And if you can't ring, write.'

'Yes, yes, yes.'

'Don't just say yes. Do it.'

'You sound like me talking to my platoon.'

'Promise me, Dave.'

He sighed. 'I'll be phoning and writing and emailing you whenever I can. OK? I promise.'

Jenny turned back and they studied one another's

faces, consuming every detail, each storing the other's features with the urgency of hoarders who knew that a famine was coming.

She said: 'I bought you a going-away present.'

'Why?'

'Because I love you.'

She turned on a light, got up and opened a drawer. Then she sat on the side of the bed and handed him a small package.

'What is it?'

'Open it. I didn't wrap it. I just put it in a canoe bag.'

'Is it a canoe?'

'Open it.'

Inside the bag was a camera.

'Shit, Jenn, I need one of these!'

'There's a spare memory card and all the stuff you need to take lots of pictures. Then when you get back you can show them to me. And I'll try to understand.'

He put an arm around her.

'Not sure you ever can.'

'I want to try.'

'Why the canoe bag?'

'In case it gets wet.'

He grinned at her in the dark. 'I'm going to the desert, Jenn. My camera won't get wet.'

She shrugged. 'Isn't there a river there? And canals? Well, you might fall in.'

She took the camera over to his Bergen, which had been sitting in the corner of the room all night like a threat. She opened the Bergen and saw his night-vision goggles.

'I'll put them in the canoe bag too, then you'll have dry goggles and a dry camera.'

'Always a good idea in the desert, waterproofing your kit to keep it dry,' he said.

She made a small sound like laughter and she was back in the bed before he realized it was a sob.

Jenny did not go to the square to see Dave off. Some of the women, Leanne for example, waited while the men threw their stuff on to the buses and gave them a final kiss goodbye, and then waved frantically as the buses drew out of the camp square. She posed with some of the other wives for the photographers who were going to document Steve's journey.

Jenny, however, was not one of those women. She hugged and kissed Dave in the hallway and watched, biting her lip, while he lifted Jaime high in the air and then swung Vicky around a few times before hugging and kissing her again. And then he was gone.

She hated the way the door slam was followed by such a deep silence. It was the kind of silence which hung around like a bird of prey hovering. You couldn't do anything in that silence. You just had to observe it.

Vicky and Jaime were both watching her. She knew that if she gave way to tears they would cry too.

'Right then!' she said as soon as she could, her voice as firm as she could make it. 'Today you can help me make some lemony biscuits, Vicky. And then we'll take the biscuits over to Adi's and you can share them with Adi and the other children for a few minutes while Mummy goes out.'

'Where Mummy going?' demanded Vicky, beady as ever.

'Tinnington,' Jenny told her airily.

But when the time came to leave for Tinnington, Vicky did not want to let her go. Jenny had tried on half of the clothes in her wardrobe before she had found a sensible combination. She had applied her make-up carefully.

'You look terrific!' cried Adi. 'All you have to do is get out of the car and they'll give you the job.'

But now here was Vicky, her fingers sticky with lemony biscuit, her face smudged by tears, her mouth a caricature of itself, grabbing Jenny's cream blouse and blue jacket and refusing to release her.

'Please, Vicks, Mummy has to go,' said Jenny. But Vicky only wailed more.

'Just leave!' Adi ordered her.

Jenny managed to extract herself and run out of the front door, the sound of both her crying daughters chasing her down the path and into the car. This is what working mothers had to do. Did she really want to be one of them?

She had already rehearsed the drive to Tinnington. It was only a couple of miles from the new nursery but whichever way you went there were winding back routes involved.

The village had modern houses on its periphery and stone cottages lining the lane at its centre. A sign said Tinnington House and she swung into a gravel drive. It went on for at least half a mile. It felt like driving up to Buckingham Palace. A large, solid, ivy-covered house was visible at the end.

As she drew closer, Jenny began to feel intimidated. Where was she supposed to park? Right outside the house? Surely that was only for people who lived here and the curtains alone told her that people did live here. Maybe in the yard by the side? It was surrounded by stables and barns and was probably where stable girls parked. Then she saw a car against a wall just before the house and she pulled in next to it.

She looked at her phone. Five minutes early. Dave's plane would be taking off from Brize Norton about now. She dialled his number but Robot Woman invited her to leave a message. So he was probably already in the air. She said another small farewell to him inside her head, checked her make-up in the mirror, switched off the phone and climbed out, her feet crunching on the gravel. Her stomach was doing strange, violent somersaults.

She looked around and felt as though she was in another world. A world of trimmed lawns and tidy views and gnarled, ancient apple trees and wooden fences. Then an Apache flew low overhead. Helicopters were always flying over camp. She looked up, feeling the strange warmth of familiarity at the sight of its rocket pods and the sound of its beating rotor.

She was standing by the car, smoothing out her skirt, when she saw a man walking towards her. He was tall and his white hair at first made him seem aged but the vigour of his walk and unlined face told her when he was closer that this was not such an old man.

'Mrs Henley?' he asked, his arm outstretched. 'Thanks for being on time. You're the only applicant to manage that today.'

Jenny held out her hand and tried to shake his firmly. She nodded and smiled. But instead of words she simply swallowed.

'Most people seem to have had trouble finding the place,' said the man.

Jenny wanted to reply but a strange, rasping sound emerged from her throat. She coughed. 'I did check the route a few days ago, actually, otherwise I probably would have got lost too.'

He nodded approval.

'Good preparation, well done. I'm General Hardy.'

Jenny said: 'Oh!'

Although this was a military area and probably full of retired generals and a large ivy-clad house here might be expected to contain one, she was still astonished to find that the job had any army connection.

They walked towards the house together.

'My husband's a sergeant,' she said.

The general was interested in this, and asked about Dave's regiment and commanding officer.

'But don't they have a company going back into theatre this week?' he asked.

'Today,' said Jenny.

They were inside the house now, walking down a long hallway. There were rugs on the floor which might be from Afghanistan and the whole place smelled of polish and dogs. An old sand-coloured Labrador strolled out amiably to be stroked. Jenny obliged and saw the dog's hairs settle on her blue skirt. No time to pick them off; she was being led further through the house. She glimpsed rooms with high ceilings and tiled floors and large paintings on the walls.

'But your husband didn't leave for Afghanistan today?' demanded the general.

Jenny nodded. 'First thing this morning. I think he's in the air by now.'

'I'm surprised you're here!'

'I'm glad I'm here. I hate the day he goes away,' she admitted.

'Well, if you'd cancelled the interview I would have understood,' he said. 'I very much appreciate your coming.'

He sounded as though he meant it.

And now they were in a large office. One entire wall was almost nothing but window. It looked across fields in which were grazing a couple of horses wearing brightly coloured rugs on their backs.

'Oh, this is lovely!' said Jenny involuntarily, and then wondered if it was OK to comment. But the general looked pleased as her eye swept along the wooden desks, the oil paintings, the nest of tall, jungly plants in one corner and the noticeboards thick with photos and lists.

'This is where you'd be working. It's a bit dusty at the moment because Linda's on holiday. She cleans and does practically everything around here. Usually you can expect it to be cleaned at least twice a week. That's my desk. And that's my assistant's desk. Please, sit down.'

She didn't feel nervous any more. The room was warm and brightened by the weak winter sun which had suddenly emerged through the grey clouds. The general was friendly. In fact, he sat shuffling through papers now in a way which suggested he was more nervous than she was.

'Er, well then . . .' Shuffle shuffle shuffle. 'What have you been told about the vacancy, Mrs Henley?'

'Nothing. I'd got hold of the idea you're an IT company. But now I don't think you are.'

He laughed.

'Ha! IT company! Ha! One reason you're here is because I'm baffled by IT. Although my daughter says I'm baffled because I want to be.'

'I wouldn't say I'm brilliant with technology myself,' said Jenny. 'Tell me what the job involves and I'll tell you if I think I can do it or not.'

'Well, don't laugh . . . I'm writing my memoirs.'

Jenny didn't laugh.

'I've had an interesting career and I think it sheds light on some political and military problems. Don't suppose anyone will publish it but if my grandchildren all have a copy I'll be happy. Anyway, I write in long-hand and I need someone to type that up. In addition, I'm on a defence committee which reports to Parliament. And a few other committees as well. That's what they do with old buffers like me when we leave the army: they put us on committees. I'm always getting emails and I can open them and read them but my typing's very bad and very slow because I have slight arthritis in one hand. So it's hard to reply. And then all this report stuff has to be typed and submitted by email. I do have other things, letters, form-filling, the usual. And my personal accounts are quite straightforward but I haven't had a chance to do them for ages and the taxman's getting annoyed with me. Oh, and the filing. I'll be honest. I've just been chucking it all into that box there and someone really needs to sort it out.'

Jenny watched his face as he spoke. He was hardly the old buffer he pretended. But he did look very despondent.

'So ... things have got into a bit of a state ...' he concluded, looking at her helplessly.

'Is there any particular reason for that?' she asked gently.

His face looked ever sadder.

'Well, it's since my wife left. I've been completely saturated in divorce stuff. And memoirs. But now I've emerged from under the ruling, everything else is in a mess.'

'Right,' said Jenny. 'Well, I think I can do all that.'

'Can you really?' asked the general. He sounded as if this might be too much to hope for.

'Yes, I think so. If you were patient with me at first.'

'Something which is very important is confidentiality.

192

I would not want you to talk about anything you type or read in this house with anyone outside it, especially not anyone in camp. And I'm afraid that includes your husband. I know that's a big ask.'

'It wouldn't be a problem for me.'

'Even if your husband wanted to know things?'

'He wouldn't. There's a lot of stuff I don't ask and he doesn't tell me about work. So we're used to that.'

The general watched her. She thought that he had a kind face.

'Why are you applying for jobs, Mrs Henley?' he asked.

Jenny was ready for this one.

'I've got a three-year-old and a baby. My husband's always going away and I'm always at home. I do love being with the girls but I'd like to get out of the house and use my brain a bit. I've managed to put some good childcare in place.'

'I dare say the money would come in handy, if you're on a sergeant's pay.'

Jenny hadn't meant to but she found herself explaining why Vicky had left the camp nursery and telling him about the new nursery and how her earnings would be spent.

'I know that nursery. It's near here and my daughter sends my granddaughter there. She speaks very highly of it. But isn't there a huge deposit?'

Jenny nodded. 'Yes. It's going to take me a while to earn that much.'

'But it would be ideal if you could drop your child off at the nursery and come on to work here . . .' said the general, thinking. He took a pen and wrote down some swift calculations while Jenny looked around the room. There were a few pictures, in frames, of an attractive blonde woman. The ex-wife, it had to be.

'Right, Mrs Henley,' he said, looking up at last. 'May I call you Jennifer?'

'Everyone else calls me Jenny.'

'Ah, but I'm not everyone else and I think Jennifer is a pretty name. Would you mind if I call you Jennifer?'

Jenny felt herself reddening slightly.

'Not at all,' she said.

'Well, I'd like to offer you the job for twelve hours a week as my assistant. I've been seeing people all day and you're the applicant I'd most like to work with. I'm going to propose that I loan you the money to put down your deposit and secure a nursery place for your child. I'll deduct it in small amounts from your pay over the next six months. Here are the sums: take a look.'

Dave was busy checking in at RAF Brize Norton when Jenny rang. Processing had taken a long time at South Cerney and they had arrived at Brize Norton an hour late. He did not pick up his phone until they were waiting to board and saw that he had missed a call from her.

The other lads were all making their final calls home and Dave dialled the house first. No reply. Where was Jenny on this gloomy Monday, and why wasn't she waiting for his call? Maybe at the playground. He dialled her mobile. It was switched off because it went straight to her voicemail.

'Where are you? I'm at Brize Norton and we're about to board. We're running a bit late. I love you, Jenn. I won't be gone long. Give the girls a massive cuddle each from me tonight. And every night. I'm thinking of you. 'Bye.'

His knew his words weren't enough to express the emptiness inside him. Yes, he wanted to go back into theatre because he was a soldier, and when he arrived at Bastion he would be happy enough. But that other Dave, the Dave who was a husband and father, was experiencing a loss so great that it felt like grief.

On board, counting heads, watching his men, he could tell they were all feeling the same thing. The flight was a quiet one. Men played games and read or talked in low voices. No one slept. After about five hours, when they reached Afghan airspace, they stowed the games and put on helmets and body armour. The talking stopped. It was too dark to see anything but Dave knew what lay below them: wave after wave of snow-capped mountains sweeping so evenly across the landscape that they might have been made by some massive mountain machine. Then the mountains would give way to desert, occasionally painted green by rivers. This was Afghanistan.

The Tristar began its descent into Kandahar, a massive complex of lights and airstrips. They were told to remain on the aircraft until their Hercules was ready. In total silence the men transferred to the big, old flying bus, a pigeon of a plane.

The ride to Bastion was bumpy and noisy. No one could communicate over the sound of that engine but no one had anything to say anyway. Suddenly they descended in total darkness, swooping down through the night like an owl. Men who had never experienced the night landing into Bastion looked around, wide-eyed and alarmed. Even those who were used to it had forgotten the intensity of the drop into this other world. Then they were on the ground. The rear hatch of the Hercules opened and they tumbled out into the mysterious pitch-black night of Helmand Province.

16

Dearest Dave,

Well, you've gone and you don't need me to tell
you how empty the house feels without you and
how cold the bed is. I've found the present
already. That's because the clue was crap. The
answer couldn't have been anything but a nappy.
I'm just glad you chose a clean one. Anyway,
thanks, darling, they are gorgeous and I love you
for always knowing which jewellery to choose.

How's Steve managing at Bastion? Leanne says
he's getting really pissed off because they aren't letting him out of the gates. He's only been there one
minute. He seems to think you'll sort it because
apparently you sort everything. But you never said
he could do anything but Stores, did you?

Jaime has another tooth, she looks like a hyena
and laughs like one whenever Vicky shouts
'Washing Line' at her. Their little private joke. I
miss you so much. I wish you were here laughing
away with the girls about washing lines. Phone
me from Bastion before they send you out to the
back of beyond.

From your loving, lonely wife,
xxxxxxJ
PS I had a job interview. If you ring me, I'll tell
you all about it.

Darling Dave,
You are such a fucking bastard, why don't you
ever phone? Sol called Adi the moment you all
got to Bastion so I know you're OK. Steve rang
Leanne. Rose McKinley got TWO calls. Stop being
nice and letting everyone else in your platoon use
the phone before you. Not telling you about my
job interview until you phone me. I love you and
miss you. Vicky has a message for you. It's:
'WASHING LINE!' You know what you're
supposed to do next. Go on. Ha ha ha ha ha ha.
   Lol xxxxxxxxxJ

Dear Dave,
Got some kind of a phone phobia? Thought of
discussing it with a doctor? But until the pills
start working, you could always SEND A
LETTER!!! I really like writing you e-blueys,
they're so easy. Or maybe you're not actually
getting them, even though the tracking system
says you are. So maybe you think I haven't
written. Maybe that's why you don't write back.
Would you please just ring and tell me if you're
getting the letters? A yes or no will do, then you
can slam the phone down before your phobia gets
the better of you.
   Vicky is pretending to write things. It's all just

scribble but don't tell her that. She sits there
reading this scribble out loud to me. Of course,
she's making it all up as she goes along. I know
that for a fact because today she picked up her
scribble and said: 'Oh look, Mummy, it's a letter
from Daddy!' Then she read it to me. Fascinating.
Apparently you have been washing your socks.
And hanging them out on the WASHING LINE!
Ha ha ha.

   xxxxxJ

PS Did I mention that I got the job? I start next
week. And you don't even know what the
fucking job is!!!

Darling,

It was so good to talk to you and hear your voice
again. I can tell a lot from your voice. I can tell it's
already getting hot out there. I can hear dust in
your throat. I can tell that you've been shouting at
your men a lot. I can tell that you're really, really
fed up with Steve. A pissed-off Steve is not a nice
Steve; ask Leanne.

   I wish you sounded more pleased about my
job. General Hardy's very nice and quite old and
I think he's got some wound which is why he left
the army. I'll just be typing out his memoirs and
letters and reports for him and sorting through
receipts and bits of paper and stuff and making
the odd cup of tea. I won't be changing his
catheter or anything; he's not ill. So I don't know
why you're making a big fuss. And stop thinking
the kids will suffer, it's for twelve hours a week and
Vicky will be at nursery most of the time and

Jaime's asleep for two hours in the morning and anyway they'll be fine with Adi. I hope there's not some stupid law which says she has to register somewhere before she can take care of the kids. It's just a friends' thing. Now Leanne's at the bakery she's leaving the boys with Adi too and sometimes they overlap and it's bedlam. But happy bedlam, you know Adi.

xxxxxxJ

Hi Jenny,
I'm sorry I don't ring you more often. I know I'm really bad about ringing. It's because it doesn't help to think about all I've left behind. Better just to get on with it. But I do think about you a lot, whether I want to or not, and I've taken a lot of pictures with the camera.

I've been asking around about General Hardy and someone said he was a right bastard. Can't you find a job in a café where you can talk to a lot of people and dazzle them with your looks and charm? Why dazzle just one nasty old man in the privacy of his own home? I know you're trying to make your life more interesting but what's interesting about him and his bits of paper? Why does he need someone to help? And by the way, he's not that old.

Also, where have you taken the deposit for the nursery from? Tell me you haven't cashed in our meagre ISA account.

We're supposed to be moving off to the FOB soon. Not a lot has been happening at Bastion. We've been involved in two operations but we were a long way from where it was all happening.

The Americans are busy eradicating the poppies and we fill the spaces they've left.

When I get to the FOB it's going to be even harder to phone and you're going to be even angrier with me when I finally get through. After that it's a patrol base and there's no phone and you'll be REALLY angry. Deliveries irregular, and that includes e-blueys.

I love you. I will do anything you ask except leave the army. But if the sergeant major keeps borrowing I mean nicking my shower gel that day could come soon. You can buy everything at Bastion but he prefers nicking mine.

All my love to you and the girls. I mean that. All of it.

Dave

PS Glad you like the earrings. They reminded me of tears. Wear them instead of crying.

PPS The drawing is for Vicky and in case there's any confusion, it's supposed to be a WASHING LINE. Ha ha ha.

Dear Dave,

I don't understand why you didn't write before you left for the FOB. I understand about the queues for the phone but is there just the one writing pad at Bastion? And you have to take it in turns?

General Hardy likes to write letters to people. He writes loads and loads of letters BY HAND. Then I have to decode them. Then I have to type them. Then I start on his memoirs. They're really interesting. When I get to know him better I might offer to teach him to type. Except then he won't need me any more, and I'm enjoying the job. I'm going three times a week for four hours, on Monday, Wednesday and Friday, in the mornings. On Monday and Wednesday, Vicky goes to nursery. She is really happy there. Everyone is kind and she has made a little friend. Unfortunately the friend is also called Victoria.

General Hardy's very nice. He lives in a big house with ivy all over it in Tinnington village. Actually, today he wrote a letter to someone about getting the ivy off. I told him it was a shame because it looks really nice. He said it damages the brickwork. So I typed out the letter but then he ripped it up because he said he'd been thinking and I was right, the ivy does look nice, so it could stay a bit longer. He says my spelling and punctuation are very good, much better than his. I didn't tell him about Spellcheck, ha. He said there were forty applications for this job. FORTY!!! He interviewed five people. And he chose me out of all of them. Are you impressed? Maybe you'll be impressed enough to write?
xxxxxxxxxxJ

Dearest darling Dave,
So you did write before you left Bastion. As usual, our letters crossed. Who told you that

General Hardy's nasty? They're wrong; he's really kind. Whatever you heard about him it's not true. Apparently there was a General Hardacre who no one liked and people always get them confused.

He has a granddaughter who lives in town and there are lots of toys here and he's loaned some to Vicks and Jamie. One of them is educational, little coloured rod things which all add up to ten.

He told me to call him Eugene (weird name, sounds like You Jean. Leanne calls him General YouTube) but I don't call him anything at all. There's an old picture of him on the noticeboard with Tony Blair and other famous people. And he's on some sort of committee and today I had to type a letter from the committee to the Secretary of State for Defence. Kept Spellcheck busy. And don't tell me the job isn't interesting, because it is. I really screwed up the other day – sent something confidential to the wrong person. I thought he'd sack me but he was very nice about it.

Adi says the kids are fine all the time I'm out – though as I said mostly Vicks is at the nursery. Yesterday Adi had the two of them and they started grizzling, so Adi got out your washing line picture, which Vicks carries around in a little bag, and Vicks couldn't stop giggling and that set Jaime off. No one could have that many pairs of big, baggy pants, not even the British Army. Adi is helping Vicky do a washing line for you. With more, bigger, baggier pants.

xxxxxxxxxxJ

PS Are you getting on better with the platoon commander?

PPS Leanne says that Steve's persuaded them to let him out of Bastion in a few weeks! Only for a photocall, though. There's going to be a picture of him in a magazine. Not sure which one.

Jenny,
I got my hands on a phone and rang you twice and there was no reply. So I suppose you were at work. Take care of yourself around General Hardy; he is a useless git. Iain Kila has remembered all about him. His name used to be General Howard-Hardy but he dropped the Howard because people were calling him Coward-Hardy after what happened. It was here in Afghanistan in about 2003 when he was still a brigadier. He had enough troops and weapons to take Chalee, a Taliban town at the centre of the opium-growing area, and at the last minute he backed down. Apparently he got some intelligence that the Taliban were going to put up one hell of a fight. He just lost his bottle – he could never produce any reason. The soldiers were really frustrated because they were out of Bastion and ready to go. We didn't take Chalee for a few years after that, and then it took a long time and cost lives. So he may be nice but he's not popular.

By the way, I notice that you don't mention Mrs Hardy in this ivy-covered house of his. What are you actually doing, apart from discussing horticulture?

We are at the FOB with our friends, the Afghan National Army, and it is the shittiest FOB ever, just a lot of Hesco and a bunch of holes in a rock face. The Americans called it FOB Carlsbad after some famous American caves but only a few of the holes are big enough to call themselves a cave. I wouldn't put it past the Taliban to tunnel their way through from the other side. Should take them a while, so hopefully I won't be here for Groundhog Day when their smiling turbaned faces poke up through the floor. The word is that we should be back in Wiltshire soon after Easter. So you can save me an egg, thank you very much. A big one will do.

  All my love,
  Dave

Darling Dave,
I just got back and I did 1471 because I had this feeling you'd rung and you had. I just want to cry when I miss your calls. Why don't you call my mobile? Why don't you leave a message at least? I was at work and then I went to pick up the kids and Leanne was at Adi's picking up the twins too, so we all had a cup of tea. Kids everywhere. Leanne likes her new job at the bakery. She's losing weight. She's already lost a stone but don't tell Steve, it's going to be a surprise. For God's sake phone again before you leave the FOB.

  xxxxxxxxxJ

Hi,
We are still stuck in our cave FOB with the Afghan National Army and two blokes have had

204

iPods nicked and we all know who's doing it. I am getting seriously pissed off with them. Some of the Afghans just don't care. They don't follow orders and they bunk off whenever they can. And one of them was chasing after Jack Binns, that little blond bloke from Dorset. He was shit scared to come out of his cave. Iain Kila's put up some wire and banned the ANA from our side of it. Some of them are all right. But not all of them. The storesman was convinced the ANA was nicking kit. He stayed up all night trying to catch them but they're too crafty for that.

Every day we go on foot patrol around here. We have to do it with the Afghan National Army. Every patrol must have an Afghan face; they tell us over and over again. Sometimes, when we patrol through the town, the Afghan face gets overcome by the Afghan Bazaar and they forget all their training and put down their weapons and start buying stuff.

I am trying to get on with that tosser Chalfont-Prick but I don't like him and he doesn't like me. Seems to prefer one of the corporals but doesn't talk to any of his men if he can help it.

We like to pretend that we're keeping the area clear of Taliban but it's all shit. They tax the stallholders at the market. They probably run the place, they're the mafia but they look like everyone else. We only know they're Taliban when they fire at us. Don't worry, I won't let them shoot me.

Remember in Iraq I had a mate called Doc Holliday? He was a doctor who'd been in the Special Forces but he got an injury so he became a medic again. Well, he's our company medic and it's good to see him. We have a laugh but he's always deadpan so it's funnier.

All my love,
Dave

Hi,
Just picked up your message on voicemail, must have been upstairs and left my mobile in the kitchen. But I still can't understand how I missed you. Don't sound so pissed off. I'd give anything to take your call. Vicky has a cold. She's running a temperature and she's been sick, so I don't want to go out and leave her with anyone, not even Adi. I have to ring Eugene and ask if it's OK for me to come another day. Have to go. They're both wailing at once.

xxxxxxxxJ

Dear Jenny,
Where are you? I rang again and there was no
reply. Then I tried your mobile and I got voicemail. Didn't leave a message, what's the fucking
point? I deliberately booked a slot in the evening
when I thought you'd be home. What's going on?
   All my love,
   Dave

Dear Dave,
I'm really missing you today. Sometimes it's
worse than others. Vicky's still not well and I
think Jaime's going down with it and I've had the
odd sniffle too. Eugene's being very nice and
understanding. He dropped by this morning with
a pile of stuff so that I could get on with things at
home if there's a spare moment. Which there
isn't. Not until Calpol time in the evening when I
collapse into a heap. But I'll try to do a bit of
work tonight.
   Leanne came round on her way home. They've
asked her to do extra hours at the bakery but she
doesn't want to do early mornings. She wears
blue bakery clothes which look like she's a doctor
just off to do an operation. And she smells of
bread. She says she doesn't ever eat it, or the
cream cakes, and she's telling the truth because
she's really losing weight.
   That picture you've just sent – was it supposed
to be a washing line hanging outside a cave?
Won't show it to the girls yet or they'll puke all
over it. But you ought to know that Washing
Lines are OUT and Post Offices are IN. Remember

Vicky had a thing about them a little while ago? Well, they're back in fashion. Nothing much makes Vicks laugh at the moment but before she got this bug for some reason the idea of Going to the Post Office was hilarious. Can you draw an Afghan Post Office? Thought not.

  xxxxxxJ

PS What exactly are you doing hanging around in a cave like a bunch of bats? Doesn't sound healthy to me. Glad you've got Doc Holliday to take care of you. I remember you talking about him before.

Darling Jenn,
Still haven't heard from you and that doesn't feel good. You don't answer my calls and you don't write. I suppose about ten e-blueys will all arrive at once. I notice that no one writes to Chalfont-Prick. Maybe even his mum doesn't like him. There's no communicating with the twat. He just thinks a sergeant is too far beneath him. The other day I tried to explain something to him about arcs of fire and he wouldn't listen. He actually said: 'My parents spent a lot of money on my education, Sergeant, so I don't need you to educate me too.' Something like that, anyway. Incredible. He always calls me Sergeant. Not sure if he knows my name. I'm trying to build up a relationship like Major Willingham said but it takes two. Anyway, I'm very polite and try not to argue. Just like I am at home.

The ANA is driving us crazy. Some of them can't shoot straight, or they can't be bothered to try. I caught a guy leaning his rifle against a rock and firing it one-handed. I mean, just pointing it in the general direction of the enemy and spraying. After all the training, they do that. They love firing on automatic. Saves your finger so much effort. And the other night they were on stag and something spooked them, God knows what, and they all jumped up and started firing. Like mad things. Just firing into the dark. We got out the night sights and there was nothing to see and no one fired back and nothing happened but we only got them to stop by taking away their ammo. Reminds me of that dog your mum had which wouldn't stop barking for no reason.

Jenn, answer the phone.

All my love,

Dave

Dearest Jenny,

Had a call booked for you but we were on minimize because of an incident. You probably heard that a bloke was killed and two were injured. IED very near Bastion. Not sure if you know that Steve Buckle was on board the vehicle and he was only going to the ranges to zero his rifle and have his picture taken. The thing is that he got away with cuts and scratches and a bit of shrapnel but the explosion must have brought back his memory of the last IED because apparently he's going a bit crazy at Bastion. Does Leanne know about it? He's not in a good place. They may have to send him home. Poor bastard. Every time he drives through the gates at Bastion, someone blows him up. Anyway, just to warn

you that if he comes back he won't be easy to
deal with.

Love D xxx

Darling,
I can't believe you wasted a whole letter asking me
where I am in a pissed-off tone instead of telling
me what's going on out there. By the time I get
your letters, I can't remember where I was. At the
playground, driving to nursery, picking up the kids
from Adi's, shopping at the supermarket, maybe
even at work, I do all those things . . . not that I'm
getting out much at the moment. Vicks is better
(except for hacking cough and runny red nose) but
Jaime's got the bug now. Vicks keeps asking when
she can go back to nursery. She loves it there.

Eugene brought some more work over today.
He stayed for a coffee and, guess what, he fixed
that drawer in the living room which keeps on
sort of dropping every time you open it and then
won't go back in. Took the whole thing apart,
which meant taking out ALL the drawers and
seeing the mess inside. I'm OK with him as long
as I forget he's a general. Having a general fix
your drawer feels peculiar. He loves kids and
stayed a while having a laugh with Vicks (Post
Office ha ha ha).

BTW, I love you lots and lots and lots. I'm
always in a hurry when I write to you and I
probably forget to say that sometimes. But it's
true. I love you and miss you, all of you including
your body. Not long till Easter and then you'll be
home and I'll feel your arms around me again.

You. Chocolate eggs. Mmmmm.

xxxxxxxxxxxxxxxxJ

PS Eugene's middle name is Howard. He was never Brigadier Howard-Hardy, so that stuff about dropping the Howard because people called him Coward is a load of rubbish, and anyway, they would never have made him a major general if he'd run away.

Dear Jenny,

At last a few letters have arrived from you. Sorry to disappoint everyone but no, I can't draw an Afghan Post Office. I asked the interpreter what they look like and he said there aren't any here. Not sure if he really understood. He's a bit shifty, to be honest.

How are the kids? Did you catch whatever Vicks had? When she can't go to that expensive nursery, do they still charge you?

We are still snuggled up in our caves with our friends, the Afghan National Army. All mod cons, especially hot and cold running Afghans. I'd like to shoot some of them. Then I get talking to a few and I like them. Then more iPods get nicked, and other stuff too. It may be something to do with this interpreter who I don't trust. I'm sure he's thieving and he might be telling his mates everything we do and think as well.

The ANA've been firing all over the place and the other day Iain Kila got out some targets and said we'll do a bit of practice. At other PBs there have been a few green on blue incidents, when ANA soldiers go crazy and start shooting us, so we were a bit wary at first. They were a bit wary too, mostly because they couldn't hit the targets. I mean, they were terrible. So much for the legend of the deadly Afghan fighter who's genetically programmed to hit a blade of grass half a mile away. A few of them are pretty good, though; they're the local lads who started handling weapons when they were about twelve.

Our job soon will be to guard Afghanistan's most unpopular guys – the tractor drivers who've been hired to spray weedkiller over the poppy crop. So we can expect a lot of trouble. If we all get slotted it will give Poppy Day a whole new meaning.

We'll be here a while on poppy duty until the tractors move further up the province. Then we have to hang around a bit to keep the Taliban out of the area until Helmand's covered in withered yellow stalks and dead Taliban. Then we extract out. I mean, home. Thank God. I want to be with you and the kids again. This is a boring tour and it's not the same sharing your rations with the ANA. Now I know what they teach them at school here. Scowling.

Love,

Dave

PS Have you seen Steve yet? Is he at home with Leanne?

Dear Jenn,

Another letter arrived. Yep, I remember the drawer which keeps on sticking, it's the one I keep meaning to fix. So a general dropped round and did it for me. I've told you what people say about him. And apparently there isn't a Mrs General any more; they're divorced. Right? So he lives all by himself, right? With you visiting him for twelve hours a week? Right? Did it ever occur to you that you got the job out of all those applications because you're the prettiest? Be careful, Jenn.

I love you.
Dave

Dear Jenny,
I'm really sorry about Easter. I would rather be with you and the kids at home than anywhere. I don't want to be in this rat hole.

I'm sorry. Try to save me an egg.
Love and sadness,
Dave

Dear Dave,
I'm going to be very pissed off if you die for a handful of poppies. And make sure you don't get any weedkiller on you, that's not good either. We're all better now, not even runny noses. Seems a long time since we all had those colds.

Lol xxxxx J

Dear Dave,
Maybe the guys in the ANA who can't shoot straight need glasses? Do they get any medical attention? I thought of that because Leanne told me about how everyone thought she was thick

when she was a kid but it turned out she couldn't see properly. Well, it's just a thought. The girls send their love too. Vicky says Post Office.

Love, J

xxxxxxx

Dearest Dave,

Steve came back but he only stayed a day. It was awful. I didn't see him arrive so I didn't know he was there. He wouldn't go out at all and when I tried to drop something off for Leanne he didn't come to the door. Leanne says he's totally withdrawn and doesn't even notice the boys, but that could be the drugs they've given him. And he's miserable. He cries a lot. I can't imagine Steve crying. He won't talk about anything, though. Leanne couldn't go into work that day because she couldn't leave him alone. Then a psychiatrist arrived, then a car came and took him to Headley Court. I hope they make him better. He got a bit larger than life before he went to Bastion and he's come back small as a mouse. It's horrible. It's horrible for Leanne and the kids.

xxxxxxJ

Dearest Jenny,

Well, by the time you read this you'll have got my message. It rang a few times and then went to voicemail as if you grabbed it and switched it off. What the fuck is going on? It was night time, you should have been in bed.

Same thing as usual here. We go out on patrol.

We get shot at sometimes. If we get intelligence
that there's a nest of Taliban we go to the
compounds and start by sending in the Afghan
face so it can get blown up first, I mean so they
can chat to the locals. The locals don't feel chatty.
They open fire. The ANA gets into a firefight and
half the time we're not allowed to join in.
Sometimes we watch the insurgents escaping
through the back of the compound and we're not
allowed to stop them. It's fucking ridiculous.
What are we here for? Then, after not fighting, we
come back to our cave. No sign of the poppy
sprayers yet.

Chalfont-Prick is still a prick but there aren't so
many officers for him to cosy up to here, so he's
having to mix with his men a bit more. Not that
he likes it. Whenever he talks to them he screws
his face up. Maybe he has a pain in his bum. I'm
prepared to bet that the man doesn't know a
single name. Except Aaron. He likes Aaron Baker.

Love,
Dave

Dear Dave,
No, there isn't a Mrs General, she pissed off with
some bloke who was giving her tennis lessons.
Eugene has taken a couple of years to get over it.
His friends ask him out to their dinner parties
and introduce him to women but he isn't
interested, still mopes for Mrs General. So much
for being a womanizer. There are pictures of her
all over the house. Very slim and pretty in a posh
sort of way.

And I got the job because I'm clever, actually. Nothing to do with my looks.

Eugene is an unhappy man, very complicated – maybe that's how generals are, in which case I don't think you're going to be one after all ha ha. The other day he took his shoes off and there were holes in his socks. It's sort of sad. I like doing his letters and sorting his receipts into piles and I've learned to use Excel and you probably don't even know what that is. Well, you can't load it into a gimpy so I don't expect you'd be interested anyway. Oh shit, let's stop having a go at each other. Anyway, Eugene's memoirs are very interesting. I'm looking forward to typing the bit about retreating from that town. Except I bet he didn't. I'm absolutely sure that he's no coward.

Why haven't you rung me? Vicky says there must be post offices in Afghanistan or they couldn't send their letters, could they, duh? How is Chalfont-Prick?

Leanne went to Headley Court to see Steve and she says he's no different. Hardly said a word to her.

Love from your loving wife who loves you a lot,

xxxxxxxxJ

Dear Dave,

Just got your letter. I did not hang up on you. Why would I do that? I wait for your calls every fucking day and all fucking night. I answered and there was no one there, you'd already hung up.

Please ring again, please, please, please.
  xxxxJ

Dear Jenny,
Adi told Sol that the other day General Coward-
Hardy came to pick up our kids from Adi's to
take them to his house because you were working
overtime there. Is it true? I don't like him being
alone with the girls. I don't know him and I don't
like it. I rang you again and there was no reply
and I am getting so fucking pissed off that
everyone's remarking on it. What's going on?
Why aren't you telling me things?
  Love from Dave

Dear Dave,
I'm putting the phone down on you if you try
speaking to me like that again. You do not have
the right to shout at me from thousands of miles
away when we can't even see each other and put
our arms around each other afterwards and say
we're sorry. Anyway I'm not sorry. I haven't done
anything wrong. You should say sorry for speaking to me that way. Since you weren't listening to
a word I said, I'll write it all down so you can
read it when you're not shouting.
  I was typing out a really long, important
document which HAD to be sent that afternoon.
And Adi couldn't take the girls any longer
because one of her kids had a doctor's appointment. And Leanne had already gone out. So
Eugene said he would pick up Vicky and Jaime
and bring them to me at his house, even though it

217

took about an hour to sort out the car seats. Surprise, surprise, he did not take them to Tinnington Woods and murder them. He brought them straight home and they watched TV and played Post Offices and stuff while I finished the document. Now just stop it, for Christ's sake. I know you imagine all sorts of weird things when you're far away but you'll just have to trust me. I know Eugene and you don't. It was a one-off event and he's safe with the kids and I didn't leave him for long, anyway. And I was in the house the whole time.

As for the theme park, I wasn't going to tell you because I knew you'd get hold of the wrong end of the stick. If Si and Tiff Curtis saw me there, why didn't they come over and say hello? I certainly didn't see them. Anyway, the theme park sometimes invites army families to come for free and I got an invite and so did Eugene. Unfortunately the main man in my family wasn't available to join me, he was thousands of miles away, as usual. It's hard to do those theme park things by yourself and Eugene's got a little grand-daughter and so we agreed it was easier for both of us to do it together with the three kids. It was a day of simple, innocent fun and you can just take back all those disgusting things you said.

Let's face it: you don't like me having a job. But I enjoy it. I enjoy getting out of the house and seeing into someone else's life for a while instead of looking at our magnolia walls all day long. Eugene's nice. The memoirs are interesting, so are the letters and I'm learning things. And the most important thing of all is that Vicky loves the new nursery and can't wait to get there in the morning and my job's paying for it.

Why do you begrudge me a life of my own when you're away? Do you have any idea how fucking lonely and boring it gets without you?

I love you. Why don't you trust me?
J

Dear Dave,
Yes, you're right, it's true. Eugene loaned me the deposit for the nursery and I'm paying it back each month, bit by bit, from my wages. There's nothing to read into that. It's a normal arrangement. I'm sorry I put the phone down instead of telling you. I just don't know what to do when you start shouting at me and making accusations. And the way you ask me questions. As if you've been trying to catch me out and you finally managed to. Dave, stop it. I'm not having an affair with Eugene. I love you. Stop it. Please.
xxxJ

Dear Jenny,
I never thought it would be like this between us. I didn't think I could be so angry with you. I am fucking livid. Would like to ask for some compassionate leave so I can come home and sort it all out but there's no way. Things are hotting up here now that the poppy sprayers are arriving. So I'm stuck in a cave, thinking my thoughts. Don't make me worry like this, Jenn. It's not fair when there's such a lot to worry about out here anyway.

You know how much I love you and the girls and now it's all started falling apart. It was OK when I left. And now we're shouting at each other and I've got a horrible feeling people are talking about us. All over the FOB and all over camp.

For God's sake tell me what's going on.

D

Dear Dave,

I am not having an affair. There is nothing going on. Why can't a woman work for a man without people gossiping about them?

Since you ask – NOT, the girls are fine and the nursery school thinks that Vicky is very advanced for her age and she enjoys every minute there. Jaime is so proud of her teeth that she grins a lot. She is adorable. Sometimes she says stuff that sounds like words.

And, by the way, stop complaining about me to your mum. She rang me last night and the reason why was obvious.

Love,

Jenny

17

Everything about FOB Carlsbad was too small. Men tumbled out of their cots when they turned over in their sleep and hit the rock walls. Some preferred to sleep outside, no matter how low the night temperature. Food was served in a space so tiny that only about ten men could eat there at a time and most didn't bother to try. The washing area was practically inside the Control Post. The Hesco never seemed to be more than an arm's reach away. And the communal caves where commanders addressed their platoons were barely big enough for two sections, let alone three, so men spilled out into the eating area and had to keep asking other platoons to keep quiet so they could hear.

The night before the spraying operation began, 1 Platoon tried to crush on to the floor of the largest cave, feet digging into each other's backs, as the boss gave orders. Chalfont-Price, at the front, was the only man with any space around him.

'It is the Afghan National Police's job to run the poppy-eradication programme and it is our job to protect them and the tractor drivers who are actually spraying the crop. I repeat: We are not here to engage in prolonged battle, search compounds or open fire on the Taliban. There is no role for the ANA because our mandate is simply to ensure that everyone involved in eradication can do their job, but let me emphasize again that we are not responsible for eradicating the crop. That is not the reason we are in Afghanistan.

'Now, at 0700 hours we will be joining the convoy of tractors at the point where it turns off Highway One . . .'

He had asked Aaron Baker, commander of 2 Section, to hold the map and indicate the route. Dave, standing at the side of the cave, his arms crossed, thought that should be his job. But for some reason the boss was still asking the corporal to play the sergeant's role.

'It's fucking insulting,' Dave had complained last week to the sergeant major.

'Only if you take it that way,' Kila had replied. 'I'm just relieved Chalfont-Price actually likes someone.'

Baker, the man whose map-reading skills were well known to be non-existent, was now showing the company Highway One, the FOB, the poppy fields and the route they would take to the RV.

'Is that clear?' Chalfont-Price asked the men when Baker had finished. He did not pause for an answer. 'And I can assure you that our journey from Highway One to the poppy fields at least will be safe. The area has been thoroughly cleared of personnel and mines.'

When the boss used the word 'safe', Dave uncrossed and crossed his arms. Noticing, the young officer turned his small, thickset body aggressively towards Dave.

'Do you have some sort of problem with that, Sergeant?' he demanded. 'Perhaps you'll share it with us?'

And then there was that silence, the one Dave was

learning to recognize, the special silence which fell among the men when he and Chalfont-Price were confronting each other. It wasn't just that nobody talked. Nobody moved either; maybe they didn't even breathe. The entire platoon was holding its breath.

Dave looked out of the cave towards the bright daylight. Helmeted heads were silhouetted against it. He saw Doc Holliday, watching him laconically, leaning against a rock. Doc raised his eyebrows. He disliked the boss even more than Dave did.

Dave turned to the men. 'You heard what the boss said. The Americans have cleared the area. But don't start thinking you can relax. You can't. Stay alert and stay sharp. Nothing's actually safe here.'

Chalfont-Price did not thank Dave before he continued. Instead he left a long pause which said the interruption had been unnecessary.

'Let me remind you once more. If the tractors come under fire, the vehicles will intercept. At worst, gunners on top can put down suppressing fire, but this is to be kept to a minimum. Men inside vehicles must not dismount and treat this like an operation. The poppy fields are not to become battlefields. Is that clear?'

No one said a word.

'I repeat. This is simply a protection exercise. Now does everyone understand what we are and are not doing?' demanded Chalfont-Price. There was a cough. Dave smiled to himself. No orders would be complete without Billy Finn asking a question.

'Sir, are you saying that we should *only* put down suppressing fire?'

The boss's face darkened. Dave had to hand it to the man, Chalfont-Prick could use his eyebrows to maximum effect. His voice, when it came, was suppressing fire itself: 'That is indeed the intention, Lance Corporal.'

'Even in an ambush, sir? Even if there's an ambush, do you want us to stay in the vehicles and not fire back?'

It had taken a while, because they were used to the open and approachable Gordon Weeks, but somehow the new boss had stopped the men asking questions. Sticking your neck out usually got it stamped on, so now people seldom did. Dave suspected that some of the lads found Chalfont-Prick more intimidating than the Taliban. But not Billy Finn. Dave knew he should put the lad in his place but he remained silent. He tried, unsuccessfully, to look disapproving.

The boss couldn't lower his eyebrows much further but he expanded his chest and there was a small but noticeable rustle of anticipation all over the cave before the men became motionless, waiting for the eruption.

'I can see,' growled Chalfont-Price, his voice taut with irritation, 'that I'll have to go over everything again as some of you have not been listening.'

He sighed expressively and then spoke slowly and clearly, as though to a child.

'We have been ordered to put down suppressing fire because the farmers will certainly attempt to protect their illegal crop from the sprayers. However, we know that these poppy fields are invaluable to the Taliban; they are some of the best in the province. We may therefore come under sustained attack, which may go beyond small-arms fire or anything local farmers can manage. There is even the possibility of serious ambush. Naturally, if that occurs, there will be fighting which requires more than suppressive fire. I should have thought that would be obvious, Lance Corporal.'

'Ah! So then it's all right for us to get out of the wagons?'

The boss's eyes flashed angrily and he turned to Dave.

'Sergeant, could you please deal with this man,' he snapped.

Dave thought the best way of dealing with Finny was to slap him on the back and buy him a pint.

'That's enough, Finny, you've made your point,' he said. He tried to sound tough but knew he hadn't succeeded.

The boss glared and then synchronized watches before stalking out to join the other officers in their cave. He did not look to right or left. His departure was immediately followed by a pause and then there was an outbreak of voices as the men scrambled to their feet and began to file out of the cave. Some of them gave Finn a thumbs-up or a high-five.

As Billy Finn passed him, Dave raised his eyebrows.

'Sarge, he sounds good but he talks bollocks,' muttered Finny.

Dave's voice was low. 'Billy Finn, I'm letting you off shit duties for a week for that,' he said. 'But be careful.'

Iain Kila strolled up.

'All right, mate?'

Dave nodded.

'Have a word?'

Dave followed the sergeant major outside and they found a place to sit under camouflage netting. Kila's tattoos were covered by the criss-cross of shadow tattoos from the netting.

Kila leaned across the table. 'Are you sure you're all right, mate?'

'Yessir. Why?'

'Because I was watching you in there and you looked seriously pissed off. Finny was cheeky and you didn't tell him to wind his neck in, and that's not like you.'

Dave shrugged. 'I thought the boss deserved it.'

'We don't let our lance corporals grip officers in the British Army, and you know it.'

Dave's face remained expressionless.

'Yeah. Yeah, you're right, Iain. Sorry.' Probably better not to mention he had actually rewarded Finny.

'I know why you're pissed off. We all do,' said Kila. 'It's not just Chalfont-Price.'

Dave felt his heart beat faster and he turned to face the sergeant major.

'What do you know?' he asked.

'Everyone's talking about it. The women are talking about it back in Wiltshire and they chatter on the phone to their husbands here and the next thing you know the blokes are all talking about it too.'

'Talking about me.' This was a statement, not a question, because Dave didn't want to hear the answer. It came anyway.

'About your Jenny. People think she's doing a bit more than typing with this general she works for over at Tinnington. Coward-Hardy.'

Dave's elbows were on the table. His chin was cupped in one palm. Now he closed his eyes. The gesture could be mistaken for defence against the long, low rays of the sun.

'Do you want to go home?' asked Iain Kila.

Dave looked up. A few lobster-coloured men passed carrying oil cans. The land still froze at night but in the day men took their shirts off whenever they could. Dave had handed out sun cream and a few used it.

Others just turned red. He made a mental note to talk to them about that again.

His eye ran over the Hesco and beyond it the rocky hillside down which, distantly, a small, brown-skinned boy clambered with a couple of goats.

'Nah,' said Dave. 'I don't need to go home.'

'Maybe you should.'

'It wouldn't be good for the lads if their sergeant sods off,' said Dave.

'We'd manage here. We'd call it R and R.'

'Everyone in camp would know why I was back.'

Dave tried to imagine arriving home in an army car, the whole street peering through their nets at him as he pulled up outside and went in. And for the next week the camp would be studying their every move.

'Steve Buckle's going home from Headley Court soon. It would help a lot if you were there.'

'No, Iain. That's not a good enough reason for me to go back either. We've got Welfare in camp for Steve.'

Kila scrutinized Dave's face now. Dave, aware that he was being appraised, closed his eyes again.

The sergeant major said: 'The worst thing is rumours. Rumours can drive you crazy because you think there's no smoke without fire and you run around looking for the fire. But sometimes there is no fire. People are just talking shit.'

'Jenny admits it,' Dave told him.

The sergeant major sat upright and wrinkled his brow. He was the only man in the FOB who stayed clean-shaven, and that included his head. 'Jenny? Admits she's having an affair?'

'Jenny admits that she sees this man because she works for him. She admits that he's picked the kids up once when she was working late. She admits that

227

they've been out to the theme park with the kids because they got some special army tickets or something and he took his grandchild. But she says she's not having an affair.'

'Christ,' said Kila. 'It's sounding like a fucking affair to me.'

Dave was silent. In the last few weeks he had been finding he had less and less to say. And the less he said, the more other people talked. About him. And Jenny.

Finally he spoke. 'I trust her.'

Kila raised his eyebrows. 'I hope you're right.'

'Until now, I'd have said we're a happily married couple.'

Doc Holliday appeared in time to hear Dave's words. He slumped down beside them, got out a cigarette and lit it, inhaling deeply and slowly. Then he said: 'I used to be happily married and look at me now.'

Dave looked at him. He saw a stocky, hairy individual blowing smoke rings.

'I'm looking. What am I supposed to see?'

'A single bloke.'

'Ah. You're telling me that you were happily married but it didn't last.'

Holliday shrugged. 'Face it, mate, none of it lasts.'

Kila assumed the same world-weary expression. 'One of the things I've learned about women is, the more you think you can trust them, the more you can't. I'm sorry, Dave. But it's true. There are women I would have put my hand on the Good Book for and said: Aye, she's faithful. Well, those are always the very ones who've let me down.'

Dave remained silent. Doc Holliday blew perfect smoke rings into the still Afghan air. Lounging about outside a cave was a group of men with nothing to do.

Dave could hear that they were talking about women too, but in a different way. An unmarried man sort of a way, their voices full of vigour and humour.

'Let me tell you a story,' Iain Kila persisted, 'about my first wife. Long ago. She was such a meek, pretty, wee thing and butter wouldn't melt in her mouth. And she was a good wife too, or so I thought. Every man in the mess took me aside and tried to tell me she was working her way through the entire regiment and I didn't believe them. And when she ran off with a colour sergeant I was knocked for six. I was distraught. I didn't go out for nearly a year. And it took a few more years for me to learn all she'd been doing when we were married and who she'd been doing it with. And even now, as I sit here, it's unbelievable to me.'

Doc Holliday's brown eyes swivelled around to Kila.

'Iain, isn't it your job to persuade him everything's all right at home?'

Kila smiled. 'I'm his mate too.'

Dave said: 'Not all women are like that wife of yours, you know. There are some women you can trust.'

Doc drew on his cigarette. 'If you trust her, why is she making you so fucking miserable, Dave?'

Dave sighed in answer.

'I often used to think,' said Kila, squinting into the sun, musing out loud, 'that if I'd listened to the blokes who were trying to tell me about my wife, if I'd confronted her and come on a bit heavy and kept her in line, we could still be married today.'

'Nah,' said Holliday. 'A woman like that would carry on, only she'd carry on in secret.'

Dave squirmed. He said: 'The thing is, Jenny's not like that.'

'The only reason I might agree with you,' continued

Kila, 'is that they're so public about it. He calls at your house, he picks up your kids from the corporal's wife, they go to some theme park . . .'

'Yeah, that's not furtive,' said Doc.

Dave couldn't imagine Jenny being furtive. He couldn't imagine her being anything but his wife. Except that recently he had tried to stop imagining her at all because whenever the idea of her appeared inside his head he felt angry and sad.

The sergeant major leaned forward and said in an undertone: 'Between you and me, I don't think we'll be here for much longer. The sprayers are due tomorrow; I reckon we should soon be home after that. And then you can sort out this General Coward-Hardy bastard. He ran away at Chalee and a lot of people despise him for it and I reckon that's when he left the army. But running away from the Taliban's one thing; having an affair with a bloke's wife while he's away fighting is even more fucking cowardly. So when you get back, you go to his posh house and punch him on the nose. And tell him to stay away from men's wives while they're in theatre.'

Jenny had given the girls their tea but they showed no sign of going to sleep. She ran upstairs to the drawer where she hid the money to pay Adi for childcare. Then she put the children in the buggy and took them to the park, hoping some friendly mothers would be there. They weren't. Only Sharon Kirk, who was just pushing her buggy smartly away. She gave Jenny a peremptory wave without stopping.

When they had played enough Post Offices, Jenny steered towards Adi's to pay her. At least Adi was always welcoming. And then, as soon as the girls were

230

asleep, she would put them to bed and sort out the mess at home. It had been that way since she started working. There was less time to get things done and the children had become more demanding when they were with her. Suddenly there were always piles of laundry and washing up. Sometimes when she got home from Eugene's she found dirty nappies which had been left on the changing table as she rushed out in the morning.

'Thank you, darling!' said Adi, as Jenny handed over the cash. 'You come in and have a cup of tea.'

Jenny went inside gratefully, only to find the Buckle twins on the rampage.

'Leanne'll be here soon for them,' said Adi. 'She had a staff meeting after work at the bakery.'

Leanne was always busy these days. Dashing off to work, up the motorway to see Steve, to the camp nursery, to the supermarket. Jenny barely saw her, and if their paths did cross as they picked up their children from Adi's house, Leanne was invariably just rushing out.

'You know what I'm saving up for?' demanded Adi as she made the tea.

'A new car?'

'I need one of those too. And that's what Sol thinks I'm buying with the money. But he's wrong. It's a big secret and a big surprise. I know you can keep a secret.'

Adi poured the tea. Jenny waited.

'A trip home to Fiji!'

'Oh Ads, what a great surprise for Sol.'

'You know what I'm going to do when he gets off that bus in the square at last? I'm not going to be holding a Welcome Home banner. I'm going to be holding the family's air tickets!'

'That's lovely, Adi.'

'So you girls can do all the overtime you want. You're buying me my tickets home. I'm thinking of writing to British Airways and telling them that Sol's a front-line soldier. Maybe they'll give me a discount . . .'

Leanne burst in. She was still wearing her blue bakery clothes.

'Hi Adi, hi Jenn.' She whistled to her twins. 'Time to go home, boys!'

Ethan and Joel rushed off, giggling, upstairs.

'How's your Steve, darling?' asked Adi. She and Jenny were sitting on the floor, surrounded by small children.

Leanne's face drooped suddenly.

'I dunno. I still can't get much out of him.'

After Steve had spent just one day at home from Bastion, a car had arrived to take him to Headley Court. He had few physical injuries beyond a small piece of shrapnel, which had now been removed. But the explosion had opened another kind of wound, the sort you couldn't see and which Steve never admitted was there.

'Any idea when he's coming back from Headley Court?'

Leanne shook her head.

'No, but I'm trying to get in all the overtime I can before he does.'

Adi smiled. 'When do you need me?'

'Can you do tomorrow morning, Ads?'

'Certainly. Eight o'clock?'

Leanne nodded, a pleading look in her eye.

'No problem. Ethan and Joel can have breakfast with us.'

Hearing their names, the twins returned, trying to squeeze between their mother's legs as she stood in the doorway.

232

'Stop that!' roared Leanne, scooping one up under each arm and holding them horizontally so they looked like tiny warheads. She turned to Jenny. 'I'll miss Tiff Curtis's charity coffee morning tomorrow. Could you stick a quid in the pot from me, Jenny, and I'll pay you back?'

Jenny looked blank.

'You must be going!' said Leanne 'She's invited everyone!'

Jenny blushed. Adi was quick: 'Jenny's too busy, but I'm going. So I'll put something in the jar for you, Lee.'

Leanne swung the twins a little to prevent them from reaching round her to pull each other's hair.

'General YouTube asking you for overtime again next week?' she demanded. Her tone was harsh. Jenny's blush turned from pink to red. She buried her face in the baby's hair. Jaime snuggled up against her.

'Well,' she admitted, 'Eugene did ask if I could stay on Monday afternoon. The nursery says they can keep Vicks all day . . .' She looked at Adi; the same pleading look Leanne had given her. 'I've been trying to get his tax stuff up together for the accountant ever since the tax year ended but we haven't even done last year yet . . .'

'OK, Jenny, no problem,' said Adi evenly. 'You want to drop Jaime before nursery on Monday and I'll keep her all day?'

'Is that all right?'

'Of course.'

Leanne was retreating now, roaring her thanks and goodbyes over yells from the kicking boys.

'I'd better go too,' said Jenny. She had been kneeling on the floor and as she stood up Vicky tried unsuccessfully to wrap herself around her mother's arm and then a leg.

'Come on, Vicks, let Mummy go or she'll fall over,' said Jenny. But Vicky did not disentangle herself, so Jenny shuffled forwards to give Adi a hug. For no particular reason.

'Darling, this job of yours is taking a lot of time and you're not seeing people like you used to,' said Adi. 'I mean, is it good for you?'

Jenny stepped back in surprise.

'I would go to Tiff Curtis's charity thing but she didn't invite me.'

Tiff had not spoken to Jenny since she had spotted her at the theme park with Eugene. It wasn't that Tiff was obviously avoiding her, but somehow she was always walking down a different street, using a different checkout at the supermarket. And she wasn't the only one. Rose McKinley and Sharon Kirk always seemed to be walking in the other direction from Jenny these days.

'Sometimes I think Tiff's forgotten what it's like for the rest of us – she's got her Si home,' said Adi. 'You have some sort of argument with her?'

Jenny shrugged. 'I don't think so.'

Adi's face creased itself up into sadness and sympathy. 'Jenny, I hate all this tittle-tattle in camp but let me tell you she's saying that you saw her in town and crossed the road.'

'Oh!' said Jenny.

'And, according to Tiff, she called out a greeting but you didn't reply. Of course, I don't believe her.'

Jenny hadn't heard Tiff call any greeting but it was true that she had crossed the road. Because the fact was that since Tiff had started to avoid her, she had been avoiding Tiff. It was the Curtises who had told Dave out in Afghanistan that they had seen her with another man. And what kind of a friend would do that?

234

Adi was looking at her closely. She said: 'Jenny, darling, are you all right?'

Jenny shrugged.

'Of course!'

'Listen, if you ever want to talk . . . I mean, it doesn't matter what you tell me, I won't judge you and I won't tell anyone else.'

Jenny forced a smile.

'There's nothing to tell, Adi. Everything's fine.'

She passed Agnieszka's house on the way home. It was empty. No buggy outside; no curtains at the windows. In fact, there was no indication that Jamie and Agnieszka and Luke had ever lived there at all. Soon another army family would move in and later another and they would be spared any information about the Dermotts' tragedy. After five, ten, fifteen years, who would remember them?

Agnieszka was always the outsider, even when Jamie was alive. Only now did Jenny understand how you could feel completely alone in the middle of a busy army camp with people and vehicles buzzing all around. And it wasn't like being alone in a city where you knew no one. It was a different sort of alone.

Agnieszka had become isolated when Jamie was away and people thought she was having an affair. People talked about her a lot but they didn't talk *to* her any more. At the playground greetings and conversation were so restrained that Agnieszka started to avoid everyone: Jenny had seen the Polish girl dive down a side street rather than talk. And now she had done something similar herself. Because most people were still polite to her but there was a new restraint. And if there was any conversation at all, it was full of the small, everyday things they didn't want to say

235

because there was so much they didn't dare to say.

As for Leanne, sometimes Jenny wasn't sure if she was too busy to talk or if there was a new distance between them. But Leanne was a friend. She wouldn't listen to gossip about Jenny. It must be that she was distracted by her job and by Steve.

Jenny turned up her front path and re-enacted the usual battle between the step and the buggy. At the sound of her key in the lock and the hollow click of the door opening into an empty house she longed to hear Dave, making a brew, watching TV, messing around on the computer. Then the house would feel like home.

She tried to ease the children from the buggy but they were falling asleep and remained motionless. And then, into the deep silence, there was the intrusion of the phone. Her heart leaped. Dave! It must be! And this time the call would be gentle and loving and they would apologize to each other for the terrible things they had said.

Jenny left the children in their buggy in the hallway and rushed to the kitchen, grabbing the handset breathlessly.

'Hello!'

There was a pause on the line, the pause which always preceded the snap, crackle and pop of the satellite phone from Afghanistan.

'Jennifer, is that you?' demanded a crisp, clear voice. It did not belong to Dave and it did not have the strange hiss of transcontinental miles. It was a wealthy, educated, sure-of-itself voice.

'Eugene! Yes, it's me.'

'You sounded rather unlike you for a moment there. Is everything all right?'

236

'Oh, I just got home to an empty house, that's all,' she said, aware that her tone was flat and lifeless.

'Where are the children?'

'Here. They're asleep in the buggy.'

'Did you realize you left your bag here?'

She looked over her shoulder instinctively to the corner of the hallway where she always dumped the handbag on arriving home. It was empty.

'I mean the big brown leather one which contains literally everything, possibly including a kitchen sink?' he continued. 'I've seen you get out a purse, nappies, make-up, pens, notebooks, a magnifying glass, scissors . . . and since you are the sort of woman who is always prepared, I suspect it also contains a screwdriver.'

She smiled. 'Well, as a matter of fact, I do carry a small screwdriver around with me.'

'I thought so. I knew that without looking in the bag, Jennifer Henley.'

'I'll come over and collect it now.' She would have to carry the girls back out to their car seats, strap them in whether they cried or not, drive down the darkening lanes . . .

He interrupted her thoughts: 'You said the children were asleep!'

'They are, but they're still in their coats so I could . . .'

'Put them to bed, Jennifer.' He sounded kind and capable. 'I'm on my way over. Have you eaten?'

She paused.

'Well, sort of.'

'What does that mean?'

'I gave the children tea.'

'Don't tell me. You ran around them eating the crusts and the leftovers?'

'Something like that.'

'Right, well, I've got a nice casserole which Linda left me . . .' Linda was the woman from Tinnington village who came in to clean the house and make a few meals and feed the dogs if Eugene was in London. She had worked for the Hardys for many years. She regarded Jenny with beady-eyed suspicion and Jenny was sure Linda would not be pleased to know that Jenny had eaten her casserole.

'I'm not really hungry and I need an early night—' she began but Eugene's kind voice interrupted her.

'There's more than enough for two and I'll only stay half an hour.'

'But—'

'It won't take long to heat up. I'm on my way.'

She put the phone down and stood quietly in the dark kitchen. The hall light shone on the children, fast asleep in their buggy. By the same light the mess in the kitchen was visible. Mostly it was piled up around the sink but it had spilled on to the table and the high chairs because she had gone straight out to the park after tea. Eugene would see it all.

As she carried the sleeping Jaime up to bed first, she recognized that she was not just ashamed of the mess, of what Eugene would think about it. She was ashamed that everyone in the street would see him park outside and walk into her house.

18

The tractors which arrived to spray the poppy crop looked as though they belonged on the prairies of America. Dave had seen pictures of the harvest there, a line of mighty machines sweeping up the continent from south to north. But these machines were not going to harvest crops, they were here to destroy them. Because this was Afghanistan where, Dave thought bitterly, everything was back to front, arse over heels, upside down, inside out. And since he had been here, his life had been the same way.

They came under intense fire while they were escorting the tractors from Highway One. They were ordered to continue but the enemy was determined to stop them and had enough PK machine guns and RPGs to do it.

Eventually they halted.

Finn passed Dave as he looked for a firing position.

'Seems we're out of the wagons! For an ambush!' said Finn happily to Dave. 'So much for the boss's fucking safe journey!'

Dave had been thinking the same thing himself.

They fired back at a fast rate but the attack did not let up. The RPGs were badly aimed and no one was hurt, although Dave saw Doc Holliday busy with bandages in Kila's wagon.

He told the section commanders to keep an eye on the new boys in 1 Platoon. In their daily patrols from the cave they had been involved in skirmishes but as soon as there was any serious fighting they were always ordered to fall back and leave it to the ANA. This was frustrating for the seasoned soldiers but he had sensed relief from the new sprogs.

So they had never been at the heart of a battle before and now here it was. RPGs lighting up the sky, the desert surface dancing with rounds as if it was crawling with some deadly, bouncing bug, the smell of cordite, the flash of enemy fire occasionally giving away their position in a confusing crescendo of wraparound sound, hot weapons and burning fingers and, above it all, your own heartbeat thudding in your ears as it pumped neat adrenalin around your body.

Sol said: 'Hemmings is doing OK. He started off slowly but he's into it now. Blue Balls has barely fired a round.'

'What the fuck is he doing if he's not firing?'

'He's in a firing position, he looks as if he's firing, but nothing's happening.'

Frozen. The first time they found themselves in battle some men went into overdrive, some men retreated into themselves, some men laughed uncontrollably, some men surprised themselves by turning into cool, calm fighting machines and some men just stopped – as if all their limbs were locked.

'I'll sort him,' said Dave.

'I've tried shouting and I've tried coaxing.'

'Coaxing! Sol, for fuck's sake, it's the Taliban out there, not a Sunday School picnic!'

Dave found Slindon, who was just as Sol had described him. Staring at the enemy and locked into a firing position – but with the safety still on. Dave didn't bother to shout. He got behind the motionless soldier, touched the safety, checked his aim very roughly and then pulled his finger on the trigger. Slindon seemed astonished by the rifle's report, but at least it woke him up.

Time to shout now. 'Fucking get on with it, Blue Balls!'

Slindon came to life and continued to fire.

'And,' Dave added, 'try to target the enemy. Not the whole fucking desert.'

He ran up and down the platoon, carrying ammo. He barely had to yell at anyone: no one was slacking or taking their time over reloading. Their rate of fire was intense and fast and he admitted to himself that it felt good to be back in the thick of a battle instead of hanging around in the background while the ANA did all the front-line work. The concentration on the faces of the seasoned soldiers, their rapid selection of firing positions, their disciplined shooting, all of it pleased him. Even the boss, who had positioned himself in the line-up, was confronting the enemy in a professional, focused manner. Dave just wished he dealt with his men as well as he did the enemy.

After an hour, the Taliban showed no sign of retreating or easing their attack.

'They really, really don't want us to spray their fucking poppies,' said Bacon to Binns.

'Never seen them fight this hard over anything,' agreed Binns. 'Not even when they were holding Martyn hostage.'

'Think we'll be here all night?' Mal asked Angus.

'Don't care if we are,' Angus replied. He had handed the Minimi to Finny and positioned the sniper rifle now. He thought if he was slow and careful and accurate there was a chance the flapping dishdash of some distant raghead might flitter across his sights and he would have the pleasure of seeing the enemy stop mid-pace and fall.

'That's what they want. They want to keep us here until it's too dark to spray,' Mal said.

Finny, pausing for more ammo, looked over his shoulder and something caught his eye. Two tiny beetles on the horizon. He nudged Angus.

At first Angus couldn't see them. When he did, he smiled and tapped Mal on the shoulder. Bacon realized the others had stopped firing and turned round too. Hemmings next, and then Binns. Sol, who was bending over and sorting out ammo, looked up and grinned. In 1 Section only Slindon continued to fire doggedly as two massive flying war machines approached overhead.

'You can stop now, Blue Balls,' said Sol on PRR. Slindon continued.

'Christ,' said Dave. 'First he was locked out of firing and now he's locked into it.'

He crouched down by Slindon and it was a moment before Slindon looked at him, his eyes struggling to refocus on a near target.

'Stop now, Slindon,' said Dave. 'I'd hate you to shoot down an Apache.'

The Apaches were American. The men watched as they found their target and instantly dropped their fire-power like wrath down on it. The desert beneath the helicopters seemed to move upwards towards them in flashes of sand and black smoke. The bombardment only lasted a couple of minutes. Then, smoke still spiralling from the ground, they disappeared. The thump of their engines became a distant patter until there was silence. The enemy had been annihilated. The whole operation had only taken a few minutes.

'Are they dead?' asked Hemmings. 'Or did they hear the Apaches and run away?'

'Do we care?' replied Finny.

'Dead?' said Angus. 'They're fucking roasted.'

After a few minutes, Dave heard Major Willingham's voice on the radio, brisk and clear.

'Right,' he said. 'Well, after that little interruption, let's carry on.'

Sergeant Liam Barnes from 3 Platoon waited for his men while Dave waited for 1 Platoon.

'They never send an Apache that fast if men are in trouble. But they'll do it for poppies,' said Barnes.

'I guessed the Taliban wouldn't let us near the poppy fields without a fight,' said Dave. 'I don't know why our platoon commander told the men we'd have a safe journey.'

'He was right. We're fairly safe with Apaches on standby,' said Liam.

Dave rolled his eyes.

'Listen, Chalfont-Price's a pain. Just accept it,' advised the other sergeant.

'Want to swap him with your platoon commander, then?'

Barnes gave a humourless laugh. 'No fucking thanks, he's all yours. I mean, I know it's not easy for you because you're having a bit of trouble at home yourself, but don't let that sour your work here.'

Dave was unable to reply because engines everywhere were starting. He climbed up beside the driver again and they continued their journey towards the poppy fields. But the other sergeant's words kept ringing in his ears. Did every serviceman in the whole of Afghanistan know about his trouble at home? Tittle-tattle about the sergeant's wife who's seeing an awful lot of a retired general. A nice little chatting point for a man and a woman who had nothing better to say to each other over a crackling phone line.

He felt a new surge of fury. What was Jenny playing at with this man Eugene, getting herself talked about across ISAF forces? It was so unlike her. In fact, deep down he still believed it was impossible. She loved him; he knew she did. The marriage mattered, it was the centre of her life and she would do nothing to jeopardize it. He had always been sure of that. Until now.

There was soon more enemy fire and the gunners on top returned it but the convoy followed instructions and kept moving. Dave's wagon was attempting to run alongside the third massive tractor in the convoy. The terrain was rough and the poppy fields were eight more kilometres away.

'Fucking hell, I'm not enjoying this much,' said the driver. 'It's all right for the bugger in that bloody great contraption but it's shit running around him down here.'

Dave's eyes followed the landscape but his mind was outside a big house, covered in ivy, staring in through the window at Jenny laughing with some bloke who dandled Jaime on one knee and a giggling Vicky on the other. When the huge bolt of lightning hit it felt as though his own anger had caused it. He took a few moments to recognize that an IED had exploded near the third tractor.

'Fucking hell!' said his driver.

Dave didn't know if he had screeched on the brakes or whether the bomb had halted them but now they were stationary and rocking wildly.

'All right, everyone?' he barked.

After a pause, Sol's voice came: '1 Section's good.'

He heard Aaron Baker say: '2 Section's good.'

'3 Section all OK,' said Si Curtis's replacement, Jason Smith.

'It missed the tractor,' Dave pointed out. 'Detonation was about fifteen seconds too late.'

'But the driver looks a bit surprised,' Sol said.

'Let's get Doc Holliday to look at him,' Dave ordered. He radioed to Doc, who answered laconically.

'Don't know why you're speaking to me on comms when I'm right outside your cab.'

Dave opened the door and there was Doc, waiting with hands on hips. Dave grinned. You could rely on Doc to be where you needed him. He had become an almost legendary figure among the soldiers, a fearless medic who retained exceptional infantry skills. No one knew his exact story but the rumour was that some crazy student game at medical school had got him thrown out just before he completed his final exams. Instead of qualifying as a doctor he had become a soldier, then a Special Forces soldier with a useful medical background. After an injury, he had left Special Forces but remained an army medic.

'Who's hurt?' he asked now.

'No one. Tractor driver's shocked.'

'I've got something for shock,' said the medic, grinning. 'It'll make him drive his tractor very fast.'

Suddenly voices were shouting from the wagons.

'There he goes, get him, get him!'

'Bastard!'

245

'He detonated it, go for him!'

A motorbike was speeding away from them across the rocky desert, its rider leaning forward as though that would make the bike go faster.

Dave said: 'Hold firm. Hold fire.' Even though he, too, was sure from the position of the motorbike and desperation of its rider that he was responsible for the IED. As he spoke, there was a quick burst of machine-gun fire. It might have come from Streaky on top or from one of the gimpys further behind. It coincided with the sound of a single shot. The motorbike powered on for a few seconds. And then it hit a rock.

Its front wheel was suddenly travelling skywards. It had almost completed a full circle backwards in the air when it dropped like a stone. The rider fell first. Then the motorbike fell on top of him. It reminded Dave of the cartoons he sometimes watched with Vicky, except in the cartoons the characters always got up and ran on, even if they were a different shape, while the motorbike and its rider had become a motionless heap of scrap in the desert. One wheel still spun at an unnatural angle to the ground.

Dave waited. The driver looked at him. Dave said nothing. His ears were still ringing from the explosion but he was aware of the diminishing roar of engines from the first part of the convoy, pulling ahead as if nothing had happened.

'Well, don't just sit there, Sergeant,' snapped a voice in his ear. It was Chalfont-Prick, barking into his microphone as if he was in charge of the whole fucking army as usual. 'You're by far the closest to the motorbike. You'd better see to the rider. He may still be alive.'

'I've got the medic. We'll need an RMP,' replied Dave mechanically as the driver started the engine. Doc climbed in and they swung out across the desert, carefully following the route that the motorbike rider had taken. Dave was sure the man could not still be alive. Maybe that last, single shot had killed him. His death would mean an investigation, more form-filling, endless questions to answer and detailed discussion about the Rules of Engagement.

A Panther pulled out from the stationary convoy and followed them slowly.

'On my way with the RMP,' came Iain Kila's voice.

They reached the wreck and Dave got out. The temperature was rising daily and it hit him now like a warm wall. Today was nothing more than a balmy spring day but, like everything else in this country, even spring threatened to get out of hand.

Mal was first out of the back of the Mastiff. He was team medic and he went straight to help Doc with the casualty. While Mal and Doc were disentangling the bike from the body, the other lads covered. The sergeant major arrived.

Doc had been feeling for a pulse on the crumpled young man.

'Nah, nothing,' he said.

As a small crowd of men gathered round, Doc went through the usual procedures.

'This is a complete waste of fucking time,' he told Dave breathlessly as he pumped on the rider's chest. 'But it looks professional.'

'Good if he's dead!' said Finn, joining them. 'The fucker tried to kill us all.'

'Not necessarily,' said the Royal Military Police officer gravely, shaking his head. 'He was under fire before anyone could be sure he was responsible for the bomb. And if he *had* detonated the bomb, he was no longer a threat. I'm afraid this lad's death is totally contrary to the Rules of Engagement we are currently operating under.'

There was a silence while people exchanged pained glances.

Mal said: 'So he's allowed to kill us . . . but we're not allowed to kill him. Duh.'

Slindon stood up straight. 'That's not fair, is it?'

'No,' said Angus, shaking his head. 'That's not fair.'

'We must account for Afghan deaths and satisfy ourselves that they're justified,' insisted the RMP. 'We can't just come to Afghanistan and spray rounds everywhere because we don't like the look of someone.'

The men said nothing.

'Who actually gave the order to fire?' demanded the RMP.

No one answered his question.

'Hmmmm,' said the officer.

'I heard Sergeant Henley tell them to stop,' said Kila.

'He was slow to give that order and it was not effective,' said the RMP.

'Anyone would be stunned so close to a large bomb,' Kila pointed out. 'The large bomb which that boy probably detonated.'

But the RMP was stubborn. 'We don't know that.'

'If he wasn't detonating the IED, why would he be running away like that?' demanded Binns.

The police officer continued to look grave. 'He might just have been a curious kid watching the convoy.'

'He was running away,' insisted Binns.

'He might have been rushing off because he knew his mum would be furious with him.'

Doc Holliday, who had been looking at the boy, stood

up. 'I'd say he's about sixteen. Although it's hard to tell with these Afghans.'

The body was stretched out on the ground. There was a thin covering of sand over thick rock here and at a gust of wind the sand blew across the dead face. The boy's eyes were closed. He looked peaceful.

'Search him,' ordered Dave. Angus and Streaky stepped forward to check the body for weapons or ID. In a thin hide purse, which had perhaps once been around his waist but was now tangled with his clothes, they found a printed card. They handed it to the interpreter. In another bag, which had probably been slung over his shoulder, were two mobile phones.

'One of those is your detonator,' said Dave.

'Not necessarily,' insisted the RMP officer.

'Why would he have two phones otherwise?' asked Doc.

'We'll have to investigate that.'

Dave, Kila and Doc exchanged glances. Whose side was the RMP on? Did the Taliban have their own military police to tell them off every time they killed the enemy?

'I heard a gimpy. Who fired it?' asked the RMP officer, looking around the faces of the men.

'Me,' confessed Streaky. 'Someone said get him, so, man, I got him.'

'Hmmmm,' said the RMP officer.

'No you didn't,' said Doc quietly.

'I did!' protested Streaky.

'You didn't, mate,' Mal told him. 'There are marks on him from the bike. But there's no sign he got hit by a round. It was an accident.'

'You fucking missed, Bacon!' roared Angus. 'And

249

how far away was he? One hundred and fifty metres? And how many rounds did you fire? Huh!'

Streaky's face curled itself into a mixture of disbelief and embarrassment.

'Shit!' he said. 'So it wasn't me! But someone else fired a rifle . . .'

'They missed too,' said Mal. Doc nodded agreement.

Kila said: 'For once I'm glad our marksmanship is so fucking awful. He was killed when his bike hit a rock and no one . . .' The sergeant major turned pointedly to the police officer. '. . . no one can get us for that.'

'Hmmmm. But he seems to be unarmed. And did he swerve and hit the rock because he was under fire?'

Everyone turned to look at the track left by the bike but by now it had been obscured by wagons and men's feet.

'I was watching and he didn't swerve,' said Dave.

'Hmmmm. But was he riding recklessly because he was fleeing under fire?' asked the RMP.

Suddenly Jamal, the interpreter, spoke up. 'This card says that he is seventeen years old and he is committed to the Taliban.'

'Streaky, you wanker,' said Finn. 'How could you miss the bastard?'

'I thought I hit him,' said Streaky mournfully.

'You shouldn't have been firing! This platoon obviously needs a reminder about the RoE,' said the police officer.

'We didn't kill him,' Dave insisted. 'I saw it all. The bike was going in a straight line. It didn't swerve. It went straight into that rock and bounced.'

Iain Kila gave the police officer a triumphant grin. 'Well, your police report should be straightforward enough. Taliban fighter dies riding his motorbike recklessly while trying to escape from a bomb he detonated. Look, here comes his family now.'

A man was roaring towards them on another motorbike. Behind him was a small, dusty pick-up truck. It looked as if it had been made in a factory in Eastern Europe many years ago. It bounced unhappily across the hard, desert floor.

'How do we know that truck's not full of suicide bombers?' asked a gloomy voice from the circle of men around the body.

'Usually there's just one suicide bomber in a vehicle, Blue Balls,' said Dave patiently. 'It's a bit of a waste to blow up a truck full of your own men.'

Slindon looked more closely.

'Oh yeah,' he said, seeing that the ancient vehicle was packed full of people. It screeched to a halt nearby and five men climbed out. They ran to examine the boy's body. One was yelling and crying and jerking at the boy's arm as if to wake him. All of them talked at once. Some were shouting at the soldiers.

Jamal the interpreter joined in. Dave listened to the sound of their angry Pashto but cutting through it all, as though there was complete silence all around, was the grief of the man who tried to tug the dead boy awake. This was certainly his father, Dave thought. Then he became aware of the man who had arrived by motorbike. He had not dismounted but sat very still, his face impassive.

Dave looked at him and the man looked back. Unlike almost any other Afghan Dave had seen, he wore glasses. Dave realized the glasses masked a strong emotion, and the emotion was not grief. It was hatred. There was nothing he could do or say to stop this man hating him. His instinct was to explain that the boy had died because of a rock, not a round, but probably the interpreter was saying this now and the news was having no effect.

He continued to watch the motorcyclist. There was something unswerving in his gaze and in his hatred which made him a threat.

'Make sure you cover the geezer on the motorbike,' he said to the lads. 'He may have a pistol.'

The man became aware that the attention of the soldiers had shifted to him and he gave a half-smile which spoke as plainly as words. *I despise you.*

Meanwhile, the other Afghans were locked in an angry discussion with Jamal. They yelled and the interpreter fired back a volley of words. What were they saying? Emotions were running high but Pashtuns often sounded just as passionate when they were exchanging routine pleasantries. Dave wondered how soldiers sounded to these people who judged them only by tone, volume and facial expression.

'Have you said that he drove into a rock?' Iain Kila asked the interpreter.

The terp nodded and continued rattling away in Pashto. The men shouted back. Jamal raised his voice more.

'I don't trust that bloke on the bike,' Dave muttered to Kila. Jamal heard him.

'He is an elder. Look at his turban.'

Metres of dark blue fabric were wound around the man's head and then hung loosely over one shoulder.

'If he is a village elder, he has power to resolve disputations and sort out marriages and other, various personal affairs. You only have to look at him to know that he is important man in community.'

'Try speaking to him,' Dave suggested. He was

unsettled by the man's hawkish stare. 'Explain to him how the kid died.'

Jamal ignored the clamour of the other Afghans and addressed his words directly to the elder. The man listened. Then, when he spoke, his voice was deep, slow and precise. Jamal paused before interpreting the man's words.

'What? What? What did he say?' demanded the sergeant major.

'Well, I'm just noticing from his accent that he is not from this village or this area. His accent is different. He comes from somewhere else, somewhere in the mountains probably. I think he may have travelled far and next I must ask him why he is here in Helmand . . .'

Iain Kila was impatient. 'But what did he say?'

'He said: This boy died because your men fired at him. Allah gives those he loves good aim. The aim of your men is poor but it was enough to frighten this young boy into riding badly. Your rounds did not hit him but because of them he is dead.'

The other Afghans had heard his words and were all speaking at once again, indicating their approval. The man spoke again and they were silent.

'In our culture we take revenge for such a killing,' Jamal translated. 'And remember, Allah gives good aim to those he loves.'

The man looked from face to face as if committing their features to memory. He stared at Dave long and hard; Dave felt uncomfortable, but he looked back into the man's eyes unwaveringly.

Jamal fired a question at the motorcyclist. Dave guessed he was asking why he was so far from home. It was clear that Jamal suspected the man was an insurgent. The man uttered a few words in reply and

253

Jamal did not translate them. Dave thought the interpreter reddened.

'He not tell why he's here,' he said.

'What did he actually say?' asked Dave. It could drive you mad working with interpreters who had conversations they did not translate.

'He says he has more right on this soil than you,' Jamal muttered reluctantly. His face was so red now that Dave guessed the man had criticized him for working with the army.

Iain Kila gave a gesture of impatience. 'OK, Jamal, do they want us to carry the body somewhere or do they want to deal with it?'

This was translated and the questions produced another angry torrent from the group.

'Let's go,' said Jamal.

Exasperated, Iain Kila demanded: 'But what did he *say*?'

'He says keep your filthy infidel hands off this son of the village,' said Jamal. 'And he says that you must pay for your crime before you have travelled much further.'

'This son of the village tried to blow us up! He's the one who committed a crime,' said Dave.

'To such a man your very presence in this country is criminal,' said Jamal. He looked back squarely at Dave. Was he echoing the anger in the tone of the Afghans or was this the interpreter's own fury? Not for the first time, Dave asked himself if this Jamal, who lived and worked with them, was trustworthy.

The interpreter pointed to the crumpled face of the dead boy's father.

'I think we leave him to grieve.'

They returned to the wagons. They were almost at the poppy fields now: close enough for these men to be the poppy farmers. Dave glanced back at the strange tableau in the desert. The group of village men, clustered around the elder on the motorbike. The tangle of dusty metal and human flesh on the ground. The father bent over his son, almost lying on top of him, sobbing. Dave felt sympathy pull at his heart. Then he remembered the elder's threats and decided that instead he should be doubly alert.

19

Leanne appeared at Adi's house at 7.45 a.m.

'You're early, darling. That's not like you!' said Adi when she answered the door, cereal box in one hand, spoons in another and giving the strange impression of having a third hand attached to a small child. The twins twisted out of Leanne's grasp and catapulted into the kitchen.

'Shit, Adi!' said Leanne. 'Oops, sorry.'

Adi looked at Leanne's face and then looked again more closely.

'What's happened?'

'I've had a call from Headley Court.'

'Is Steve all right?' Although Adi could tell from Leanne's face that he wasn't.

'They've asked me to go and pick him up.'

'Oh! When?'

'Soon.'

Adi nodded. 'So they think he's better.'

Leanne's loud response was half a scoff, half a sob.

Adi said: 'I'll take the boys when you go, and of course you won't have to pay me.'

'Thanks, Ads. I'd like to go early and spend a bit of

time at Headley Court. See the doctor. About how to deal with him.'

'Oh Leanne. Will you be able to cope when he's home?'

Suddenly the house seemed very quiet. Even the children, who had just been quarrelling in the kitchen, were quiet.

Leanne looked close to tears. Strands of hair were escaping from the clips around her blue bakery cap. Her face was white and doughy. Adi pulled her off the doorstep and inside the house, shutting the door.

'He used to be so angry but it's all gone out of him now. Like a burst balloon. I mean, ever since he got back from Headley Court the first time he's been a fucking balloon, sorry, Adi, bouncing around everywhere full of air. And now the air's all out and the balloon's gone down. I think it's gone for good . . .' She dabbed her eyes with a ragged tissue. Adi put an arm around her.

'What does the psychiatrist say?'

'She doesn't know anything!'

'But what does she say?'

Leanne took a deep breath. 'That he's never really accepted he lost a leg. And when the second explosion happened it was a sort of reality check.'

Adi watched Leanne's features pulling themselves into new shapes as if someone was pummelling her face.

'Well, I think that's what she said. I can't understand all that psychobabble.'

'They must think he's better or they wouldn't let him come home,' said Adi, patting her friend comfortingly.

Leanne looked back at her with red eyes. 'What does better mean? Better than he was before? Or back to how he used to be?'

Adi said: 'It takes time, darling.'

Leanne had not completely given way to tears yet, although her eyes were very damp.

'That's what the shrink said. She said this is all part of recognizing and accepting change. But if this is change, I don't want to accept it!' Her voice rose. 'Steve had to fight to go to Bastion. Then he had to fight to be let out of the gates just to zero his rifle. Then he gets out into the desert and . . .' Her words cracked and a water valve seemed to burst. '. . . another fucking explosion! And now all the fight's gone out of him!'

'I'm glad you're working at the bakery,' Adi told her between sobs.

Leanne, sniffing loudly, nodded. 'I just hope I can leave Steve and get to work. It's the only thing which keeps me sane. And they like me! The customers like me! Shit, I'm going to be late, sorry, Adi.'

'Leanne, when Steve comes home, we'll all help.'

'Oh Ads, I'm dreading it. I wish they'd keep him longer. It was awful before he went to Bastion; he was yelling all the time. But ever since the second explosion . . .'

'Darling, that was the worst luck.'

'. . . since then he's just been in this quiet depression. I don't know what he's thinking, I don't know if he's thinking anything. It's scarier than when he's angry.'

'I'll help and Jenny'll help . . .'

At the mention of Jenny's name, Leanne's face changed. Her tears stopped.

'No thank you! I don't need Jenny Henley's help.'

Adi pursed her lips. 'She's your friend.'

Leanne began to dry her face fiercely with the ragged tissue.

'Yeah, well, Dave's been good to us and I don't like

the way Jenny's treating him. Steve and I can't talk about much but we talk about that. And it makes Steve really livid.'

Adi looked lost, or maybe she was pretending to. 'What makes him livid, Leanne?'

'Did you look out of your window last night when Jenny went home?'

'Well . . . I don't think so.'

'His car was parked right outside. General YouTube was there for about an hour.'

'Leanne, they work together.'

Leanne rolled her eyes significantly. 'Yeah, right, they work together,' she sneered. 'And they were working together at the theme park when Tiff saw them. They were working together last night. Jenny does all this overtime and it's because they're *working* together. While her man's on the front line. You can believe they're working if you want to, Adi, but no one else in camp does.'

As they approached the poppy fields, they once again came under small-arms fire. The convoy bumped on along the rutty tracks, past a knot of women and children who were stumbling with bags of shopping and a goat on a leash.

'Incredible the way they keep firing despite the presence of civilians,' said Chalfont-Price over the radio.

Dave doubted the boss was talking to him but he replied anyway: 'Poppies are worth more than people to the Taliban.'

But Chalfont-Price exclaimed: 'Just look at this!'

As Dave neared the fields he, too, saw the huge carpet of poppies stretching out as far as the eye could

259

see. They were still green and many weeks off flowering but it was plain that here was industrial agriculture, a crop planted by large machinery. It was evenly spaced in rows and the rows were evenly spaced too. It looked like something growing in Wiltshire, far from the patchwork of small fields and animals he was used to here.

'Christ!' he said. 'What's the street value of that?'

He wasn't speaking to anyone over the radio in particular but Chalfont-Price replied: 'Millions, probably.'

'They needed some bloody big machinery to get it in the ground.'

'Make no mistake, this is as big an agricultural business as you'll find in the UK,' agreed the boss.

'The compounds are evenly spaced around the edges. They must have been built to guard it.'

'Probably. Even before the Americans decided to eradicate the crop they had enough people trying to steal it.'

Dave was so busy staring at the poppies that it was a few moments before he realized that he and the boss had just held something which might pass as a normal conversation. For the first time.

Each of the huge, green American tractors unfolded the sprayer it carried behind like a great metal butterfly opening its wings. They spread out across the field and began their work. The spray nozzles were angled directly at the ground and the air was still but nevertheless there was a fine chemical film, like a spider's web, all around the machinery.

'I can smell it,' said Bacon from the top of the Mastiff.

'No way! They've only just started!' Sol told him.

'I can smell it too. It's fucking horrible,' said Slindon. 'Makes me want to puke.'

Finn rolled his eyes. 'Listen, mate, you're new so you

don't know this, but there's a puking order around here and Binman always goes first. Got it?'

Slindon looked nervously at Binns.

'You want to puke?' he asked.

Binns's face was pale as usual. He nodded silently.

Dave spoke into their ears.

'Lads, we're running along the edge of the field now. If there's any trouble we'll need to get between the tractors and the compounds and that means driving across the irrigation ditches. So expect one shitty, bumpy ride.'

'Great,' said Sol miserably. 'Now we'll all be puking.'

'This smell is *disgusting*!' moaned Streaky. 'I can feel it scratching the back of my throat. It's like a hand with claws.'

Sol rolled his eyes. 'Mal, is the smell affecting you?'

Mal grinned. 'Nah. Nothing affects me.'

'Get up there on the gimpy instead of Bacon then,' Sol said and the men scrambled to change positions.

The firing which had accompanied their arrival at the fields ceased as the crop spraying started. But within five minutes the Mastiff slowed. A small group of men, their loose clothes fluttering behind them, was rushing towards the vehicle. The man at the front was waving his arms for them to stop.

'That's nice. It's the welcoming committee coming to offer us a cup of tea,' said Dave.

'They're offering something but it's not tea. Where's the terp?' demanded the driver.

'Coming up behind,' said Dave. 'But it's the Afghan National Police we need, if this lot want to argue. It's not our job. Where the fuck are the ANP?'

'Guarding the flatbeds with the chemicals,' said the driver.

Dave radioed for the ANP but the Afghans had surrounded the Mastiff now and were all gabbling simultaneously. Dave told Sol to organize cover and Jamal the interpreter appeared. In the absence of anyone else, Dave got out of the cab to join him. Jamal was trying to go through the usual Afghan pleasantries but these men were having none of it. They surrounded the interpreter, stabbing their fingers in the air, their voices rising.

'Let me guess. They want the spraying to stop?' suggested Dave.

'They say that these crops are everything they have. If they don't take money for this poppy then many families are hungry. But most of all they need to sell the poppy to the Taliban. This is because, see, the Taliban lended to them the money to buy seed from which this crop grows. And if they don't pay money back to Taliban, big trouble follows.'

Dave looked around the thin faces of the men. Their skin had been turned to animal hide by the intense sun and the merciless winter cold. Their eyes surveyed him hopefully, as if he could tell the sprayers to stop. He thought: Poor bastards. They're just trying to scratch a living in the only way they know. They probably get paid a pittance for growing the Taliban's drugs.

'Er, Sergeant Dave, please, I explain this crop is very bad and illegal and Afghan government not allow them to grow it?' offered Jamal.

'OK. But it won't help.'

In the distance, along some other track, two crops away and behind some trees, Dave glimpsed movement. A truck. A motorbike. It was the group of men who had confronted them earlier returning with the body of the dead lad who had detonated the IED. And then they were gone. They had disappeared inside the baked mud walls of the village. They would be picking their way through the labyrinth of compounds, tracks and alleyways known only to the locals.

At that moment an Afghan National Police Land Rover pulled up.

'We are representatives of the drug-eradication programme,' said the first to climb out, adjusting a shabby uniform. 'You must leave this discussion to us, please. But please I ask you to protect us while discussion takes place, please.'

'No problem,' said Dave. Jamal said a few words to the Afghans and a heated debate took place in Pashto between the farmers and the police. Dave watched them for a while and then climbed back into the wagon. Chalfont-Price demanded to know what was happening and Dave explained that they were offering protection to the ANP, who were involved in a confrontation with the locals.

'Get back to Tractor 3 as soon as you can,' said Chalfont-Price. '2 Section can't cover two tractors.'

Dave wanted to reply that firing was unlikely while the farmers were all clustered in the poppy field. It would probably start a few minutes after they returned to their compounds. But, as usual with Chalfont-Price, he judged it better to remain silent.

Tractor 3 roared past them, shaking the ground, destroying the drainage ditch as its great wheels crossed and leaving behind a strong aroma of bittersweet chemicals.

'Oh yuck, yuck, fucking yuck,' Dave could hear from the wagon.

The confrontation ended when the ANP climbed, jaws clenched, back into their Land Rovers. The farmers shouted abuse after them and then, following a final flourish which was probably very rude in Pashto, they turned and made their way back to the compounds. Throughout the conversation their eyes had followed the mesmerizing progress of the giant sprayers up and down their crop. Five minutes later, firing started.

Tractor driver 3 had covered his face with a balaclava but his fear was still easy to detect from the way his body hunched behind the wheel.

'Are we protecting Tractor 3?' came the boss's voice.

'Yes, sir,' said Dave over the net. Over PRR he said: 'Hold on tight, lads.'

The men on top were put on rapid fire and, pitching up and down over the drainage channels, firing fiercely back at the compound, they cut through the poppies towards Tractor 3.

'Please stop 1 Section behaving like pirate buccaneers, Sergeant,' said Chalfont-Price. 'The object of the exercise is to suppress enemy fire, not to destroy the local farming population.'

'Slow your rate of fire,' Dave told them.

There was no appreciable change.

'Sol, pull the lads back. That means you, Angry, and you, Bacon. We're trying to warn them off, that's all.'

There was silence in his ear as they were tossed up and down by the drainage ditches through the poppy field. But Chalfont-Price hadn't finished yet.

'I hope I didn't see you attempting to engage with the locals back there, Sergeant,' he said. Dave thought that, since they were under a lot of fire, this was a bad time to have this conversation and he wanted to say so. Instead he replied: 'No, sir, I simply got out of the vehicle to explain that we were waiting for the Afghan National Police.'

'You had specific instructions not to get out of the vehicle. It is very important that in an operation like this, we show only the Afghan face.'

Fuck off, thought Dave, as an RPG whistled past. Tractor 3 ground to a halt so abrupt that its sprayer bounced dangerously behind it and the masked driver was almost lying on the steering wheel. The Mastiff driver stopped too.

'We need to get out, Sarge,' said Sol.

'Yeah, do it,' agreed Dave.

They sat still in the open, flat field, their bodies shielded by the Mastiff, returning fire, and at a fast rate. The tractor driver, shouting, suddenly jumped out and ran to the comparative safety of the Mastiff. Dave craned his neck.

'What stopped him?' he demanded.

His driver eased forward alongside the tractor, inch by inch. 'Will you look at that!' he said.

In front of the tractor, sheltering down in an irrigation channel just centimetres from its mighty wheels, were three Afghan women.

'Fucking hell,' said Dave. 'They nearly got a lot of horse power through those headscarves.'

He jumped out and ran, bent double, all around the tractor, gesturing for Finn and Mal to follow. The drainage channel was full of water. The women, who were standing in it up to their waists, their clothes drenched, looked miserable. They were carrying washing and had evidently been on their way back to the village from the river when the sprayers had arrived. Dave shouted to them to get behind the tractor and they stared at him as if he was the scariest thing of all. He saw that one was carrying a baby.

'Come here!' he roared. 'You'll get killed if you stay there.'

They hung back in that demure Afghan woman way, treating him like a monster who had come for rape and pillage instead of a man who was trying to save their lives.

'Fucking civilians won't move!' said Dave to Billy Finn and Mal.

Finn leaped into the ditch behind them. 'Goooo on, goooo on, get up there!' he cried, as if they were frightened horses. The women seemed rooted to the spot. Finally, amid bouncing rounds, they scrambled rapidly up the bank, their wet clothes clinging to them.

'Some very fine arses hidden inside these baggy old burqas, boys,' Finn announced.

Mal immediately jumped into the ditch behind him.

'For fuck's sake,' growled Dave.

He gestured to the women to shelter under the tractor. They looked very young, their eyes wide with terror.

'Think she's the baby's mother? Or elder sister?' Dave asked Mal.

'Mother.'

'Christ, how old is she, Finny?'

Finny took little time to consider. 'Easy,' he said. 'She's fifteen.'

There was a shout from Mal. 'IED!'

He was still in the ditch.

'What? Right where they were standing?' said Finny.

'Maybe they planted it.'

'No way!'

Mal was insistent. 'I can see it! In a wooden box thing.'

Firing from the compound had become frantic and it

266

was all falling in Mal's direction. Dave radioed for the Mastiff to drive forward further to protect them.

'So I'm half in the fucking ditch? And half out of it?' demanded the driver disbelievingly.

'Yeah,' said Dave.

When the Mastiff was in place, he and Finny joined Mal in the ditch.

'See, Sarge, they were going to try to blow up the tractor.'

Mal pointed to a box, covered in earth but just visible above the waterline of the drainage ditch.

'It can't be an IED. They never would have left their women sitting in front of it.'

'Maybe they don't like those particular women much,' suggested Finny.

Protected from the battle, Dave began to pull at the earth around the box. It gave way easily. The box had only recently been buried here.

'If it's an IED we're all dead,' said Finny.

'It isn't,' Dave assured him. He glanced back at the faces of the women. They no longer looked frightened, just angry, or even sulky. They didn't want him to open the box. Suddenly he remembered hiding Jenny's green dress in the box he had made to look like a book and placing it on the bookshelf at home. Jenny. In the green dress at the Dorchester Hotel, looking like a movie star, smiling for the cameras. He started, as though the memory had teeth and had bitten him.

'Open it,' he told Finny.

20

'I've made you a cup of tea,' said Jenny, carrying two mugs into the light, bright office.

Eugene smiled. 'Thank you, Jennifer.'

She smiled back. 'I spoke to the builder about the tiling on the stable block; he says he can start in a week.'

'That's good. Normally we have to wait months for him to do anything.'

'I told him that the roof was going to collapse on the horses' heads if he didn't get here soon. He likes horses so he's coming.'

'Amazing!'

'I phoned Barclays to ask for replacement statements for the missing tax years. They will supply them, but they're charging.'

Eugene grimaced. 'They would.'

'If I show you online banking, then it won't happen again.'

The general looked unenthusiastic.

'And Robin Douglas-Coombs called to say that he needs you to check the last committee minutes as soon as possible. The date of the next meeting's been changed; I put it in your diary. And he said to remind you about the deadlines, so I printed them out and pinned them on the noticeboard.'

'You exhaust me, Jennifer. I don't know how you get so much done.'

Jenny sat down at her own desk. It was antique and covered in ancient marks and blemishes which all told their own story. Jenny did not feel entitled to be part of the story so she'd brought a coaster from home to put under her hot mugs of tea.

'I can do it for you,' she said. 'I just can't do it for me. My house is a complete mess.'

Eugene watched as her fingers clattered over her keyboard.

'Maybe I should send Linda to give you a hand with your housework . . .'

Jenny laughed. 'I'm a sergeant's wife; I do my own housework. Otherwise they court-martial Dave.'

Eugene didn't seem to understand that Linda was devoted to him alone and would never agree to help Jenny. But he laughed too and they both settled down to their work. Eugene was writing something in longhand on a large, lined pad and Jenny clattered out emails. There was a tap at the door and it burst open. Linda stood at the threshold, looking from Eugene to Jenny and back again. Her face was red, as though something had embarrassed her.

'Morning!' Jenny said cheerfully.

Linda threw Jenny her habitual look of hostility. 'Post's arrived, General Hardy.' She handed it to him.

'Thanks, Linda.'

When she had gone, Eugene muttered: 'What was all that about?'

'Linda does everything quickly.' Linda's token knock had given them no time to prepare for her entrance. Her face had been flushed with embarrassment at what she might find.

But Linda had found nothing. Because there was nothing to find. Why, thought Jenny, does everyone think a man and a woman can't simply enjoy working together? Why is everyone so suspicious?

'Right, this is for John *Cardingham*.' He stripped a page from the pad, swivelled in his chair and threw it in her direction. It floated gracefully towards Jenny's desk and she caught it neatly.

'Not John *Cardimann*,' she said. One of her first mistakes in the job, and there had been a few, had been to send a confidential document intended for one committee member to the wrong man. 'John Cardimann's phone call when he got that email must have been one of my top three most embarrassing moments . . .'

Eugene grinned and sipped his tea.

Jenny felt herself colouring at the memory.

'I thought you were going to sack me. I wouldn't have blamed you.'

'John was as good as his word; as far as I know he's never mentioned the contents to anyone.'

'When I realized, I couldn't sleep all night.'

'Oh Jennifer, you have enough keeping you awake at night, worrying about that husband of yours in his FOB. You shouldn't let my stuff stop you sleeping.'

'I used to be so efficient. If I'd made a mistake like that at the travel company, someone flying to Alicante would have ended up in Agadir. So I was sort of worrying that I'd lost my touch.'

Eugene started sifting through his post, absentmindedly pulling the junk mail to one side. He looked around at her and smiled. 'You haven't lost your touch.'

She smiled back at him. The first time she had met him, she'd thought he was an old man just because his hair was white. Now she knew that it had turned white before he was thirty. In fact, he was in his fifties, but he had the physique and clearly defined jaw of a younger man.

He looked back down at the mail and she saw him suddenly recoil. He was holding a large, white envelope.

'Everything all right?' she asked.

For a moment he did not reply. Then he half swallowed, half coughed.

'It's from the court. I think it must be my decree absolute.'

'Your divorce?'

'Yes.'

He still did not move. Jenny said gently: 'Sometimes when something arrives which I don't want to open, usually a bill, I don't. I put it aside and get used to the idea and then I open it when I'm ready.'

Eugene said nothing for a long time. Then, carefully, as if it might break, he passed the letter to her.

'Would you mind . . . ?'

'You want me to open it?'

She was taken aback, although she tried not to show it. But he knew her too well.

'You do mind,' he said.

'Of course I don't.'

He watched her as she tore the envelope open.

Gingerly, Finny's fingers worked at the stiff iron clasps on the box. Dave looked around impatiently: at the angry faces of the women; at Streaky on the back of the Mastiff, rattling back fire with the gimpy; at the RPG which the enemy had just sent a hundred metres past its target. And he was in no doubt that they were the target. The women had been supposed to look as if they were just on their way back with the washing when the sprayers came, when actually they had been stationed in the ditch so that the tractor would swerve around them, clear of the box. And, looking at the size of the box, Dave was pretty sure he knew what was in it.

Mal was helping Finn with the last clasp, both men concentrating so hard that they were oblivious to the battle going on around them. As another RPG splintered brightly in the air nearby, the women squirmed further under the tractor with their washing.

'We could do with a bit of WD40, mate,' said Finn.

'Let's try gun oil,' suggested Mal, but at that moment the clasp snapped back.

Finny tugged open the lid. It was unexpectedly heavy.

'Fucking hell!' said Mal when he saw the contents.

Dave looked over their shoulders. The box was full of weapons.

'A fucking arms cache!' said Finny. 'Hidden in a box in the middle of a fucking field.'

'Some of those are really old,' Dave told them. 'I reckon there's some old bolt-action rifles. And look at that—'

The explosion from another RPG lit up the air and this time it was close. Finny and Mal, noses in the box, ignored it.

'No time to look now,' said Dave.

But Finny and Mal could not tear themselves away.

'A few AKs,' said Finny.

'There's stuff in here a lot more interesting than AKs,' Mal told him. He reached in. 'See this one—'

'That can wait,' insisted Dave. 'Close it up and get it in the wagon or it's going to be blown to smithereens and you with it.'

The lads reluctantly shut the box. With difficulty they passed it across the drainage channel. As they carried it around the tractor under fire, the women shared agonized glances. Dave wondered if they would be in trouble. Instead of protecting the arms cache, their presence had drawn attention to it.

'What's that?' demanded the boss, who was with 2 Section but had sighted their activities from across the field. 'Just what are you doing?'

'We've found an arms cache, sir,' said Dave into his radio. He received no reply, or maybe he just didn't hear it because when he turned around again he was astonished to see that the Afghan women had crawled out from under the tractor and were walking towards him, their washing under their arms and on their heads.

'Christ, you can't go out there!' he shouted. They ignored him and showed every sign of wandering around the Mastiff and across the field.

'Shit!' said Binman as they passed him. He jumped to his feet and tried to restrain the youngest of the women, the one carrying the baby. She wriggled and screamed something at him in Pashto, her voice squeaky and horrified.

'Don't touch them!' yelled Dave to Binman.

'But they're going to walk out there! With a baby!' roared Binman more loudly than anyone had ever heard him shout before. A couple of the lads were so surprised that they stopped firing and stared. In the meantime, the woman had pulled away from him and was following the others out from behind the Mastiff into the field of fire.

Dave radioed everyone to stop firing. They did so, swearing. Dave felt helpless. He shouted at the women again to stop but they ignored him.

Fucking, fucking women. That's the way they were everywhere, all around the world. High-pitched, irrational, emotional: they had no place in theatre. Jenny appeared inside his head, her hands on her hips, her chin jutting forward, looking furious with him. Her angry stance, last seen in the kitchen late one night. Quickly, he made her disappear.

'What the hell is going on?' demanded an angry voice on the radio. Not the boss but Major Willingham.

'We couldn't stop them, sir,' said Dave.

'Unbelievable. We can stop a bunch of Taliban who are trying to intercept the poppy-eradication programme? But we can't stop three women and a baby?'

'Not without manhandling them, sir.'

'Jesus fucking Christ.'

The women had fallen into line now and were walking across the field with the washing and the baby as though deaf to the battle. They did not look back and they did not look around them. Dave debated following and detaining them but their presence had not stopped the firing from the village. In fact, there was a prolonged burst of small-arms fire. And then something different.

Afterwards, Dave could not remember what came first. The whoosh just by his head as the deadly trajectory of a round missed him by centimetres? The burning feeling in his cheek because the round had come so close? Its distinctive heavy thump as it hit the soil nearby? Or the report? It was a deep-sounding, single shot. He was unable to identify the weapon. Not a normal rifle, something heavier and nastier. A Dragunov?

He found that he had stepped neatly back behind the Mastiff. For a moment he stood there, stunned. He had followed the women into the open and, by trying to stop them, had exposed himself to enemy fire. He had been a target, and not the target of some spray-and-pray, automatic-loving Taliban lad. He had nearly been killed by a specialist marksman with a marksman's weapon.

Finn and Mal joined him behind the Mastiff.

'That was fucking close, Sarge,' said Mal. Dave noticed he was breathless.

So was Finn. 'Fuck me if those ugly bints weren't trying to lead you out there!'

Binns asked on PRR: 'Anyone shot the civilians yet?' He sounded hopeful.

'Nope,' said Sol. 'Amazingly. They must be insane.'

Angus was alert. 'Sarge, what weapon was that?'

'Not sure,' said Dave. 'Could have been a Dragunov. Listen.'

He listened for the deep, deadly bass note of the rifle which had nearly killed him. He did not hear it. The enemy's rate of fire was easing and the women had crossed the field now and were melting into the thick mud walls of the village.

'OK, lads,' said Dave. His voice was weary. 'Get that tractor driver back in his cab as soon as you can.'

The driver ran out, pulling down his balaclava. Dave's glimpse of his face told him the man might be Turkish. He started the engine. The Mastiff reversed to give the sprayer clearance and immediately small-arms fire broke out. The Mastiff moved forward again but wide of the sprayer this time and the driver released a huge puff of chemicals before plunging across the drainage channel where the women had been hiding.

'So what is this arms cache?' came the voice of Major Willingham.

'Haven't had a chance to look yet, sir. It's in the back now. About twenty weapons, AKs and some others.'

'Well done, Sergeant,' said the major. 'No dead civilians and twenty enemy weapons.'

Dave said: 'Sir, I think there's a sniper out there. With a Dragunov or something similar. Did you hear it?'

There was a pause. Everyone was listening. Light-arms fire had started again. It was a part of the patina of daily life and all the men were used to its sound. Here at the poppy fields the enemy was firing AK47s from too far away to aim accurately. Rounds were, as so often, going everywhere. And, as usual, the Taliban were leaning heavily on their automatics. So it was spray and pray and anyone who was hit could blame bad luck as much as enemy skill. Dave had told the ANA often enough that pointing your weapon is not the same as aiming your weapon but someone out there had already learned that lesson. They had fired just one single shot with high precision and it had missed him by a whisker.

He remembered the dead boy, the sobbing father, the elder on the motorbike. The elder had been wearing glasses. Behind them, his cold eyes had studied Dave's face, trying to remember it. Dave felt the hairs on the back of his neck stand up.

'Sergeant—' began Chalfont-Price, his voice pompous. Then he stopped. Because there it was again and he had heard it too now. That sound. An isolated, throaty, single shot from a heavy rifle. Its report was instantly discernible over the patter of other weapons. And the marksman had fired just one because he knew he was a very, very good shot.

The radio crackled but no one spoke.

Dave knew from the sound of the weapon that he had not been the target this time. He wondered who was. His question was answered by more crackles over the radio and then yells from 3 Platoon. A casualty. He listened and understood that the platoon commander, who had been darting around in a Jackal, had been hit in the neck. The radios became frantic with orders and reports as Doc Holliday's wagon screamed across the poppy field.

Major Willingham's voice was fast and crisp. 'Gunners take cover. Anyone exposed take cover,' he said. 'Get the tractor drivers. There's a serious sniper out there.'

But before the OC had finished his sentence, Dave heard the marksman fire again.

Another roar went up.

'Man down!'

This time it was 2 Platoon. Another Jackal had been hit. After some confusion Dave learned it was the gunner.

'Sniper! Get down, everyone, get the tractor drivers inside. Sniper!' he repeated as Iain Kila's wagon scooted towards the second casualty.

Dave waited in the Mastiff, listening for the sound of the rifle again. Despite the surge in firing, he knew its voice would speak clearly. And when it came, with deadly accuracy, it picked off the tractor driver 3 Platoon was protecting: he had gone back to his vehicle and been trapped there by the sudden outbreak of firing. Then he had opened the door to try to make a run for it. But he hadn't even got down the steps. Dave watched with horror as the body, far away, tumbled from its seat to the ground.

So the Taliban had produced a fighter who was so well trained and highly skilled that he could hit a man from a distance with almost every shot. His three well-aimed rounds created chaos. All crop spraying stopped and men rushed around the casualties, radios were busy and the soldiers, with a new anger, fired on the compounds.

'Two can play at snipers!' roared Angus, sliding out of the back of the Mastiff with the L115A3.

'Oh man, you've been itching to use that thing,' Streaky said. 'Itching in your fingers.'

Sol shook his head. 'I think you're too late.'

'I've got to try,' Angus insisted.

'Just make sure you keep your head down, Angry, or you'll be next,' warned Dave.

But there was no target for Angus. He trained the sights all over the village, peering at any exposed walls of the compounds; no one was to be seen. He detected movement and swung towards it. But it was only a couple of women, walking along a track on the far side of the compounds, going about their business as though nothing much had happened.

'If the women are out that means they know it's over,' said Sol.

The enemy had almost ceased firing. And there was silence from the sniper.

'I reckon that bloke knows he's caused total mayhem and he's packed up and gone home now,' said Binns.

Far beyond the noise of the radios, the shouting and the soldiers' gunfire could be heard the eerily compulsive whine of the call to prayer from the village mosque.

'Gone to pray, more like,' said Slindon. 'He's just shot all those people and now he's gone to thank Allah.'

Finny said: 'He probably gets a special place in Paradise for all those direct hits.'

On the radio, news came through of the casualties. The tractor driver, an Iranian, had been killed outright. The commander of 3 platoon was seriously injured, the gunner of the Jackal less so.

'Another centimetre to the right and he would have had it,' said a voice over the radio. Dave sighed. He heard that every time there was a casualty. A centimetre to the right, ten millimetres to the left, fifteen seconds earlier, ten seconds later, and everything would have been much better or much worse.

'Anyone still firing back there is just wasting time and ammo,' said Dave.

'Yeah,' said Bacon, 'but it makes me feel a lot better, Sarge, just doing some, you know, bang bang, back at those bastards.'

'Well, stop with the bang bang, Streaky,' Dave ordered. 'MERT's coming in.'

'We should raid the fucking compounds and get their fucking sharpshooter! Let's do it!' roared Angry.

'Duh, yeah, like their top man's going to be sitting there waiting for us to come and get him,' groaned the lads.

Chalfont-Price said: 'The Taliban will probably have whisked him away. We've had reports of an exceptional sharpshooter elsewhere in the province. The Americans encountered him near Sangin. But no one was aware he had moved to this area.'

'Might be more than one of them,' said Dave.

'The Taliban certainly could be moving their best marksmen in to counter the poppy-eradication programme,' agreed the boss. 'But there have been rumours for a while now about one outstanding sniper. He's constantly on the move.'

279

'I'd like to show the bastard what outstanding snipers from the British Army can do,' roared Angus.

'Angry, why don't you shut up and have a brew while we sit here and wait for the heli,' said Dave wearily.

'Brew's on, Sarge,' said Hemmings.

'I can't drink nothing,' said Binns.

'How's your allergy, Streaky?' asked Dave.

'I'm all right when I'm firing. Then when I stop I feel sick.'

'Get a brew inside you,' advised Dave. 'Cures most things.'

Mal added: 'And we can take a look at that box full of weapons while we're doing it.'

A Chinook could be heard thudding nearby. Iain Kila was directing the soldiers around the stretchers. Sol gave Dave and the driver a cup of tea. The driver produced some peanuts and he and Dave sat in the front of the Mastiff, crunching in silence. They watched the helicopter land and the hatch at the back open. Soldiers with stretchers began running towards the team of waiting medics inside.

Dave felt a new weariness. He didn't even ask the boys in the back what they were finding in the arms cache.

Chalfont-Price's voice came over the radio. It was a smaller, less sure voice than usual. 'Thank God the sniper didn't turn his sights on us. We're the only platoon to escape.'

The commander of 3 Platoon was being loaded right now into the back of the helicopter, gently as though the stretcher was made of glass. Dave knew the officer and liked him much more than he liked his own commander.

Dave spoke hesitantly into the radio now. 'Well, sir . . . he did. Turn his sights on us.'

'What? The sniper fired at someone from 1 Platoon?'

'At me.'

'When?'

'When I was out in the field trying to persuade the women to come back. He very narrowly missed me, I felt the round close to my cheek.'

He heard his own voice. Tired. Shocked. The sniper had only just missed. All his subsequent shots had hit their target. His legs suddenly weighed more than metal. He dropped his heavy hands to rest on his knees. Even his eyes were leaden. For a moment, he allowed himself to close them. And waiting for him inside his head were Jenny and the children. In all the hurt and arguments and half-heard phone calls and too-brief blueys you could forget how precious they were. How there was nothing more important in his life than these three: a woman, a small girl and a baby. How it was his job to love and care for them and how it was difficult to do that when they were far away, the distance doubled by angry words and foolish actions. He knew then that he had to contact Jenny soon and tell her how much he loved her and how much she meant to him, whatever she had done.

'Are you sure about that?' Dave became aware of Chalfont-Price in his ear. The boss's voice was sharp, as though he had been repeating the question over and over. 'You're saying he fired at you and missed?'

'By not much.'

'Jesus Christ.'

Dave had not heard the boss nonplussed before. No matter how bad his own cock-ups or other people's,

Chalfont-Price's confidence never wavered. And now, suddenly, his voice shook.

Dave said: 'Luckily I was the first target. He was still adjusting his sights.'

'The practice shot,' said the boss shakily. 'And the only one he missed. It seems 1 Platoon has had a lucky escape.'

And for a moment, no, a fraction of a moment, Dave heard Chalfont-Price recognize his sergeant's value. He should have enjoyed it, but just talking about the near miss was exhausting.

When he saw Jamal, the interpreter, Dave hauled him to one side.

'Remember the man on the motorbike this morning?' he asked.

Jamal looked hostile. 'He was only a boy.'

'Not the one who died. The man who arrived with the boy's family. He wore glasses and you said he was a village elder.'

'Oh yes. I can't forget that man,' said Jamal, with unusual spontaneity.

Dave said: 'And I can't get the thought out of my mind that he's the sniper.'

Usually Jamal looked away or at the ground when he spoke but now, for the first time, his brown eyes stared directly into Dave's.

'I have had the same thought,' he said. 'That man spoke of revenge for the death of the boy. And he looked at you so carefully. I think he may be a sniper. And if it was your body which they put into the helicopter, I could be absolutely sure of it.'

21

The letter had an official court stamp which gave the contents weight and finality. Jenny read it quickly.

'Yes, you're divorced,' she said softly. 'That's all it says.'

Eugene did not respond. Outside, a horse wearing a blue rug suddenly threw up its head and chased a grazing horse wearing a red rug, teeth bared. The grazing horse jumped and ran off and the pair cantered around the field, nipping at each other. Were they playing or fighting?

Jenny said: 'You don't have to read this. I'll put it away in the divorce file and we'll be able to close it now. We can take it out of the filing drawer and put it in the cellar with all the other closed files.'

He nodded. He did not look at her. Her heart beat sympathy and sadness around her body. Didn't his wife know how lucky she was to be loved by a good man like Eugene? Was she snuggled up with her tennis coach somewhere now, feeling twinges of regret for all she had given up and all the pain she had inflicted?

'Eugene?'

'Twenty-five years of my life. A closed file,' he said at last.

'Closed files mean you can open new files.'

'Some people go out together and have a divorce lunch when their decree absolute comes through,' he said, snorting at the impossibility of doing such a thing with his ex-wife.

'You'll be friends one day,' Jenny assured him. Not because she knew this would be the case, but because she wanted it to be. She found the idea of a partner of twenty-five years turning into a stranger unbearable, no matter what they had said or done.

'That's rather hard to imagine. You know my financial position as well as anyone. Fiona had nothing when I met her and she seems to be rather well off now. I've had to borrow vast amounts to hang on to Tinnington. I had hoped it would stay in the family for my children . . .'

Jenny did not know what to say.

'I'm sorry,' she murmured.

He stood up abruptly. 'I'll walk the dogs now. When I get back, I wonder if you'd be kind enough to have lunch with me?'

She nodded as if she would like nothing more in the world, while inside her nodding head she was doing childcare calculations, about the nursery, about Adi. The longer she was out of the house, the harder it was to re-establish a comfortable home with the children. After lunch she would pick them up and then there would be that moment when she walked in through her front door, Jaime crying, Vicky whining and a stack of chores waiting.

'Are you sure you can organize your children?' he asked.

'I think so.'

'I'll try not to drone on too much about Fiona,' he promised.

'I don't mind, Eugene. Say whatever you like.'

'We'll go to the White Horse, over by the river at Fulton,' he said, walking out of the room. 'Could you ring and book a table for one o'clock?'

'I'll do it now.

He paused in the doorway. She looked him full in the face and admitted to herself that, yes, he was still a handsome man, but he was old. His eyes looked hollow, his skin puckered as though someone had hit him.

'Jennifer, a piece of advice,' he said. 'Don't ever get divorced.'

Back in their caves, the men were subdued. A simple protection exercise had left them with three men down. Only the arms cache stimulated interest. Everyone wanted to have a look and get their mates to photograph them with enemy weapons.

'You look right Taliban with that AK!' said Slindon, snapping Mal.

'Yeah, put on a dishdash, wrap a scarf round your head and I'd open fire,' Angus told him.

Binns and Mal exchanged glances, reminded that Angus had told them several times that he intended to deal with Aamir in Wythenshawe as soon as they were back in the UK.

'Can you print that picture when we get to Bastion?' Mal asked Slindon. 'So's I can send it to my mum?'

'Oh man, take one of me with the AK for my mum, too!' pleaded Streaky.

'That's enough,' said Iain Kila, standing over the box of Taliban weapons. 'EOD's on the way and they don't need to see us poncing about with the arms cache.'

'What's in there?' asked Dave. Kila had promised him phone access as soon as possible, but of course all the phones in Helmand were down while relatives of the dead and wounded received their bad news.

Doc Holliday was leaning over the box.

'Er, twelve Kalashnikovs,' said Kila. 'And . . .'

'Two, no, three pistols, semi-automatics,' said Doc. 'And four PK machine guns. And will you look at these bolt-action rifles?'

'That one's old,' said Dave.

'Lee-Enfield,' Kila said.

Dave held it and felt the weight. 'It's the sort of weapon that sniper today could have used. Nice long range.'

Doc took it and lifted it into a firing position. 'Got to be World War Two.'

'Some lads from B Company found an arms cache with a Lee-Enfield from 1915,' said Kila. 'And the Taliban were still using it. There was a stash of .303s right by it.'

'I think they found a Martini-Henry too,' Doc told them.

'Fucking hell!' said Kila.

'Late nineteenth century, left over from the last time the Brits tried to fight here. But it wasn't in good working order. Probably couldn't get the ammo any more. It takes .450s, I think.'

'Well, that's been out of production for a hundred years.'

Dave drew one of the PK machine guns from the box.

'Look at the stock. Laminated. Is it plywood?'

Doc took it and examined it, blowing out cigarette smoke.

'Well, it's an old PK variant and the stock must have snapped a while ago. So they've sorted it with a few strips of metal and some nails. Bloody amazing. These little old guys squatting outside holes for workshops are probably doing this kind of thing all the time.'

'Wouldn't want to shoot with it,' said Dave.

'It's usable,' said Doc. 'But not very accurate.'

'How do you know so much about these old weapons?'

'I've always had an unhealthy interest in old weaponry,' said Doc. 'I've got a collection at home. Totally illegal, of course.'

'It's not more unhealthy than your cigarettes,' said Kila, flapping his hand across the funnel of smoke which rose from Doc's mouth.

'I know, I know. But everyone's allowed one vice.'

'You've got several,' Dave pointed out.

'My wife would say I've got the lot.' Doc drew out an AK47. 'This old lady's in a state. Pitting, corrosion. But I bet if we opened it up we'd find the working parts are all oiled, up together and ready to use.'

'They probably pass them down from father to son,' said Dave.

Doc said: 'If I passed my collection down to my son, he'd shoot me with it.'

EOD came for the box of Taliban arms the next day while the company was back in the poppy fields. This time spraying continued in the face of only small-arms fire. The sniper had apparently evaporated.

As they made their way back to the FOB, rain began to fall. It did not start slowly and then thicken: the clouds suddenly released a torrential downpour. At first the lads inside the Mastiff, hearing it pattering on the vehicle's armour, thought that they were under fire.

When they realized it was rain they were delighted. Rain would freshen the FOB, replenish water supplies and deaden the dust.

It was still raining without showing any sign of easing when they arrived back at FOB Carlsbad. After another hour the lads were beginning to feel that was enough rain. But the skies remained uniformly leaden.

Kila came to Dave.

'Phones are open now. I've got one for you.'

This was a favour, since the men were given very limited opportunities to use the satellite phone at the FOB.

Dave dialled his own number slowly and deliberately. He was not going to blow this call. He wanted to hear Jenny's voice. Even the way she said hello would tell him everything he needed to know. And he had a lot to tell her too. Not the fallen men, the arms cache, the sniper, the job or the rain had distracted him from his resolution to make sure she understood that he still loved and cared for her. She had been a good wife. He was not going to allow his anger to drive her away. He had known that for sure when the sniper's round had nearly killed him and he had kept the know-ledge alive in his mind until he could phone her.

Click clunk. He was through to England. Ding ding. He was through to home. Across mountains, seas and land masses, the phone in a hallway, living room and bedroom in Wiltshire was ringing. His heart seemed to beat in time with the rings. He waited, waited, for her voice. Ding ding. Ding ding. After a few more rings it seemed to mock him. And after a few more came a man's voice: 'Hi, we can't answer right now so leave a message after the tone.'

A confident, happy family man. Sure of his world,

sure of his wife. The Dave Henley he used to be before this fucking country had turned his life upside down.

He did not answer his own invitation to leave a message. He hung up and dialled Jenny's mobile instead. Ding ding. He hated the fucking ring tone. Hated the way it went on and on and on and on. Until: 'Welcome to voicemail!'

He hung up and went back out into the rain. It dripped down his neck from a rock edge and he did not care. He stood still until he was drenched.

'What's up, mate?' asked Doc Holliday, appearing at his side.

'Fucking women,' said Dave.

'What did she say?'

'Nothing. Because she's not there. As usual.'

Doc Holliday's head was wet now. Rain dripped from the end of his nose. He had not shaved for some time and his facial hair was matted by water.

'Fucking women,' agreed Doc.

The next day, Gerry McKinley from 2 Section took Dave aside.

'Sarge, I'm not sure if I should tell you this . . .'

Dave paused. He had been loading ammo for today's tractor protection and keeping it dry in this weather was a problem. The earth was pooling now because the rain had not stopped overnight, so you couldn't put anything down.

'The thing is, Rose saw Leanne Buckle yesterday. You know Leanne leaves her boys with Adi while she's working. I think your Jenny does too. Anyway—'

Dave braced himself. He put his hands on his hips. Gerry's voice began to fade a bit, as if he was wondering if he should have started this.

'Well, a couple of days ago, Jenny rang Adi and asked her to keep the baby for the afternoon.'

Dave shrugged. 'She probably had a good reason.'

'Yeah. She said she was going out to lunch with her employer.'

'Oh.'

It was important not to show any emotion. It was important to make that 'oh' empty of pain, of shock, of anything, to keep it as clear as a piece of ice.

'Well . . .' Gerry backed off rapidly. 'I just thought you'd want to know.'

'Thanks, Gerry,' said Dave, starting with the ammo again. 'Thanks for telling me. It's good to get news from home.'

They loaded up and set off to meet the tractors. And all the time Dave's heart was thumping with anger. Lunch. Employer. Adi telling Leanne fucking Buckle, who for a fact would tell half of fucking Wiltshire. There had been a postal delivery that morning and from Jenny there was nothing, nothing at all. As if being angry with one another could make the other person just cease to exist. He felt his heart harden again. The reordering of priorities he had experienced after his near escape from the sniper was already disintegrating. If Jenny wanted to play stupid games with him, let her.

22

Leanne drove into Headley Court. Usually she zoomed up the motorway feeling anxious, wondering what mood she would find Steve in. But when she arrived she always relaxed. Headley Court didn't feel like a hospital. It was normal to be wounded here. One-legged, no-legged servicemen buzzed around, busy and focused on a tight work and exercise regime. Nobody stared or made excuses for them or looked at them with pity. Only when he got back to Wiltshire was Steve distanced from everyone else by his injury.

She went to look for him and passed another patient she recognized.

'Hi, Sergeant Smi!' she said and Smi spun around on his prosthetic leg, grinning at her. He was an immense Fijian, broad as well as tall. He'd had a reputation for being a tough sergeant before he was blown up but Leanne couldn't imagine him being anything but fair and generous. If only Steve was more like Smi. He had accepted the loss of his leg with a sweet grace and devoted his time to supporting and encouraging others.

'Hey, Leanne! You coming to take the boy away?'

She nodded. He frowned.

'Well, baby, you don't seem too pleased about it.'

That was all it took. Smi's concerned look, his sympathetic voice and suddenly, without warning, she was crying.

'Oh shit, Smi, sorry!' she sobbed.

He gestured to a seat in a corner away from all the busy people.

'So what's the problem?' he demanded. 'Is it harder to love a man with only one leg?'

Sobs shook her. 'No!'

'Well, that's a relief for a one-legged man to hear.'

She still could not speak. Smi waited. Finally he said: 'You won't believe this, but Steve had everyone laughing till their prosthetics fell off yesterday. In a group session.'

She did not believe it.

'He's a funny guy,' said Smi. 'If he wants to be.'

Gasping for breath, as though the sobs had robbed her of air, she said: 'He used to be. He hasn't been funny for a while.'

'Listen, I've seen him make roomfuls of people laugh quite a few times.'

Steve: relaxed, chatty, thinking out loud, coasting further and further with some mad idea while anyone around him picked up the thread and followed it, laughing loudly. She had seen it often enough. But not lately, and certainly not since that second IED.

'He's not like that at home, Smi. At home he's really angry or he's really withdrawn. And when he laughs it's not nice. He's laughing to make a point or he's laughing at me. And he's ratty with the kids.'

'Was he ratty with the kids before he lost a leg?'

Leanne considered. Well, actually, yes. 'Sometimes,' she said cautiously.

'Before his accident, if he'd been sitting around at home or doing things he didn't enjoy, how would he have been?'

That one was easy: she only had to think about Steve with flu or Steve off work to do a bit of DIY. 'Impatient and nasty.'

'So it's not losing a leg which is a problem for Steve, it's losing all the things he used to do. Listen, Leanne, I can't talk for Steve, I can only talk for myself. I was a good sergeant and I want to be a good sergeant again and I want to be useful and busy and work hard and look after my family. That's all it takes to make me happy. I haven't changed that much, personally. I still want the same things. I just have to achieve this in a different way.'

She pulled out a matted tissue. Her pockets were always full of disintegrating Kleenex these days.

'I wish Steve was a bit more like you.'

'Oh, baby, I wish I was a bit more like Steve. That is one clever guy! But it seems to me that all the problems he's got now he's always had. He dealt with himself by joining the army, soldiering, doing a job he loved. Now he has to find a different way, that's all.'

Leanne allowed herself, briefly, to think the unthinkable. That Steve had not been a lamb before his accident but difficult, demanding, bad-tempered. That the army had channelled his anger and aggression. Shit, it was true. He had masked it with his humour and his charisma; that's why she had married him. And now the mask had gone.

Smi seemed to read her thoughts.

'Let's not be too harsh. Before he lost that leg, apart from being difficult, was he kind?'

'Sometimes.'

'Was he generous?'

'Very.'

'Was he funny?'

'Yes.'

'Did he love you?'

'Yes.'

He put a weighty arm around her shoulders. 'See, the psychiatrists keep telling us we have to accept change. I think what we amputees have to accept is that nothing's changed. It's just some of the things we used to cover up are exposed now.'

She nodded and blotted the tissue over her damp face once more.

'And one other thing,' said Smi. 'You've probably noticed. Booze doesn't help.'

When she found Steve, it seemed to Leanne that he was more relaxed than he had been for a long time. He kissed her fondly. She hugged him for longer than he expected. Then, after all the noisy farewells, they got into the silent car. They were alone together.

Until they reached the motorway they said nothing. Steve was the first to speak.

'I'm having a week off,' he told her.

'Good. Then what?'

'I have to phone Welfare.'

'What will they do? Visit us?'

'No, I have to phone them about a job.'

'In Welfare?' She tried not to sound surprised. One gram too much surprise and the scales could tip dangerously towards fury.

'Yeah, they think I've got a lot to offer other wounded soldiers and their families.'

'Oh!' Careful. Not too enthusiastic. Not too astonished. 'Well, I'll bet you do,' she said.

'Just part-time initially.'

'To see if they like you?'

'Yeah, and to see if I like Welfare.'

'Good! Should be interesting. You could really make a difference there.'

She thought she had got that just about right: she had sounded interested without going overboard. She sneaked a glance at his face and was relieved to see his features were still even and relaxed.

They drove on in silence, Leanne occasionally breaking it to talk about the twins or about the nursery or about the bakery. He listened to her but asked no questions.

'Adi's been fantastic about taking the boys. Considering she quite often has Jenny's kids there too,' she said.

He gave a snort of derision.

'So the cow can spend time with General Coward!'

Leanne wished she could rewind the conversation and erase the mention of Jenny. Steve's face was darkening and his voice had a dangerous undertone which threatened anger.

'So she can work,' she said soothingly. She agreed with Steve, but she didn't want to go there if it made him angry.

'Jenny Henley's cheating on her husband and everyone in camp knows it,' he said.

'What makes you so sure of that?' demanded Leanne evenly, uncomfortably aware that she had made a contribution to camp knowledge on this subject.

'Si Curtis. He phoned me the other night. What a slag! She's been seen out all over the place with her general and apparently she dumped the baby with Adi for hours the other day because she was going out to lunch with him.'

Shit! Leanne took her foot off the accelerator for a moment with the realization that she herself had given Tiff Curtis that information.

'I can tell you what they were having for lunch,' said Steve, his voice full of implication. She knew he was spiralling into anger and she wanted to stop him. Only she didn't know how.

She tried: 'It's none of our business.' But this just angered him more.

'Of course it's our fucking business! Dave's been a good mate to me. The best. They're having a rough time out in theatre and what's she doing to support him? Bonking half of fucking Wiltshire, that's what.'

'Calm down,' said Leanne. She knew it was a stupid thing to say before she had even opened her mouth. It was like lighting a touch paper.

'Leanne, I will not fucking calm down. Jenny Henley's cheating on my mate. I've never really liked her. I only got on with her for Dave's sake. I always thought she was a snotty bitch.'

'Stop it, Steve.'

'Look at how the camp nursery isn't good enough for her kids. Look at the way she was all over the cameras at Martyn Robertson's party. Couldn't keep away from them in that million-dollar dress she got poor old Dave to buy her. It was embarrassing. He was embarrassed, I could tell.'

Her voice was smooth-calm. Icy-calm. 'That's not true.'

'She's a slag, and you can't deny it,' said Steve, more quietly. It was all too familiar to Leanne: after the anger came the withdrawal.

'I hardly speak to her these days,' said Leanne.

His voice was a near-whisper now. 'I won't be speaking to her at all.'

They drove on in silence, Leanne thinking of Smi, the man who could find a smile and a kind word for everyone. Smi had probably always been that way. And, underneath, maybe Steve had always been like this. So he was unlikely to change.

She sighed. At least the sun had arrived extra early this year. The car was full of light and the steering wheel was hot to touch. Thank God. It meant Steve would be able to spend plenty of time out of the house.

23

'Does it usually rain like this here?' the men asked their
ANA counterparts when they got back from the poppy
fields.

Jamal, the interpreter, said: 'It's spring. Rain can fall
in spring.'

'When does it stop?'

Jamal shrugged. His features closed up the way they
so often did. Dave always watched his face carefully,
because he could never resolve the question: Can I trust
this man? Jamal frequently threw sidelong glances at
Dave, as if he knew that Dave was unsure of him. Even
if they only discussed the weather, suspicion flared up
between them.

'All I know,' said Jamal, 'is that now it rains.'

The rain did not stop in the night. The morning skies
were a thick, crusty grey and large drops still fell at an
even rate. They went on patrol and the people they
passed peered out at them from inside damp clothes. In
the town, water ran in rivers down the streets. It was
mixed with raw sewage.

'This smell makes Binman puke, right, Binman?' said
Angry as they tried to wade along the main street.

'Right,' said Binman. 'I just want to get back to our nice clean cave.'

'Yeah, at least we're not stepping over turds there,' said Slindon.

''Cept you're a human turd, Blue Balls,' Angus told him.

Streaky Bacon looked miserable: 'Chemicals, shit – this is the smelliest tour ever.'

Finn asked: 'How does Wolverhampton smell, then, Streaks?'

'Wolverhampton smells of weed. And aftershave. Wolverhampton smells nice,' Streaky told him nostalgically.

'What does Chelsea smell of, Tiny?' Finn asked.

'Money,' said Tiny Hemmings. 'I think they mint it there.'

Everyone thought the rain must stop that night but it did not, nor the next.

'Is it going to rain all fucking week?' they asked Jamal.

'Maybe,' he replied. 'Maybe all month.'

They stared at him in disbelief. 'Without stopping?'

Jamal shrugged.

The walls of the caves were soon shiny. Water dripped through the rock on to men as they slept. They were always hanging kit out to dry but nothing ever did. They were sent to the poppy fields again and the vehicles slipped over the tracks. When they arrived they found the usually powdery Afghan soil had turned to solid, sticky clay. Tractors got stuck as they tried to cross the drainage ditches. The drivers spent less time spraying and more time pulling each other out of the mud. An armoured group arrived to tow the tractors with Scimitars. The soldiers became bored and frustrated.

'Did we join the fucking Land Army?' they asked.

'Do we want to be, like, *farmers*?'

'Are we here to fight or what?'

All spraying was halted. At the FOB they were told to stand by for humanitarian work, since the rain was causing mudslides which were endangering some mountain villages.

'Rescuing Taliban fighters, that'll make a nice change from killing them,' the lads said.

Chalfont-Price was not amused.

'Apparently families and their goats are in considerable distress and we will be winning hearts and minds by helping,' he told his men. 'The rain has given us a good opportunity to show the caring face of the British Army.'

His words were greeted with silence. There was only one dry place in the FOB, a small cave in such solid rock that no water penetrated and the floor remained dusty. Chalfont-Price and a couple of other officers occupied it. Even Major Willingham cast jealous glances at the dry cave, although he stopped short of demanding it for his own use.

'Will the boss be showing the caring face of the British Army to Afghan goats, then?' Dave heard someone say in an undertone.

There was a muttered reply: 'No fucking way, he'll be staying in his cave and sending us to do it.'

Among themselves the lads agreed that doing humanitarian work in the floods would be more interesting than the wet, quiet patrols through the town. The rain had sent the Taliban indoors and now there was almost no action when they left the FOB. Men complained of boredom.

'This weather's reminding me of Wiltshire. It's

making me think of being back in camp with Adi and the kids, watching TV with the rain banging against the windows,' said Sol. And that was all it took to make everyone think of home. Once the thinking and talking had begun, they could not stop.

'I'm even feeling nostalgic for Tesco,' said Danny Jones.

'Me too! Fucking FOB Tesco!' said Gerry McKinley.

'Steady on, lads,' Dave told them.

'When it rains like this on Saturdays, I get up, go for a run, get back into bed with my bird and stay there all day,' Jonas said.

'You can't do that once you have kids,' Andy Kirk told him.

'No way. You're lucky if you get a run, let alone a shag,' Gerry McKinley said.

'I'm not never having kids,' said Jonas. 'Not if they get in the way of my sex life.'

The married men exchanged wry glances but said nothing.

They were told that Major Willingham wanted to speak to them all. The gravity in the 2 ic's tone made Dave certain there was some big announcement coming. It might be about humanitarian aid to flood victims. Or maybe the OC would tell them they were going home to Wiltshire. Home. It was a while since he had communicated with the place. Home was a new, strange, bleak landscape, full of emotional complexities he would have to resolve and, at its centre, a woman he seemed not to know any more.

The lads were ready for what the OC was going to say.

'We're going home! That's what it is, we're going home!' they said. There was a buzz of excitement as

301

they gathered for prayers. Dave's gut twisted quietly inside him.

The men who couldn't fit under the rock, which was most of them, tried to stand under the tarpaulin they had rigged up outside. The rain seemed to drip right through it. Dave remembered the way Slindon had said he would just open his mouth in Brecon to save carrying water and how he had bawled Slindon out, saying it never rained in Afghanistan. Christ. Slindon being right was almost as irritating as Chalfont-Prick being dry.

Major Willingham entered the cave and, apart from the steady drip of water on all sides, there was complete silence, the silence of anticipation, the silence of men who waited for good news.

'First, although we have been standing by to aid the flood victims, I understand that the Paras have the situation under control and our services won't be required,' he announced. 'Next, I think you will all be relieved to hear that we are scheduled to leave FOB Carlsbad by the end of the week.'

A cheer went up but the OC did not smile reassuringly.

'We will be saying goodbye to our friends in the ANA, who will remain here when B Company replaces us. We will initially be spending a couple of days at Bastion, where you will be glad to hear there is no rain. And I understand that there has been very little rain at our next destination.'

There was a buzz of anticipation.

'So that would be Wiltshire, then, sir?' shouted someone. Dave didn't need to look to know who.

'No, Lance Corporal,' said Major Willingham, shaking his head at Finny. 'No, it would not.'

A new silence fell. Its texture was different. It contained both disappointment and apprehension. If the good news was the weather forecast, what was the bad news?

'We'll remain at Bastion for a couple of days, which will give us all a chance to dry off, phone home, take a hot shower. Then we'll be moving to FOB Nevada.'

The men waited. They had heard of Forward Operating Base Nevada but no one knew much about it.

'As the name suggests, it is currently occupied by the Americans. They, however, will be moving north with the sprayers on eradication duty. The FOB is on the edge of Mas'qada, a town at the heart of Taliban opium operations. The Americans have succeeded in driving back the Taliban from Mas'qada and they are very anxious not to lose the ground they have taken while they concern themselves with the rest of the poppy crop. There are a number of patrol bases within a twenty-five-kilometre radius of the FOB and we will also be expected to hold these. At times the Taliban have shown a determination to win the area back and it is possible we will come under considerable pressure. Alternatively, the Taliban may concentrate their efforts further north in order to preserve what is left of their crop. We will, of course, be joined at the FOB by the ANA but due to a manpower shortage this will not be for two weeks.'

When the major asked for questions there was a long pause. Sol coughed and then spoke: 'Sir, we were originally told to expect a two-month tour. We've been here a lot longer than that now. Do you have any idea how long . . . ?'

Every head craned towards the OC for his answer.

Major Willingham's mouth seemed to snap shut as if it was on a hinge.

'No, Corporal, I don't.'

Jenny dropped Vicky at nursery with some labelled sunblock and a sun hat. Then she drove on to Tinnington, a route she had come to love. Bluebells lined the woodland floors she passed like a startling blue carpet and the bright light made curling shadows beneath the branches. Overhead, the leaves had the special freshness of the very young.

'I love the trees at this time of year,' she told Eugene when she was at her desk. 'I've never spent so much time in the country.'

Eugene, sitting in front of a pile of hand-written pages, smiled. 'Fiona used to say that the newly unfolded leaves were the colour of fresh bank notes.'

Jenny's face fell. 'Fiona did seem to think a lot about money.'

'Sorry. I keep promising not to mention her again.'

'I don't mind.'

'Anyway, soon I'll be so busy that I won't have time to think about the divorce. Which means that you'll be busy too, I'm afraid. After various questions were asked in the House of Commons the Government has moved our deadline for the report forward. Brace yourself. It has to be finished by Monday morning.'

Jenny had been filing while they spoke but now she paused.

'It's Wednesday today. You can't mean next Monday.'

'I do. Well, Sunday night really, because it should be on desks by nine a.m. Monday.'

'But we haven't got all the notes and amendments in yet!'

'Everyone has promised them by tomorrow. Which means that they'll still be coming in on Sunday. I can guarantee that Robin Douglas-Coombs will be last.'

'I'll have to work on Sunday, then.'

Eugene looked away. He looked past her out of the window, past the horses, heads down on the shining grass, towards the newly green woods with their show of bluebells.

'Jennifer, I don't like to ask you but I don't have a choice. Of course you'll be on double time – and I'll certainly give you time off in lieu as well. I hope you hadn't got anything planned that day?'

Jenny saw that the horses' rugs were off now. They tore greedily at the bright grass, the sunshine bouncing from their smooth coats. No, she didn't have anything planned. She never did these days. She simply tried to enjoy Sundays with the children, although weekends weren't much fun without Dave because wherever she went, to town or playgrounds or the children's farm park or the indoor play gym, she encountered whole families, not the splinter of a family like hers.

'I don't mind working Sunday,' she said. 'I don't much like Sundays.'

'You could bring the children but of course that might mean we get less work done. And we may have to work into the night.'

'That's all right.'

'You wouldn't have to come in on Monday, obviously. But knowing how some of these committee members leave everything to the last minute, I'd say late working is a strong possibility.'

Jenny sat down to think.

Eugene watched her. 'The children could sleep here. Although moving small children to unfamiliar

305

surroundings to sleep can create more problems than it solves.'

'I'll try to arrange to leave them at Adi's for the night.'

He straightened his back and swivelled his chair in an unnatural, embarrassed movement. He said: 'Please don't take this the wrong way. But if it's late and you're tired, you would be most welcome to stay here. I have at least three spare bedrooms at the moment and they're all very comfortable.'

Jenny did not want to blush. If there was any way to stop her cheeks from reddening now, she would have paid a lot for it. She bent over her computer, hoping her hair covered her face.

'Thanks, Eugene.' She did not look round. 'If I'm really tired I'll stay. But I'll try to get home if I can.'

When she next looked round, he was deep in his work.

At lunchtime, as she switched off the computer and stood up to go, he said: 'I hope you don't mind my inviting you to stay. I'm only trying to make life easier for you.'

'I know, Eugene,' said Jenny. 'It's a kind offer and I may take you up on it.'

He opened his desk drawer and instead of pulling out more pieces of paper or a stapler, he produced a bottle of wine. 'You were telling me about your friend? How her husband lost a leg and returned to Bastion, then was unlucky enough to be caught in a second explosion?'

Jenny remembered that she had talked about Leanne and Steve over lunch that day.

'Is he back from Headley Court yet?'

'He's been back a few days but he hasn't seen anyone or left the house yet.'

306

'This is a particularly nice bottle of wine. People think soldiers only drink beer but in my experience everyone appreciates a fine wine. Please give it to him with my compliments and say welcome home.'

'Oh, but he doesn't know you!'

Eugene shrugged. 'He doesn't need to know me. Our wounded have many well-wishers and I'm one of them. You don't even have to give him my name.'

Jenny felt herself reddening again, as if he had given *her* the bottle of wine. 'That's very kind of you, Eugene. Really kind. And of course I'll tell him your name.'

'That's up to you.'

'I was planning to visit tomorrow. I'll take it then.'

That afternoon, she looked over to Steve and Leanne's house several times. No one went in or out. She remembered how it had been when Steve first returned last year from Afghanistan, via the military wing of Selly Oak hospital. There had been a welcome party and banners and the twins had been running around in badges which said: 'Yes! He's our dad!' Today there was no one, maybe not even the twins. People stayed away because they knew that the second bomb blast had left Steve with a different kind of wound, the kind you can't see and for which there are no prosthetics.

Jenny thought of calling in briefly with the bottle but she was stopped by Leanne's new coldness towards her. They hadn't quarrelled and Leanne hadn't explained herself but she seemed to be avoiding her friend. Or maybe she was just very busy now she had a job. It couldn't, surely, be that she listened to gossip? No. Leanne was the kind of person who would tell Jenny the rumours and ask outright if they were true.

In the back garden in the sun with the children, a

large bowl of water and some bubbles, she wondered if the Buckles' old resentment had resurfaced. They both believed that when Steve had lost his leg, he had taken the blast for Dave. Because just a few seconds earlier Dave had been on top cover, the position which proved most vulnerable to the blast. He had fallen back when his weapon had a stoppage and Steve had replaced him, only to be blown out of the wagon. Jenny thought this resentment was unfair. What was Dave supposed to do? Cut off one leg and hand it over to Steve? But they were still feeling repercussions from that bomb, so it might explain Leanne's haste on the phone, her rapid departure from Adi's if Jenny arrived and her strange reluctance to meet.

The garden was a sun trap which eliminated any late spring chill lingering in the air. The children were happy splashing and blowing bubbles. She took some pictures with her phone and only when she looked at them did she notice how Jaime had grown. Jenny wanted to hug her and hold her at this age for ever. She decided to email the pictures to Dave. No message, though. Not until he phoned and apologized for the things he had said and the way he'd said them. But she would send the pictures. According to Adi, who dropped these things into conversation in a way which suggested Jenny must have known them too, the boys were going to Bastion soon, where Dave would have internet access.

The next day was sunny again. It seemed the warm, summery spell would never end. Jenny tucked the bottle of wine into the buggy and they walked to the playground. On the way back, they stopped at the Buckles' house. Jenny taught Vicky to say, 'Welcome home, Steve'.

She got the bottle out ready. She felt nervous, because Steve had not been easy to talk to for some time. But her visit would be brief.

She lifted Vicky so that she could push hard on the bell. It had been broken so long that Leanne had given up asking the army to fix it. And then they had taken her by surprise one day by arriving with a new bell.

'I can hear it!' said Vicky as the bell rang loudly inside the house.

'What are you going to say?' Jenny asked her.

'Welcome home, Steve.'

'Good.'

Jenny had not anticipated that it would take Steve long to get to the door, even if he was in the back garden. Previously he would have bounded to answer the bell just to prove that he could.

They waited. At first they heard nothing but, after a couple of minutes, there was movement inside.

'He's coming!' said Vicky.

They continued to wait, Vicky rehearsing the words she was to say over and over to herself in a whisper.

The noise stopped. No one came.

'Let's ring again,' said Jenny doubtfully. Vicky held out her finger and Jenny lifted her and once again they both heard the bell ring. It was greeted by silence.

'No one home. Leanne's at work and maybe Steve's gone out,' said Jenny at last. She tucked the bottle of wine inside the buggy once more and took Vicky's hand.

They were crossing the road to their own house when Vicky said: 'Mummy, look!'

Jenny turned and there, in an upstairs window, hands on hips, watching them, was Steve.

Jenny waved. 'Hi, Steve, welcome back!'

He did not wave. He looked for a moment longer. Then he turned away and disappeared from sight.

Jenny waited. Was Steve going downstairs to answer the door? After a long pause she continued to her own front door, ready to be stopped at any moment by Steve calling her back from across the road. But, puzzlingly, he neither appeared nor called to her.

24

Dave was having a cup of rich, dark coffee with Kila and Doc Holliday in the NAAFI at Bastion the day before they left for FOB Nevada. It might not have been anything special in the UK but after months in FOB Carlsbad and with the immediate prospect of more months at FOB Nevada, it tasted exquisite.

Dave closed his eyes and let the coffee's strong, bittersweet flavour envelop him and drive all thoughts from his head. So the big screen in the corner of the room had probably been talking about Afghanistan for a while before he noticed. It had already caught everyone else's attention and Kila and the medic were watching it intently.

'Fucking hell,' Kila was muttering.

An American serviceman had been exposed by the Afghan soldiers he was supposed to be training. Somehow they had got into his day sack and found ears there: human ears.

The serviceman had admitted that when he had cornered and killed a small group of Taliban fighters he had cut off their ears and kept them as a trophy. He had previously been regarded as a hero for his role in the well-publicized close-quarters combat, in which other Americans had died. Now he was shamed.

'President Karzai has expressed his disgust, on behalf of the Afghan people. Secretary of State Mrs Clinton has also said that all Americans will feel revulsion and shame at the serviceman's lack of respect. She has described him as a "lone wolf" who ignored all army procedures and she has indicated a prosecution will follow. But nothing the courts or the politicians can do will turn this bad publicity around in Afghanistan,' said the news commentator, her face serious.

'Dickhead,' said Doc Holliday. 'How many women did he think he was going to impress with an ear collection?'

'And why would you keep them where anyone can find them?' added Kila.

'So the Afghans are right,' said Dave. 'They think we're infidel barbarians, and now that bloke's proved we are.'

Doc Holliday grinned ghoulishly. 'Sure thing. I'm an infidel barbarian and proud of it.' Dave suspected he wasn't joking. Who knew what went on inside Doc Holliday's head?

'Glad it was an American and not one of ours,' said Kila.

'You think most Afghans can tell the difference?' Dave took another sip of the coffee and Kila passed them each a square of chocolate.

'This is fucking marvellous with coffee,' he said. 'Jean sent it. We won't taste anything this good for weeks now. Not at FOB Nevada.'

There was silence for a few moments while they submitted to the dark flavour of the chocolate. Even sitting upright at a table felt like a luxury after FOB Carlsbad.

Dave said: 'The Taliban are going to get revenge for those ears.'

Kila raised the place on his forehead where his eyebrows should be. 'You think the Taliban will be after our ears now?'

'Or balls, or dicks. But body-part collecting has to be the new fashion.'

'Better not get captured at FOB Nevada, then,' said Doc Holliday, looking at his watch and getting up. It was time to prepare to leave the luxurious tented accommodation, Wi-Fi and warm showers of the sprawling Camp Bastion.

'You heard from that wife of yours?' demanded Kila as they walked out into a cloud of hot dust. There had been no rain at Bastion, in Helmand's north-eastern corner. The whole base seemed to be built on dust and rising winds were throwing it about now.

'Nope. She sent me some pictures of the kids. Without any fucking message from her.'

'For Chrissake, Dave. I don't know what comms are like at Nevada, but just break the fucking silence.'

'I tried to phone from Carlsbad and as usual there was no reply. She's out all the time or she doesn't pick up when it's me.'

'Try again.'

Dave sighed and his mouth filled with dust. Kila suddenly tugged him into one of the camp's air-conditioned offices while Holliday disappeared without breaking his stride. The office was quiet and busy and its cool temperature felt as good as a hug. Kila summoned a member of the staff, a woman whom he seemed to know well and, when she nodded after a muttered conversation, he strode up to a phone and grabbed it.

'Do it now, Dave. Just do it. We're not going to have an easy ride at Nevada and if anything happened to you and you'd left things like this . . .'

'I can't, Iain. I've got to get my platoon sorted—'

'I'll go and shout at your men. Phone her.'

Dave was surprised at the way his heart thudded as he dialled the number. It was thumping out a battle rhythm. Ridiculous. He was phoning his wife, not Taliban HQ.

Click. He had crossed one continent. Clunk. That was the second continent. Ding ding. Welcome to the UK. When she picked up the phone, his heartbeat was so loud he could barely hear her.

'Jenny?'

There was a pause. Was that a satellite pause? Or was it her?

'Dave . . .'

He had thought that just by the way she said his name he would know everything. But from this short, faint statement he could glean nothing except perhaps surprise.

'Jenny.'

Keep it bland. Gauge the enemy's position before firing and giving away your own.

'Are you at Bastion?'

Hmm. The enemy was reluctant to reveal anything. But maybe, maybe, there was a certain softness there.

'Yes. Thanks for the pictures. The kids have grown. Jaime's grown a lot.'

'We've been having this amazing sunny weather. They looked so sweet playing in the garden . . .'

'We've been having rain.'

'I thought it didn't rain in Afghanistan.'

'It rains on FOB Carlsbad. All day every day.'

314

They were talking about the weather. About the fucking weather! In polite but restrained tones. He had managed to forget what a formidably tactical enemy Jenny could be.

'I'm going away very soon,' he said carefully.

'Right.'

'So I thought I'd ring. To say goodbye.'

'I hoped you'd ring. To say hello.'

There was a silence. Nothing wrong with the line. It was doing that convenient crackling thing which might make her think he was talking and she couldn't hear him. Except he wasn't saying anything.

'Any news?' he asked at last.

'No. Well, Steve Buckle's just come home.'

'How is he?'

'I don't know. I went over there but he didn't answer the door.'

'Doesn't sound good.'

'Maybe he was asleep. Except he wasn't because I saw him in the window.'

'Where's Leanne?'

'At the bakery.'

'Jenny . . . ?'

'Yes?'

'I love you.'

Fuck fuck fuck fuck, he had just put the enemy in an absurdly advantageous position.

'I love you too, Dave. But I'm waiting for an apology.'

'What the hell do I have to apologize for?'

'The letters you wrote, the things you said. The way you shouted, the way you keep suspecting me of doing things I wouldn't do, the way you don't trust me.'

'Fuck it, Jenny, what am I supposed to think? Blokes

315

walk up to me every day and tell me something else you've done.'

'Done! What am I supposed to have done?'

'Hmm, let's see what the most recent bit of gossip is. Oh yes. You left the baby with Adi all afternoon while you went out to lunch with General Coward-Hardy.'

He was shouting, he knew it. He was trying to shout quietly, so that the office staff didn't hear.

'His decree absolute came through and he was very upset so I stayed and had lunch with him. And his middle name is Howard.'

'He was very upset! *He* was very upset! Does he pay you overtime to hold his fucking hand?'

Evidently shouting quietly wasn't a successful strategy because the office staff who were nearest were looking up from their computers at him now.

'I did not hold his hand.'

'Jenny, I don't know what you're up to but this old geezer, this *coward*, has got some sort of a hold over you and I don't like it.'

'You don't like it? You were away six months and you were only too happy to fuck straight off for more! I don't like that! But what do you care? You go away all the time and, guess what, while you're gone your kids grow and you don't know your wife any more because you never see her, she's just someone people gossip about.'

'That is not fucking fair! I didn't know this tour would last so long.'

'Why should I be fucking fair? You haven't been fair to me! You believe every piece of rubbish people say and you ring me and shout at me instead of phoning me to ask me how—'

'Now who's being unfair? Whenever I phone you, there's no reply!'

'Sorry about that. I'm trying to have a life here by myself.'

Every single face in the office had turned towards him. With a great effort, Dave dropped his voice.

'Are you having a life by yourself? Or with him?'

Her voice dropped too.

'Stop it, Dave. Just stop it and apologize.'

'I've got *nothing* to apologize for. I just want to hear the truth.'

'I've told you the truth. You keep asking me the same thing over and over again, interrogating me until I give you a different answer. That's what torturers do.'

'Great. Now I'm a fucking torturer. I have to go, Jenny. I may not be able to ring you for a while.' Was she coughing? Or was that an explosion of fury at the other end? He managed to regain something like normality in his voice when he realized it could be many weeks before they spoke again. And, as Iain Kila had reminded him, that anything could happen in that time. He was jolted back to that day on the poppy fields when a sniper had targeted him and barely missed.

He said, slowly and clearly: 'Jenny, I don't understand what's happening to us. But it doesn't really matter what you've done or what I've said. I want to tell you that I love you and I'll always love you. I want you to know that you've been the best wife any man could ask for. I apologize for all the hurt I've caused.'

He did not wait to hear her reply. He hung up, left the phone on the nearest desk and walked out of the office.

25

FOB Nevada was large. it was on the edge of the sprawling town of Mas'qada. Its rows of exercise machines stood inside the Hesco, pointing towards the town's walls like a line of cavalry ready to charge.

As soon as they arrived, the men established their firing positions and grabbed their places to sleep while the sergeants and officers mined their American opposite numbers for information. Soon, the smell rising from the cook area told Dave that the lads were hitting their rations. He wouldn't mind joining them but there was a strange sense of urgency around the Americans. Dave guessed something was up. The Yanks were usually relaxed and laconic inside their forward operating bases.

The American OC was called away frequently and then he began taking his aides aside. Soon the Americans were running around, rushing off for urgent calls, busy with ammo, or just standing and talking intently in small groups.

Major Willingham asked pleasantly: 'Has anything happened? Or is it always this busy here?'

His American opposite number said: 'Well, it's been a

pleasure to meet y'all and I wish you success. But it does seem our departure may be more imminent that we thought.'

Dave looked around. The airspace around the FOB was buzzing. It seemed to him that the Yanks were already departing.

'You may be aware of a recent scandal which is putting American relations with the Afghans under strain,' said the OC.

'Is that . . . Eargate?' asked Major Willingham.

'It's the ears. The effect on relations means we have to get up-country fast.'

'But what about the patrol bases?' asked Major Willingham. 'We haven't had a chance to—'

'I have to ask you to prepare your men for immediate occupation of the PBs because we're drawing down the Marines who are currently holding them. We are drawing down right now.'

'Our stores haven't arrived!' the major objected but the American commander was temporarily deaf.

He said: 'You should get guys out to all the PBs within two hours and the men taking over the furthest bases, that is PBs Red Sox, Giants and Mets, should get moving right now.'

The major turned to his men: 'We'll have to send advance parties to the PBs. Their relief parties can follow as soon as stores arrive.'

The American consulted his watch: 'If you can get your advance out to the PBs within forty minutes, we'll allow three hours for all our guys to get back to the FOB and that will be the point of our final departure.'

'Forty minutes,' echoed Major Willingham, with a hint of irritation.

'Sorry about this. However, we have a special steak

lunch organized today and those of us who haven't left the FOB by 1300 hours will go ahead with it. Any of your people who are at the FOB at lunchtime are more than welcome to help us eat steak.'

Faces all around Dave lit up.

'Thank you,' said Major Willingham stiffly. 'We'd be delighted.'

'I can assure you and your men of a quality meal, Major,' said the American and then suddenly the British were invisible as the Americans rushed to organize their departure and their steak lunch. The air throbbed as first Black Hawks and then Chinooks appeared.

To keep his team away from the running, shouting Americans, Major Willingham took them over to the exercise bikes and leaned against the handlebars of one to talk.

'The Yanks never miss a chance to get into a tailspin. I can't imagine why they've been given orders to move so quickly, but evidently it's related to the diplomatic crisis. Since they are drawing down their men sooner than thought, it's vital that our advance parties are ready to take over the patrol bases at once. It would be highly embarrassing to lose those positions.'

The 2 i/c handed him a clipboard. 'Now. All the PBs are irritatingly named after football teams.'

'I believe, sir, that they're actually baseball teams,' said the 2 i/c.

'Thank you, Captain. Men, you will have seen from the plan that Boston Red Sox is the patrol base furthest from the FOB.'

He turned to Chalfont-Price.

'Second Lieutenant, 1 Platoon has been detailed to PB Red Sox and since this is the most exposed, send your advance party there as well equipped as possible. Now,

I expect this exposure to be brief. Stores should arrive imminently and we hope to get the rest of the party on their way within a couple of hours, possibly much sooner. But please prepare with the knowledge that there are often delays.'

'Yessir,' said Chalfont-Price.

The major organized the advance parties to the other PBs: the New York Mets and San Francisco Giants were also distant. So the advance would travel together, dropping parties on the way until 1 Platoon was left to travel the final few kilometres to PB Boston Red Sox alone.

The commanders and sergeants turned to go back to their men.

'God, I'm looking forward to renaming the PBs,' Dave heard the major groan to his adjutant.

'English football teams would be better, sir,' said Captain Bryan.

'Which is your team, Captain?' asked the major.

'Charlton Athletic, actually, sir.'

Dave and some of the others paused long enough to hear the OC scoff loudly. 'There's no way I'm naming a PB Charlton fucking Athletic, Captain.'

The men within earshot guffawed and at the same moment Dave realized that Chalfont-Price had stalked off towards 1 Platoon without him. The sergeants of the other platoons were setting off together with their commanders to gather their men, deep in conversation. The only commander to walk ahead, ignoring his sergeant, was his own. And since they were the platoon going to the furthest PB, they had the most to talk about. He glared at Chalfont-Prick's departing back. He certainly wasn't going to run to catch up with the man.

'Sir,' he said loudly, 'the most vulnerable party is the

advance to PB Red Sox and it's important to take the right kit with you . . .'

He felt ridiculous, calling to the commander's retreating back about red socks.

The man replied over his shoulder, without turning around: 'Not with me, Sergeant. I'm not going.'

Dave suspected that this might have something to do with an American steak lunch.

'Why not, sir?' he demanded.

'There will be limited spaces and taking the advance party will amount to little more than a menial admin job. The bulk of the work will be here at the FOB when stores arrive.'

Dave was so surprised that he broke his stride.

'Right, sir,' he said, with effort. 'Then I'll have to go to PB Red Sox since one of us should be there. Because it may be a bit more hairy than a menial admin job if the relief party's held up.'

Chalfont-Price had reached the cook area now, where the men, startled by his face and urgent approach, were jumping to their feet.

'The relief party will be right behind. You heard the major,' the officer snapped, turning to Dave at last.

Dave said: 'A lot of things could delay the relief. And if the Taliban take advantage of the situation . . .'

'I doubt the Taliban are on the ball enough to capitalize on a very slight and brief dip in manpower during the handover,' said Chalfont-Price crushingly. 'It may be as little as thirty minutes before the relief gets to you.'

Dave reddened with the effort of not contradicting him. He felt sure that the Taliban were on the ball enough to recognize any chink in their armour.

'How many men can I have for the advance party to Red Sox, sir?'

The lads were all on their feet, staring at them, looking from face to face, trying to gauge the degree of tension between the commander and his sergeant. But Dave had no intention of wasting time arguing. He had a nasty feeling that if they did not arrive at the PBs when the Marines were told to draw down, the Americans were capable of just going, leaving the British to win the bases back again.

He waited for Chalfont-Price's reply and the man looked away from him as usual, running his eye over the low concrete buildings, the desert sands which had taken a little rain and changed everywhere to a new, darker colour, the distant hills and the glittering Helmand River, snaking across the valley.

'Take 1 Section to the furthest PB,' the commander finally ordered. '2 and 3 Sections follow with the equipment when it arrives. It may be that a few of us are kept back in the FOB.'

'Right, I'll need two Mastiffs to go to Red Sox,' said Dave. 'With a .50 cal on one of them. I'd like a tripod for when we arrive, ideally.'

'You can't have everything. Tripods are limited until stores get here and there are other advance parties,' snapped Chalfont-Price.

Dave sought Sol's eyes among the faces which were turned to them: '1 Section, get your ammo and weapons sorted out for immediate departure. I'll be coming with you.' He swung round to meet the stony gaze of the young officer. 'And you will be following with the relief. Right, sir?'

He heard his own insistent voice. Even Chalfont-Price could not ignore its tone, but he sighed in protest.

'Yes, Sergeant, I have already told you that I will do my best to accompany the relief.'

323

Angus put up his hand. 'Sarge, can't the US Marines stay at this Red Socks place until Stores arrive and we can all get there together?'

'No, Angry,' said Dave patiently, 'the Marines are drawing down fast. That's why we have to get moving now.' He said to Chalfont-Price: 'I'd like to take a generator. I doubt that the Marines will leave us theirs.'

'Sergeant, you're overreacting to this situation. You will be fine for half an hour without one. We will send a generator in the relief wagons.'

Dave did not argue. He had thought of something much more important than a generator.

'I'll need a signaller and a medic.'

Chalfont-Price rolled his eyes.

'You will have eight men! Rifleman Bilaal is very capable with his bandages if one of you trips over your boot laces. Isn't that enough?'

'Mal's good but in the circumstances I'd like to take Doc Holliday. With any luck he'll be able to operate between all the outlying PBs. But I'd like him based at Red Sox, at least until all the relief parties have arrived.'

Chalfont-Price shook his head. 'I'm surprised at you, Sergeant, hogging so many resources for yourself. You certainly can't have a signaller and the main medic.'

Luckily, at that moment, the sergeant major arrived.

'I want to take Doc Holliday to PB Red Sox, sir,' said Dave.

'Fucking right you should,' said Kila without hesitation. 'If the Taliban aren't watching every step of this handover and don't start flexing their muscles to impress the advance party, I'll eat my hat.'

Involuntarily everyone glanced at his cap.

Chalfont-Price scowled but did not challenge the sergeant major. Anyway, Kila was already walking away. 'I see you've got things under control in 1 Platoon as usual. I'll sort out Doc,' he said over his shoulder. Dave knew the compliment was meant for him. But probably Chalfont-Prick would assume it was his.

A few minutes later Dave was checking off ammo and handing it around 1 Section to distribute the load. Each man carried fifty rounds for the Minimi. The UGL men had twenty-two rounds each. 'If anyone's got any room in their day sack, take some more Minimi rounds!' roared Dave, throwing ammo into his own Bergen. 'Mal, can you find me a couple of .66 rockets?'

Mal disappeared.

'Sol, have they all got pistols?'

'Pistols and two magazines each,' confirmed Sol.

'Slindon? You got your pistol?'

'Er . . .'

This desert FOB was certainly front line, its PBs were front, front line, and now they were going to the furthest and most isolated of these, undermanned and underequipped. Just Dave's luck that, of all the men in the platoon, Slindon was going too.

'Found it, Sarge!' said Slindon happily, producing the pistol from his webbing with a look of total surprise and an enormous smile.

'Amazing, Slindon. The Taliban had better watch out now. Is everyone carrying hand grenades?'

'Yes!' chorused 1 Section.

'How many?'

Sol said: 'Should have two each. Slindon, have you got your hand grenades?'

Slindon was thrown into confusion. He grabbed his Bergen and began frantically searching through it. Dave ignored him.

'Night-vision goggles, everyone?'

'Yes!'

'Laser light markers?'

'Yes!'

'Hand-held illumes?'

'Yes!'

'How many?'

'Two each, Sarge.'

Mal was returning with the rockets as a Lancer from the Kings Dragoon Guards appeared, looking miserable. He was a tall man with a long face. He yawned.

'Sergeant Henley? I'm Lancer Dawson. I'm driving you to this bed socks place,' he said unenthusiastically.

'You don't look too pleased about it, Lancer Dawson,' said Dave, shaking hands with him.

'Yeah, well, the Yanks are doing steak while they wait for the men to get back from the PBs and they're serving up to anyone left in the FOB,' said Dawson. 'And that was supposed to be me. Except now I'm going to the back of beyond with you lot instead.'

'Sorry about the steak, Lancer. But I think you'll find my lads are always ready to divvy up their MRE Lancashire Hot Pot.'

'Great,' said Lancer Dawson wretchedly. 'That's just fucking great.'

'We're taking two Mastiffs. Who's the other driver?'

'Lancer Reed. Here he comes, look.'

Another forlorn face appeared.

'Have you heard about the steak?' he said to Dawson. 'I mean, they're serving up fucking steak and we're going to miss it!'

'Morning, Lancer, I'm Sergeant Dave Henley and we're scheduled to depart in five minutes.' Dave tried to remain cheerful in the face of the men's gloom.

Lancer Reed's shoulders sagged. 'Morning.'

'Lads!' yelled Dave to 1 Section. 'Use each wagon. Who do you want on the heavy machine gun, Sol?' Then he turned back to the drivers. 'Let's just check one thing: batteries. We've got no generator. Have we brought enough batteries for the radios?'

'Yeah, yeah, yeah.' The two Lancers, sounding more bored than doleful now. 'Sorted.'

Doc Holliday arrived. 'Hi, Dave!' he said happily. 'A distant PB with insufficient men and equipment? It's looking like fun.'

Dave grinned back but the drivers looked at him with disgust.

'Yes, yes, oh yes, we're heading for action!' said the medic. He rubbed his hands.

The drivers shook their heads. 'Glad someone's happy about missing a fucking good steak dinner.'

'Who cares about steak when Taliban's on the menu?' asked Doc Holliday. 'If all the rumours about PB Red Sox are true, I reckon I could double my ears collection.'

Dave looked around rapidly for Americans but luckily none of them was close enough to overhear.

The men were ready and waiting now.

'Streaky on the HMG,' said Sol.

Streaky Bacon's face lit up and he scrambled into position behind the .50 cal at the back of one Mastiff. The other had a gimpy on top.

'Angus, you go on the GPMG.' Angus's face broke into a smile.

'The rest of you inside,' Sol told them. 'Now.'

The men heaved their Bergens into the backs of the vehicles. Binns could barely lift his and Angus had to help. The packs bulged with weapons and ammo. Sol gave them all a hand and then jumped into the front of the second Mastiff beside Lancer Reed.

'You're commanding, are you?' asked Reed. 'Owing to the manpower shortage, I don't even get a proper commander.'

Sol grinned broadly at him.

'I'm proper,' he said cheerfully. He was happy, thought Dave, because he was going into serious action at last. All the men knew this might not be an easy journey but no one looked nervous or apprehensive. They looked sharp, keen and alert. They seemed only distantly related to the lads who had stood around in the pub in Wiltshire one icy night moaning about wives and girlfriends and wishing they were still at the front line.

The other wagons in the convoy, taking other sections of other platoons to their advance positions at other PBs, were revving up. Dave joined Lancer Dawson at the front of the Mastiff with the HMG and the two 1 Section vehicles fell in at the back of the line. Iain Kila watched them go from behind large sunglasses, his arms folded. He nodded to Dave. Further back, Chalfont-Price was visible, leaning on an exercise bike with another officer and a couple of high-ranking Americans. He was deep in conversation and did not turn to see his men leave.

Dave knew the boss couldn't hear him but he roared, 'Enjoy your steak!' anyway. Then they were out of the main gate and surrounded on three sides by featureless desert. They had to cross the Helmand River. It lay ahead of them, shining in the sun, snaking through the heart of the strange green world it nurtured.

26

Their route took them over many bridges – across the river, its tributaries and canals. Dave knew that the Royal Engineers had put most of these in. They were counted a success story because the locals were using them as if they had been there for ever. Today there were children and old men herding goats over them, women returning from market on foot, the occasional overloaded car passing and, on one, a camel that had got halfway and was refusing to go further despite the men who surrounded it shouting and waving sticks.

Gradually the convoy got shorter and 1 Section found themselves nearer the front as two wagons peeled off each time they passed a PB. Dave checked in at the bases without stopping. There were no incidents. The Green Zone was lush and quiet today. He heard a few shots but the firing was not close to them.

'They don't sound serious. Maybe they're just out bagging a rabbit for lunch,' suggested the driver. He cut up the tracks with confidence. 'We've got an easy run. They didn't have much rain here, the mud's all dried out and the Yanks have pretty well guaranteed this route is clear of mines.'

'I've heard that one before,' said Dave.

'Their surveillance systems are fucking good these days.'

The driver was right. It was a warm spring day, the chance of IEDs was slim, the Taliban apparently couldn't be bothered to fire, the fields looked fertile after some rain and the newly dampened ground was a lot less dusty than usual. There was no reason not to relax and enjoy the ride. Except Dave couldn't. He shifted from right to left. His body was tense. When his neck started hurting he became aware that he was sitting at an awkward angle. Christ, what was wrong with him? Was it that phone call to Jenny? Or was it that uncomfortable feeling he got inside when things were kicking off? Because, right now, nothing was kicking off anywhere. Nevertheless, he felt his gut do a little back-flip inside him.

'You're clutching your stomach, Sarge. Not going down with D and V are you?' asked the driver anxiously.

'Nah,' said Dave, trying to sound relaxed. He knew that thinking about Jenny could cause a bit of gut twist these days. Which is why he didn't think about her if he could help it.

They checked in at Detroit Tigers, Chicago White Sox, Texas Rangers, Pittsburgh Pirates, Cincinnati Reds. The PBs varied from concrete bunkers wrapped in Hesco to old compounds to a row of deserted shops. Then they climbed up to the edge of the Green Zone, driving around a sand and rock cliff to resume their journey along the other side of the zone. The track now ran alongside a wide canal. The sun glimmered on its surface. They passed women with baskets of washing. At the sight of the convoy some of them ran to hide behind the bushes, others continued their work with stoicism, ignoring the soldiers and wagons. The children who played nearby stared and a few waved. Dave threw a boy a sweet in a red wrapper and the child caught it neatly and then opened his hands to survey it with awe.

'You always keep sweets in your pockets for kids?' asked the driver. 'That's nice.'

'You never know when you may need to bribe them,' Dave said.

The convoy had begun to feel very short now. Ahead was PB New York Mets, some three kilometres further on PB San Francisco Giants and about three kilometres after that lay PB Red Sox.

'See you later, 1 Platoon,' said the commander of 2 Platoon over the radio as his Mastiff peeled off. 'Good luck out there at Red Sox.'

'We're thinking of renaming it Charlton Athletic,' said Dave. 'See you later.'

When there were just 1 Section's two Mastiffs left, Dave felt small in this huge landscape. He had seldom been so far from a FOB so unprotected. He reminded himself that the Taliban didn't know how few men he had in the back. Anyone watching them might assume their force was twenty men strong, including the vehicles' drivers, gunners and commander. If he had twenty men instead of just eight, a medic and a couple of drivers, would he sit differently, would he look more confident? He rearranged himself to look big, strong, certain, just in case the enemy had a body-language expert peering between the trees.

To Dave it seemed a long, windy road. They passed a small village, wedged between the track and the canal. Across the canal a group of children minded the goats, sitting in the shade with sticks, drawing

331

in the sand. They jumped to their feet when they saw the soldiers. One tried to run alongside the canal but his friends called him back.

'No sweets for them?' asked the driver.

'They'll only land in the canal,' said Dave.

They rose up a slight incline, the track curved and PB Red Sox came into sight. It was about two kilometres away, a small compound, reinforced with Hesco on one side, with two vulnerable-looking wooden towers rising up from inside its mud walls.

'Welcome to your new home,' said Lancer Dawson. 'All mod cons. Friendly neighbours. Fine views.'

Angus's voice came on PRR.

'Is that falling-down load of mud shit what the Yanks call a patrol base?'

'Home sweet home,' said Streaky Bacon.

Suddenly the road dipped alarmingly. The PB began to disappear over the horizon.

'Shit!' said Dave. 'Stop.'

Lancer Dawson groaned.

'Now!' Dave insisted.

The Mastiff screeched to a halt, and behind it so did the second vehicle.

Dave asked on PRR: 'Streaky Bacon! Can you still see PB San Francisco Giants behind us ?'

There was a pause.

'Just about,' said Streaky. 'It's going to disappear any minute. This is quite a dip we're in here.'

'Can you see PB Red Sox ahead of us?'

'The lookout tower. But that's going to disappear soon.'

'We're going into a dead zone,' said Dave.

'Oh fuck,' said Lancer Dawson.

'It won't take long to Barma it,' Dave told him.

But Lancer Dawson had been once more overtaken by gloom.

'I hate stopping. I'm a driver and that's what I like to do. Except when it means I'm missing a steak lunch.'

Dave said on PRR: 'OK, Binman and Tiny, you're our minefield men and we're in a dead zone. You need to check out any parts of this track which don't have enough visibility from Red Sox or Giants to stop our friendly local Taliban from planting an IED.'

There was a pause and then Binman and Tiny appeared, covered by Sol and the men on top of the Mastiffs. They edged forward slowly, swinging the Vallons back and forth in front of them over the dusty, stony track.

While the engines stayed off, Dave drank in the silence. He couldn't even hear the kids playing now. Where was the boy who had run alongside them? Had he been told not to go near the track because it was mined?

Lancer Dawson began to look tense. 'How do we know nothing was planted overnight? Do the Yanks check it every morning?' he demanded.

'Yep.' Dave clicked on PRR again. 'Slow down, Barmarers, you're moving too fast. The enemy is active round here and there's a good chance you'll find something.'

But they found nothing. They reached the top of the incline and took a good look at the PB and then Barmaed a short way down the track before turning and checking again all the way back to the vehicles.

'Thanks, lads, get on board,' said Dave.

The local Taliban seemed remarkably quiet. There were some houses wedged between the track and the canal not fifty metres away. They were the perfect place for an ambush to hide while visitors Barmaed the track.

Perhaps the locals were friendly after all. Dave made a mental note. More candy for more children.

Tiny and Binman gave Dave a thumbs-up as they passed him to climb back into the wagons. Sweat was dripping down their faces. Barmaring was intense, scary work. It felt routine but if you relaxed for a moment and missed a faint signal, you or your mates could be blown up.

They drove on, back up the incline and along the canal. After about fifty metres they swung left at ninety degrees to the compound. As they neared it, the gate opened for them. Inside were the Marines' vehicles and men in American desert camouflage were piling kit into the back of them. There was little room for the Mastiffs.

The very first thing Dave noticed was that the walls here were so high they wouldn't be able to use the heavy machine gun on the back of the Mastiff. And they couldn't take it off because they had no tripod for it. Shit. He looked around for a sand bank to drive the Mastiffs on to: there certainly would have been one in a UK-run compound but here there was none.

Dave hailed the American officer, aware as he did so that the US Cougars were almost fully loaded and Marines were throwing the very last of their kit inside.

The OC barely greeted Dave.

'I'm Captain Grant Rider.' He did not pause for Dave to give his own name. 'We've been told to leave straightaway. We're just about ready to go. This is my sergeant, Gunny McGunn.'

Dave held out his hand and Gunny McGunn shook it, but he did not allow Dave time to give his name either.

'I have five minutes to tell you everything I know about this place, so let's get going, pal.'

He strode ahead and Dave followed him while the

lads dismounted and stretched and looked around them.

'How long have you been here?' Mal asked a Marine.

'Three months.' With their beards, their kit and their loud voices they filled up the crumbling compound. The lads sat down on the ground, backs to a wall.

'Going home?' asked Bacon enviously.

'Nah, we do longer tours than you Brits. We're going north now, up towards the mountains.'

Dave stepped out of the bright spring day into the compound behind the US sergeant. It was dark and dingy. Gunny McGunn led Dave through empty, dirt-floored rooms.

'We used this for ammo, because it was the only place to stay dry when it rained, but you probably won't have any more rain now. This is the kitchen. We had a rat problem but we've sorted them out. Just stay vigilant because you got one rat, you got a thousand.'

In the courtyard he pointed out the towers.

'They do not afford good protection. Got to keep your head down in there when things get hot outside . . .'

'Do things get hot around here?' asked Dave. And for the first time the man stopped and looked him full in the face.

'You're British but you're not talking about the weather, right?' he asked, squinting slightly.

We're on the same side, thought Dave, but we're different.

'No,' he said, 'I'm not talking about the weather.'

'This is a seriously active PB,' said Gunny. He fired his words rapidly, without expression. 'Some days the local Taliban are quiet. Like Friday. So we think they're very religious. But Sunday to Thursday they're, like, not religious.'

'Mostly light arms?' asked Dave.

'If only. They often have machine guns and RPGs and sometimes there are a lot of them. We've had to call for air support on average once a week.'

Dave asked about the Taliban's usual firing points. Gunny discussed the terrain.

'Visibility is good on the whole. Remember always to watch those rocks. They don't seem a whole lot higher than this compound, but they are, and it's a favoured enemy position.'

He led Dave up the tower. 'It feels like you have visibility in most directions,' said the Marine, 'but don't be fooled. Did you notice a dead zone on the track?'

'Notice it? We Barmaed it,' said Dave.

Gunny nodded.

'That's correct. You should always Barma the Bronx. That's what we call that area. We just can't get a line of sight on it; it's too low and on an angle. So the enemy sneaks in with their IEDs and they plant them in the Bronx. We do a clearance route every morning. We cleared for you a few hours ago.'

'Thanks,' said Dave.

'We prayed to the Lord that you would remember to stop and check the Bronx.'

'Thanks,' said Dave again. 'But you didn't need to. It's basic drill to check a dead zone.'

'We should have put in another PB down at the Bronx and we've been meaning to the whole time we've been here. But I guess no one ever had a chance. The Taliban kept us too busy,' said the American.

'You'll be going back to the FOB through the Bronx,' said Dave evenly. 'But don't worry, we'll pray for you.'

The sergeant seemed to take his words at face value.

'Thanks, but actually we're turning right out of the gate and taking the other route back.'

'It looked like the track came to a dead end here.'

'It used to but we've cleared it so we can go around to the FOB in a big circle. The first mile's difficult but it's OK after that.'

As they went back through the kitchen area, he gestured to a box.

'We left you some stuff. We know how you Brits love our rations so there's some over there. You guys don't get M&Ms in yours, right?'

'Right,' said Dave, putting his hand in the box and pulling out some M&Ms. 'Thanks a lot.'

McGunn was making his way back through the compound now. Outside, the Marines were revving their vehicles. Men were climbing on board, shouting to one another, radios crackling.

'Oh, and if a guy called Raham Dil tries to sell you goat meat, don't eat it. No matter how good it looks,' Gunny said, climbing into the back of the vehicle.

The lads watched them manoeuvre around the Mastiffs. The American Cougars were not only built with good mine resistance but they had mine flayers on the front too.

'You lucky, lucky bastards,' said 1 Section to the Americans' retreating backs.

'Why do the Yanks always seem more tooled up than us?' asked Binman.

'Because they are,' said Angus.

Before the last vehicle drove off, a Marine leaped out of the back and ran up to 1 Section. He chose Slindon and pressed a bag into his hand.

'Guys,' he said, his eyes sweeping the assembled faces, 'I don't know if you already have one of these, but

I really recommend you take a look at it. God bless your stay here.'

He pressed the bag into Slindon's palm. Then he ran back to the truck. The Cougar roared out of the entrance like a big, vicious animal which had been released into the wild.

'Gates!' yelled Dave and Tiny and Bacon ran forward.

Meanwhile, Slindon pulled down his headphones in surprise. Distant, tinny music issued from around his neck.

'Why did he give this to me?' he asked blankly.

'Because you were nearest. Maybe it's a box of M&Ms!' Angry pulled it out of Slindon's hand and drew a book from the bag. He saw the cover and then dropped it as if it was contaminated.

'Christ, what is it?' asked Mal, picking it up. 'Oh. One of those.'

The other lads crowded round.

'A *Bible*!'

'Shit!'

'He must be one of them Bible Belt soldiers.'

'Reckon he scatters them all over Helmand Province?'

'Well, I'm not reading it.'

'Me neither.

Sol and Dave, after rapid discussion, showed the men their firing positions and somehow by the time this was completed the Bible ended up on the ground in a dusty, dark corner of the compound.

'I'll tell you something,' said Mal. 'If that was the Quran and everyone here was Muslim, there's no way it would be lying there like that.'

Most of the lads were messing with iPads or listening to iPods and did not hear him.

338

27

Dave's words at the end of their phone call had made Jenny cry. He had said he was sorry in the most loving and graceful way possible. Overnight, she examined her own behaviour. Had she been unkind or unfair? He had said he was leaving Camp Bastion and she could tell from his tone that he was going somewhere dangerous. Had she told him she loved him? Probably. But not in a truly loving way. She did not fall into a deep sleep until morning, shortly before it was time to get up.

She prepared the children and went over to Adi's. She had arranged to leave the girls there when Adi got back from church. The Kasanita family had gone to the first service. Somehow Adi had managed to dress herself and all the children nicely and pile them into the car at a ridiculously early hour while Jenny still slept. But now Jenny had seen her scooting home and she braced herself to take the children over and ask another favour of Adi – an enormous one.

'I'm a bit early. I thought maybe we could have a chat for a few minutes,' she said when Adi answered the door.

'Come in, darling, we'll have a cup of tea. But watch

out, because I've started cooking and I've already burnt something and the whole place smells horrible!' laughed Adi, leading her to the kitchen, where children were scraping leftover cake mixture from bowls with wooden spoons. Jaime was asleep so Jenny left her in her buggy in the hallway. Vicky sat down in front of the TV with some of the other children as though this was her second home. Which, thought Jenny guiltily, in a way it was.

'I think our boys are leaving Bastion,' she said.

Adi, who was making a pot of tea, swung round to her.

'You've spoken to Dave!' she said, her face breaking into a wide smile. So Adi knew how little communication there had been between them. Because Adi always knew everything.

Jenny nodded. But she doubted that the phone call from Dave yesterday was like any phone call between Sol and Adi.

'How is he?'

'Fine. They were getting ready to leave Bastion to go somewhere.'

'Another FOB, I believe. Did Dave tell you when they might be coming home?'

Coming home. Not a subject they had broached.

'I don't think he knows.'

'Well, I'm glad you two have spoken.'

The water boiled and Adi poured it into the big teapot, stirring it with the same energy she applied to everything. Jenny couldn't smell anything burnt in the kitchen. It felt like a warm, welcoming, sweetly scented Adi sort of place.

'Can I help you with anything here?' asked Jenny.

'Don't you have to rush off to get ready for work?'

'I've got a few minutes. I'm just wearing jeans, since it's Sunday.'

'Hmm, well a bit of peeling maybe?'

Adi plonked a tray of vegetables and a peeler in front of her.

'Now then, Jenny, what time do you think you're going to finish tonight?'

'Well, you know that Eugene's on a committee?' Jenny began.

'Ummmm,' said Adi.

'They're writing a report.'

'Oh yes? Is that what you type? I thought it was his memoirs.'

'That too. But the report's really urgent. It's for the Government.'

'Ooooh.'

'And I think I told you that the deadline's moved forward and it has to be finished tonight? Well, that might mean working very late.'

Adi was pouring the tea but now she paused and looked at her.

'So, what are you trying to tell me, Jenny?'

Jenny could not look up. She picked a large, bell-shaped squash from the tray and tried to peel its thick skin but the peeler kept sliding over the hard, smooth surface.

Adi delivered a cup of tea to Jenny and then scooped up a small child and placed him on her hip. She stood swaying gently with the child in front of Jenny.

It was difficult to say this. It was difficult to peel the squash. 'I'm not sure what time we'll actually finish.'

'Well, we agreed I'd have the children this afternoon . . . I can keep them until their bedtime this evening . . .'

'The thing is, we might not finish until, well, midnight or even later.'

Adi stared at her.

'Oh. I see. So what you really want is for me to take the girls all night.'

Jenny was making headway with the squash now. She had found it was possible to peel it using sheer brute force, pushing the blade into the skin. She pressed as hard as she could and at that moment the blade slipped down the squash to her other hand, which was holding the vegetable, and along the back of one finger. Jenny could see the white line of peeled skin.

First there was pain and then there was blood.

'Oh Adi, I'm sorry, I'm making a mess of this!' Jenny did not want to admit how much her finger hurt. She tried wrapping a tissue around it but by the time Adi had reached for her first-aid kit, the tissue was soaked in blood.

Adi put the child down and rummaged in the box until she found a bandage and without a word started to wrap it around Jenny's finger. Jenny took her silence for anger. Usually Adi was all noise and sympathy at the slightest mishap. This cold, quiet Adi was like a reprimand.

She stood up.

'It's OK, Adi, don't worry about my finger.'

Adi looked up at her. Jenny took the bandage out of her hand.

'I'm causing nothing but trouble. I'll see to this at home and replace your bandage. And don't worry about this evening either. I'll be back at five for the girls.'

'Now, Jenny, don't be like that.' Adi's voice had lost its customary warmth.

'I've put you in a very difficult position. I've asked too much. I'm sorry.' Jenny was moving towards the door now.

'You've put me in a difficult position because you've asked me to take your kids for the night. So that you can work late with this man, Eugene. Jenny, do you have any idea what people are saying about you? And what they'll say if they find out I've looked after your girls so you can be alone with him at night in his house?'

Jenny looked through to the living room. The children had all left the kitchen now and were sitting in a tight circle in front of the TV. She leaned towards Adi. They were both standing and Jenny had to bend to speak quietly to the small, solid Fijian.

'I don't care what people say, because I know none of it's true. I do care when my friends, or people I thought were my friends, are ready to believe lies about me.'

Adi stared back at her.

'Is it all lies, Jenny? I didn't want to believe it but so many people have seen you in public with this man. You spend such a lot of time alone with him in his house, he visits you here, he picks up your kids. And you hardly speak to your husband.'

Jenny continued to search Adi's face. Of all the women at the camp, she loved Adi the most but now none of the familiar features she cared for were visible: the ready smile; the warm, shining eyes; the comfortable curved cheeks. Adi's face had become all cold, jutting angles.

'We're alone in his house *working*, Adi. I don't stop from the minute I arrive to the minute I leave and that's why he picked up the girls once, because I was *working*. He's been to my house once, because I left my handbag. We've been out twice together and both times there's been a good reason. He's never held my hand or kissed me or spoken to me in any way he shouldn't. That's the truth.'

While she was speaking she saw Adi's face change again. The angles began to soften, the warmth returned to her eyes.

'I believe you,' she said. 'But Jenny, Jenny, why couldn't you be more careful?'

Jenny was ready to bolt for the front door but Adi stopped her, suddenly throwing her arms around her. 'Oh darling, you know how people like to talk and say bad things. Why do you give them so much opportunity to gossip?'

Jenny shrugged inside Adi's hug. 'I didn't know they were going to start talking about me. I thought people liked me.'

'The best thing, and you won't be happy but I'm saying it anyway, the best thing would be for you to stop working for Eugene.'

'I don't want to. I love the job.'

'It's not fair on Dave. All this gossip. He hears it out in theatre and it's not right.'

'I can't give up work.'

'Is it true he's loaned you money?'

'What?'

'Eugene. Is it true he loaned you the deposit for Vicky's nursery?'

Jenny drew back.

'It's in my pay package. He deducts the money each month.'

In the next room, the children's programme was ending with the usual music. Adi and Jenny knew the tune well; it was part of the soundtrack of their lives. Its conclusion usually signalled the onset of hunger, restlessness or some other demand from their children, which meant adult conversation had to end.

'Jenny, listen.' Adi spoke rapidly and softly. 'If you're staying there because of the loan, don't. That money I'm saving for our trip back to Fiji, I'll never have enough before Sol comes home. I'll loan it to you, I know you'll pay it back when you can. If it helps you to give up the job, then take it.'

Jenny was touched.

'Oh, Adi.'

'Don't decide now, Jenny. Think about it. OK?'

Jaime was moving in her buggy the way she did just before she woke. Around the TV, the tight circle sprung a leak as children broke away.

'Thanks, Adi. I will.'

'Listen, come back at bedtime this evening to say goodnight to the girls and then leave them here and pick them up in the morning. I'll deal with the gossip as best I can.'

'Adi, thanks, I—'

'Jaime's waking up. Don't let her see you or she'll cry when you go. Hug Vicky and leave now, Jenny. And take care of yourself.'

Vicky ran for a cuddle as Adi followed Jenny through the hallway. At the door, Jenny kissed the half-asleep Jaime and then remembered something. She reached down into the buggy's carrier and pulled out a bottle of wine.

'Jenny, you know I don't touch that stuff!' exclaimed Adi.

'It's for Leanne and Steve. You see Leanne much more than I do these days. Would you pass it on?'

'Well, of course.'

'I told Eugene about Steve coming home and he sent this bottle to wish him well.'

Adi immediately held the bottle differently, as though it was something dangerous.

'You want me to tell them this is a present *from Eugene*?'

'Well, yes. It's supposed to be really nice wine.'

'Darling, I'll think of something else to say.'

'Why?' Jenny was putting Vicky down now and the little girl was clinging to her leg.

'That's what makes me sure you're not having an affair, Jenny Henley. You just don't know how to lie. Or when to lie.'

'I thought Steve and Leanne would be pleased to have a nice bottle of wine!'

'If they think you're having an affair with this man, they won't want presents from him, will they?'

Jenny stroked Vicky's hair and gently lifted her back into the house. 'Is that really what they think?'

Adi looked her straight in the eye and nodded.

'But how do you know?'

'I saw Steve for a few minutes yesterday. And he expressed an opinion. So did Leanne.'

That was why Steve hadn't answered the door. Jenny felt hot and defensive. 'I don't know about Steve but I thought Leanne was my friend. We've always helped with each other's children, we've got keys to each other's houses and we do a lot together . . .'

'The last thing you two did together was go shopping for party dresses,' Adi reminded her. 'Months ago.'

Jenny realized she was right.

Adi rolled her eyes. 'See you at bedtime.'

Vicky burst into tears and Jenny kissed her again, and then Adi tugged the little girl inside. They turned and waved as Jenny walked back down the street clutching the remaining ball of bandage with the half-bandaged finger. She looked back once to see the pair of them waving, Vicky's face tear-stained, calling her name. She heard Jaime's wail as she woke too. She swallowed, waved and turned towards home.

As she swung up the path she felt that Steve might be standing at his window watching her once more, disapproving of her, perhaps even hating her. She did not turn around towards the Buckles' house; she did not even glance in that direction.

28

The section took over the Marine latrines, the Marine cooking area and the Marine wall posters.

'Personally,' said Finn, 'I don't need to know so fucking much about the finer details of the female anatomy.'

'About the what?' asked Angry.

'Girls' bodies. I just like nice pictures of, sort of, the whole body. Not little bits of it which look like they're out of a doctor's manual.'

'Those pictures probably belonged to the geezer who left the Bible,' said Binman.

'I got some interesting female anatomy here. This chick ain't out of no doctor's manual but I can't get her to stay up on these walls,' said Mal wrestling with his poster.

'That's because she got all wet in the cave. She didn't like it back there,' Bacon told him. He turned to the poster and cooed: 'Did you, baby?'

As if in reply, there came a volley of fire.

'Shit, not yet!' said Mal and Angus.

'Hold on, Terry Taliban,' said Slindon. 'I haven't unpacked.'

'Get to your firing positions,' shouted Dave.

'Come on, come on, come on, we only just showed

them to you,' Sol yelled. But it was the usual arrival chaos. People who were still arguing with each other about where they were to sleep could not focus on the real enemy outside. They stumbled about looking for weapons and ammo.

'Shit!' said Dave. 'This always happens the moment we arrive anywhere so why aren't we *ever* ready for it?'

Men bumped into each other as they looked for their firing positions.

'This place is barely large enough to swing a cat. How can you get lost?' roared Dave.

Finally the men were in place. At first the firing was spasmodic as if a couple of Taliban lads were laughing and joking together and firing when they remembered to. Then suddenly their dads seemed to arrive and the fight got fiercer, until it echoed from all sides. Dave was fairly sure that the enemy was in the rocky outcrop the Marine sergeant had pointed out but he could not be sure that this was their only position. The compound seemed to be in a giant bowl and noise echoed around inside it. This made it difficult to gauge just how strong the enemy was, since every report echoed once, twice and maybe three times.

'If only we had the tripod for the .50 cal!' he moaned to Sol.

Sol, leaning over a rifle, turned to look at him. 'Well, why don't we?'

'I was told we couldn't take it.'

Sol looked incredulous. 'Who told you that?'

Dave did not reply, so Sol guessed who. He shook his head sadly but said nothing.

'Is there any way to position the wagon so we can fire the HMG?' Dave asked the driver.

Lancer Dawson shrugged.

'Nothing wrong with my position. The problem is the walls are too high. S'pose you might scare the ragheads off a bit if you fire it into the air. But you're not going to hit anything.'

Dave felt exasperated.

'We haven't got enough ammo to just piss it away,' he said.

'Well, what else are you going to use HMG ammo for?'

There was no answer to that.

'If you ask me, the ragheads saw the personnel handover,' continued Lancer Dawson. 'And they're giving us a warm local welcome.'

Dave silently agreed with him. The enemy were trying to gauge their manpower and this was the opening of a conversation, the only sort you could have with the Taliban. It would continue throughout their time here. He wished he could start the conversation with a firm statement and there was nothing better than an HMG to say: 'Fuck off.'

The Minimi chattered angrily and so did the gimpy but it wasn't enough. The enemy answered with their own machine gun. Dave could almost hear them laughing. They had been watching the place; they knew the arc of fire of a big gun and where it had to stand for maximum effect. And they couldn't see it and they couldn't hear it so, despite seeing it arrive, they were already guessing it was out of use.

He called Dawson and Reed.

'We've got shovels. See if you can build up some of this sand, enough to reverse the Mastiff on to it and get the HMG above wall level.'

If the Lancers had looked miserable at missing their steak lunch, now they looked wretched.

'In this heat?' demanded Dawson.

'We need to give them a show of strength.'

'There isn't enough sand in this courtyard. We'll never get it high enough!'

'There's rubble stacked up around the edges, and more in the other courtyard. Try using that, then sand.'

'But the relief should be here any minute,' said Reed.

'Listen,' Dave told them. 'We've got twelve men, that's including me, you two drivers and a medic. As far as I know, stores haven't even arrived at FOB Nevada yet. So it might be a while.'

Moaning, the drivers went off to examine the rubble.

Dave went through the compound to the next courtyard to join in the firefight.

'Up your rate of fire,' he told Sol. 'And move the lads round a bit. We don't want the enemy to know how few of us there are.'

'It's fucking horrible up here, Sarge,' shouted Binman from one of the towers. 'I've got my head down all the time and it's fucking raining rounds.'

'All right, you can get down,' Sol said. 'Streaky Bacon, go up there.'

Streaky didn't hear him at first. He was doing that Streaky giggling thing under heavy fire. In fact, it was the sound of those giggles which focused Dave on how serious their situation was. The enemy was testing them for firepower and manpower and if they guessed resources were really limited then this could turn into a sustained attack. As their own rate of fire had increased, so had the enemy's. Anything we can do, thought Dave, they can do better, and that's what's giving Streaky Bacon the giggles.

Dave got on the radio to the OC and gave a sit rep.

'You're not the only PB to come under attack. PB

Detroit Tigers is having a hot time,' the OC said. 'Good thing you've got the .50 cal.'

'It would be if I could use it,' said Dave.

The OC's voice turned electric. 'Why the *fuck* can't you use it?'

Because my twat of a platoon commander told me I couldn't have the tripod, sir. Dave said: 'There's a technical problem, sir.'

'A technical problem?'

'We're working on it, sir.'

'It sounds as though all your men are busy firing, Sergeant Henley, so I can't imagine who's dealing with the technical problem.'

'The drivers should soon have it sorted, sir.'

The OC's sigh was audible.

'Are you likely to be requesting air support?'

Dave hesitated. 'Not yet . . .'

But he was just thinking that it was reassuring to know air support was there when Major Willingham said: 'Could be a dust storm starting at Bastion. You may have noticed it was a bit dodgy when we left this morning. So let's hope support's available if we need it.'

Dave felt a pit form in his stomach.

'A dust storm?'

'Yes. Stores have arrived and we're loading up. The Americans are anxious to get away while they can, so most of them have had an early lunch and left.'

Dave wanted to ask the major whether he had enjoyed his steak. Instead he said: 'Will the relief be able to get out of the FOB to us, sir?'

He heard the major hesitate.

'If we don't have a dust storm here. If we do, they can last for days.'

Dave tried not to think about the possibility that they

could be cut off here without supplies or support for days. He decided to renew his attempt to frighten the enemy into backing off for a while. He told Angus to fire a .66 rocket. When it reached its target and turned into a plume of smoke and noise there was a satisfying silence at last. For two minutes. Then it all started again. As if the enemy knew he had only one .66 rocket left.

Dave hoped the skirmish would run its course within about forty minutes. Previous experience with the Taliban told him that when they attacked camps and bases it was often just a show of strength which only lasted until fighters melted away for food or prayers. Except this lot weren't melting anywhere. The two sides exchanged fire for forty minutes. Then fifty. Then an hour.

After ninety minutes of small-arms fire, Dave began to suspect that the enemy was making a serious bid to take the patrol base. It had seemed like an amateurish, low-key show of strength at first but he guessed that reinforcements were still arriving. And then the guy with the grenades showed up.

The first was rocket-propelled and exploded over one of the outer mud walls, throwing up a lot of dust and mess but barely denting the wall. Its arrival was met by a burst of machine-gun fire. Mal was on the gimpy. When he paused you could hear the higher pitch of the Minimi still chattering away. Dave waited for Binman to pause for breath too. But he didn't. The Minimi fired on and on and on, madly, relentlessly. Sol went up to him and shouted: 'Binman! Stop! You're not firing at anything! You're just firing!'

Binman looked at him as though Sol had shaken him awake.

'We don't have so much ammo you can just throw it down like that!' said Sol.

Binman had turned that special Binman shade of pale.

Sol asked: 'When did you last eat?'

Jack Binns stared back at Sol blankly.

'Where are you, Binman?' shouted Sol over the noise. '*Dorset?* Stop firing and get some food inside you, for heaven's sake.'

That was as close as Sol ever came to swearing but still Binman did not move. Sol reached into his own webbing and pulled out an energy bar and a couple of packets of peanuts. He took the Minimi away from Binns.

'Thank you very much,' said Doc Holliday, taking it neatly. 'You see to my patient and I'll see to the enemy, Sol.'

'Don't expose yourself. I can't afford to lose you,' Dave told him.

Doc laughed and trotted off happily with the Minimi while Sol and Dave sat Binns down in the safest place he could find. He handed him the food. Dave found an energy bar too and threw it over to Binns, who sat opening the packets and shoving food into his mouth silently and mechanically.

'Has he been checked for diabetes?' asked Dave.

'Yeah. Doc says it's just low blood pressure.'

Doc Holliday had found himself a good firing position through a slit in the wall which had been made by the Marines or someone else, maybe even the Taliban. Because before this was a PB it might have been an enemy stronghold. Dave had a strange vision of the Taliban and the Americans and the British constantly rotating firing positions in a sort of deadly dance. He watched as another RPG sailed overhead and exploded beyond the compound.

'They're in those rocks,' said Sol. 'But their firing point's very hard for us.'

'And they know it.'

'They know everything about this place. And they know we've only just arrived.'

'They're fucking bastards, Sarge!' shouted Slindon, who was now up the tower. 'Every time I put my head up I get ding dong ding dong on my helmet. It's like being inside Big fucking Ben.'

'They're throwing it all at us!' yelled Finn, his voice battle-excited.

Doc Holliday was silent. He was a focused marksman, sitting still for minutes at a time and then suddenly erupting.

'OK, Slindon get down. Mal, get up there,' Sol said. When Slindon slithered gratefully down from the tower, he attracted a shower of rounds from the enemy.

'I wish we could use the HMG,' said Sol, weariness in his voice.

'I'll find out how they're doing.' Dave had seen the drivers moving in and out of the courtyard carrying rubble, red-faced, shaking their heads in disgust, complaints drowned by the firefight, so he expected little.

He passed through the compound where the noise was temporarily deadened, glancing into the box of food the Marines had left to see that the MREs were still there but all the M&Ms had gone. The sun and sound of firing hit him again when he emerged into the yard – where he saw a small hill of sand and rubble with the Mastiff backed on to it so that the HMG could clear the walls. The two drivers were sitting in the cab, doors open, having a smoke.

They viewed his astonishment with open satisfaction.

'How long has this been ready to roll?'

'About five minutes, Sarge. We were just going to come and tell you.'

An RPG lit up the sky. There was a break in firing from the compound and then the boys responded simultaneously with grenades, the Minimi, the gimpy and rifles. Dave didn't hesitate. He climbed up to the HMG himself, fearing that his weight might disturb the vehicle's precarious balance.

It rocked a little under him as he fed the belt into the .50 cal, which cleared the high mud walls with only centimetres to spare. But centimetres were enough. Within moments, he was firing up the hillside at the muzzle flashes which kept appearing from around a group of big, pink rocks.

The entry into the battle of the big gun at first silenced the enemy. Then an RPG dissolved in mid-air into a flash of angry light far beyond the yard. Dave knew he was the intended target and, aware that next time the enemy's aim might not be so poor, he upped his rate of fire on the machine gun, its deep bass thundering under rifles so it sounded like a man among boys.

The enemy stopped firing back. Dave guessed they had taken cover and he stopped firing too. There was a long pause. Everyone waited. The pause got longer. The silence continued. Was it too much to hope that the HMG had made the enemy decide to go away and fight again another day? He remained alert, watching the large boulders on the hillside. The rocks were motionless. The ground around them was motionless. Only the sun moved a little.

Over PRR he told Sol to get someone to relieve him

on the heavy machine gun. He slipped down and went back to the men, passing Angus in the compound heading for the .50 cal.

'They've gone home, Sarge,' said Angry miserably. 'Now I won't get a chance to fire the .50 cal at them.'

'There'll be lots more chances.'

Out in the compound yard men were sitting down by their weapons relaxing and smoking. A few had their hands in their ration packs and steam puffed from a kettle.

'It's all over,' Streaky Bacon said sadly.

'You were giggling like a maniac,' Sol told him.

'Oh no I wasn't.'

'Oh yes you was!' everyone shouted.

'That wasn't laughing. That was crying. Because I only killed one of them.'

'How do you know you killed any of them?' asked Slindon. 'I didn't see the enemy, not one.'

'It was amazing. I got this clear line of fire right between the rocks.'

'You never!' said Finn. 'I was aiming for that gap but it was too fucking hard.'

'I did, Finny, I really did,' said Streaky.

'So how do you know you killed one?'

'Because from my position I could see clear through the gap. Then suddenly I couldn't. So it must have been someone moving in the way. So I fired and then there was a couple of moments for him to die and then it was clear again.'

'That doesn't mean nothing,' said Finn. 'He might just have moved out of the way.'

'I killed him, man!' insisted Streaky. 'I know I did. Because the enemy started slowing up after that.'

'You think you changed the course of the battle?' demanded Sol.

'I fucking did!'

Finn looked at Streaky sceptically.

'All right, Streaks, I believe you. Thousands wouldn't.'

Sol said: 'It was the HMG which shut them up. And Doc on the Minimi scared them too.'

Suddenly there was a familiar, crackling voice in Dave's ear. It sounded smug. The sort of smug which could follow a good steak lunch.

'Well, Sergeant,' said Chalfont-Price, 'stores arrived, we're kitted up already and we're leaving the FOB now with supplies as agreed. We should be with you shortly. So you see, there really was nothing to worry about.'

Dave scowled into the mic.

'I'm glad you're on your way, sir, because we're badly in need of the ammo.'

The OC's voice cut in.

'Patrol Minimize has now been called,' he announced.

'Oh no!' said Dave involuntarily. Operation Patrol Minimize meant that dust storms would keep air support confined to Bastion and the FOBs. Patrol Minimize meant that men on the ground should limit their exposure to the enemy.

'Right, sir,' said Chalfont-Price. 'We'll turn around and come back, then.'

For a moment, Dave was speechless. Then he echoed, helplessly: 'Turn around?'

'Please repeat, Second Lieutenant?' demanded the OC, as if he hadn't quite heard.

The boss's voice sounded a bit less steaky now. 'Since we've only just left the FOB and Operation Patrol Minimize has been announced, we'll turn around.'

'No fucking chance, Second Lieutenant,' snapped Major Willingham. 'You're through the gate, now get out there to your men.'

Dave wanted to shout: 'Thank you!' Somehow he remained silent. So did Chalfont-Price. When he spoke the officer simply said: 'Continuing to PB Boston Red Sox. Sir.' Dave's face broke into a smile.

'What's going on?' asked Sol. The men could not hear this exchange but they had been watching Dave closely throughout.

Dave said: 'The rest of the platoon should be here in just over an hour. But there's no chance of any air support from Bastion: the dust storm's grounded them.'

The men looked out of the compound across the desert for signs that the sand was moving here, too. If there was a sandstorm, the chances of further attack diminished. But although a warm wind blew around the compound, there was no disturbance in the sand.

29

In Wiltshire the weather was changing. The temperature was dropping and a cold wind blew darkening clouds across the sky. Severe weather warnings were issued. Parents took their children out to play before the torrential rain hit the south. Adi bundled all her charges into their coats and somehow managed to move her entourage to the playground and they all scattered at once. The place was full of mothers and children.

'Might not get outside for days now,' they were saying as Adi pulled the buggy and a snake of children through the gate.

She saw Steve Buckle and Si Curtis. 'Hi, boys. Haven't we been lucky to have such a run of good weather? I've loved every minute of that sunshine.'

'Glad you enjoyed it. That was summer,' said Steve dismally.

'It's even been raining in Afghanistan,' said Si. 'So God knows what it's going to do here.'

Steve and Si were the only fathers at the playground: most of the others were away fighting. They stood together, separated from the mothers by swings, while their kids rushed around.

Si Curtis's leg was out of plaster. 'How's it doing?' asked Adi.

Si looked miserable. 'This leg isn't what it was.'

'Whose is?' Steve said.

'Sorry, mate, I shouldn't moan. But I thought I might get out to Afghanistan and they say it's still not strong enough.'

Adi said: 'It will heal.'

'Well,' said Si, 'I can't even run on it yet.'

Steve had been looking into the buggy. Jaime was sitting up and grinning at him. He did not grin back. 'That's Jenny Henley's kid, isn't it?'

'It's Jaime!' said Adi, stroking the baby's cheek.

'You've got her kids on a Sunday!'

'Well, yes.'

'And who's she off with?'

'She's not off with anyone. She's working.'

Si and Steve looked at each other.

'Like hell she's working,' said Si. 'Was she working when we saw her laughing and giggling at the theme park all over that old bloke she's having it away with?'

Adi looked at him with extreme disapproval.

'Simon, please. There are children here.'

'They can't hear us. Only Dave's poor little kid and she's too small to understand.'

'Poor little kid,' echoed Steve. 'What a mother.'

'Don't tell me,' said Si. 'She's got to work late and she's asked you to take the kids all night.'

Adi knew she looked shocked at their accuracy; she just hoped she had managed to hide this before the men noticed. But Steve was too quick.

'She is! She is!' he howled.

Adi said truthfully: 'She's coming back at bedtime.'

That seemed to stop them for a moment. Then Si sneered: 'Whose bedtime? Theirs or hers?'

'Now just stop it, you two. You're spreading gossip.'

But Steve's eyes were narrowing and his cheeks were growing shadowy with anger.

'Dave's been a good mate. I don't like to see his wife making a fool of him. If I could put a stop to it I would.'

'You can't stop a slag being a slag,' Si said.

'Nah, there's probably no stopping her,' agreed Steve.

'Now then, that's enough,' Adi told them sternly. She glared at Si and he began to look sheepish.

'Sorry, Adi. We were both out on the piss last night and our heads are hammering today.'

'That's nice for Leanne and Tiff,' said Adi.

'They married soldiers,' said Si. 'What did they expect?'

'We miss our mates. They're fighting and we're stuck back here. Of course we go on the piss,' said Steve.

'I'm a section commander with no section! And I still worry about them and about how Jason Swift's managing. I worry all the time,' added Si.

'Here's how I get through,' Steve told her. 'I take pills when I wake up in the morning. And I get rat-arsed at night.'

Adi shook her head disapprovingly. 'That's not a way of getting through anything. I saw enough of it in Fiji.'

Si and Steve exchanged glances.

'Hair of the dog,' Si said. 'Gets us over last night. And it means I can avoid my mother-in-law. We'll start this afternoon at the Duke's . . .'

'Moving on to the White Horse . . .' added Steve.

'And not forgetting the Eclipse in between. So by the time I get back, my headache will be over and the mother-in-law should have gone home.'

* * *

The lads from 2 and 3 Sections of 1 Platoon were relieved to be out of FOB Nevada. The Americans had a way of possessing the place with all their hurry and shouting. The British had crammed themselves into the corners trying not to take up too much space while the Americans rushed around yelling into their radios. Even when the steak lunch had been served, the British had clustered around the far edges of the cook area.

Stores had arrived and from the second they touched down 2 Section's Corporal Aaron Baker had been pushing the men to load up and get away fast. He knew there was a firefight going on out at the FOB and he knew Dave was undermanned and he just wanted to get there.

But after their big lunch the men had moved slowly. He and the acting corporal of 3 Section, Jason Swift, had shouted and cajoled. The platoon commander, who had got into some kind of political or strategic discussion with a group of American officers, had occasionally torn himself away from it to shout at the men too. But it seemed to Aaron that everything was happening too slowly.

However, the lunch had been very good. To prove it, after about ten kilometres, Jonas and Gerry McKinley had a burping competition as they bumped along in the Mastiff.

'That's enough,' said the corporal. 'I can't stand it no more.'

'But why don't we get steaks like that?' Danny Jones demanded.

'Because the Americans like their soldiers and think they're worth it,' Patrick O'Sullivan told him. 'All the

British think we're worth is damp, falling-down houses and not enough peanuts in our rations.'

'Here we go,' said Aaron Baker. O'Sullivan never missed a chance to moan about the army and the way it treated them.

'And the Yanks get M&Ms,' added Jonas miserably. 'It's not fair.'

Andy Kirk suddenly produced a small, brightly coloured candy bag from his webbing. He threw it at Danny, whose face lit up.

'Holy shit! Who gave you these, Skirt?'

'No one. I went round nicking them out of their day sacks.'

Everyone looked admiringly at Kirk.

'How did you do that, Skirt?'

'When they served the steak. I could have nicked their wallets and their pistols and everything because nobody cared about nothing but getting that steak in their mouths.'

A few of the lads began to throw Kirk suspicious glances.

'Sure it was just the Yank day sacks you went thieving from, Skirt?' asked Max Gayle.

Kirk looked mysterious. He had very fair skin and red eyebrows, which he raised now, stretching the skin across his face.

'That's for me to know and you to find out.'

'What? What!' said the lads, tearing through their day sacks to check their rations.

A shout went up from O'Sullivan: 'Where's my peanuts?'

Andy Kirk could barely suppress his laughter.

'Wassup then, Sully?' he hissed, heaving with the effort of not corpsing.

'WHERE'S MY PEANUTS?'

A snort escaped Kirk. O'Sullivan was famously partial to peanuts, so partial that he had been known to buy up all of 2 Section's peanut rations. Sometimes he tried to buy them from the whole platoon.

'You've had my fucking peanuts, Andy Skirt! I'll kill you for this!'

He jumped up and grabbed Andy Kirk, and Gerry McKinley and Aaron Baker pulled him back.

'Sit down, Sully.'

'He's thieved my peanuts!'

'Give him back his fucking peanuts before I go mad,' Baker ordered.

Kirk opened his day sack and produced handfuls of small silver bags which he began hurling at O'Sullivan. They slithered around his legs and between his knees like silver fish as he tried to catch them.

'What *is* going on?' demanded the boss's voice on PRR. 'Corporal, is there some sort of a fist fight in the back? If so, please sort the men out.'

'For Chrissake! Everyone sit down and shuddup,' said Baker, trying to sound like Dave, whose orders the men always followed without question. The Mastiff fell silent.

Aaron looked around. Faces were hot and red and dusty. He glanced at his watch. Only another few kilometres to go.

'It's fucking roasting up here,' moaned a voice in his ear. It was Mara, up in the turret.

'OK,' Aaron radioed back. 'Come down and I'll go up on the .50 cal for the last few k.'

Once on top he realized they had nearly passed through the Green Zone. They were going around some sort of a hill or a cliff. Behind them the next vehicle kicked up a cloud of dust. The river below them moved lazily through the heart of the Green Zone like a long, curling reptile in the sun. Men, women and children stumbled along tracks of their own around the crops, apparently deaf to the convoy.

At least they don't hate us, thought Aaron, who had been spat and shouted at by people in the streets of the last town they had patrolled. But that had been in the heart of the poppy-growing area. Here there were a lot of poppies but other crops too and the farming was less organized. The fields were smaller and looked as if they had many different owners. Compounds were more scattered among them.

Chalfont-Price was evidently thinking the same thing.

'This area doesn't feel like such big business for the Taliban,' he said on PRR.

Baker felt a moment's disappointment.

'Maybe there won't be any action after all,' he said.

'Apparently this is an important trading area for poppy resin,' the officer told him. 'And there's been a lot of action so far. 1 Section has been under almost continual fire since arriving at the PB.'

At this, Aaron looked around him more keenly. He saw PB New York Mets disappear into the distance as PB San Francisco Giants came into view and then the last vehicles in the convoy peeled off and 1 Platoon was alone in the two Mastiffs, heading towards PB Red Sox alongside some kind of tributary or canal right on the edge of the Green Zone.

After less than ten minutes, Aaron Baker could see in the distance a compound which the boss immediately identified as the patrol base.

'Looks like home, sir,' Aaron said, although he could

barely distinguish the base from the desert out of which it had grown. When he next turned to look back at PB Giants, it was already gone.

He looked ahead, across the rocky desert again and, to his surprise, PB Red Sox was no longer visible. He scanned the horizon. They were plunging into a dip. He could see no PB behind and no PB ahead. They were in no man's land.

Aaron waited for the boss to stop the convoy. When he did not, the corporal said quickly: 'Sir, we're in a dead zone here. We're not overlooked by either patrol base.'

'I'm sure Red Sox will reappear imminently,' said Chalfont-Price. He sounded sleepy, thought Aaron. That good steak lunch had done more harm than good. 'It's only about two k away.'

Jason Swift from 3 Section in the Mastiff behind came on the radio, as if he had not heard Aaron Baker talking to the boss. Since he was only acting commander in Si Curtis's absence, most of the time he was unsure of himself. But now his voice was sharp.

'Sir, we're in a dead zone here. Should we stop and Barma, sir?'

Chalfont-Price yawned.

'I'm sure there's no need.'

'It's out of sight, sir. The ragheads could have planted an IED.'

'It's all right, Swift. The Americans have only just cleared the area. They will be aware of the personnel change and I believe they have been monitoring this dead zone from the air. We'll just keep an eye out for disturbed earth.'

There was a silence on PRR as his two corporals digested this. Aaron Baker was asking himself whether they could really ignore their own drills and expect the Americans to take care of them. They were about to ford a small stream which ran from the canal across the track to a field which stuck out into the desert like a green thumb. How could they see disturbed earth under water? Jason Swift, behind, was so alarmed they were abandoning drills that he was actually on the radio repeating his request to Barma when the IED went off.

The bomb exploded into the silence suddenly and massively. Baker held on to the machine gun as though it was a lifebelt. He felt no surprise. They were in a dead zone. Of course the enemy had seeded it with mines and now one was exploding. It was utterly predictable. He thought all this in the fraction of a second before he saw kit flying past him and felt his head exploding like another small bomb. He waited to see bits of it falling off him, an ear hurled this way, a nose that. The Mastiff rocked violently from side to side. Still clutching the machine gun with one hand, he reached up with the other to hold his face on. He could feel his features inside his glove. The skin of his face came alive under the harsh touch of the glove. So, he thought, it's still there, then.

His ears ringing, his head throbbing, his eyes aching from the mighty flash, he wiggled his toes and bent his knees. The impact had gone all the way up to his head but that didn't mean his lower limbs were still there. Except they were, because he could move them.

Aaron heard a voice in his ear, demanding to know if anyone was hurt. It was his own voice. He was on PRR talking to the lads, hearing their dazed, stuttering replies.

Everyone was alive; everyone had all their limbs.

Aaron remembered his own arms, hand and fingers.

He wiggled them. So they were there too. He knew that Aaron Baker, the real Aaron Baker inside him, was shocked and scared and reeling from the noise and thrust of a massive blow. But Aaron Baker the soldier was already on the radio, telling everyone to stay put, instructing McKinley to pull the Vallon kit out and start clearing back so they could all extract to vehicle two. He told O'Sullivan to cover McKinley. He was aware, dimly, of strange background music. Was it inside his head? Was his iPod on? Then he realized it was the Muslim call to prayer, released from some distant mosque and haunting the landscape for miles around.

30

At PB Red Sox the world was quieter. The enemy was still out there. Every so often they took a pot shot. But it sounded to Dave as though the heavy men had gone home, leaving their sons to watch the PB. And the sons were too busy playing Angry Birds on their iPhones to care about firing too often.

Far away there came the call to prayer, a deep bass voice singing across the desolate world beyond the Green Zone.

'Good idea! Fuck off and go pray!' said Mal to the invisible enemy from the Minimi.

Dave had put the two drivers up the tower on stag. They had moaned a bit but Dave had not needed to shout because the other men had turned on them: 'We don't have enough manpower for you two to lounge around all day!'

'But we—!' Lancer Reed had begun, before the men interrupted him.

'There's no driving, so get your fucking finger out and help, pals! Even Doc's firing for us.'

Dave thought the drivers were like fish on dry land if

you asked them to use their infantry skills. They were fine behind a wheel, but looked awkward as they climbed the tower with their hands and legs in all the wrong places. Then they had to be reminded to keep glassing throughout the time they were up there. And they were less keen to fire back at the enemy than the infantrymen.

Finally, Dave told Slindon and Bacon to take over up the tower. Gratefully the two drivers started to climb down. Lancer Reed, who was behind, caught his rifle strap on the edge of the Hesco, almost suspending himself in mid-air. He managed to disentangle it but the moment's vulnerability unleashed a volley of fire from the enemy. Over on the HMG, on the other side of the compound, Binns answered them.

'You bastards,' moaned Reed, falling awkwardly to the ground. He stumbled on to one foot and yelped in pain.

Mal, who had just come off stag on the main gate, looked around for Doc Holliday. He was asleep under his basha. Mal did not wake him but walked over to the driver.

'I saw you. Your foot twisted outwards.'

'Shit!' said Reed, grasping his ankle and flopping down on to the ground. 'I would've been all right if my kit hadn't pulled me over.'

'That's the trouble with all this kit. Whenever you fall, you fall harder.'

'Should have fired more!' yelled Finn from behind the gimpy. 'Then you wouldn't have been carrying so much fucking ammo.'

Mal started to take off Reed's boot.

'What you doing?' demanded Reed. 'Just wake up, Doc!'

'No,' said Mal. 'I'm team medic and I'm only waking him up if I think it's broken.'

'Mal's a fucking good medic,' said Streaky Bacon from the tower. 'He knows what he's doing.'

Reed allowed Mal to run his hands over the ankle and pull his leg in various directions and flex his foot.

'Ow, fucking ow!' he said. 'Look, it's swelling up already.'

'I think you've only twisted it,' Mal told him.

'Is that all? Oh fucking fantastic,' groaned the driver. 'What happens when you try to walk on it?'

Mal helped Reed to his feet. The driver stood on one leg and then very gingerly tried to put his weight on the other. He moved forward slowly like a crab, bending sideways to avoid putting any weight on the twisted ankle.

'If I can find anything really cold I'll put that on it. Lie down and keep it elevated and I'll bind it up,' said Mal.

'I hope you know what you're doing,' said the driver. 'I'd rather Doc put my bandage on.'

Mal started to argue but everyone was distracted by a cry from the tower. It was Slindon, peering through the binoculars.

'I can see them! Two fucking Mastiffs!'

He sounded like a man marooned on a desert island who had just seen a ship. A loud cheer went up. Slindon continued to watch. Mal handed the driver a couple of tablets.

'Anti-inflammatories,' he explained. The driver swilled them down quietly.

Slindon reported: 'They're in the Bronx now, Sarge.'

Dave had half a mind to get on the radio and tell the relief party to check for mines in the dead zone. But it was so routine, such basic drill, to Barma a track for mines when it couldn't be glassed that the boss would probably bite his head off if Dave tried to remind him.

Sol appeared, his face puckered with concern because he'd found a leak in their water supplies. Then Finn suddenly responded to a single AK shot from the enemy with a long volley on the gimpy.

'You're late! Get yourself off to the fucking mosque!' he roared.

Dave thought he had heard the deep thud of an explosion somewhere behind all the noise. He listened, but Finn let the gimpy loose again now that he knew more ammo was just a few kilometres away.

When at last there was a pause, Dave heard Slindon say: 'Holy shit!'

Blue Balls Slindon was capable of turning a packet of dropped biscuits into a T4 tragedy but this time his voice had a breathless undercurrent which made Sol stop in mid-flow and the lads in firing positions turn to stare at him.

'What?' Dave asked.

Slindon remained silently glued to the binoculars, his mouth open.

'What's happened?'

Before Slindon could reply, Binns appeared, running through the compound into the courtyard.

'Did you hear that?'

They turned to him speechlessly.

'I could hear it clearly from out by the wagons!' he said.

'What, what, what?'

'A big bomb. A few kilometres away, I'd say. Probably anti-tank. I'm just hoping it's not . . .' Binns did not finish his sentence. He did not need to.

The radio crackled into action. Dave knew it would be Chalfont-Price. It had to be.

'Charlie One Zero to Zero. IED. Wait, out.'

'Oh fuck!' said Dave. 'Oh fuck! They've hit an IED in the dead zone. Chalfont-Prick didn't stop to Barma it. Why didn't I tell him to? Oh Christ!'

Sol had not moved throughout this exchange. He said: 'You shouldn't need to tell him to Barma the dead zone. It's basic drill.'

Anyone in 1 Section who wasn't firing gathered round, their faces grave, waiting for Dave to tell them more. Dave was silent and still, only his heart moving inside his chest, thudding away like artillery. How many lads were hurt? Or worse? He waited for those terrible words. Man down. He was so focused on the radio for news that it felt like a part of his own body.

They waited. Each moment was not a moment of real time, it was a moment lengthened by the anticipation of pain. Was it seconds, minutes or hours before Chalfont-Price came back on?

'No serious casualties. Slight casualties. No burning.'

Dave was so relieved that he felt lightheaded, and then realized this was because he had been holding his breath. Slight casualties only! He passed on the news, hearing his own voice shake.

'Those Mastiffs are amazing!' said Sol, his face breaking into a wide smile. Dave looked around and suddenly everyone was smiling. Something was plucking on unused muscles in his own face. He must be smiling too.

'Fucking good thing Andy Skirt didn't get banjoed because he owes me a tenner!' said Finn and people started to laugh. It wasn't funny, but Dave found himself laughing anyway and now his face was hurting.

The muscles along his cheeks and around his eyes and under his ears were painful, they were so unused to laughing. His throat hurt too. It felt like weeks, no, months maybe, since he had smiled. Let alone laughed. And now he was laughing so that his stomach hurt. He clutched it. Other men were doubling up and Streaky Bacon and Binns were so helpless that when they could no longer hold each other up they fell dramatically to the ground like a pair of drunks. Doc rolled around under his basha. Angus bent over the gimpy, roaring.

Dave had begun to reorganize his face and body back into its normal shape when there was a further exchange over the radio between the OC and Chalfont-Price. Dave could tell that the platoon commander was shaken but he kept coolly to the information he was asked to supply without spiralling off the point the way some men did after a shock. So the first vehicle, Chalfont-Price at the front, had driven through a small stream and apparently the bomb had been planted there. It had been blown up under its front left wheel station and was now blocking the track.

'Sure you're not hurt, Second Lieutenant?' demanded the major.

'I have a slight wound on my arm from a flying object, sir,' said the boss.

'Has the medic looked at it?'

'Yessir. When do you estimate EOD can get here?'

'I can't get you EOD soon,' the major told him. 'They're all elsewhere dealing with other incidents.'

'We are likely to come under attack if we wait here long, sir. We are vulnerable without air support.' Dave detected a hint of accusation in the young officer's voice, because the major had told them to continue even when air support had been withdrawn. It was just like

375

Chalfont-Prick to blame the major, thought Dave, when it was his own fucking fault for not Barmaring.

'I'll get you some firepower as soon as I can if you need it,' said the OC.

'No EOD and no air support, sir, plus the bomb has caused us a few equipment failures – for instance the Vallon has been damaged and so we only have the mine-detection kit from the other Mastiff. If I deny the vehicle, sir, then we could move forward to PB Red Sox,' said Chalfont-Price.

Dave hated to see vehicles destroyed by their own forces. Not just because it was like torching a bank vault full of fifty-pound notes but because destroying your own kit always felt like a small defeat. He hoped that the OC would refuse permission.

There was a long pause before the answer came.

'No. Don't deny it. Just stay where you are. When Patrol Minimize is lifted we'll send you some firepower.'

'Have you any idea how long that will be, sir?' the young officer persisted. Dave thought he was pushing his luck with the major and, sure enough, the OC snapped back at him.

'I'm not the fucking Met Office, Second Lieutenant. They say the dust storm will only last a few hours but of course no one really knows.'

'Sir,' Chalfont-Price confirmed stiffly.

'I'll get you recovery as soon as I can,' the major told him more amicably. 'In the meantime, Sergeant Henley must stay alert in PB Red Sox.'

'Yessir,' said Dave quickly. 'Of course, we can't cover the dead zone. But we're watching the area.'

'The IED was in a dead zone?' demanded the major. 'Charlie One Zero, can't you currently be seen by either PB?'

'No, sir.'

'An insurgent's paradise. Were you Barmaring when the IED exploded, Second Lieutenant?'

'No, sir. The Americans Barmaed a few hours ago and I understood that they were then watching this area from the air.'

'Who told you that? Because there are no Americans in the air. By now everyone is grounded.'

'At lunch, one of the American officers I ate with said they were watching the track to the PB. I assumed they were using a drone.'

Dave thought: That fucking steak has a lot to answer for.

'Precisely which officer told you that?' demanded the OC.

'Er . . . I didn't catch his name, sir.'

There was another ominous pause.

'It is unwise to abandon standard drills on the basis of intelligence which an unnamed US Marine throws around over a rib-eye, Second Lieutenant. However, we'll discuss this later.' The major's tone was even. Too even. It meant that he was furious and trying to keep his anger under strict control, for now anyway. Dave felt his own anger surge. The men's lives had been risked because their twat of a commander had failed to follow drills. Thank God no one had been badly hurt.

Jenny remembered the first time she came to Tinnington House, for her interview. How she hadn't known where to park and had felt small and intimidated by its size. Now she parked at the front of the house next to Eugene's car and let herself in.

Eugene heard her and came down the long corridor to greet her.

377

'I'm wearing jeans because it's Sunday. I hope that's all right,' she said.

'Of course. What have you done to that finger?'

'Peeled it.'

'Ow.'

'I'll feel it for a few days. But I've managed to tie the bandage so it won't affect my typing.'

They were walking through the house together now but instead of going to the office, he led her to the dining room. She had never been in here before. There were pictures of people from long ago around the walls. It had high ceilings and arched windows, and an enormous log fire crackled at one end.

'I lit the fire first thing this morning to make sure the room was warm enough to work in. Is it OK?' he asked.

She nodded. Across the middle of the room was a huge, polished dining table.

'Look,' he said.

The table was groaning, but not with food. With piles of paper.

Jenny turned to him and grinned. 'What that table says to me is that we'll be working all night.'

'Don't panic. It's not as bad as it seems. First we have to collate it all. Then we have to type it up with all the comments and changes people have made.'

'Has everyone given them to us?'

'Except Douglas-Coombs. No surprises there.'

'Have you rung him?'

'Yes, he says he's working on it now and we'll have it in a few hours.'

Jenny put down her large leather handbag, the one which contained everything including a small screwdriver, and began to walk along the table, peering at each pile.

'Shall I make us a coffee?' asked Eugene.

'I'd love one. And while you're doing that, I'll start.'

She began to leaf through individual piles, nodding occasionally. When she glanced up, she was surprised to see he was still standing in the doorway, watching her. She moved to the next pile and when she looked up a few minutes later he had gone.

31

The wheel station was blown on the front mastiff. When the ground around it had been cleared for mines, the driver examined it, shaking his head.

'If we could get the other wagon in front we might just about be able to tow it . . .' he said doubtfully. With the one functioning Vallon the men had made a track within the track between the two vehicles. It was marked with blue spray paint. Now the driver joined Sections 2 and 3, who were crouched inside a wobbly blue line around the second Mastiff, having a brew and heating rations.

'I think it would be better to blow the thing up but the major's not having that,' said Chalfont-Price gloomily, looking at the other Mastiff. 'He's determined to fix us here.'

Aaron thought that for once the man seemed human. He was sitting with his platoon, his hands clasped around a mug of tea as if it was a cold day in Wiltshire.

'We don't want to blow it up if we can help it,' said the driver of the second vehicle.

The driver of the exploded Mastiff lit a cigarette. He had a bandage tied around his head and there was a small bloodstain soaking through it. 'Nah. Not unless you want to make me cry,' he said.

'It's just fucking typical that the other Vallon kit was damaged in the blast,' said Chalfont-Price. 'Right now it's the bit of kit we need the most.' His arm was bandaged towards the top and there was an obvious tear in his camouflage. But the graze was slight; Aaron Baker knew that, because he had bandaged the boss himself.

'We could be fixed for a while,' sighed the second lieutenant. 'And unfortunately my kit's right over there.'

He pointed to a Bergen which had been blown thirty metres into a field from the top of the Mastiff as if a giant hand had picked it up and dropped it there. Nearby were strewn two others.

'So's mine,' said Mara, indicating his own kit.

'So's mine,' said O'Sullivan, his voice heavy with misery.

'A lifetime's supply of peanuts lies rotting in that field,' said Danny Jones. 'It must be killing you, Paddy.'

'Want to risk your life Barmaring out to it?' suggested Gayle.

'Maybe we should sound the Last Post for all them little silver bags,' said Andy Kirk.

O'Sullivan only said: 'I'm hungry.'

'All right, all right, it's coming,' said Jason Swift, who was cooking something nearby for the men whose rations were now lying in a field.

As they ate, Aaron noticed the boss throwing anxious glances at his kit bag.

'What crop is that?' Chalfont-Price suddenly asked irritably.

The men shrugged.

'Not poppies,' said one.

'Not marijuana,' said another.

'We rely on Jack Binns from 1 Section to answer our burning agricultural questions,' said Jason Swift.

By way of explanation, Jonas added: 'He's from Dorset.'

'Ah. No wonder,' said the boss.

A voice said: 'I think it's cotton, sir.'

They all turned to look at Gerry McKinley, who reddened slightly.

'Really? Are you from Dorset too?' asked the boss.

Aaron thought it was amazing that Chalfont-Price had no idea where any of his men were from. But of course he never asked or showed the smallest interest in them. Aaron was sure that was one of the reasons Dave hated the commander. You could see it on the sergeant's face at prayers, whenever the boss gave orders or was seen swaggering around at Bastion with his officer mates. And you could see Dave biting back angry, sarcastic retorts when the boss was rude to him. Aaron Baker didn't know how Dave stopped himself from criticizing the boss in front of his men but he never, ever did.

'No, sir,' said Gerry McKinley. 'I'm from Norfolk. But I saw cotton growing in America once and this looks a bit the same.'

The boss nodded. Aaron noticed that he continued to throw anxious glances at his kit.

The radio crackled into life. Reports came in that the FOB was under fire. Gradually the reports became more urgent. The FOB was under determined and sustained attack.

'This isn't looking good,' said Jason Swift. 'No air support and now they won't be able to get out of the FOB to us either.'

It was hard to believe that there was a battle raging back at FOB Nevada. They were surrounded by silence. Just once or twice they heard the distant bass of artillery.

When it was time to change the men on stag, Aaron took Fife off the .50 cal and told O'Sullivan to replace him. The HMG had been lifted off the compromised wagon and carried back down the blue lane and mounted on to the second wagon instead of the gimpy.

There was the rustle of noise and activity when the men changed over and settled into their new positions. People moved around inside the blue line as though it was a high electric fence which they must not touch instead of some spray paint on the desert floor. The call to prayer sounded across the Green Zone and the desert as if it was swelling out of the ground. Then the voice stopped and the men were still and the afternoon was quiet again. Nearby were a couple of compound walls and from inside came the occasional shout of children playing and then a woman calling. Aaron Baker thought that women yelling to their kids sounded the same all over the world: the voice could belong to his mum telling his kid brothers to get inside for their tea.

The boss was still listening to the radio, his face alarmed.

'There are now four PBs under attack as well as a very major assault on FOB Nevada,' he said. 'This is certainly a Taliban strategy in response to the handover from the Americans.'

'They probably worked it all out a long time ago. They've just been waiting for a personnel change,' said Aaron.

'Four PBs and a FOB, that's a lot of ragheads,' said Swift.

Danny Jones shook his head. 'They couldn't have

planned for a fucking sandstorm grounding air support. You have to ask yourself whose side Allah's on.'

'The ragheads don't have to ask themselves. They *know*,' said Gerry McKinley.

'Wish I could be so sure of anything the way they are,' muttered Andy Kirk.

The second driver rearranged his back against the wheel of the Mastiff, kicking up a small cloud of dust with his feet. 'I'm sure of one thing. If Allah keeps Terry Taliban tied up down there, it's good for us. If he lets Terry Taliban drift this way, we're in trouble.'

They listened. What little battle noise they could hear sounded reassuringly distant.

The sun was sinking towards the horizon now. Further down in the Green Zone a boy chased six goats larger than he was. A man with a camel passed along a track on the other side of the canal. He did not look at them. No one came near.

'They know this track has got mines sprinkled around on it like fucking pepper,' said the bandaged driver. 'That's why no one walks along it.'

The boss wrinkled his brow. 'But there's nothing to stop someone crossing the field and taking my kit.'

'We're showing a lot of weapons, sir. I don't think anyone's going to risk nicking your kit,' said Aaron.

'Not with me on the fucking HMG they won't,' shouted O'Sullivan from the turret. 'If Terry Taliban goes near my peanuts he's dead meat.'

'Even if they send a little kid?' asked the driver of the second Mastiff.

'Ha! Especially if they send a little kid!'

'Yeah, well, let's get real,' said the driver with the bloodstained bandage. 'If they ambush us and they've got enough firepower, they can get their hands on the kit, the wagon and us too.'

Aaron saw Chalfont-Price's look of alarm. Trust a fucking driver to look on the bright side.

'And anyway,' the second driver went on, 'once it's dark it won't be so easy to watch those Bergens.'

Andy Kirk picked up his tone. 'The ragheads haven't been for the Bergens yet because they're just waiting until night.'

'The way the kit's sitting right out in the field, Terry Taliban probably thinks Allah just dropped a big present,' added Jonas.

'Yeah, gift-wrapped,' Fife agreed.

Aaron rolled his eyes. So all those anxious looks which the boss kept throwing at his kit had not been lost on the lads. Chalfont-Price was not popular and men loved a chance to play on his fears.

'For Chrissake, boys, we've got fucking night sights and we can keep an eye on the kit,' Aaron said gruffly.

But now the boss's attention had switched from the Bergens to the sky.

'I think it's getting dark already,' he said.

Still enjoying his discomfort, the men agreed. 'Yep. Won't be long now, sir.'

Chalfont-Price suddenly jumped to his feet.

'Look, it's not just my rations in there. It's some sensitive stuff,' he said. 'Mapping. Signals document-ation. It's all secret.'

Aaron exchanged concerned looks with Jason Swift. They had both guessed what was coming next. Senibua from 3 Section was returning with the Vallon from the area around the compromised vehicle. As he moved towards the rest of the platoon down the blue lane,

Chalfont-Price swung around abruptly to the nearest man.

'You!' he said. He was talking to Gerry McKinley. Aaron guessed that the boss had forgotten, or more likely had never known, McKinley's name. 'Norfolk Man. Grab the Vallon and Barma your way out to my Bergen, would you?'

McKinley blinked at him.

Aaron coughed a little and then said: 'Sir, since it's getting dark we should clear as much of the area around the Mastiff as we can now.'

The boss turned to him.

'I don't think you understand, Corporal. That Bergen is vulnerable to attack and it contains compromising information. Retrieving it *must* be a priority.'

There was a silence. Then Senibua started passing McKinley the protection kit.

'Sir, McKinley did a long stint on the Vallon earlier,' said Aaron. McKinley and Senibua had both trained extensively on the mine detector and were probably the fastest men in the platoon on it if there were no sappers around. But you couldn't keep twenty men hanging about while two did all the work, not when most had taken some level of Vallon training.

'I'll go, sir,' said Jason Swift.

'No,' said Aaron. It was daft to send a corporal on the boss's Bergen mission. He looked around at the men to choose someone else.

'I'll go,' offered Jonas.

But McKinley was already putting on the protection.

'I don't mind,' he said. 'It's better than sitting here and just waiting.'

'What happened to those mine-protection pelvic overpants we trialled back on the Plain?' asked Jonas.

'Yeah, it would have been a lot more useful to trial them here,' said Senibua.

'I don't need them. I'll go careful.' McKinley took the visor.

'I've got the Vallon set high,' Senibua said, 'or every little bit of shrapnel sets it off.'

'Yeah, I'll keep it high or it'll take me all night to get to the Bergen,' agreed McKinley.

He set off down the blue-sprayed path. The others watched him. He reached the damaged Mastiff and then turned. Swinging the Vallon in front of him, he stepped outside the blue paint which marked the safe zone.

The PB was quiet before dark. The drivers had put up bashas and were already asleep under them and so was Doc Holliday. Mal and Angus were cooking. Binns was on stag on the gate, Streaky Bacon had just changed places with Slindon, who was now back up in the tower, and Dave had been inside the compound with Sol reviewing the ammo and listening on the radio to reports of the mighty battles raging at other PBs and back at FOB Nevada. It was the smell of Mal's cooking which had pulled them outside in time to hear Slindon say: 'Holy shit!'

And behind his words came the thud of an exploding landmine. Its boom seemed to echo down inside Dave, so deeply that he knew instinctively that it had blasted a hole at the base of his world.

Sol looked up at Slindon.

'Where was it?'

As if they didn't know.

'There! In the dead zone! I saw the flash and now I can see the smoke. Hoooooooly shiiiiit.'

Dave did not move. He waited. He listened to the radio so intently that his whole body was nothing more than an appendage attached to his ear.

After a long silence, he heard: 'This is Charlie One Zero to Zero. IED. Man down. Sit rep to follow. Wait. Out.' It was a strangely clipped version of Chalfont-Price's voice.

Dave wasn't here in the compound any more. He was across the desert, two kilometres away, with two Mastiffs which were fixed in one spot, sitting ducks for any weaponry or explosives the enemy cared to unleash on them. The anxious faces of his men gathered around him brought him back to the present, to the compound, to the sound of his own voice moaning: 'Fuck, fuck, fuck,' to the knowledge that he was here, not there. And if he had been there, would it have happened? One of his men was down, and, without knowing which one, Dave felt the dead weight on his shoulders.

'Zero this is Charlie One Zero. Sit rep as at 1745. Zap number MK4452 has been badly injured. Can't yet assess extent. Lower limb injury. Put tourniquet on his leg himself. Request urgent medical aid at grid 626298.'

'MK . . .' said Dave out loud. He knew whose zap number that was.

'Gerry! Gerry McKinley!' shouted the men who stood around him. 'Shit, Gerry McKinley's down!'

Quietly, the group was joined by Doc Holliday.

'He's not a T4, he's injured. Lower leg. They're Barmaring to him,' Dave said, cutting off the end of his own sentence to listen to the major's voice in his ear.

'Zero Alpha to Charlie One Zero, why did he apply his own tourniquet? Can't you get to him?' demanded the OC.

'He was Barmaring into a field.'

388

'So you're Barmaring out to him now, are you?'

'No, sir, we only had one working Vallon. And it's just been blown up with the casualty.'

Dave and the major both gave a sharp intake of breath.

'Fucking hell,' said the major. 'You'll have to send the men prodding forward slowly on their belt buckles.'

'Yes, sir. A helicopter would help now, sir.'

'There are no fucking helicopters!'

'Sir, the front vehicle is still immobilized. Do you still want me to hold fast until assistance arrives? Or should I now deny the vehicle?'

The major told him to wait. There was a long pause. Finally the radio crackled back into action.

'Charlie One Zero this is Zero Alpha. You are to remain where you are until I can organize a recovery plan to get you out. Be aware that there are still no helicopters. Be aware that at this location we are under very sustained attack. Be aware also that there is sustained attack at other locations and we have casualties. Out.'

Dave was quick. During the radio silence he had been thinking rapidly and now no more thought was necessary.

He said: 'Hello Zero Alpha and Charlie One Zero, this is Charlie One One. At this location I have a CMT Class 1. I will now move from here to your grid ref with Vallons to give assistance. I will also bring tow ropes. Will I be able to pull your immobilized vehicle on a straight bar, Charlie One Zero?'

There was no mistaking the relief in Chalfont-Price's voice.

'Charlie One One, we are badly in need of Vallons and a class 1 medic and your offer is accepted. I confirm that you will be able to tow the vehicle.' His voice was

389

shaky, shocked and even, for once, humble. Dave looked up and saw that Doc Holliday was there, nodding.

'What is your ETA?' the boss asked anxiously.

Dave said: 'Well, if you're prodding your way to the casualty we should be there to help with a Vallon kit before you've even finished the job.'

Chalfont-Price did not reply but Dave paused for the major to argue with him. After all, this was a high-risk strategy. He was proposing to leave the PB under-manned and venture, undermanned, into a world of total exposure to the enemy. But without a good medic Gerry McKinley's chances of survival were insignificant.

He remained braced for a challenge from the major, but, amazingly, none came.

Dave looked around at the waiting men. He spoke quickly and firmly.

'I want to be out of here in fifteen minutes with both Mastiffs and a tow rope. I'll go in the first one. I'll take a gunner, Doc and two more men, one to Barma and one to cover him. In the second wagon we'll have a driver, a commander and a gunner: that wagon will have to bring back the men from the exploded vehicle. Shit, Sol, that's not leaving you with enough men here at the base.'

Before he had finished speaking Doc Holliday had melted away again and was even now shuffling around, gathering equipment together for their exodus. His rasping voice suddenly issued from under the basha: 'I can fire an HMG. And I'm handy with a rifle. So save yourself a man in the first Mastiff.'

Dave nodded.

'Yeah. Thanks, Doc. And when I think about it, I can

390

command from on top. So I'll take a driver, you, and two others.'

'That leaves four men here,' said Sol.

'Can you manage?'

'If you're quick.'

Dave looked around at the remaining faces. It was easy to tell who wanted to go on the mission and who dreaded they would be picked.

Sol said suddenly: 'Sarge, there's only one driver! Reed's ankle!'

Dave jumped as though Sol had delivered a small electric shock.

'Can anyone else drive a Mastiff?'

Tiny said: 'Well, I had some lessons at Catterick . . .'

'You were good!' said Slindon. 'I remember that. I was useless.'

'No surprises there, mate,' Finny told him.

'It was really basic. I'm not sure I could—'

'Lancer Reed, take Rifleman Hemmings and give him a five-minute refresher course in driving the Mastiff,' Dave instructed. Reed started to stagger to his feet. Angus tried to help by grabbing him eagerly and pulling him up.

'Fuck off, oaf!' the driver protested, pushing Angry away and hobbling painfully through the compound with Tiny. 'And as for you driving the fucking thing,' Reed said, 'do you know how long it took me just to master reversing? It's one of the most heavily armoured vehicles on active service but if you think you can just get in and drive it . . .!'

He limped off, still moaning audibly, Tiny loping awkwardly behind him.

Dave looked around at the other faces.

'Sol, can you cope with the numbers you've got? You

can bet that the moment we leave the patrol base, it's going to come under attack.'

'The moment you leave the patrol base, *you're* going to come under attack,' Sol corrected him.

'Yeah, of course. But we're only going about two k down the track. Since we've been dicking it, we won't need to Barma so we should be there in a few minutes. Then once we reach the relief, we're safe and you're going to come under fire.'

'They'll throw everything they've got at you for two kilometres.'

'I'm hoping they're all too busy fighting down at the FOB to come all the way out here.'

'The enemy has enough guys to phone for reinforcements.'

'By the time they can mobilize we'll be over in the Bronx with a tow rope, the Vallons and the medic. And before they can get here we'll be back at the PB.'

Sol's eyes rested a moment on Dave.

'That's the best scenario,' he said.

'Yeah,' said Dave. He knew he had to prepare for the worst. But what was the worst that could happen? Probably an ambush when they were isolated on the track. Surely they would have reached the relief before the enemy could organize itself to react effectively to their surprise exit?

'Who, Sarge?' asked a voice. A keen, urgent soldier's voice. 'Who're you taking?'

'You, Billy Finn,' said Dave. 'You're gunner on the .50 cal. But when we leave the compound here, I'll command from on top because I'll need a good view.'

Finn's face broke into a smile and he immediately left the group to prepare.

Dave looked at Mal. His mouth was still, while his

lean face and dark eyes were saying: 'Choose me!' Mal was the sort of fighter Dave wanted for this mission. But he shook his head.

'I can't take you, Mal,' he said. 'I'd be leaving the PB with no medic.'

He looked away quickly, but not quickly enough to miss Mal's disappointment.

His eye ran across the line of faces and Jamie Dermott came into his mind. It was times like this you needed an outstanding soldier like Jamie. Each time he looked around for Jamie Dermott and remembered again that he was dead he felt a small shock and he felt it again now.

'Right,' he said. 'I'll take Finny, Doc Holliday and Angry McCall in the first Mastiff with me and the driver.'

McCall's face lit up like Christmas lights.

'Thanks, Sarge!'

He ran off at once.

'In the second there'll be Tiny driving, Binns commanding from the front and Bacon on top with a Minimi. That leaves you with two gimpys, Sol.'

He turned to Binns and Bacon, who had not moved, as if Dave was going to give them further orders. Binns's eyes had opened wide.

'Get moving, you two,' Dave told them. 'You need to work on reversing together because only Streaky on top will be able to see where you're going. Binman, eat something now and make sure you take plenty of rations.'

'Yes, Sarge.' But Dave knew that pale, sickly look meant that Binns was too nervous to eat.

Binns turned to go with Streaky but paused. He said: 'I've never commanded anything before, ever, Sarge.'

393

'I know. But I've chosen you because I think you can do it. I'll be just ahead of you in the first wagon and Bacon will be on top with the Minimi.'

'Yes,' said Binman. 'Yes.'

He retreated into the compound, walking awkwardly behind Bacon. As if Dave had just made him into some new, different, Mastiff-commanding Jack Binns and he wasn't sure how this new Binns walked.

Sol said: 'Sure you don't want the other gimpy?' He looked tired. His solid frame was suddenly smaller.

'We'll be OK with a Minimi on one wagon and the .50 cal on the other as long as we stick together.'

Sol nodded.

'You could be the one taking a big hit back here,' said Dave. 'If they realize how short of men you are, they might bombard you instead of ambushing me.'

Sol grimaced. 'Or they might bombard me as well as ambushing you.'

Dave did not meet his eye for a moment. It was hard enough to go out there undermanned. It was harder still if he went out unsupported by his best corporal. He looked straight at Sol and said: 'Sol, I'm doing this because McKinley could die if we don't go.'

'I know. And I know that we could lose even more men trying to get to him.'

'It's a risk we have to take,' said Dave.

'Yeah. You're right. We have to do this.' Sol managed to grin. An anxious grin, but it was the gesture of support Dave needed.

The men Dave had named were all busy preparing themselves and their weapons for the mission: the PB had turned from a sleepy late-afternoon base to a hive of activity. Soldiers ran around and outside there was more firing, as if the enemy had heard every word Dave had said and was limbering up for a serious battle the moment he drove out of the gates.

Dave was ready to join the men but something was bothering him. The radio had been silent all this time. There had been no further word from the boss. Stranger still, the major, back at the FOB, apparently had no response to his plan at all.

He stared at the radio, as if that would make the major talk to him. It took a moment to realize that there was no light on. The radio was silent because it was dead.

He shouted for a new radio battery, striding off towards the vehicles, and someone threw him a spare. He fixed it into the radio and switched on thankfully.

'This is Charlie One One to Zero Alpha. Please confirm that you—'

He stopped. The radio was without hiss, crackle or splutter. He shook it a few times. No light.

'Zero Alpha . . . ?'

The radio threw dead sound back at him. It had not heard his words. It had received none and sent none.

'Shit!'

He delivered the battery into the hands of Lancer Reed, who was shouting something about clutches or brakes at Tiny. The driver's bad ankle was elevated at an awkward angle against the side of the Mastiff and he was yelling at Tiny through the open door.

'What?' demanded Reed rudely when he was interrupted. Swinging around he realized that it was Dave who had tugged at his arm and quickly added: 'Sarge?'

'This fucking battery's dead too,' said Dave. He glanced up at Tiny's face, red, shining and anxious, behind the wheel of the Mastiff.

The Lancer rolled his eyes. 'I had a nasty feeling

someone threw a dodgy one in . . .' he admitted, lifting his ankle carefully, with two hands, off the Mastiff and lowering it to the ground.

'We've got three batteries and two of them are down. Just get me the third,' Dave said.

Reed limped off to the back of the wagon.

'All right, all right, it's been on charge.'

'How long has it been on charge?' demanded Dave, following him. From the corner of his eye he saw Tiny Hemmings's long legs stamping on the foot pedals of the Mastiff and his hands busy with levers, practising something Reed had shown him. On top, Streaky was looking behind and directing him on PRR.

'Good,' Dave told them approvingly. Except it was just the ghost of a practice. They weren't really reversing or carrying out any manoeuvre. He looked at his watch and then up in the air to assess the way the sky was thickening into darkness. Last time he had looked the sky had still been a light blue. Now it was navy. Next it would be black. No time for driving lessons.

He became aware that Reed was swearing loudly in the back of the wagon.

'Fuck, fuck! Who the fuck? What fucker's fucking done this?'

'I'm guessing maybe that battery isn't charged?' asked Dave, his heart sinking, involuntarily looking back up at the sky to assess it again. Was it darker than it had been a moment ago? How long could they wait for the radio battery to get a bit of charge in it?

But Lancer Reed was howling now: 'Oh fuuuuuuuck, when I find the fuuuuuuucker who did this . . . !'

His threats brought the busy base to a halt. The enemy continued to fire but no one fired back. People began to gather around the back of the Mastiff; men who stayed in their firing positions strained to hear. Even Hemmings got out of the driver's seat and Bacon came down from on top. Reed appeared, his face bulging with fury.

'OK, who did it? Tell me? Which of you little shits decided to charge his iPod or Christ knows what with my inverter? Which of you bastards done it? Come on, own up!'

The men stared at him silently.

Lancer Dawson appeared, his hands on his hips, shaking his head.

'You bastards can*not* keep your hands off the inverter, can you? No wonder REME gets so fucking pissed off!'

'We don't have time to mess around blaming people,' said Dave. 'Right now, just put the battery on charge.'

'I can't! Because the fucking inverter's blown! I can't charge fuck all!'

There was an awful silence.

'You can't charge the radio battery . . .' echoed Dave. He looked from Lancer Dawson to Lancer Reed. 'But don't we have another inverter?'

The two drivers shook their heads in unison. Dave thought they looked like nodding fucking dogs in the back of someone's souped-up car.

'Let's get this straight,' he said slowly. 'You put the radio battery on charge but it didn't work because—'

'Because some bastard decided to use my fucking inverter for his own fucking personal use when he didn't know which way round to put the croc clips. So he's only gone and blown it. That's all!'

'Blown it . . .' said Dave, his voice very clear and very quiet. 'And so we have one knackered radio battery and two which aren't charged and no way of doing anything about it.'

'Yep!' chorused the drivers.

Driver Dawson turned to Reed.

'It was Slindon,' he said, simply. 'Before he went on stag he wanted to recharge his iPad. It was fucking Blue Balls Slindon!'

Reed looked as if he was going to boil with rage.

'I'm going to get him,' he announced, glancing over at the tower, which was just visible rising above the inner courtyard and where Slindon was even now returning enemy fire, oblivious to the greater fury aimed at him inside the base. 'And he tried to cover up what he did by putting the croc clips back on so we wouldn't notice! Fuck it, I don't care if my ankle's broken, I'm going to get that little bastard and . . .'

Dave felt a new, strange quiet.

'Shuddup, Lancer Reed,' he said. 'If anyone's going to deal with Slindon it's me. Later. You're here to deal with the enemy, not my men. I don't want fighting or arguing inside this base, not with the enemy right outside it.' He looked around. Doc Holliday was ready, silently waiting with his rifle and day sack by the other wagon.

'Are you still going?' asked Sol. 'With no radio?'

'Yes,' said Dave, glancing up once more at the sky. 'My last radio message was to the boss that we're on our way with a medic for McKinley. So that's what we're doing. Get ready to open the gates.'

Two men ran to the gates. Those who were going put on night-vision goggles and scrambled on board the vehicles. Angus got into the first Mastiff while Finn was up on top with the HMG. Lancer Dawson started the engine. Binns and Bacon high-fived before climbing into the second wagon.

'Good luck, Streaky,' said Binns, his voice bleak.

'Good luck, Binman, my friend, I mean Commander Binns. Remember I'm just on top!'

'Yeah. Remember I'm just in front.'

They gave each other grim half-grins and then took up their positions. At the front of their Mastiff, Tiny succeeded in starting the engine. He gave Dave a surprised thumbs-up.

'Go for it, Sarge,' said Sol.

'See you in an hour if it all goes according to plan,' said Dave. 'As soon as air support can take off again they'll get here when they realize we've lost comms. They could be here before we're back.'

'Yeah,' agreed Sol. He looked unconvinced but held his hand out to Dave. 'Good luck, Sarge.'

Dave climbed into the back of the first wagon. Angus, Doc and Finn were sitting there and the door slammed shut behind him.

'Ammo's ready for you on the HMG, Sarge,' said Finn.

'You're at the front with the driver,' Dave told him. Finn unstrapped himself and clambered into the front seat and Dave took up his position on the plate which raised him up behind the HMG. He had a 360-degree view. He thought to himself that he should command more often from up here.

Dave looked down at Sol, who raised a hand.

'OK, open the gates and let's go,' he said on PRR.

Dave's last sight in the base was Sol's broad face distorted with concern. Well, for Chrissake, Dave thought as Lancer Dawson drove the Mastiff up to the gates, we're going two k up the track and it's been dicked so nothing's going to blow up in our faces. We just have to pick up a casualty, some men and a broken-down truck and drive back again. It's not much different from picking up a Chinese takeaway and rushing home to eat it before it can go cold. So what's all the fucking fuss about?

But Dave's stomach ached and churned as the gates began to swing apart. He glanced at his watch again. It was less than fifteen minutes since he had first formulated the rescue plan. In that time the temperature had fallen and the sky had deepened through many shades of blue. The first stars were visible overhead. A faint crescent moon looked like a fingernail someone had bitten off and thrown skywards. This twilight would turn to darkness in just a few more minutes. It would be pitch black even before they reached the casualty. Night-vision goggles? Check. He knew they were in the day sack in the canoe bag along with the camera Jenny had given him.

The gates were wide enough now and before them the desert glimmered to one side. Ahead the leafy Green Zone looked like an immense streak of darkness. Creating a vast bubble of dust around them, they thundered out on to the track.

32

'We're working through this faster than I thought,' said Eugene. 'You really are amazing.'

Jenny smiled. 'It's a long time since anyone called me that.' Well, anyone except Eugene.

'Shall we take a short lunch break and go to the village pub?'

'As long as it's just a short lunch break.'

'I'd like to talk to you about something. I mean, something which is nothing whatsoever to do with the defence committee review.'

She picked up the leather handbag and they drove down to the village in the Range Rover. Jenny had never been in one before. Her father had owned a van so as a child she had been used to sitting high above the other traffic. But not in this sort of luxury. The Range Rover smelled nice and its engine was so quiet that they could talk without raising their voices.

They found a table and ordered rapidly.

'Don't you want to take a selection from our Sunday carvery, General?' asked the waitress.

'Sorry, Mary, not today. We only have time for a sandwich,' Eugene told her.

Jenny was aware that her presence in the pub with Eugene was attracting a lot of staff attention. They all took the opportunity to stare at her as they passed.

'Do you often eat here alone?' she asked.

'Not so much now that I'm learning to cook more. But I did when Fiona first went. Ate here and probably drank too much. The staff were all very nice to me.'

'What did you want to talk to me about?' Jenny asked him curiously.

'Thank you for being so kind when my divorce papers arrived.'

'I'm glad you weren't alone when you got the letter.'

'I explained to you that Fiona tried hard to clean me out and I only hung on to the house by the skin of my teeth. The house does matter a lot to me. I really felt that if I lost that I'd lost everything.'

'It's very big for one person,' said Jenny.

'A time will come when it's too big, but not yet. And it feels full enough when my brother and his family all arrive from Singapore.'

'It must cost a lot to run.'

'If I want to stay there, I'm going to have to produce a bit more income. That's what I wanted to tell you. Believe it or not, I might just be able to do that soon.'

Jenny looked at him. Her heart began to beat faster. She felt as though he was about to say something significant, and significant to her.

'I've been offered a job.'

She stared at him. For some reason, she wanted to object violently.

'But you've already got a job!'

'Not really. The defence committee is a one-off and we've nearly finished with that now. I do a bit of commentary and consulting . . . but not much.'

'What sort job have you been offered?' she asked.

'It's in Libya.'

'*Libya!*'

'A nation which is anxious to rebuild itself. The United Nations is sending people out to both observe and advise – in fact, the Libyans have requested it. I'd be advising them on military matters.'

Jenny felt herself plunging into sadness. She didn't know why his news affected her so deeply but she knew that if she let herself she could cry. So it was important not to let herself.

'But . . . when?'

'I'd start quite soon.'

Men were always going somewhere. They were always leaving. Dave was always piling on to a bus to Brize Norton, or he was off in some big army vehicle going training. And now Eugene was doing the same. She realized one of the things she liked about Eugene was that he was always there, always at Tinnington. And now he was going.

'Would you have to live in Libya?'

'I'd spend quite a bit of time there.'

'Is it safe?'

He laughed. 'That's a good one, coming from the wife of a front-line soldier!'

Their sandwiches arrived. Mary took the opportunity to sneak glances at Jenny, grinning broadly.

When she had gone, Jenny asked: 'Eugene, do you want this job? Or are you just doing it for money?'

He laughed again. 'Well, money isn't such a bad motive for doing a job, is it? I certainly wouldn't do it for *no* money. It will be both very interesting and very demanding. I simply don't know what to expect out there but not only will my experience be useful to the

Libyans, everything I learn might be interesting for the British.'

Jenny felt desolate. She did not know why. She said: 'You're speaking as if it's all signed and sealed.'

'It isn't. Yet. But if I agree to take it, I'll be away for the best part of six months. My daughter and her family would come and live in the house for that period. My problem, Jennifer, is what to do about you.'

She sighed. 'My job's not looking very long-term all of a sudden, Eugene.' Was anything long-term? Or was life just a series of brief events, full of fleeting relationships and friendships which could be easily snapped?

'That's something we should discuss.'

'Let's wait until we know for sure that you're going,' she said wearily. 'Today we should concentrate on the report.'

His eyes found hers. He reached out and, just for a moment, stroked her hand.

It was like driving into a swarm of killer bees. Within a few metres of the gates, rounds began to bounce off the Mastiff. Dave's stomach turned and turned again, like a washing machine. Misgivings about the expedition assailed him as inside his head he heard Sol's voice, worried and puzzled: 'We could lose even more men trying to get to him.'

McKinley. Dave focused on him. Didn't he have two, or was it three, little kids with reddish hair? Dave had a vague memory of coming home to find the living room full of red-haired people. Rose McKinley and her kids were having tea with Jenny. And he remembered seeing Gerry and Rose on the dance floor at the Dorchester. Rose was the shy, smiling type who didn't say much if she didn't know you. Now she had a husband without a leg. And if the Mastiff didn't get there in time, maybe no husband at all.

They were heading due west. In a moment, just before it hit the canal, the track would turn ninety degrees and from there it was a straight line south to the relief party and McKinley. Firing was coming from the south-west at the moment. He swung the Heavy Machine Gun around and let it rip in that direction.

'That gave the ragheads something to think about,' said Finny on PRR into the silence.

'Can you speed up, Lancer Dawson?' asked Dave. 'They're chucking the fuck of a lot at us.' Had the enemy been silently massing its forces? Or had they been here in such numbers all along? Waiting quietly?

The driver accelerated. 'Ever wonder if they listen to our radios? I mean, it's like they knew we were coming.'

Firing started again from the enemy. An RPG exploded a hundred metres to the north-west of them.

Dave did not fire back because both gimpys were suddenly busy from the base.

'We're covering you,' came Sol's voice on PRR. A voice could be heard swearing near him. Dave was not sure who it was but there was certainly some confusion audible in the background before Sol clicked off.

The enemy was throwing rounds at the Mastiff now, like handfuls of deadly dirt. Dave went back to work on the HMG.

Then Sol came on again: 'Problem on the second wagon. Can you hang around a bit?'

Lancer Dawson heard this and groaned. 'We're not hanging around in this, look!' At the same moment, an RPG crossed their path before exploding in the desert just behind them, throwing up an ugly storm of stones and dust.

'See,' said Lancer Dawson. 'If I'd been "hanging around" that would have—'

'The second wagon still isn't out of the base!' Dave yelled.

Sol said over PRR: 'Mastiff's stalled.' Voices, possibly those of Tiny and Lancer Reed, could still be heard shouting in the background.

'Well, restart it!' ordered Dave.

'Trying. He's flooded it or something.'

'Won't restart?'

PRR in these conditions was so short range that Dave knew they would very soon be losing contact with the base.

'We can't do this alone,' he said. 'If the second vehicle isn't out of the gate in thirty seconds, we'll have to turn back.'

'Oh fucking hell,' said Lancer Dawson. They had nearly reached that point where the track hit the canal and bent round to the south. Dave estimated that the corner was about a quarter of the way to the wrecked vehicle, the casualty and the relief party. A quarter of the way and if they now drove back through their own dust storm they would have covered half the distance and got nowhere. Shit.

'That bend's the place to turn,' said Dave. 'It's wide enough.' The bend had been fattened by a succession of vehicles cutting the corner.

The driver repeated: 'Fucking hell.'

Dave demanded: 'Is the other vehicle moving yet?'

'It's not starting,' confirmed Sol. 'And we're coming under very heavy fire in here. So are you. We're still trying to cover you.'

'OK, we'll abort. Close the gates until we get there,' Dave told Sol wearily. So that was the end of their mission. And maybe the end of McKinley too. Rose McKinley's face appeared inside Dave's head. She looked quiet and sad. Dave silently apologized to her.

'I knew that big lanky kid couldn't drive a Mastiff,' said Lancer Dawson. 'I just fucking knew it.'

'Turn back,' Dave ordered him firmly. 'It's not safe to go on.'

'It's not safe to go back,' Dawson muttered as they approached the bend.

'Ready with the gates?' Dave asked Sol. There was no reply. So they were now outside the range of PRR. No radios and now they couldn't even talk to base. They were alone in the desert without comms, under fire. He suddenly remembered that night extraction exercise on a cold, snowy Welsh landscape. How the signaller had tried to change radio batteries and found he had damaged the spare when he fell on it. Goater. And he had said: 'We'd never be out in the middle of nowhere without comms in theatre, Sarge. Not ever.'

Dave knew the driver could no longer hear him on PRR but he roared down into the Mastiff: 'Turn here! And don't go off this track. Doesn't matter if it's a ten-point turn!'

Even if he had heard, Lancer Dawson would not have had time to react or argue. Only Dave was high enough to see the RPG skimming low across the desert towards them and it took him just a split second to know this would be a direct hit.

He grabbed the handles by the hatch and dropped his body instantly down from the top. His actions were so fast that afterwards he could not remember thinking about it and he had barely a memory of doing it. He swung inside the Mastiff just as the world around them lit up. The huge vehicle seemed weightless for a second, rising up before it was flung, with everyone and everything in it, in a violent circle through the air. Dave felt as though he was flying with suicidal force, his body following somewhere behind him. He was still holding on to the handles as the massive vehicle rolled and twisted, hurtling towards the water of the canal. He saw the splash go up like a flash of light. The water seemed so bright he shut his eyes. The Mastiff squirmed for an instant and then it was still and there was silence.

33

'Holy shit!' breathed Slindon. He was up on the tower but he was not the only one, or even the first, to see the Mastiff crash. The focus of the battle had moved to the other side of the compound now because everyone else was covering Dave's Mastiff from the courtyard by the main gates.

Sol and Mal had been nagging at the enemy with the gimpys as the Mastiff cut across the desert towards the canal at breakneck speed, pursued by enemy fire. When it was clear that the second Mastiff would not move out of the compound and Dave had aborted the mission, Sol watched and waited for Lancer Dawson to slow the first Mastiff and turn it around. But instead it had continued, at speed, towards the canal.

Tiny Hemmings, Lancer Reed and Binns were still arguing about the stalled Mastiff and hadn't really got into firing positions. However, Bacon, on top of the useless Mastiff, had been rattling away with the Minimi.

He saw a bolt of lightning, which must have been an RPG. Then there were sparks flying from somewhere under the vehicle like a welder's shop. A brief pause for the impact on the wheel to take effect. And finally the incredible sight of five thousand kilos of heavy metal rolling on its side once, twice and into the canal.

It settled on its left side, rocking slightly. And then it was menacingly still. Even the enemy was astonished into silence. All weapons at the PB stopped firing.

The men at the base climbed up the Mastiff or gaped through firing holes in the mud walls. They were waiting, waiting, with every corpuscle in their blood vessels, for any sign of life to emerge from the wounded metal monster. But there was none.

Mal erupted suddenly: 'We've got to get out there to them!'

'We can't,' said Sol.

'We've fucking got to!' shouted Streaky.

Tiny Hemmings, his face distraught, said: 'The engine'll start in five minutes. I won't flood it again. I won't get it wrong again.'

Lancer Reed was too shocked to contradict him.

Sol said quietly: 'We're not giving the enemy any more corpses today.'

Binns had started to shake. 'They're not corpses. They're not dead. Sarge isn't dead, neither are the others.'

The men fell silent. Those who were not wearing night-vision goggles yet put them on. No one said a word as they watched for some sign of life in the Mastiff. But there was none.

The enemy had opened fire again, gleefully, energetically. In a few minutes they would start moving forward towards the vehicle.

'Get to your firing positions,' said Sol. 'And give them all you've got.'

Everything was still inside the Mastiff. Everything was quiet.

Dave experienced total helplessness. He was in a new world without sound and without movement. The depth of silence was something he had never known before. Was this the quiet of the grave?

His life spread itself out before him like a tablecloth groaning with good things. Jenny, tall and strong, a small child on one hip, another at her side, smiling at him. There was love in her eyes. Anger and differences were all forgotten now. This was his beautiful Jenny and he loved her and knew that she loved him. But in a short while she would hear the knock at the door and know instinctively what news awaited her. Then, gradually, over many years, she would age. She would be old one day. Jenny would be old without him there to love her and look after her. The girls would be tall and strong and beautiful like their mother and she would have to learn to lean on them for support.

Here were his mother and stepfather in their allotment, proudly examining some bulging vegetable they had plucked from the neat, fertile rows. His mother's mobile phone was ringing, the phone call which would bring them the news of his death and shatter their lives. And here was his own father, a sad and hopeless drunk, who had heard the news and was sitting outside a pub, an empty pint in front of him, his head in his hands. They would all be shocked; their lives would break into small pieces. For a while. Then they would regain their strength and start to rebuild. The world would continue in its own way without him.

Dave felt a sudden, piercing pain inside him. He realized he was grieving for his own lost life. And then he opened his eyes.

He could see the inside of the Mastiff, but the vehicle was at a strange angle. A corner of the dusty windscreen in the cab at the front was visible, splattered with round bubbles of water as if pairs of glasses had been dropped all over it. But something was hiding most of it.

He moved a hand. It was trapped underneath him as if it had not kept up with the twists and turns of the vehicle. He disentangled it without difficulty. He waved it in front of his face. It was gloved but it was certainly his hand, and it had life in it.

He remembered his toes. He moved his head into the strange, horizontal position which enabled him to see his feet. There were his boots with his feet inside them, amazingly still attached to his body.

So he was alive. He turned his head through a curious arc and realized that the cold feeling along his left arm was water. It was impossible to understand if the Mastiff was upside down or sideways on but beneath him was water and the water was rising.

'Fucking hell!'

It was the voice of Angus McCall. That's how Dave knew for sure he was alive.

'Fucking, fucking hell,' breathed Angry again.

'You all right?' Dave asked him gruffly over the sound of sudden and renewed firing. It came from the enemy. It came from the base.

'What happened?' asked Angus.

'IED?' suggested Doc Holliday. Dave was glad to hear the medic's low, grating voice.

'No, RPG,' he said. 'I saw it.'

Rounds were bouncing off the Mastiff's armour. He could hear the rattle of angry answering gimpys from the base.

'The ragheads must think it's Christmas,' came the gloomy voice of the medic again.

So Angus and Doc were talking. Dave felt something

like electricity flow through his body and brain when he realized they had heard nothing from Finny and Dawson in the cab. The electricity powered him. He jumped up. How long had he just been lying here feeling the water rise along the left side of his body when he should have been checking on his men and getting them off the besieged vehicle? A minute? Or sixty minutes?

He was upright now. His right leg hurt but he didn't care. He was tearing at the big box which blocked Finny and Lancer Dawson into the cab. It contained ammo for the .50 cal and it weighed a tonne and neither his pulling hands nor his shoving shoulder shifted it.

He peered around it. Dawson was under water. Finny was on top of the driver, his head not quite submerged.

Yelling their names he continued to tug at the box. It remained firmly wedged, even though Angus had released himself from his harness and had wrapped his fingers around one corner and was tearing at the box with all his strength.

'Pull!' yelled Dave but even a concerted effort could not move the ammo.

Angus peered through the crack.

'Finny's sort of moving,' he reported. He yelled Finny's name.

Dave felt panic and desperation start to pound deep inside him but he did not indulge it.

'Open the back. Angus, lay down fire; Doc, get round the front to Finny and Dawson.'

But of course Doc had anticipated this. He already had the rifles out and, armed with his, he had succeeded in opening the back door. The enemy had seen him and were firing with renewed zeal. Dave heard the rat-tat-tat of a PK machine gun. It was answered by a GPMG from the base.

'Don't get out there until Angus can cover you!' yelled Dave, but he was too late. The door had been opened up in the air and the medic was leaping out. He turned smartly to run around the back of the Mastiff where enemy fire could not reach him. Angry grabbed a rifle and followed, Dave behind him. Dave had no time to look at the PB but it seemed to him that a roar of delight at their emergence had gone up from the boys. Maybe he imagined it. It was hard to hear because the lads were firing energetically back at the enemy.

The mighty Mastiff lay on its side, half submerged in the canal like a great, fallen beast. The left front wheel-base had been taken out by the RPG: it must have zoomed right under the vehicle.

Doc had climbed on to the side of the Mastiff and was wrestling to open the door through the vehicle's armour. Angus, crouching in the dark shadow of the wagon in a pocket between the cab and the back, fired almost continuously.

Dave vaulted up just as Doc opened the door upwards. By now Finny, inside the cab, had worked out which way was up. He was righting himself, his eyes wide and shocked. Had he released himself from his harness? Or hadn't he been wearing it?

Dave slipped into the cab, wedged one foot against the windscreen, and helped him stand. It smelled very wet in here. And Dave had the sudden idea that he could smell death.

Finny began climbing out, helped by Dave and pulled by the medic.

'Shit, Sarge,' he said. 'Shit. I think I hit his head with my helmet when we crashed.'

'All right, Finny, I'm getting him out now,' said Dave, diving into the murky canal water which half filled the cab. This wasn't the moment to ask Finny if he had been wearing a harness. If not, it would have been easy for him to plummet into Dawson, knocking him unconscious. An unconscious man could drown in rising water in a few minutes. Doc would have to be a fucking magician to bring a man back from that.

He reached for Dawson's chest and pushed the release on his harness. Nothing happened. He banged it again, this time forcefully, but it continued to hold the man fast. He felt for the harness-cutting mechanism. He could not move it. After a moment he ran his finger along the belt of the harness. It remained uncut.

He would have to cut Dawson out. As he surfaced, he found Dawson's hand. The second he felt it, he knew the man was not alive. He recognized the strange, rubbery feel of the recently dead. The hand did not resist him and it was not stiff yet, but it was without humanity.

So he was too late. His own torso, his arms, his legs, his whole body, was suffused with a new weight, as though sadness was a heavy, toxic metal released into his blood stream.

Doc Holliday hung down inside the cab as Dave grabbed his bayonet to cut Dawson out of his harness. Dave was soaking and not just because he had been immersed in water but because he was sweating profusely. He could feel sweat rolling down his cheeks and more sweat streaming down his back in hot rivers.

He kept sawing at the harness and suddenly it gave way. Lancer Dawson was released into his arms. The body floated up through the water but it retained the shape of a man driving, his arms stretched to a ghost steering wheel.

'He's dead,' Dave said.

'Get him out!' shouted the medic. Without consciously thinking about it, Dave was aware of the rattle of the enemy machine guns getting closer. As he tried to lift the body, Doc's words echoed in his head: 'The ragheads must think it's Christmas.'

'It's too late.' Dave heard the lifelessness in his own tone but he continued to heave Dawson towards the pair of hands reaching for him. The body banged against the open hole to the sky and the medic let it sink back down.

'Shit, we'll have to turn him around. This isn't good!'

'Can you get down and do your medic stuff in here?'

The medic paused to consider this.

'Not really. I need a floor not a fucking swimming pool.'

Dave managed to turn the body through ninety degrees and then lift it again. Lancer Dawson was a big man and now he was a big deadweight. Dave gritted his teeth. His arm muscles strained and bulged the way they did at the gym when he was too ambitious with the free weights. He knew what the pain was saying: this is too much for you to lift. And he knew he had to lift the body anyway. Just in case the medic really could work his magic and bang some life back into Dawson.

Every muscle in Dave's body tensed and swelled to bursting point. Just when Dawson was almost out of the Mastiff, the huge machine rocked. At that moment a 7.62 gun round made a distinctive deep plonking noise, hitting the vehicle's armour right by them. Dave did not know if it was the rocking vehicle or an instinctive attempt to duck that threw the medic off balance.

'Shit!' Doc roared, breathing out, releasing the body and buckling slowly. 'Shit, my fucking knee!'

Dave wedged Dawson's body against the battered

seating inside the Mastiff. It was a relief to ease the load. Except that by now he was so tense that his muscles remained taut.

'Did it get you?' he demanded.

'Nah.'

The medic's face had disappeared inside his own pain. He closed his eyes. He could barely speak.

'What then, Doc?'

At last Doc said: 'Old injury.'

So that was the injury which had pitched Doc out of Special Forces. There were a lot of rumours about the nature of the problem and the way it had happened.

Dave roared: 'Angus, you help me get the driver out! Doc, cover us!'

'I can cover,' said a voice which sounded like Billy Finn's, only a bit fainter than usual.

Dave felt his heart pump hopefully. Billy Finn was back in business.

'Two minutes ago you were fucking dead,' he grunted.

'I've already got my rifle, Sarge,' said Finny, firing to prove it.

The medic slid gratefully down the side of the Mastiff and disappeared beneath it where the shadows had already joined together to make deep night.

Angry clambered up to help Dave, drawing renewed firing from the enemy. He was bigger and stronger than Doc and he and Dave gritted their teeth and groaned and between them pulled Dawson's body out. Even though Dave was sure he could not be revived.

A round whistled past Angry and skimmed the edge of the driver's arm.

Angry yelled: 'Did you see that! Fuck it, he's been hit!'

Dawson did not bleed.

'He's already dead,' Dave said, lowering the body to the ground where Doc waited under the Mastiff.

The medic leaped on the body and dragged it beneath the vehicle like a big animal tearing at a piece of meat. He began the vigorous process of resuscitation, pumping at Dawson's chest.

'Looks more like he's killing him,' said Angus. His hand was shaking.

Suddenly the medic stopped and some water came out of the dead man's mouth.

Angry jumped as though he had received an electric shock.

'He's alive, fuck it, he's alive!' It should have been a shout of joy but there was horror in his voice. His words were punctuated by gunfire reverberating around them, from the base on one side to the enemy on the other and from Finny's rifle nearby.

'He moved!' shouted Angus.

The medic shook his head.

'Nah. I'm getting nowhere. Wasting my time.'

Finny stopped firing.

'We had to try,' he said.

'Yeah,' agreed the medic. 'We had to try.' He flopped down by the side of the body.

Dave looked up. Night had fallen across the desert now: the shadows had grown longer and longer until they were spun together in a dense, dark fabric. He wanted to sit and watch the night deepen and wonder exactly how Dawson had died. He hoped he had drowned quietly and unconsciously, without struggle, panic or pain. He looked down at Dawson's strangely peaceful face.

'Sarge?' It was Finny, speaking to him as though to wake him.

'OK, we can't stay here.' His own voice sounded a long way off again. He had the strange sensation that someone else was talking. Who was this quick, decisive commander? And what was he going to propose next? 'We're under fire and they'll soon be closing in on us. Get ready to move.'

'Sarge, I'm pretty sure they're closing in on us already,' said Angus.

Finny agreed.

'Are we going home, Sarge?' asked Angus.

'Where's home?' Finn asked. 'You talking about that load of shit and mud compound?'

'PB Boston Red Sox,' Angry said. 'That's the place I'm calling home right now, mate.'

He turned and looked longingly towards the muzzle flashes which defined the dark base. There was extremely heavy enemy fire aimed at the Mastiff and the base was firing back with the two GPMGs. And when there was a dip in the enemy's energy, Dave noticed that Sol kept the boys going, creating all the cover they could. Because Sol had worked out that they had no choice but to run for it.

'Keep firing so the boys know we're still here,' he told Finny.

Doc Holliday asked: 'Where are we heading, Dave?'

'Back to Red Sox?' said Angry.

'No,' said Dave. 'We're dead meat if we do that. And we're dead meat if we stay here. We came out of those gates for a reason. And now that we're a man down, it's even more important to finish the job.'

Finn stopped firing again and looked up from his rifle butt. Angus stared back at Dave, expressionless. Doc Holliday nodded.

'We're going to run across the desert to the relief

party? To help McKinley?' asked Finn. He straightened. His tone was unconcerned and matter of fact. He sounded relaxed. 'Right, Sarge.'

Angus looked more nettled than Finny. Dave looked at him with concern. He remembered how, near the start of his first tour, Angry had panicked a couple of times. Since then he had been brave to the point of fool-hardiness. All that big man talk must have been hiding panic and fear. Dave would have to grip him, or it could surface.

Now Angus said: 'If we run to the relief, we're running right into the arms of the enemy!'

They stopped talking as the air around them turned from falling night to wild, effervescent daylight. Dave estimated that the fireworks were caused by two RPGs from the enemy and a rocket from the base, all explod-ing more or less simultaneously. When the darkness came back, it seemed deeper. There was silence all around them. Dave knew it would not last. It was one of those battle spaces which just happened, as if every-one was taking a deep breath.

'There's a lot of mines hidden under this desert. They go back years,' came the medic's voice, calm and sensible, as if there had been no interruption.

Dave said: 'That's one reason we can't cross it. We have to move through the Green Zone. We've seen children, goats, camels, on the other side of this canal – it's clear.'

Angus looked horrified now.

'They'll find us in the Green Zone, Sarge. Even if it's dark. That's where they fucking live and they've all got fucking dogs.'

Dave said: 'McCall, stop talking and get any ammo for the SA80s that you can find, and get the day sacks

420

too. Everyone should have their night-vision goggles on in two minutes. Do it now.'

Angus did not move. Dave thought: Shit, I'm losing him. He had seen men overcome by fear before but he could not afford to carry such a man now. They were all shocked – by the crashing Mastiff, by the death of Dawson, by the danger which lay ahead – but shock would have to wait. Four men could not move through this terrain, surrounded by the enemy, if one of them was paralysed by fear.

'Get on with it, mate,' Finn told Angus. 'I've been firing all by myself.'

'Move,' Dave ordered.

'Yes, Sarge.' Angus dropped, picked up his rifle and slithered along the metalwork of the Mastiff. Dave was relieved that he looked more like a soldier and less like a panicking kid who was going to get them all into a lot of trouble.

Then Angus stopped and looked back. 'Sarge, why can't we just stay here?'

Dave said: 'In fifteen minutes this vehicle will be taken by the enemy.'

'Oh. Yeah.' Angus continued his journey along the great slumbering vehicle.

When he was almost lost in darkness, Dave called sharply: 'I want you back here within two minutes, McCall.'

Angus leaped into the back of the Mastiff just as the firing started again. It burst out of the base with gusto. The enemy returned it at once. Finny joined in the fray.

'How long before the FOB gets someone out here?' Dave muttered to Doc Holliday, who was sitting by Dawson's body, his legs flat out in front of him. It was a rhetorical question so he was surprised when the medic answered.

'Hours and hours. As soon as we lost comms they would have started to worry but the dust storm has to end at Bastion or the firing has to stop at the FOB. I reckon nothing's going to happen before morning. So the best chance for McKinley is still us.'

Dave listened to the crack of enemy weapons. In the distance a dog barked. Above them the night sky was brighter, as if layer upon layer of stars was being peeled back.

'You've chosen the right plan,' said Doc Holliday. 'I reckon that's why Sol's leading the battle out there. He's giving us a chance to move off.'

Dave looked down at Dawson. The dead man's face seemed to glow white in the dark.

'Shit, I hate leaving him here.'

'I hate leaving his rifle for the bastards.'

'We'll take it and hide it in the canal.'

'Wish we could hide the fucking HMG.'

Dave asked Finny: 'How is the HMG?'

'Wet,' said Finny. 'Very wet.'

Angus reappeared at that moment with the day sacks. 'Wet? It's under fucking water. Just like these day sacks were.'

Finny opened his and reported: 'My night sights are useless, Sarge. They're wet through.'

'Everything's wet, fucking wet,' said Angus.

Dave pulled his out. They were dry. Why? Because they were in the canoe bag along with the camera Jenny had given him. Fucking well done, Jenny. He remembered opening the camera at home. He had said something sarcastic like: Waterproofing's a sound idea in the desert. Did she have second sight or something?

422

Jenny. His Jenny. So far away, doing God knows what, but always inside his fucking head. No matter what stupid thing she had done back home in Wiltshire, she was a girl worth fighting for.

He pulled the GPS out from his webbing. He remembered that when the Mastiff had rolled, flinging him about, there had been crunches around his body. He had wondered, fleetingly, if it was ribs or equipment. Now he knew. It was the GPS. It was both crushed and wet. So he would be navigating using his sense of direction. That snowy, cold night in Brecon reappeared inside his head again, the whole platoon lost and exhausted. Training. Training with no enemy around except possibly his own platoon commander. It seemed like some kind of a game now.

Doc was ransacking Dawson's wet webbing.

'I'll get his ammo,' said Dave, stuffing some of it into his own sack and throwing some of it at Angus.

Finny found space and Doc took a lot more. They rearranged the contents of their day sacks and stuffed rations into their webbing while Dave spoke to them.

'The enemy'll realize we've left the vehicle when we stop firing. The moment they get here they'll send their dogs after us. So we'll have to throw them off the scent by wading down the middle of the canal.'

'We've got a lot of kit here,' said Finny.

'If we can't carry it, we'll have to dump it. They'll expect us to head south towards the relief vehicles. That's why we're heading north.'

It seemed to Dave that under the Mastiff there was complete silence at that moment, even though Sol and the enemy were at full throttle just a few hundred metres away. He could see the eyes of Finn and Angus, shining in the dark, staring at him in disbelief.

Then he heard the reassuring voice of Doc Holliday: 'Good plan.'

'We'll tab back to the relief party through the Green Zone.'

'Right, Sarge,' said Finn. It sounded as though he was trying to make his voice firm and strong. But underneath Dave knew it was wavering.

'They'll find us! What are the chances we can go tabbing for miles and miles without no one seeing us and no dog smelling us?' demanded Angus, that undertone of panic audible again.

It was more of a statement than a question but Dave had begun answering it in his mind before Angus had even opened his mouth. He had decided they had a 50 per cent chance at most, probably a lot less, of reaching the relief party alive. He would have liked to ask Doc's opinion. But not in front of Finny and Angus.

'Odds are looking good,' said Finny rapidly.

Angus blinked at him. Doc looked surprised.

Dave explained: 'Billy Finn's our platoon's gambling expert.' He did not add that Finn had been banned from taking bets all the time they were away.

'Anyone who wants a flutter on our survival chances is welcome to lay a bet,' said Finny. 'I'm offering nine to four on.'

'Yeah, I'll bet a thousand that we arrive,' said Doc quickly. 'Since you won't be collecting your winnings if we don't.'

'That's enough,' said Dave. 'We should go while Sol's covering us. Knee OK to move off now, Doc?'

Doc shrugged dismissively. Probably because he knew that, even if he was in agony, they had to move.

Dave said: 'Finny at the front, then me, then Doc, then Angus. Complete silence. If you *have* to say something or stop, tap the man in front. Use hand signals. Keep checking the guy behind you.'

He looked around at their faces: Finny's battle-sharp, Angus's blanked by anxiety, Doc's expressionless.

Finn asked: 'Should we fix bayonets, Sarge?' His eyes moved quickly in the starlight.

'No, but keep your bayonet where you can get your hands on it fast,' Dave ordered. 'Before we go, let's give them a fireworks display for a few minutes and use up some of the ammo which we can't carry. So they don't get it. And so they know we're still here.'

They had been under assault from the moment they had left the base. Ever since the Mastiff had pitched into the canal the enemy had been attacking them with glee, like the fans of a football team two-nil up who knew the ref was about to blow his whistle. Dave had been too busy with a dead man, an injured medic and a near-panicking rifleman to focus on the constant ping and whistle of Taliban rounds coming too close for comfort, bouncing off the Mastiff's armour, throwing dust up in the ground nearby. But now it felt good to return some of that fire.

The two gimpys from the base joined in and for a while the enemy were silenced by the concerted British effort. They might have assumed, Dave realized, that the wrecked Mastiff was in some kind of radio contact with the PB as well as the FOB. Maybe they had no idea that a dust storm in Bastion meant no help could come from the air. It probably didn't occur to them that out here were four soldiers who were as isolated as the great metal wreck which lay by itself at the desert's edge.

For a grand finale, he switched Dawson's rifle grimly to automatic and pretended it was a machine gun. He changed the magazine once and the weapon got so hot that he thought the barrel was drooping. He wouldn't do it to his own rifle but this one would soon be in the canal anyway. He turned up the night sights and gazed at the rocks where the muzzle flashes were coming from, at the base of a ridge to the south-west. Then the goggles picked up a man, his loose clothes flying behind him, running from one rock to the next through the dark, exposing himself to enemy fire for about three seconds. When the man fell, Dave hoped it was his shot which got him. Although it could have been one from the gimpy at the base behind.

'OK, let's leave it to Sol now,' Dave ordered reluctantly after a few minutes, looking up from his rifle. He realized that the men had stopped firing and were watching him, ready and waiting to go. Finn immediately moved forward under cover of Sol's gimpy fire. Maybe Sol guessed what they were doing, or maybe his night vision told him that the distant, silent forms were slipping away from the side of the vehicle, but the gimpys were now in overdrive. Dave hoped the barrels wouldn't melt.

Swinging left when they reached the canal might confuse the dogs and confound their handlers. For a while. The drainage in this area had mostly been built by the Americans and they favoured the grid pattern of American cities, so finding your direction was as easy as east on Third Street and then north on First Avenue. After about ten minutes down the canal, they were to climb out on the right side and cross the fields going east. When they hit the next drainage channel, they would turn left and go north again. They would walk for at least an hour through the water where the dogs couldn't smell them. Only then, if all was quiet, could they consider looping back through the Green Zone to the relief party.

Dave estimated that the silence meant the enemy would realize the Mastiff was deserted within five minutes, ten at the most. And, despite Sol's efforts, within another fifteen they would be swarming all over it, stealing its weaponry, learning its secrets. He wished he could blow it up instead of leaving such a fat prize for the enemy. Less than ten minutes after they took the Mastiff, the Taliban would get dogs here to sniff out the trail of the departed men. Which meant that the four of them could be caught within thirty minutes.

He decided that he would rather be dead. If the Taliban came close enough to catch them alive, he would give each man a choice. They could hope the enemy would be kind to them. Or they could accept his offer to kill them first. Dave hoped he would have time to kill himself too. It would be better for Jenny to learn from a knock at the door that he was dead than to watch his brutal execution online.

Dave took a last glance at Dawson. He saw the others do the same, all except Angus, who ignored the still body. Then they rounded the great, lumbering shape of the Mastiff and, as they did so, Dave decided that the enemy were welcome to it. But he was fucked if they were having any of his men too.

34

Jenny had brought the computer into the dining room and was bashing the keys without looking at them, her eyes fixed on the paper by the keyboard.

'I don't think we'll be finished by the time my kids go to bed,' she said.

'What time is that?' asked Eugene.

She paused. The room went silent.

'Well, seven o'clock at the latest, preferably earlier.'

'Are you going to fetch them so they can sleep here?' he asked, getting up to throw another log on the fire.

'No, Adi said she'd keep them all night.' Jenny did not look at him. Her eyes tried to make sense of Robin Douglas-Coombs's scribbled handwriting.

'Good!'

'But I'll have to ask you for an hour's break later so I can go and say goodnight to them.'

'Certainly. Are you sure you wouldn't rather bring them here to sleep?'

She paused to consider.

'No thanks. This house is much bigger than any-where they've slept before. They might not settle down.'

'Will you have to pay your friend to look after them for the night?'

Jenny nodded in response.

'It's just a friendly arrangement; she's not a registered childminder. But of course I pay her.' She started typing again.

Eugene said: 'This time I'll pay her, obviously. And will you stay here or go home?'

Jenny stopped typing and looked at him.

'I think it's better if I go home. Don't you?'

He looked back at her.

'No.'

Her voice dropped. She was embarrassed to look at him. He was such a good man that she couldn't bear to remind him what other people were like. She said: 'You don't know how the camp talks.'

'Why do you care what they say?'

'I don't. That's the problem.'

'What problem, Jennifer?'

She sighed. 'They're talking in camp about me because I spend so much time here. Just as we left the pub today, someone I half know, someone from the RMP, came in and saw us together. She lives in camp. So by Monday, everyone will know I had lunch with you.'

He came and sat next to her at the long table with its centuries-old patina.

'Why do you care about their gossip?'

'Because I have to live with it. There are women in camp who've made up their own minds and they avoid me. Even one of my best friends has been steering clear of me because she disapproves of me spending all this time with you.'

He sighed. 'I enjoy your company and I haven't seen

any reason to hide that. But maybe I should have done, for your sake.'

She felt her face softening the way it did sometimes before she cried.

'We have nothing to hide,' she said.

Eugene leaned towards her. This time he did not just reach out and stroke her hand for a moment. He took it in his.

'Yes we do,' he said.

She looked at him in surprise.

'I've been meaning to tell you, Jennifer, how much I appreciate all you've done for me. I look forward to the days when you come to work. You're always bright and cheerful even though I'm sure there are many reasons for you not to feel cheerful. Sometimes you literally seem to bring the sun in with you. My house was a gloomy place before you arrived and my life was a lot more gloomy too. You've made a big difference to me.'

Jenny did not know where to look. At the oil paintings of men in waistcoats and women wearing impossible dresses or down to the carpets, which might have come from Afghanistan? Along the table at the piles of paper or out of the windows where the rain was pattering as if thrown against the glass by a giant hand? She looked at none of these and all of these, aware that her hand was in Eugene's as he spoke.

He said: 'I'm sorry for embarrassing you. I just want you to know that I hold you in very high esteem. And I will add, at the risk of embarrassing you further, that I think you are a lovely – no, a beautiful young woman.'

She looked into his eyes. They shone with a mixture of sadness and laughter. The wrinkles at the corners made him look mature and wise. He smiled at her now with even teeth, the skin stretched tightly across his

430

cheeks with no hint of that loosening around the jaw and the neck which aged most men. Yes, he was an attractive man, although it was something she had always chosen to ignore.

'You've been good and kind and generous to me,' she said.

He squeezed her hand more tightly. They smiled at each other.

She said: 'Let's get the report done now.'

He nodded and released her.

Dave walked into the still, dank water of the canal behind Finny. It retained something of the day's heat. As it rose up to his knees, thighs and then waist he was suddenly, strangely, reminded how he and Jenny had found a hidden lake in a wood when they were camping in Scotland a few years ago, before Vicky was born. They had waded in together. It was September and they had prepared themselves for cold's sting but instead they had found summer's heat waiting in the water for them. Jenny had stopped walking and in one even motion had lifted her feet and started swimming, breaking the membrane of the lake's surface with her smooth stroke. The memory of that warm, balmy water and Jenny swimming in it made Dave's heart ache. Briefly, as the cold canal water closed around his stomach, he ached for home and for Jenny and for all things safe.

He heard the smooth entry into the water of Doc behind him. At the back, Angus's splash was less muted. Big man, big splash. Not that it mattered here because the noise of the battle was deafening and the chances of meeting any civilians minimal.

Within a few minutes they had achieved a rhythm

which enabled them to walk forward noiselessly into the unknowable dark.

With every step their clothes dragged them back. The bottom of the canal was soft and clung to each boot as they lifted it. The water felt viscous like treacle.

Dave paused to drop Dawson's rifle into the mud. He buried it with his foot as best he could. He hoped that by the time it was found, when the water level dropped at the height of summer, it would be useless.

Dave looked back frequently through his night-vision goggles. Behind Doc was Angus's face, expressionless in the way that faces went blank because the minds behind them were busy. Angry McCall was a complicated soldier. Brave as a lion one minute, furious to the point of apoplexy the next, often nasty, frequently rude. Angry wanted to be good at his job and he was both experienced and well trained but there was something about him which made him unreliable. Dangerous, even. He was the weak link in the file and Dave resolved again to keep a close eye on him. Angus was thinking so hard now that he had forgotten to breathe quietly. Dave could occasionally hear him taking sharp intakes of air.

Ahead, Billy Finn moved forward soundlessly with the confidence of a man who could see in the dark. He had been brought up to cut through streams and slip through woods at night, poaching and stealing in the countryside. The lads used to call him the Nike Pikey and for a long time he was the first to be suspected if anything went missing. But the others had soon learned that Finny was loyal and talented. And no one could move across terrain as stealthily while totally aware of everything around him.

On either side were cultivated fields. Crops grew at

waist height and there were agricultural ditches cut from the canal into which the water flowed sluggishly. Dave knew there must be houses near here. He could occasionally hear dog barks. But there were no lights. Because there was no electricity. Because apart from their twenty-first-century weapons, the Afghans were still living in the Middle Ages. *Why are we here, fighting these people?* Dave knew the answer he was supposed to give the men. They were protecting the Afghan people from the Taliban and at the same time protecting the West from the terrorism which was spawned here. But the Afghans' sullen distrust, sometimes even hatred, never made him feel like a protector. It made him feel like the enemy. And he had no doubt that Afghan civilians who encountered the four of them would do nothing to take care of them. No, they would be far more likely to alert the Taliban. Who would then kill them.

Dave tapped Finny on the shoulder and signed to go right. Finny nodded and scrambled up the bank by a drainage ditch in one swift, smooth movement. Dave did the same and then waited to help the medic up. Doc was limping, although only slightly. He took off his day sack and threw it to Dave, along with his rifle. He lumbered clumsily out of the canal, but he did it alone. Dave gave him back his kit and watched Angus, who was big enough almost to step out of the water. Then they set off along the edge of the field. Dave did not know what the crop was. The leaves were large and leafy. Was it something you ate or something you smoked?

The sound of firing at the base was distant now. After a while the rhythm of his walk in this quiet world extinguished thought from Dave's mind. He focused on meeting the next canal. When they reached it, the channel appeared so suddenly before them that Finn stopped short and Dave nearly pitched into him. The gap between Dave and the medic had widened and they had to wait for the last two to arrive.

Angus signalled that he had something to say. They gathered round, their heads close together. They had all shaved back at Bastion and now their faces were shining with sweat in the dark.

Angus knew how to talk in the dark. He breathed the words: 'Sarge, I think they've got to the Mastiff back there.'

Finn nodded: 'Yeah, he's right.'

Dave and Doc simultaneously looked at their watches.

'Shit,' said Doc Holliday. 'It only took them twenty minutes.'

Dave wanted to plunge on into the dark at once. But he asked: 'How do you know?'

'Sol went fucking mental from the base. He had the lads throwing all the big, exploding toys out of the pram. But when they got answering fire, it was definitely closer.'

'I s'pose they'll help themselves to the HMG,' said Finn gloomily.

'Glad they won't have a fucking tripod for it.'

Dave said: 'Everyone all right?' He didn't wait for an answer. 'Let's move north again, then.'

'How long will we go in the wrong direction, Sarge?' asked Angus. He threw the words out like a quick barrage of nervous fire from a Minimi. Dave suspected this question was the real reason Angry had stopped the file.

'If they've got a pack of dogs, we'll need another hour probably,' said Dave, speaking so quietly that he breathed the words.

They plunged down into the next canal. It was deeper and muddier than the last. The water reached up to their chests. There was too much splashing as they entered it. Dave looked around anxiously and held his finger to his lips.

The world seen through night-vision goggles was a world of dull greens, as if they were travelling under water. He could see a green compound across the green field and dogs in it started to bark. He hoped their owners would not release them into the fields to investigate and that no human had heard the suspicious splashing. After a few minutes, the barking stopped.

Dave signed to Doc behind him any difficult areas or big boulders. He was alert, listening intently, and he soon knew for sure that the Taliban had got to the Mastiff, found it empty and were hunting them with dogs. Because in the distance was the barking of not one dog but a whole pack.

Dave felt instantly cold, even though walking through the canal water was such an effort that he was sweating. He knew the others would have heard the dogs too. He did not turn around to look at Angus.

As they walked on, the sound of the dogs did not lessen but at first it seemed to get no closer. He imagined the big, fierce animals the Afghans favoured rushing around the Mastiff, noses down, tails wagging, eyes hungry. He thought Sol would probably shoot a few and he hoped their handlers would encourage them to sniff south of the canal.

After another ten minutes the dogs were still barking like a pack of wolves, yelping and howling. The sound was blood-curdling. It was the voice of animals who would show you no mercy. They did not seem further away, as Dave had hoped. He was aware that their own pace had slowed significantly as the canal had narrowed and deepened and the muddy bottom had grown softer and harder to walk on.

Only this morning they had been at Camp Bastion. It seemed like a week ago, a month ago. And almost half a year before that, they had been at home in Wiltshire, standing around on an icy night saying how much they wanted to get back into theatre. He recalled that he had stomped off to the pub after some stupid row with Jenny. That Dave seemed like some other person now. Someone young and stupid enough to think that the front line was exciting without being any real threat to his life. Jenny and the other wives back home could smell the danger better from Wiltshire than the soldiers who were fighting. They lived with the possibility of men's deaths, while the men themselves chose to ignore it, as if death didn't apply to them. Until they found themselves in a situation which they were unlikely to survive.

The next time he turned routinely to check on the others he found that the space between him and the last two men had widened again. Each time he turned they had fallen a little further behind; now the gap was so great that he had to tap Finny on the shoulder for him to wait while the others caught up in the long stretch of darkness. Doc arrived at last, limping significantly. Angus behind him looked worried.

'What's up, Doc?' Dave asked.

Doc Holliday's face was white and sweating. He could not catch his breath to answer.

'You in a lot of pain?' Dave demanded.

Doc nodded and grimaced. 'It's the knee.'

'Twisted?'

'Yeah. I've had surgery three fucking times and it's never really been right.'

'We can't go south until the dogs stop barking,' said Dave, 'but we can cut down the journey a bit and stay safe if we go east again. Think you'll be able to walk on dry land?'

'It'll be easier.'

'You're carrying too much weight.'

Dave could tell that the medic did not want to admit he was right.

He said: 'Get rid of everything except essential medical stuff, a few rations, your rifle and a bit of ammo. If it didn't get blown up with the relief wagon, they'll probably have a lot of the medical gear you need for McKinley.'

Doc sighed. 'Shit,' he said sadly.

'Everything. Hurry up. Into the canal. It's the only place where they won't find it any time soon.'

The medic opened his sack and pouches and began throwing things out into the water. The first splash was loud.

'Shhhhh,' hissed Dave.

A few minutes later his pouches no longer bulged and his day sack was only half full.

'All that great kit under water,' he said miserably.

Angus tapped them on the shoulder: 'Come on, come on, let's go!' he breathed quietly.

'First we'll listen,' hissed Dave. They all stood motionless. It felt good to stand still. It was a relief not to experience the water's resistance. They did not even breathe.

They could hear that there was still some distant firing, sporadic now and so far away it might have been further even than PB Red Sox. Dave hoped they wouldn't arrive at the relief to find it under fire. But there were no longer any dogs. One barked but it was far away, a lonely dog in a compound further north. Otherwise the starry night was soundless. They all let out long breaths.

'They're not coming this way,' said Finn. 'They've given up looking or they've hared off south.'

So the plan was working, Dave thought. So far. Except that the plan had brought them miles in the wrong direction, one of them had an old injury, they still had to double back on themselves and pass through a populated agricultural area by night and they had no way of knowing whether the party they were trying to reach had been ambushed and overrun by the enemy. Apart from that, the plan was working.

He said: 'OK, no dogs. Let's start heading back. We'll go east and at the next canal turn south.'

He saw Angus's face break into a smile. Now at least they would be heading in the right direction.

Finny was an athlete, emerging sleekly out of the canal without a splash like a quick, black shadow cutting through the water. Dave and Angus scrambled out less gracefully. Then Angus turned to help Doc without being asked. Usually he was a selfish soldier, so Dave felt pleased. It was amazing how some serious fear and the smell of death could make a man grow up quickly.

Doc swung his day sack up first and Dave held it and was surprised by how light it was. He and Angus each took an arm. The medic did his best to clamber up the bank but there was a moment when Dave knew he and Angus were taking the man's full weight. Then Holliday regained his strength and balance for long enough to swing upright. He stood still for a moment, halted by pain, his face twisted.

Dave whispered: 'How fast can you go, Doc?'

'Faster than you think now I'm out of that fucking water.'

Finny indicated that he wanted to go south-east, cutting across the middle of the field, but Dave shook his head. The crop here grew in neat, lush rows and if they damaged it someone might guess that four big men had passed this way. He hoped to be far away by the time morning could shine its light on their path. But Doc's limp was worrying him. He turned back frequently to look at it. He estimated that the relief party was now 4 k away in a straight line. And 6–8 k away if they took a safer, more circular route.

It seemed a long tab to the next canal, a long tab in wet, heavy clothes in the wrong direction. When they reached it, Dave took Doc's day sack from him. The medic did not object. His look of relief, even more than his limp, told Dave how much pain he was in. With a thudding feeling he admitted the truth. This man did not have 8 k in him.

Dave tapped shoulders until he had everyone's attention. They gathered round while he whispered: 'Now we're going south we're moving into a much more populated area. It isn't just people in compounds and their dogs. It's blokes who come out to work the sluices at night. So for Chrissake be quiet.'

They nodded and Finny slipped into the canal. After a moment he turned, grinned and put his thumb up. This drainage channel was shallow. It would be easy to walk through it.

The others followed him in. They were going more and more slowly now, Finny and Dave stopping constantly to wait for the medic, who was limping so badly it was difficult to prevent the water lapping around him in tiny, noisy waves.

Behind him, Angus's face was creased with concern.

They had been progressing for ten minutes when Dave heard a splash ahead.

Finny was suddenly motionless. He held up a hand. Dave stopped and held up his hand to the others. Nobody moved. Nothing moved. Dave peered ahead through the bottle-green world of the night goggles. To the left was a field of some tall, large-leaved crop which could easily hide a man: in places the crop fell across the ditch. To the right the crop was only knee-high.

After a few minutes of silence Dave was tempted to move off but he had too much respect for Billy Finn's instincts to ignore the sign he was making for them to hold firm. He waited with Doc and Angus, scarcely breathing.

Starting so slowly that Dave was hardly aware he was moving, Finn eased his body forward through the water. His hand was still in the air to keep the others holding firm. He seemed not to break the water's surface or cause a ripple. About ten metres ahead, he froze again.

Dave knew that someone must be here. He waited. Finny was motionless.

Then there was another splash. This time he heard it clearly. It could be an animal, like a rat, jumping into the water. It could be someone moving, like them, through the water. It could be someone throwing something at the water, perhaps in an attempt to attract them into an arc of fire. It was close, that was sure. Sound travelled on a quiet, still night but the splash could not have been much further ahead than Finny.

Very, very carefully, soundlessly, Dave fingered his bayonet. He could reach it easily. Then slowly, so slowly that he hoped even a fish would not hear, he moved up behind Finn.

He arrived alongside him just as Finny leaped up the bank. Billy Finn was a slim, powerful, cat-like animal with the patience to watch its prey and the killer instinct to know when to pounce. He erupted out of the water and fell neatly on something in the bushes. Dave saw a man roll beneath the soldier, helpless with surprise. Finn threw his weight on top of him, twisting the man's arm behind his back and clamping the man's hand across his mouth. He could keep the top half of his victim silent and still but down below the legs began to thrash. They were dangerously close to the water, dangerously close to attention-attracting splashing.

Dave jumped on to the man's legs, holding them firm. The man could not make a sound. He could not move. Nor could he see his captors. But nevertheless protest throbbed through him.

Shit, thought Dave. What do we do with him now? He could see Finn looking at the bayonet, waiting for Dave to draw it. They both knew that the man could not be released, or their journey would soon be over. This unlucky Afghan had to be kept quiet and the only way to do that was to kill him. Except, Dave knew, there was no court in the world which would acquit him of killing a civilian who had no weapon and had committed no crime.

They would have to find a way to detain their victim, at least for a few hours, while they made their escape.

Dave heard more water movement, but this time it came from Angus and Doc. The medic had handed a First Field Dressing to Angus and was now drawing something else from a pouch and handing this over. Angry began to wade towards them. He moved too quickly to be silent and as he did so he opened the field dressing with his teeth. As soon as he was close enough, Dave saw that as well as the bandage, Doc had handed him plasticuffs. Plasticuffs! What a fucking fantastic idea!

They gradually released the man's hands and feet as Angus plasticuffed them. Being Angus, he was rough. Finn kept his hand over the man's mouth and Dave covered his eyes but it was not easy to maintain this while Angus bound them in the dressing. The eyes blinked open for a second but before they could take in the sight of three British soldiers looming over him, Angus had the bandage across them. The man was ready to yell the second Finn's big hand was removed from his mouth but Angus was too quick and only a short, strangled sound, like the sudden quack of a duck, escaped.

Angus ran the dressing tightly under the man's chin as well to discourage him from emitting any throat noises but by the time Finn and Dave had thrown him into the bushes the man had been shocked into silence.

The soldiers gave each other the thumbs-up and continued on their journey. Doc seemed to have benefited from the rest and was moving a bit faster now.

When a dog barked nearby Dave knew they had to change course. They were crossing a drainage ditch and could have swung west for a field width, taking them away from their target. Dave took a deep breath and changed his plan. Instead of circling cautiously around their destination, it was time to head for it. Sooner or later they would have to cut through the dense population to get to the relief. It may as well be now. He told Finny to head due east.

So they continued to cut their zigzag course through

the Afghan darkness, around the occasional field but mostly along canals and drainage channels, watched by a fingernail of a moon and a million stars.

35

Jenny drove out of Tinnington through rain and high winds. The roads were running with water. A few trees were down. She pulled up outside Adi's house at last and got soaked just running up the path.

'Come in, come in, don't bring the gale in with you!' Adi pulled her through the door and slammed it shut.

Most of the children, including her own, were in night clothes. Vicky ran to her, wrapped her arms around her mother's legs, and burst into tears. Jenny lifted her up.

'Now, Vicky, what's all this?'

Seeing her sister in tears, Jaime started to cry as well. Adi rolled her eyes. 'They've both been happy as Larry until you walked in!'

Jenny sat on the sofa with both children in her arms and tried to explain to them why she was leaving them at Adi's. She did not expect Jaime to understand but the baby seemed to take in every word, blinking her big, blue eyes. Vicky maintained an obstinate silence. Jenny tried to persuade them it would be fun sharing a room with the Kasanita children but Vicky just said: 'Want to go home.'

'I'll tell you what,' said Jenny. 'If it's not too late when I've finished, and if Adi's still awake, I'll swing by and scoop you up so you'll wake up at home. How's that?'

After a bit of persuasion, Vicky accepted this offer.

'Mummy put you to bed now?' asked Jenny.

Adi intervened. 'It's chaos up there with the extra mattress. I'll put them all to bed together. They'll have a bit of a giggle and then they'll fall asleep.'

Jenny got up to go. Vicky looked stricken. Jenny hugged and kissed her goodnight. At the door, Adi asked: 'What time do you think you'll finish?'

'Another five hours or so. Do you want me to stop by for the kids at midnight?'

Adi laughed. 'You must be joking, darling. I'll be dead to the world at midnight!'

Jenny thanked her again and left before Vicky could come padding into the hallway in her pyjamas. She turned the car around and drove slowly past her own house, which was in darkness. The Buckles' house was lit up. Maybe Steve was helping Leanne put the boys to bed.

At the end of the road she turned into the camp main street, with its small arcade of budget shops, a dry cleaner's, a café and a counselling centre. On the corner was the Eclipse. She was picking up speed when she saw two figures, oblivious to the rain, striding out of the pub. Under the street lamp she could see them clearly. Steve Buckle and Si Curtis. The two most reluctant members of the rear party: nobody wanted to be in theatre more than this pair. They were probably drowning their sorrows together.

As soon as she was out of the 30-mph limit, she accelerated towards Tinnington.

* * *

'The fucking slag!' said Steve Buckle when he saw Jenny's car swish by in the rain. Its wheels threw back a fine spray which had left a thin film of water on his prosthetic leg.

'I don't get it,' said Si.

'That was Jenny the Slag Henley. A stuck-up bitch who wants to send her kids to a stuck-up nursery. Well, in my humble opinion, she isn't good enough for Dave Henley.'

'I'm confused,' said Si.

'He'd be better off without her – in my humble opinion. She wants to run off with some general who's twice her age? Let her!'

'So . . . did she have the kids in the car?' asked Si.

'No, she didn't. Why?'

'Adi said she was coming home at bedtime. When's that?'

'Her bedtime's all the fucking time from the sound of it.'

'Not *her* bedtime! The kids'.'

'Ah. About . . .' Steve consulted his watch. '. . . now.'

'So if she's coming home for bedtime, why is she heading out of town?'

They were walking towards the White Horse but now Steve paused and leaned against a wet lamp post to think about this.

'Why *is* she heading out of town?' he echoed.

'She's left the kids with Adi. And now she's visiting him. General Coward. The bloke who ran away at Chalee.'

'Fucking hell.'

'See, she's driving in the direction of Tinnington.'

'Yeah, but she's not visiting. She's staying there. She's left the kids with Adi and she's staying the night at his place.' Steve did not move from the lamp post. 'I'm surprised at Adi. Encouraging Jenny the Slag.'

Si said: 'Adi believes her, that's why. She said she's working late. And Adi believed her.'

Steve began to laugh. A hollow, joyless laugh. 'Yeah, right, she's working late with General Coward on a Sunday night. That's really believable. Good story, slag.'

'Poor old Dave.'

Steve echoed: 'Poor old Dave. Shame he's too far away to teach her a lesson. Maybe someone should do it for him.'

Doc Holliday's limp was worsening. Finally he allowed McCall to walk supporting him and Dave knew from this that they must be reaching the medic's limit. They were moving so slowly that, although Dave remained alert, his thoughts had fallen into the dull rhythm of his walk.

He was thinking about Jamie Dermott. He was wishing he was in this mess with him now. He missed Jamie in different ways. There was the rapid, early-morning acknowledgement of his absence when he woke up and remembered that one soldier he wouldn't exchange a few words with today was Jamie. Then there were constant reminders in the working day because Jamie had been one of those key men who raises everyone's standards. Like now, a time of peril when top-level soldiering was required. And then there was that painful level of personal loss. Jamie was a mate but he was gone now, out of Dave's life and all the other lives where he mattered. He had simply disappeared. You had a stock of memories, stored away like snapshots, which you could pull out of the albums from time to time. But the stock dwindled as months passed and there would be nothing more to add to it. Until all you were left with was a sense of the man, a sort of cipher which your mind recognized as being Jamie.

He wondered if he was thinking about Jamie because he was a dead man and death felt uncomfortably close right now. The water had lost the day's heat and their slow movement through it and the freshness of the Afghan night air had caused body temperatures to fall. They were cold and hungry and they had a very lame man. They would have to stop soon.

Then Finny did stop. But so suddenly that Dave almost ploughed into him.

Finn held up a hand and all four of them stood, tense and motionless, in total silence. All the thoughts which the long walk had generated were left behind. Their senses strained ahead of them. The only sound Dave could hear was his heart thumping.

Just a few metres down the canal something started to splash. It was followed by a strange, deliberate scraping sound. There was someone just ahead.

Dave knew one thing. Whatever the scraping sound meant, the splashing was unselfconscious. It did not come from a crouching enemy but from a human who had no idea they were here. Dave reminded himself which pouch his plasticuffs were in. It seemed like poor drill to leave a trail of plasticuffed people lying across Helmand Province, but it was a lot better than leaving a trail of dead civilians.

Then he heard something which sent an electric impulse through his every nerve: the sudden and un-expected sound of a human voice a few metres away. For a moment Dave could not hear the voice over the thump of his own heart. He felt engulfed by a sense of crisis. The voice must be talking to someone, maybe to two or even three people. How could the soldiers fall on so many, keep them quiet, tie them up and, even if they managed this impossible feat, get away at this slow pace before one of these people was missed? And how many First Field Dressings did they have between them anyway?

As he listened the voice became clearer and Dave formed an impression of the speaker. He was old. He did not suspect the soldiers' presence. He was chattering and the tone of his voice was a moan. In fact, it sounded a bit like Dave's dad. Involuntarily, Dave rolled his eyes.

He waited for someone to reply. No one did. Maybe it was like the way his patient mum and stepfather sat and listened when his dad showed up at their house unannounced and drunk, droning on about how unfairly life had treated him. The pause went on a long time. Perhaps there was a woman with the old man. Perhaps Afghan women were so oppressed that they never spoke back to their husbands. Dave caught himself thinking it wouldn't be a bad thing if British women were a bit more like that.

The old man started speaking again. The scraping noise began again too. Then there was a sudden thump and a brief silence followed by angry muttering. Dave couldn't speak Pashto but he knew the tone: the man was swearing. To himself. Because no one else was there.

When the scraping started again Dave decided it would drown more distant sounds, so he moved forward until he could see the man in his night sights, crouched down on the other side of some reeds. The scraping and thumping were the sluice boards of a channel the old man was trying to open so that water from the canal would flow along it. He was the night irrigator. Dave's stepdad watered his vegetables at night during hot weather so that the crop was immersed before the water could evaporate, and Afghan farmers did the same.

Finn looked at Dave, waiting for orders. Dave could see he was ready to spring. But that might not be necessary. Because the old man had turned now. His back was towards them and he was kneeling, his back almost parallel with the ground. Dave was sure neither his dad nor his stepdad could hold such a position: the old man had been doing this all his life. It took a few more moments before Dave realized the man was praying. The sluice was being stubborn and the man was praying for help. Dave could hear him mumbling to Allah irritably, expecting Allah to sort it out when all he probably needed was a screwdriver.

Dave could tell that Finn thought this was a good moment to pounce on the old geezer but instead Dave gestured him forward. The sluice was jammed in a barely open position and the water was trickling very slowly but noisily beneath it and the board was banging. This would help to cover up any noise they made. If the man was devout he would be praying for a few minutes and in that time they could be gone.

Finn looked surprised and disappointed, but followed orders. He disappeared silently and swiftly down the canal ahead. Dave put his finger to his lips and gestured for Angus and Doc to do the same. Doc did his best to move fast. From behind, Dave could see just how lopsided the medic had become. He was leaning heavily on Angus.

Dave followed them, heart in mouth, his eyes fixed on the old man's crouching figure, his ears focused on the old man's muttering. Doc and Angus were the noisiest movers and, as they crept past the praying man, he seemed suddenly to sense their presence. He stopped mumbling abruptly and Dave could tell that he had become alert. Angus and Doc were beyond him now, continuing up the canal, their passage hidden by reeds. But Dave was still level. He froze. After a moment the man began to mumble again and Dave was just about to move when he finished his prayer. He remained kneeling but his back straightened slowly.

Dave had a choice. He could dash on behind the others and risk the old man turning. Or he could wait here quietly until the Afghan had finished his sluice work. Either way, it might mean plasticuffs.

Dave decided to take a risk and the split second he made that decision he knew he had to act on it. Gambling on the possibility of arthritis, the unhurried pace of old age and the man's general air of weary dissatisfaction, he pressed on through the canal water. He wanted to forge ahead, stomping fast, splashing, making waves. But he could move only as fast as he could move silently.

His eyes on the kneeling man, the water swelling all around him, his heart beating and his nerves tingling, he waded slowly ahead. When he nearly tripped over an underwater boulder he decided to look where he was going and keep his weight balanced. He tore his eyes away from the man. Not until he was under the safe cover of some reeds thirty metres on did he stop with the others and look back.

The old man was bending over the sluice, seeing if Allah had helped solve the problem. He was muttering to himself. He had no idea that four British soldiers had just passed a couple of metres away.

36

They had to divert twice more for barking dogs. Dave listened constantly for the chilling sound of a hunting pack but they must have dispersed or were looking in the wrong place. The threat now was the compound dogs. The nearer they were to dogs, the nearer they were to humans.

All the time he was watching and listening, Dave was thinking. He did not need to cajole or scare Doc forward the way he would a younger, more inexperienced soldier. He knew the medic would walk until he dropped. And he knew that wasn't much further.

When he turned round and found that the medic had halted completely, he tapped Finny on the shoulder and made his way back. Even big Angus looked exhausted. He had been bearing Doc Holliday's weight all this time, often loping alongside in places where the canal was scarcely wide enough for two.

'Are you finished, Doc?' whispered Dave. He breathed the words, barely forming them, but it seemed to him that they were loud in the Afghan night. Everywhere was quiet now. Firing had stopped and there was no distant thud of artillery.

Doc Holliday hung his head miserably. His face was white. His leg dangled limply. One arm leaned on Angus, the other on a stick. He didn't look like a man who was on a mission to save another man's life.

'We only have about two k to go,' Dave breathed. He hoped he was right. Without GPS he couldn't be sure of anything.

The medic said nothing but shook his head.

'We'll rest. Then we'll start off first thing,' said Dave.

Doc Holliday shook his head again.

'Shoot me, Dave.'

Dave assumed Doc was joking. Finny gave a sad half-grin in the darkness.

'I'm serious. Because of me you could all be dead meat before morning. So kill me. Throw my body in the canal. No one will know.'

Dave felt a wave of nausea.

'No fucking way, Doc.'

'Think about it. You've got a choice between four dead men or one dead man. That's a no-brainer.'

'I ain't carried you all this fucking way just to shoot you,' Angus announced, too loudly. Dave quickly waved his hand in front of Angry's mouth.

'Sorry, Sarge,' murmured Angus meekly.

'You're doing all right, Angry,' Dave told him. 'You're doing more than fucking all right.'

Doc Holliday spoke again: 'I'd kill myself to save you doing it if I could.'

Finny said firmly: 'You're talking shit, Doc.'

Angus added: 'Yeah and I'm hungry, so tell me this, Doc, is it OK if we eat you after we shoot you?'

Dave said: 'Listen, Doc, you've got a twisted knee. Now stop trying to be Captain fucking Oates. Here's the plan. Remember the ridge running across the river valley and the desert? The track between PB Giants and PB Red Sox curves around it. I reckon it's just about one and a half kilometres from the relief. That's where we're staying tonight. We're there in fifteen minutes. Can you do fifteen minutes?'

Slowly, sadly, Doc Holliday nodded. 'I'll try. But I can't do it fast.'

Dave hoped he was right that they were so close to the ridge. It was a good hiding place, steep enough so that no one would have bothered to plant a mine there. Above the irrigation so there would be no night sluice workers. And near to their target. All they had to do was get there.

The last leg of their route to the ridge was the longest, slowest journey that Dave could remember. It was less than a kilometre but it felt like thirty. Finn went behind to support Doc and Dave put Angus at the front. This meant Dave had to remain fully alert at every moment. He had trusted Finn's instinctive awareness of danger but in comparison Angus was a big, blundering noise machine. He tried to tell himself that Angry had been moulded on mean streets which might have helped shape his survival instincts too. And, while Finny had been incapable of setting a really slow pace, Angus knew Doc's limitations.

What Dave had meant when he said that the ridge was fifteen minutes away was that it would be fifteen minutes if they were all fit. At this speed it would take more like an hour, Doc's body limp with agony. They continued at a snail's pace in total silence. Dave knew Angus would be getting frustrated. But when he stopped suddenly and turned towards Dave, it wasn't to voice objections or let off steam or be very angry. It was because they had almost reached their destination.

The ridge swelled above them. Dave could see it with the night-vision goggles but he wondered how Angus had sensed its presence from the canal in the dark.

Somehow they got the medic out of the water. Dave unfolded a field stretcher. Doc lay down on it gratefully and without arguing. Dave gave the injured man his rifle and day sack and Doc accepted them with fond familiarity, placing them across his body the way, thought Dave, that his elder daughter received her teddy bear at bedtime. Vicky's small, serious face, framed by wisps of fine blond hair, appeared inside his head. *Go away, Vicks. It's better not to think about you now*.

Finny and Dave stood at one end of the stretcher, big Angus at the other. Dave had remembered the ridge as rising gently to a halfway point, where it turned steep and rocky. His plan was to spend the rest of the night hidden by these rocks, before heading down before first light, earlier even than the call to prayer echoing across the valley. If they followed the canal at the extreme edge of the Green Zone, they would quickly reach the relief.

They lifted the stretcher. Holliday was deadweight heavy. Dave felt his arm and back muscles protest. The medic lay watching Dave's face.

'Shit,' he murmured, and closed his eyes.

Dave knew that casualties and fatalities punch at double their weight. He had prepared himself but nothing could prepare you for this. He forced himself to carry the stretcher up the hill, in total silence, teeth gritted, face grimacing, hot sweat running into his cold, wet clothes.

The hill was steeper and longer than he remembered it. The soft soil immediately by the irrigation canal soon gave way to sand, which finally gave way to the crunch underfoot of small rocks and then larger rocks. Finally the big boulders which would shelter them for the night loomed almost directly overhead. At first they seemed not to get any closer. Pain slashed at his muscles like a rip hook. He staggered. Dave was about to tell the others he could not go on without a rest when he realized that they had arrived. They were in the shadow of the boulders and all they had to do now was support the medic as he stood up and heaved himself between the big rocks.

It was difficult to put the stretcher down carefully. Dave just wanted to drop it and rid his muscles of the pain. A few centimetres from the ground the agony got the better of him and the stretcher touched down with a thump. Doc Holliday lay still.

'Wait, I'll recce,' breathed Finn, his slim body slipping between the boulders. Dave wanted to tell Angus to go with him but he was unable to speak. He was fighting the urge to splutter and gasp loudly for breath. He sat down next to the medic and waited.

Finny's return was announced by a slight rockfall. If anyone else was staying at the boulders tonight, they would certainly know there were some new guests checking in.

'Cave!' reported Finn.

They pulled Doc to his feet and he put one arm around Dave's shoulders and the other around Finny's and, his head drooping, hopped up the last part of the hill.

The cave had been chewed into the side of the ridge many years ago, perhaps by water when the Helmand River had been younger and more tumultuous. It contrived to see everything without being seen itself.

It looked out across the dark valley and tonight there was a panoramic view of the stars.

'Two minutes to eat and drink,' Dave instructed the other three. They sat in a row, looking out at the star show, munching in silence, while Dave reviewed the inside of the cave with his night-vision goggles.

It was obviously used by goat-herders because its gritty soil was lined with animal turds. It smelled strongly of goat, too. It went back into the rock about twenty metres but for roughly half of that you could not stand up without bending. The back part of the cave was less than a metre high. To the side, there was a ridge halfway up one of its rock walls. Leaving Doc on stag, Dave took Angus and Finn to help him climb it. They lifted him up and he saw it was not so much a ridge as an outcrop. Behind it a second chamber opened out. You could get right into the second chamber, which was low and smaller than the other.

'Fantastic. We sleep here on our belt buckles, rifles ready, heads down. One man on stag outside, one man sleeping in that corner there behind those rocks. If anyone comes in he can see without being seen.'

Dave looked at his watch. It was only 2300. Which meant that, incredibly, this was still the same day that they had left Bastion for the FOB. If they moved off tomorrow at 0400 they would get a refreshing five hours of sleep, minus stag duty. Except he knew one thing. He would not sleep.

Doc was still sitting munching and staring at the stars when they went back out for him.

'Kill me,' he urged them. 'I'd have done it while you were in there except the noise from my rifle would have blown your cover.'

'Shuddup, wanker,' said Dave affectionately, helping the medic to his feet.

'I'm serious. My wife's left me and the kids don't speak to me and she's even taken the fucking dog. What have I got to live for?'

Angus carefully placed Doc's arm around his shoulder to help him in. Dave noticed that Doc could put more weight on the knee now. Resting it must be the answer. In the morning he should be able to walk the last part of the journey.

'More wives, more dogs, that's the answer,' Dave told him.

'Not more fucking kids, though.'

'The kids you've already got at the moment will realize what a great bloke you are,' Dave assured him. 'Now shuddup. We'll get you on your ledge and you'll sleep. Without snoring.'

Finn stayed outside on stag and Angus and Dave managed to lever the medic up on to the ledge. He instantly put his rifle by his side, pushed his pouches around his body, went straight on to his belt buckle and got his head down.

'I'll go on stag first,' said Dave. 'Get up there, Angry.'

Angus asked to borrow the night-vision goggles before he climbed up behind Doc.

'Why?'

Angus looked embarrassed: 'Just so's I know there's no bats in here. I hate fucking bats.'

They still spoke in an undertone but no longer on a low, outward breath. It was strange to hear a hint of their own voices again. In fact, there were bats in the cave. Dave had noticed a small colony hanging around in the far corner of the small chamber, God knew why, since everyone knew bats were supposed to hang about in caves in the day and fly out at night. Bats or no bats, Dave would normally have told Angus to man up and lie down. But it was important for Angry to get some sleep.

'I've looked. There's no fucking bats.'

Angus's expression said he did not believe this.

'It's true,' Dave assured him sincerely. And it was. There were no fucking bats, only sleeping bats.

That satisfied Angry. Dave helped him climb up alongside Doc.

'You did well today, Angry. It was pretty tense out there but you saw what we had to do and you did it. That was fucking good.'

'Thanks, Sarge.'

Dave couldn't see Angry's face up on the ledge, but from his voice he guessed he was grinning.

Finny was sitting outside.

'All quiet?'

'Yeah. No noise at all, not anywhere.'

'I'll stay on stag,' Dave told him. 'Go in and get some rest.'

'Not sure I can sleep, Sarge.'

'Try.'

'Sarge . . . I killed Dawson.'

'What?'

'I killed him.'

Dave could see Finn's face in the dark, lean and worried, his eyes darting.

'What the fuck are you talking about, Finny?' he said gruffly. 'A raghead fired an RPG and hit the wheelbase of the truck causing it to capsize in the canal. Killing Dawson. So a fucking raghead killed Dawson, not you.'

'Yeah, but if I'd had my safety harness on, I wouldn't have hit him. See, my head hit his jaw, Sarge. That's what knocked him out. That's what happened. He drowned. He drowned because I knocked him out.'

Dave sat and thought for a moment. He looked up and saw the usual incredible blanket of stars, layer after layer, piled up into infinity. Infinity was a difficult idea to grasp, like death.

He said: 'OK, Finn, why didn't you have your safety harness on?'

Finn said: 'You know why, Sarge.'

'Let's pretend I don't know anything. Let's pretend you're up on a manslaughter charge for killing Dawson in some civilian court and the lawyer's asking you questions. So: are you supposed to wear your safety harness, Lance Corporal Finn?'

'Well, your honour, we're supposed to. And we always do in the UK. But in theatre they let us decide, see, because sometimes it's more dangerous to be all strapped up. If you're under heavy fire. You need to be free.'

'So you forgot to put on your harness today? Or you didn't want to?'

'Nah, I decided when we left the base I was better off without it.'

'For safety reasons?'

'Well, yeah.'

'Then your vehicle was blown up by the enemy and Lancer Dawson died?'

'Yeah.'

'Then the fucking enemy killed Dawson, not you, because you didn't just forget to put on your harness, you took a decision based on safety. For Chrissake, stop worrying about what can't be changed.'

It was easier to give advice than to follow it yourself. Because Dave had been haunted, on and off, by the suspicion that he never should have left the base this evening. Dawson was dead. And, over in the relief party, the man they had set out to save, McKinley, could be dead by now too.

As if he could read Dave's mind, Finn said: 'You did the right thing tonight, Sarge, taking Doc to McKinley. You didn't know it would go so wrong.'

Most people would say that venturing out to a casualty while there was no air support was risky. Some people would say that venturing out without air support or comms was suicidal. Maybe you had to be in the heat of battle to understand the decisions you made there.

'I hope we're not too late tomorrow morning to save Gerry,' said Dave.

'Will Doc be able to walk in the morning?'

'I just asked him that. And he told me to kill him.'

There was a pause. 'Sarge . . .'

'What, Finny?'

'I wanted to kill him tonight.'

'Why?'

'Because I thought he was right. It looked like a choice between having four men dead or one dead and three alive.'

'But that wasn't the choice, was it, Finny? Because we're all alive. So far.'

'Yeah.'

'And we don't have far to go in the morning. We're leaving at 0400, the bloke in the mosque starts singing them out of bed at around 0500, dawn's around 0615. I reckon we'll be home and dry by then.'

'Yeah.'

'And maybe we can bind up Doc's knee before we extract.'

'Yeah, right.'

They were silent. Then Finn said: 'Sarge, this is serious. Holed up in a fucking cave with the ragheads all over the place down there and a medic who can't walk and no comms.'

'It's serious, yeah. But we didn't join the army to learn how to make a good brew.'

There was another long pause.

'And we came through a lot of danger tonight,' added Dave. Not mentioning that they were one man down.

'Yeah,' Finn agreed. 'Yeah, if we can get through that . . .'

'We can get through anything. Now go in there and sleep. You've got two hours before you're on stag.'

But Finny did not move. Dave knew his mind was still whirring. And he knew it because his own was.

'Sarge, I reckon the hardest bit now is going to be at the end. Because there's going to be ragheads all around the relief party. They've had one blown-up Mastiff, now they'll be after another.'

Dave did not admit that Finny had voiced his own fear. His mind kept buzzing like a bee around the possibility that the relief party would be under ambush and they would not be able to approach it. Instead he said: 'Well, most of the night my ears were telling me they were still bombarding the base, not the relief.'

'I hope Sol and the boys are all right.'

'The relief lost a Mastiff but they've got a lot of men and ammo. Sol's more vulnerable, and maybe the Taliban know it,' agreed Dave.

Finny was silent again.

'Go to sleep,' Dave ordered him. 'You did fucking

well out there tonight, Finny. I knew I could rely on you.'

Finny stood up at last.

'Once Angus got himself under control you could rely on him too. He's a funny one, Sarge.'

He disappeared into the dark mouth of the cave. Dave followed him to help him on to the ledge. Angry muttered something which might have been a greeting when Finn arrived and lay beside him. But Doc said nothing. Dave hoped he was asleep.

When Dave had gone back on stag, Finn whispered: 'Angry, will you tell me something?'

Angus was grumpy as usual. 'Fucking what now?'

'Were you asleep?'

'Nope. Is that what you wanted to ask me?'

'Is Doc asleep?'

'You asleep, Doc?'

There was no reply.

'Angry, we might get killed,' said Finn. 'We might die.'

Angus took a deep breath.

'Yeah. And?'

'I want you to tell me something. If we live, I won't tell anyone, I promise.'

Angus sighed. 'What do you want to fucking know, Finny?'

'When we ran out of oil during training? And we couldn't get to Donnington . . . remember?'

'Yeah.'

'Where were you planning on going that day?'

'I told you. Got a bird up there.'

Finny shifted his weight so that a sharp rock dug into

463

his flesh instead of his spine. He said: 'I think you wanted to kill someone.'

There was a long silence.

At last Angus's whisper cut through the cave's still air. 'What makes you think that?'

'From your face when you got into the Land Rover,' lied Finny. 'Like you was on a mission, and it didn't look like that mission was shagging.'

With barely a pause, Angus said: 'All right, yeah, I was planning on killing someone.'

'For fuck's sake, Angry.'

'This bastard who deserves it, Finny. This fucking bastard who's got Mal really upset. Been throwing flames through his mum's letterbox, really trying to burn the fucking house down. With his mum and dad asleep inside! And it's the same with his brothers' taxis . . .' Angry's whisper was threatening to break into a voice.

'Shhhhh,' hissed Finny. Doc rearranged his position in his sleep.

'. . . and all because Mal's in the army fighting other Muslims. Mal can't even go home and see them 'cos it would mean more trouble. So I was going to sort it. That's all.'

'Sort it?'

'Yep. Mal knows the geezer who's doing it.'

'So how're you going to sort him?'

'I'll slot him.'

'Fucking hell, Angry!'

'Found out where he worked. Went there. Recced. Familiarized myself with the target. Real fucking sniper stuff, mate. Real Special Forces.'

'Familiarized yourself with the target? You mean you spoke to the bloke you were planning to banjo!'

'Ha! Pretended to buy a sofa from him, ha!'

'Shhhhh.'

'I ran out of time before we came back here, thanks to that fucking Land Rover breaking down. But I'll do it when I get back. And it's better. Because when I recced my face got all over their security cameras. They won't look back months and months on their security footage, though.'

'Angus, you can't do it, mate.'

'Don't you start. Mal and Binman keep saying I can't. But I fucking will.'

'Listen, Angry. Here it's war. Do it in England and it's murder.'

'Doesn't matter what you call it, I'm fucking doing it.'

'No! You'll go to jail. I know Mal's a good mate but—'

'You got families living out here with the Taliban scaring them and threatening them and we slot the Taliban. You got Mal's family in Wythenshawe living in fucking terror and no one sorts it. Not even Mal.'

'Listen to Mal. He knows Wythenshawe. Don't go barging in and—'

'Mal wants to sort it but he's promised his mum he won't do nothing. Never made no promises for me, though.'

'Get a grip, Angry, you dickhead. You'll be out of the army and into jail. For years and years.'

Angus said: 'Fuck off, Finny. It's all planned. It'll be quick and clean like a Special Forces op. I'll be miles away before they realize what's happened and they won't even know where to start looking.'

A third voice hissed at them out of the darkness.

'Lads, shuddup. It's bad enough trying to sleep here without you two yakking all night.'

The voice sounded alert. Finny wondered if Doc had been asleep at all or if he had heard the whole conversation.

The three men lay still in the cold, silent void of the cave. Finny could not sleep. The reason was not fear, the cold or the hard rock beneath him. It was the knowledge weighing inside him like a stone that Angus would go ahead with his mission to kill a man no matter what.

37

Jenny surveyed the dining-room table. It was still covered in neat piles of paper but now she could gather these up and pack them away in boxes.

'I didn't think we'd finish so early,' said Eugene. Jenny looked at her watch. She didn't think it was early.

'They'll all find it in their email when they get to work tomorrow morning,' she said with satisfaction.

'Come and sit down and have a glass of wine. You can relax for five minutes before you go, can't you?'

There were two threadbare old armchairs in front of the fire. A dog was sitting in one of them. Jenny sat down in the other. Eugene disappeared into the kitchen. Jenny watched the flames, blue, red and orange, dance wildly around the logs. She felt the fire's heat.

Eugene reappeared and handed her a glass of cool white wine. He seemed to be drinking whisky. He shooed away the dog, sat down and they clinked glasses.

'To a successful report!' he said.

'To a successful report!'

She sipped the wine. It tasted good.

'What will happen to the report now?' she asked.

'Well, a few people have a sneak preview. Then it's published. Then journalists come and ask questions and make comments and they mostly print rubbish, picking out the most sensational stuff. The Government promises to review our findings. And then nothing happens.'

Jenny closed her eyes.

'So it's all been a complete waste of time?'

'Probably. The Government generally shelves any recommendations it doesn't like. But reports like ours can go some way towards shaping public opinion. At the very least it should stimulate some debate about what we want from a defence strategy.'

The fire felt warm on Jenny's eyelids. She didn't want to open them. She realized how tired she was.

'You know you can sleep here if you like.'

'No. Thanks . . .'

He said: 'I hardly ever wish I was twenty years younger. But I do now.'

She felt herself smile.

He chuckled wistfully. 'But don't worry. I have the company of a clever, beautiful woman three times a week. I'd be an old fool to ask for more.'

She looked at him. His face was softened by the firelight.

They watched a log lose its shape and disintegrate in the grate to glowing grey ashes.

'I must go now,' she said, but did not get up.

He said: 'If I take the job in Libya, I'll be away for six months. Until the end of the year. If you're not working anywhere else then, will you consider coming back? I'd like to carry on with my memoirs. I've got a few things to get off my chest.'

She said: 'Chalee.'

He flinched.

'What do you know about Chalee?' he asked, looking at the fire.

'Nothing really.'

'So ... you tell people you're working for me. And they say: Chalee. Am I right?'

'Yes.'

'I *must* finish my memoirs. So people know the truth.'

She was careful. 'Will you tell me what happened there, Eugene?'

'In 2003 Chalee was a Taliban stronghold and when we leave Afghanistan in the next few years it will, in my opinion, become a Taliban stronghold again. It's surrounded by poppies and the trade routes from the town are good and, historically, certain powerful families are based there. I was a brigadier then and I was in a very good position to take Chalee away from them. The operation took weeks to plan and I had good support with extra helicopters, Merlins covering Chinooks, A10s standing by from Kandahar, you name it, I had it in place. On the ground, I moved six hundred fighting troops out of Bastion. We knew the Taliban would put up one hell of a fight but we also knew we'd win. Then, at the very last minute, I had to withdraw. And I couldn't tell anyone why. So there are some people who've never forgiven me because we didn't take it again until 2009.'

'Why did you have to withdraw?'

Eugene frowned into the fire. 'No choice. Special Forces had intelligence that a very senior Al Qaeda figure was in the town. At some sort of a family party. They had a hit squad lined up to go in and take him out cleanly. Killing him was more important than securing the town and trying to do both at once would have jeopardized the Special Forces operation and probably ended up with a bloodbath at the party. I was told to hold firm, then to back off completely. But since it was a Special Forces op, I couldn't tell anyone why.'

'Did they kill him?'

'Not then. Not for another couple of months. They finally managed to follow him over the Pakistan border and then they got him. But, of course, no one knew anything about that. To everyone else involved, it just seemed I had a big operation lined up and that I'd bottled out of it. They knew I was extremely concerned about ensuring there were no civilian casualties and they thought I had let women in headscarves scare me away.'

Jenny had been watching Eugene's face. From the fast, intense way he spoke, his voice lowered, she knew that he had never told anyone this before. And she could see it was painful to tell it now.

She said: 'But operations often stop at the last minute. Dave's told me. He never asks why. He knows there are good reasons and he just accepts it. Civilian casualties are a good reason.'

'I don't think anyone would have questioned it if it hadn't been for my nephew.'

'Your nephew?'

'My sister's son. In my opinion, he never should have joined the army. There was a certain family pressure, I suppose. He's a lawyer now and he loves it.'

'Was he there?'

'He'd just left Sandhurst and was commanding his first platoon. He was sent straight to Chalee, where there were always skirmishes while the Taliban held it. He was wounded and before we left Bastion for our big operation, I went to see him in the hospital. He begged

470

me to abort the whole mission, saying that the Taliban there were better equipped and had a lot more men than we thought and were likely to take civilian hostages. He wasn't experienced enough to know what he was saying, plus he was injured – I think he was being flown home that night. The least I could do was promise to consider what he said. So I patted his hand and told him I'd think about aborting the operation. Then I wished him good luck.'

'You didn't retreat because of anything he said?'

'Of course not. I had planned the operation with great care to avoid any civilian casualties or hostage-taking. But other patients in other beds overheard every word. And when the whole operation went pear-shaped, tongues were wagging all over Bastion. It's such a closed community that it doesn't take much. One word in the NAAFI. Soon everyone believed that on my nephew's scaremongering I'd turned tail and run.'

'And you couldn't tell anyone the real reason!'

His face was flushed now, not with anger, she thought, but by the memory of shame. 'It was very hard. Walking around at Bastion and trying to hold my head high, knowing what people were saying about me.'

Jenny tried to imagine the hot desert world, men and artillery and vehicles and weapons all baking in the sun, waiting to advance. And Eugene's desperation when he realized he couldn't.

'My middle name's Howard. I heard them calling me Eugene Coward-Hardy.'

She did not need to ask how that felt. She saw it in his face. He continued to stare into the fire. He said: 'Incredible how a lifetime's hard work can be destroyed in a day.'

'But you became a general.'

'Yes, I made it to major general, because the high-ups knew the truth, of course. All the same, some of the mud stuck. Later on, long after the death of the Al Qaeda 2 i/c, I could let it be known why I'd retreated that day. Too late. Reputations are strange things. They have a sort of life of their own. Sometimes the hot air is a lot more pervasive than the facts.'

Jenny thought of her own reputation. It was true. Her friends had preferred hot air to facts.

'Eugene, write all this down,' she said. 'I want to type the true story for your memoirs. And you should write about how it feels to have everyone calling you a coward.'

'There aren't words for it, Jennifer. For the way it stings. Even now, I see soldiers looking at me in a certain way and I know they're thinking: Chalee.'

'Send me your memoirs, even from Libya, and I'll type them. I want to. Please.'

He sighed. 'You know me very well, Jennifer. I think you know more about my life than anyone but me now.'

She said: 'Sometimes, if I've been typing memoirs all day, I don't know where you stop and I start.'

They smiled at each other.

Eugene said: 'Your husband's a very lucky man. I hope he appreciates you.'

Jenny did not answer.

When she got up to go her body felt stiff, as if she had been sitting in one position for a long time.

At the door, Eugene put his arms around her. It felt good, very good, to be enveloped by the warm arms of a man who cared about her. It made her feel safe and happy. She knew that he would respond if she lifted her face up to be kissed. She did not.

As she pulled away, opening the door on to sheets of rain, he said: 'It's a filthy night. Will you phone me or text me as soon as you get home? So I know you've arrived?'

'Yes.'

'Promise?'

'I promise.'

Dave sat silently, all his senses alert. He heard distant dogs barking to each other from scattered compounds. There was a spate of firing which he guessed came from a base, maybe PB Boston Red Sox. Once, far away, he heard men shouting, not at each other, he thought, but at animals. There was some occasional distant splashing and scraping which he now recognized as the sluice system.

He thought of Lancer Dawson. He didn't know anything about the man, didn't even know if he was married. He would have to visit the relatives, usually either a wife or mother, and tell them about Dawson's last hours. He wouldn't tell them about that dead hand, reaching out for the steering wheel but grasping only water.

At 1300 he went back into the cave. Finny was up and ready to go out instantly. Dave guessed he hadn't slept. The others were still and no breathing was audible, let alone snoring. Maybe no one had slept.

'Fucking freezing in here,' muttered Finn as he pulled Dave up.

On the ledge, it was very cold and very dark. When Dave passed over the night-vision goggles it crossed his mind that a grave couldn't be darker than this cave where the rocks had been untouched by sun for millennia. He settled himself into the position he had earmarked earlier, the vantage point for watchers. Rocks above and below made it hard to be seen. And still harder to sleep here. He felt the rocks with his hands. In places their ancient, hard surfaces were smooth. The river could not rise this high, so what had smoothed them? The hands of other men like him? Had this place been a hideout for bandits and warriors in a battle-torn land for centuries? And, a chilling thought, did they use it still?

He tried to fall asleep thinking about the other men who had crouched up here on cold nights, trying to sleep and stay alert at the same time. Sleep did not come. He ordered himself to sleep. He could not. He felt intense cold roll up his body like fog. Unable to fight it with movement, he tensed and untensed his muscles. Except he wasn't very good at the untensing bit.

With his face down on jutting rocks in a pitch-black cave with cold gradually seizing him and the knowledge that tomorrow morning would bring even more dangers than they had already faced, his mind threw images from the day at him.

The hot shower at Bastion that morning. Shaving, knowing that it would be his last shave for some time. Arriving at the FOB and then rushing around to leave it at once. The boss's nonchalant announcement that he was staying at the FOB and leaving with the relief after lunch. A US Marine pressing a Bible into the hands of an astonished Slindon. Then Slindon later, up in the tower, peering with the binoculars at a distant column of ominous black smoke – twice. The grateful, shocked voice of the boss when Dave radioed that he was bringing a medic for Gerry McKinley. The flash of the RPG preceding by a few seconds the Mastiff's falter. His powerlessness as he was caught up in the huge machine's twist and roll. The weight of the driver's body; how Dawson had been as uncooperative in death as he had in life. And then their silent flight up to their chests in the murky canal . . .

'Sarge! Wake up!'

'Is it 0400?'

'No, there's blokes just down in the Green Zone.'

'What sort of blokes?'

'Don't know, but I think they're coming up here.'

Jenny drove out of Tinnington, the rain slapping against her windscreen and gusts buffeting her car, with the feeling that she had just had a very narrow escape. She was relieved to reach the camp. Her eyes were tired. They felt as though they had sawdust in them.

It was strange to walk up her path without the children. Stranger still to put the key in the lock with one hand and not have a baby or buggy in the other. She stepped into the empty, childless house. She was completely alone here. The dark stillness was like a cave.

She dropped her bag into its customary corner and then, remembering her promise to phone Eugene, she fished in it for her mobile.

She went into the dark kitchen, where she planned to sit down, pull off her shoes and have a cup of tea before falling into bed. She switched on the light.

A man was sitting there.

She jumped and opened her mouth to scream but no noise came out.

'Evening, Jenny,' said Steve Buckle.

He was relaxing in a chair with his feet, one real, one fake, on the table.

'Steve! What are you doing here? You made me jump out of my skin!' Her body gasped for breath while her mind tried to make sense of this situation. And why had she spoken as if the sight of a man in the kitchen had been terrifying until she realized that man was Steve? As if he had some kind of right to be sitting here in the dark? Why was she trying to normalize something which was very far from normal? In fact it was so abnormal that she still wanted to scream. Although no one would hear.

'Well, Jenny, I thought it was time we had a little chat.'

He must have taken Leanne's key to this house. It was too easy for him.

'That's nice, Steve, but a little chat tomorrow morning would be even nicer.'

Steve took his feet off the table and swung round to face her.

'I'll tell you what really pisses me off, Jenny. It pisses me off the way you're smiling at me.'

She felt her own face harden.

'I'm not smiling. Because I'm not that pleased to see you. I'm tired and I'd like to go to bed now.'

'Did he exhaust you? Did General Coward wear you out?'

She wasn't scared any more. She was angry.

'Steve. Go home. If you want to talk to me, we'll talk tomorrow.'

She could smell booze. But his speech wasn't slurred; his face didn't have the distortions of drunkenness.

'No, Jenny. I want to talk to you now.'

'Leave this house, please. Or I'll have to call the police.'

He stood up and walked towards her. At first she did not move. She stood rooted to the spot, looking him directly in the eye, but as he got closer, bearing down on her like a large, armoured vehicle, she lost her nerve and started to back towards the door. He was too quick, darting around her on his prosthetic leg, slamming the kitchen door, standing against it.

Her heart stopped pounding and started battering against her ribs.

Steve had survived two bomb blasts. He had lost one leg. Had he also lost his sanity?

She jumped suddenly when her mobile phone started to ring. She was still holding it and tried to answer it but Steve leaped forward and grabbed her hand roughly.

'Let it ring.'

'It might be Dave.'

'Everyone knows you never speak to Dave these days. Too busy with your fuck buddy.'

She felt a new fury. The phone was still ringing but she was powerless to answer it. When it had stopped he said: 'Turn it off.'

'No.'

He twisted her wrist easily. It required little effort on the part of this big man to cause her pain. The phone fell from her hand and bounced on the floor. At that moment the landline started to ring.

'Leave it. I'm talking to you.'

'It might be Dave,' she repeated lamely, knowing that both calls must have been Eugene, anxious because she had not rung him as promised. What would he do now he had received no reply? He cared about her. Did he care enough about her to come looking for her on a wet, windy night? *Please come looking for me, Eugene. Please.*

'That's not Dave. He's fast asleep in some FOB. Wishing he hadn't married a slag like you.'

'Fuck off, Steve.'

'Don't flash those eyes at me. It might turn your fuck buddy on, but it just makes me want to hit you. I expect that was General Coward on the phone. He'll think you've fallen asleep already because you're exhausted. I saw what time you left the camp, slag, and I know what you've been doing since then.'

She kept her voice strong and firm. Although it wanted to waver. 'Why are you here?'

'I'm here on behalf of my mate, Sergeant Dave Henley. And I'm here in memory of another mate, Rifleman Jamie Dermott, 1 Section, 1 Platoon. See, Jamie was married to a slag of a wife who was with her fuck buddy while he lay dying. He knew what was going on and he suffered a lot and Dave knows all about what you're up to. He's hurting. He's hurting a lot. And I'm asking myself, Jenny Henley, who the fuck you think you are, going around causing a fighting soldier so much pain? He's away on the front line, he's fighting for you and for his country, and all you can do is get your knickers off with some old geezer who should know better.'

'Get out.'

'No. Don't expect you want to hear the truth. Don't expect you like it, do you?'

'Get out. You don't know what the truth is. You just like the sound of your own voice in my kitchen in the middle of the night. Where does Leanne think you are now? What will she say when she finds out you've been here after midnight?'

Steve hesitated and Jenny knew she had scored a direct hit.

'Leave my wife out of it.'

'Why should I? You think you can tell me how to behave? Look at your own behaviour. Ask yourself whether you make Leanne happy with all your anger and shouting.'

She didn't see his fist, only heard the crack of it against her jaw and then felt pain snapping through her face like a series of metal poles thrust through her cheeks.

Dave and Angus leaned down to pull Finny up to the ledge. He was swift and quiet.

'Give me the NVGs,' whispered Dave.

'Is Doc OK?' asked Finny.

'Fucking fantastic,' a gloomy voice whispered back. Dave felt a mad urge to laugh.

The men lay motionless on the cave's rocky ledge, straining to hear in the extreme darkness. Dave wasn't sure if that deafening thud was his own heart or the combined hearts of all four of them, thumping in unison against the rock.

Sure enough, there were voices. At first it sounded like just a couple of men. Good. With the element of surprise on their side they could deal with a couple. But then more voices joined the others, calling from outside. They were climbing the steep ridge, silenced by the gradient until they reached the cave.

Then he heard a dog bark. Shit! Another dog snapped back at it and the barking that followed reassured him that these animals were not following a scent. They were arguing over essentials like food and resting places. Dave felt the hairs on the back of his neck stand up when he realized that the men were coming to the cave to stay here. For the rest of the night, perhaps. Maybe for longer.

His heart ached. They had come so far. In their lives. And on their journey tonight. Was this as far as they were destined to travel? For a few moments he allowed himself to give in to despair. It was as black and cold and rocky as the cave itself, only despair had a much smaller exit.

Finny was lying against him and now he felt a strong pressure from that side. What was Finny trying to tell him?

He heard a sound that was half a breath. 'NVG . . .'

Shit! The glow from the goggles! He scrambled to take them off before the voices got any closer. Their faint green glow would certainly be visible in this intense darkness.

A few moments later, voices entered the cave. He did not hear anyone strike a match but a hand held up a tiny flame. By its light Dave saw dark faces, moistened with sweat, eyes bright. He could not count how many. The hand holding the match stretched out so that the light flickered around the cave walls. Dave did not breathe. He shut his eyes as the light neared his face. The other lads all had their heads down and were pretty well undetectable unless someone happened to climb up here. In which case, they were dead. Because he had time to see an AK47 thrown carelessly across a shoulder before the light blinked out.

So these men were not wandering camel-keepers or local goat-herders who had scrambled up here for the night to rest. They were Taliban. The men perceived no danger. They made no attempt to drop their voices. They called to each other and one man shouted at the dogs to get outside. They were without fear. Dave thought the whole cave must stink of terror, the terror of four silent, trapped British soldiers. But the insurgents chatted amiably among themselves, oblivious to their presence. And it seemed they preferred to keep their dogs outside. *Thank you, Allah, for that.*

What were they doing in the pitch black? Could they see in the dark? They were dragging things around and calling to each other. Were they building a PB here? Dave knew what Doc Holliday would say about that. *Fucking fantastic.* He wanted to corpse at the thought of Doc's sardonic voice. He might as well. Because all four of them would soon be corpses anyway.

He felt the return of the strange, sudden piercing sense of grief he had experienced hours earlier when the Mastiff overturned. Once again Jenny appeared inside his head with the girls. This time there was an expression of immense sadness on her face. She had received the knock at the door, the news. She reached out for him. Jaime was on her hip, looking at her mother, but Vicky, tear-stained, clinging to Jenny, was reaching out towards him too. There were his mother and stepfather again, staring at him as if he was a ghost, his mother crying. As for his drunken dad, the old man still sat outside some pub with his glass empty before him and his head in his hands. Dave loved these people, even his dad. If he died he would lose them all. He felt his guts twist painfully with grief, as if he was a silent mourner at his own funeral.

He continued to stare down into the well of darkness, where Taliban fighters not two metres away were busy dragging something around the cave floor. Then suddenly, surprisingly, he was looking into Jamie Dermott's face. Not the Jamie whom he had last seen dying, a man in agony, his body sliced by an RPG. Here was the real Jamie, tall, whole, the good soldier. Jamie Dermott in desert camouflage with helmet, webbing and rifle. Solid, always in the right place at the right time, always ready, always alert.

Jamie looked right back at him and said: 'It's not over till it's over, Sarge.'

Dave wanted to reach out and grab the man but he could not move. Helpless, he had to watch as Jamie gave him one of those strange, wistful smiles of his, and faded before his eyes. He wanted to shout to him but he could not speak.

38

Jenny was trying to get up when something hit her sharply in the chest and took her breath away. She tried to pull in another breath, like a smoker desperate for one last drag, but if there was air available she could not reach it. She fought for breath and lost, sinking back down on the kitchen floor, helpless and gasping.

Why try to fight? Stand up? Breathe? Why? Steve was big and he was strong and she was powerless.

She lay on the floor in a crumpled heap. She closed her eyes. She felt herself switch into a strange new state, floating high above the ceiling, the roof, even above the rainclouds. Far below her she could see her own kitchen. On it, her body lay curved on the floor, Steve standing over her, his back against the door. Even from up here you could feel his huge, dark, angry presence.

She saw with a detached interest that he was kicking her. He was kicking the side of her body and she was not even trying to stop him, just curling up against the force of his prosthetic foot, the foot on the end of the metal jumble which was his leg. He swung it back as far as the kitchen door would allow him and then he swung it forward again in a smooth arc which terminated in her stomach.

She listened. The kitchen was silent except for Steve's swearing, a sound as inevitable and uninteresting as wallpaper or the background music in a shop. The woman on the floor was not crying out or begging him to stop or swearing back at him. She was lying in silence while his huge foot kicked her over and over and over again.

Then the woman on the floor pulled herself up on to her hands very suddenly and pivoted sideways in a neat, circular movement and it was too late for Steve to stop the trajectory of his swinging leg and so this time he missed her. He lost his balance for a moment and in that moment the woman should have pushed him, pushed him with all her strength, and he would have toppled or fallen. But she did not. Instead she watched as he regained his balance, staring at her, breathing hard.

Clear of his leg now, sitting up on the floor, one knee under her and holding her throbbing side, she said: 'Stop, Steve. Just stop and think what you're doing.'

And Steve said: 'You fucking slag, you never thought what you were doing with your fuck buddy, did you? You never thought about Dave!'

'I think about Dave all the time! He's my husband!'

'Yeah, slag, and you forget that when it suits you.'

'I never do, Steve.'

'"I never do, Steve,"' he echoed, turning her voice into a caricature of itself, into a small, whining, little-girl voice.

He diminished her. She felt angry and this anger returned her, with a rush, to her own body. She looked up at him, his big face swollen, his eyes dark, his face shadowed. Steve, but not the Steve she used to know, a

484

different, insane Steve. She scrambled to her feet. Pain threatened to take over her right cheek, her jaw, her temple. The pain almost blinded her and she felt sickness turn inside her stomach. She was going to throw up. She fought the urge to vomit, fought the pain, and found her voice.

'That's enough. Stop now, Steve, before you do something you really regret.' Speaking hurt. It sent lines of agony across her face.

'I won't fucking regret it, slag. I might pay for it, but I won't regret it.'

'I'm phoning Leanne. I'm going to—'

She didn't see the truck which drove into her face. She felt its weight and heard its sickening crack. Tendrils of lightning flashed around her nose and eyes, into her hairline, blue streaks reverberated inside her head, and afterwards there was a series of explosions, each with a payload of pain. She did not know where on her face he had hit her. As the lightning subsided she could feel pain everywhere, on both cheeks, across her skull, stretching down her back to join up with the dull, throbbing pain where he had kicked her side. It was all connected. He had turned her body into an electrical circuit which conducted pain.

She had fallen backwards across the kitchen worktop, head lolling. Now she managed to twist so that she could fold herself across the counter for support. She tried to hold her head in her hands, but this hurt so much that she just placed her forehead directly on the cool surface.

Steve was shouting: 'Don't you bring Leanne into this. She's a fat cow but she never looks at any other man. She wouldn't do that. She wouldn't run around some bloke who's got no balls just because he's rich and

485

he's a general. She doesn't fancy herself like you do.'

Then his hands closed roughly on her head and he lifted it only to bang it down hard on the work surface. He dragged her head up again by her hair and pulled it back, back, until the skin along the front of her neck stretched like a drum's surface. Then, when it would go no further, he pushed her head forward as suddenly as a fairground ride and there was a dull thud as her face smashed into the counter and the fairground lights, powered by pain, flashed on all over her head.

'Bitch, slag, cunt, you've got everything you fucking want, you've got a man with two legs because I got blown out of the wagon instead of him, you've got another man with no balls but a big house, you've got money, you've got a baby, you've got people looking at you in your fucking dress, you've got it all and you still can't stop yourself being a slag—'

The skin on her neck threatened to rip again as he dragged her head back by her hair. All the small tubes which stretched down inside her throat reached breaking point. He was peeling the hair off her scalp. Then everything snapped forward and she heard the sound of her head crashing against the worktop again moments before she felt the pain.

Nothing would stop him now. Steve was on his own, private journey to hell and he would take her with him. All the way.

With immense sadness, a pain inside her which was deeper, heavier, more penetrating than any injury inflicted by Steve, Jenny sent Dave her love. As Steve smeared her face in her own blood she wished her husband farewell, and she told her daughters that she loved them and she would never stop loving them, even from beyond the grave. She saw Dave, standing in some over-bright FOB in that faraway desert, receiving the news from an embarrassed, unhappy officer. Dave's shock. Dave flying home to pick up the girls from a silent, bleak-faced Adi. Dave bringing them back to the empty house, a house with no heart, a house with silence at its centre because she would not be there.

For a moment she gazed on Dave. He was lying in a small, dark space. He was not moving but he was not dead. He was very scared. He was scared to move. Her heart beat harder for him.

I love you, Dave, she thought. Together, you and me and the girls, together we are a home. When one of us is missing, there is no home. I'm sorry that the person missing is going to be me. I'm sorry. Love the girls enough for both of us. Please.

Jamie Dermott, as usual, was right, Dave decided. It wasn't over till it was over. The Taliban might just be here to bury something or dig something up and if the soldiers could stay motionless and silent for long enough . . . At that moment, the lights went on.

So that's what the ragheads had been doing. Building a fire. It sprang into flame as though lit by spontaneous combustion and the men made approving noises and then settled themselves around it. Some produced flat-breads from their pockets and began to eat them. A few held the breads up to the fire and the sweet smell of warm, simple food wafted around the cave. The insurgents relaxed, passing bread to each other, although Dave noticed they were warriors enough to keep their weapons to hand. A few continued to wear them.

Dave tried to count how many were here but didn't want to move his head. And he knew there were more outside with the dogs. Attracted by the smell of the food, two big, thin, ugly mutts tried to enter the cave and voices outside yelled at them. The dogs backed off. Say, two outside. And maybe ten in here. Twelve men with eyes and ears and senses that could detect four men hiding in their midst. He had been cold a few minutes ago. Now he was sweating and he was sure the others were too. They would die if there was just one insurgent with a keen enough sense of smell to detect their sweat, or another with ears sharp enough to catch the thud of their hearts, or another with eyes quick enough to glimpse Dave's eyeballs moving.

Scarcely daring to breathe, he watched them by the light of the fire.

They're just like us, he thought. He recognized fellow soldiers, sharp-faced and battle-hardened. They're having a brew and some rations and maybe they'll get their heads down.

From time to time different men looked for signals on their mobile phones, failed to find one inside the cave, and then went outside for a few minutes. They could be heard barking or crooning into them.

Inside the men talked and laughed. Dave couldn't speak Pashto but he didn't need to because soldiers were the same everywhere. They were ribbing one of the younger blokes about something. He'd been firing and lost his footing and toppled over still firing. Dave knew that because a couple of his mates got up to imitate him. First one – everyone laughed and the lad they were teasing reddened – and then another, in much more comic and exaggerated a style, and everyone cackled into their beards even more. Dave almost caught himself joining in. Ha ha. A Taliban fighter fell over while aiming at a British soldier and almost killed his mate. Well, that was fucking hilarious.

The talk went on. It grew serious. One man was insisting on something and the others were disagreeing with him. There was a lot of gesticulating. It was turning into a stand-off, when a third man intervened. Ah, the peacemaker. Or was he just of higher rank? He said a few surly words to the quarrelling men and they lowered their heads. One looked embarrassed. The other looked sulky. Dave concluded that the third man was the Taliban equivalent of himself, a platoon sergeant telling Finny and Angry to wind their necks in.

Dave examined their faces. The man they had been laughing at was the youngest here. He was the Slindon of the platoon. After that, ages varied much more than in the British Army. One man was old, his hair white, his arms skeletal. He squatted closer than anyone to the fire. But one look at his face told you that here was a survivor of many skirmishes. He was scarred. He was hard. Once he laughed and Dave saw that he was toothless. Most of the others were Dave's age or younger. They were thin and tired and they wore sandals on bare feet but they were fighters, every one of them. He had never been sure that was true of the ANA men they worked with. Maybe the Taliban creamed off the best.

Despite the fact that every muscle in his body was as tightly strung as a violin, Dave found his mind wandering back to PB Red Sox. Had the lads watched while insurgents swarmed all over the vehicle, over Dawson? Tiny would be furious with himself for not getting the second Mastiff out of the base. When the platoon all finally met up again and Mal heard what had happened to them this night, he would be jealous because, if there was any danger out there, Mal wanted some of it.

Maybe there had been enough danger at Red Sox to keep him satisfied.

Suddenly there was a noise, too loud, too close. *Fuck!* It was Angus. Or Doc. *Fuck!*

A couple of the ragheads jumped up and stared in the direction of the rock, straight at the soldiers, squinting in the light of the fire. It was positioned near the mouth of the cave but smoke had wafted in and up, creating a gauzy haze.

The two men who had jumped to their feet hissed at the others to be quiet. But a branch in the fire fell and the logs and flames rearranged themselves, disguising further sound for a moment. What had caused the noise? Had Angus suppressed a sneeze? Had the smoke made him cough? Had Doc moved and knocked the butt of his rifle?

Sure that now they must be discovered, Dave felt adrenalin surge through his body. This was the moment to grab his rifle and start firing. At least he would slot as many of them as possible before they took their revenge.

It's not over till it's over, Sarge.

OK, Dermott.

Dave let his heart thump the moment past like a musician beating time. A few beats later, four bats swooped out of the second chamber, over Angus's bowed head, into the smoke.

Ah, said the men, so that's what it was! Bats!

Dave could understand them as if they were speaking English. It was strange to have that sense of clarity in another language. He also understood them when they started teasing the young insurgent who had slipped with his weapon today. They were saying that he hadn't turned a hair when he had thought there was

490

someone hiding in the cave but as soon as he'd seen the bats he'd been terrified. The young insurgent blushed a bit and nodded and admitted that he didn't like bats much, just as Angry McCall had done earlier.

Dave realized the noise had probably come from Angus. Because bats were surely silent. Disturbed by the smoke, they might have been flying around the second chamber for a few minutes and when one had flown close to Angus he had jumped. Thank God, or Allah, or both, that the bats had flown out into the second chamber so rapidly to explain the noise.

Their suspicions allayed, the men settled down by the fire again and Dave felt his adrenalin drain and his heartbeat ease – although the ends of his nerves were still tingling. He knew he had been close to storming out of the hiding place and blowing everything. Only Jamie Dermott's words had stopped him. A dead man had appeared inside his head and given him advice which had saved their lives. This knowledge made the hairs stand up on the back of Dave's neck. But it made him feel good, too. As if Jamie was there soldiering with him, helping him, supporting him.

Jenny only half heard the distant crash of a window. It was just something else breaking, inside her or outside her; she didn't know which and she didn't care any more because she was barely here now. She was somewhere dark and still with Dave, reaching out for him, trying to calm his beating heart.

The kitchen door banged open.

A loud, firm voice said: 'Stop this, Rifleman. Now.'

And the great weight which had been on her back, her arms, her head, was suddenly lifted off her.

She did not move. She did not look up. Steve was

shouting and there was someone else in the room, his voice crisp, compelling, authoritative. But not raised. She recognized that voice but did not attempt to remember to whom it belonged. The sound of it had brought her back to the kitchen and the kitchen was pain. All over her body but especially her head. It was the sort of pain which kept you motionless.

'Sit there. Put your hands on the table. Don't attempt to move.'

Steve was saying something, but the voice was commanding. It was a voice which had commanded hundreds, maybe thousands, of men. It said: 'Silence now, please.'

And at the sound of that voice, Steve fell silent.

Jenny had not heard silence for a very long time. It had a viscous property; it was thick like a blanket.

'Jennifer . . .' Eugene took her arm and then her shoulders and gently turned her around so that he could see her face. 'Oh God,' he said. 'What has he done to you?'

He supported her to her feet. She leaned heavily on him. Together they stepped to the kitchen table. Had she been lying looking up at the chair legs just a few minutes ago? Or hours ago? She sank on to a chair now. She tried to lean her head on her hands but she could not touch her face without small rivers bleeding pain from even the slightest pressure. Her eyes wandered across to Steve. He did not look at her. He made as if to stand up.

'You have been ordered to sit down,' snapped the general, and the rifleman sat down.

'Please put your hands back on the table as instructed,' said Eugene. Steve put his hands on the table, large palms flat, bony knuckles uppermost. Jenny

492

stared at the knuckles and remembered the sight of them rushing towards her.

Eugene found the freezer. He opened it and dug out a bag of frozen peas, passing it to Jenny. She clamped the peas immediately to her face. They did not anaesthetize her pain but they brought a certain alleviation, like a kind friend.

Eugene remained standing. 'What is your full name, Rifleman?' he asked. Jenny was surprised when Steve rattled off both his name and number mechanically and without protest.

'Rifleman Buckle, I thought so. I've heard a lot about you, Buckle,' said Eugene. Jenny stared at him. Steve looked up.

'I have helped the MoD evolve its short-term response and long-term strategy for the wounded. In that context, I have examined the records of a number of soldiers, including yours. I know that you are a brave and generous infanteer who was always at the heart of his fighting unit, who took care of his comrades in training and then in the heat of battle in Iraq. In Afghanistan, also in the heat of battle, you were blown up and lost a leg. Later, in convalescence, you played a key role in the rehabilitation of other men. You were recently used by the army as an example to the press of a man who is learning to live with his new disability. Am I right in thinking that a campaign to return to the front line got you as far as Bastion?'

Steve nodded. His eyes were large, his face swollen, as if he had been crying.

'I understand, Buckle, that on exiting Bastion the vehicle you were travelling in hit an IED. The second of your career?'

Steve nodded again.

'That's two more than most people survive. You are a remarkable man.'

Steve did not blink or remove his eyes from the general.

'You are also a wounded soldier. Asking you to adjust to a quiet life in Stores while your comrades are all back on the front line is asking too much of a man of your calibre and character. Your appalling behaviour tonight is shocking, but it is not surprising. I know, because I know the kind of man you are, and that you will be deeply ashamed of this for the rest of your life.'

Steve hung his head.

'Jennifer will have to decide if she wants to press charges—'

'No,' said Jenny. Pain shot across her face. Her voice had a strange, deep quality, as if she'd been smoking all night.

'—and she is in no state to make such a decision now. However, you are in no state to be allowed loose in this camp, either. I'm not calling the civil or the military police, but please remember that I can if you behave badly.'

Steve's eyes did not move from the general. He nodded slightly.

'I'm calling for a vehicle to take you quietly and discreetly to Headley Court. What you have done to Jennifer tonight is a crime. It is also, I believe, the legacy of combat. If, as she generously suggests, Jennifer doesn't choose to press charges, it may be possible to keep this away from the police and off your record. But you'll need to work hard, Buckle. Rehabilitation is a long, hard, lonely battle to fight, and no one gives you a medal. You will need comrades and at Headley Court there are comrades to fight alongside you.

Rehabilitation is about changing your behaviour. Buckle, you must change. Or the next time there will be police, courts, jail.'

Steve put his head in his hands. He remained silent.

'Leanne,' Jenny said.

'His wife?'

'She lives . . . across the road.' Each word cost a lot in pain. Eugene passed her the phone and she dialled the number and handed it back to him.

The receiver was snatched up as if Leanne had been waiting for a call.

'Steve, where the hell are you?' she roared. Jenny could hear her from across the table. Steve started at the sound of her voice, even this small, tinny version of it.

Eugene explained that there had been a difficulty at the Henleys' house. Steve was here now. Could she leave her children for a few moments to cross the road?

Leanne's voice was still audible.

'Oh fuck it, what's Steve been doing?'

Then she slammed down the receiver. Jenny got up to open the door. Her whole body ached as she moved. Her head felt twice its normal size. She walked very carefully in case it toppled off. When she reached the door, Leanne was already standing there. She saw Jenny's face and screamed.

'He's inside,' said Jenny in that slow, deep voice she had acquired which hurt with every word.

'Tell me Steve didn't do that. Oh Jenn. Oh fuck. Oh, tell me it wasn't Steve!' Leanne wailed.

Jenny said nothing but held open the door and Leanne catapulted through it and followed the light into the kitchen where General Hardy stood, talking quietly on the phone. Leanne looked at him and then at

495

Steve, who remained motionless at the table, his head in his hands.

'Oh Steve, Steve, my Steve, how could you do this, how could you hurt Jenny?' Leanne wailed the words as though they were part of a chant.

Steve suddenly spoke from behind his hands. His voice was small and muffled.

'I'm sorry. I'm sorry. I'm sorry.'

Leanne turned to Jenny, her face a white, horrified mask. Jenny put her arms around her friend.

'Afghanistan . . . did this to us,' she heard herself say.

Leanne drew back to stare at her once more. 'Shit, you need to get to hospital,' she said. 'Oh Jenn, your beautiful face . . .'

Eugene had completed his phone call now. He said: 'We need to tie something under that jaw and around her head.'

'No one's touching . . . my jaw,' said Jenny.

Eugene rolled his eyes. 'I've called an ambulance.' Jenny tried to protest but he held up a hand. 'It's all right. I've made sure they don't ask any questions and I've told them no siren or blue light in camp.' He turned to Leanne. 'A car will be here soon and Headley Court will be informed and ready. I'll go in it with your husband.'

Steve said: 'I'm sorry. I'm sorry. I'm sorry.'

'Please go and pack him a bag quickly now,' Eugene told Leanne.

Leanne looked at the general and nodded.

'Yes,' she said humbly. 'Yes. Thank you, sir.'

The insurgents settled back down in the cave for more bread and chatter. One of them was evidently considered a storyteller and the others badgered him until he gave in gracefully and spoke for a very long time. He paused a lot and illustrated things with his hands and used a wide range of facial expressions and the other men sat transfixed while he talked. This must be the Helmand equivalent of going to the movies.

The ending seemed to satisfy them. About half of the men rolled out some mats and fell asleep by the fire. A few carried on talking in quiet voices. More danger. When they had all been chatting loudly and laughing and telling stories there had been enough noise to disguise any inadvertent movement up here on the rock wall. Now the fire was dying down and the cave was too quiet.

The soldiers waited. Waited for the insurgents to discover them or go, waited for life or death, Dave did not know which. They waited without moving and, over the hours which followed, Dave felt a slow cramp creeping up one leg, he felt the tingling itch of a face which had lain downwards too long, he felt the urge to cough, to sneeze and then to urinate. He did not move as one by one his body's needs seized him until he could think about nothing else. The itch started by his nose and gradually, as he thought about how good it would be to scratch it, the itching spread out across his face until an army of small insects was running across his skin, rioting all over his cheeks and forehead. One scratch! Just one scratch would bring the crowd under control. He did not move. Bit by bit he won the fight to think about other things until his mind began to wander.

He thought about the men he watched, the men he had been firing at today, the men who had been hunting him, who had killed Dawson, who wanted to kill him. Now they were sitting a few metres away from him they seemed less like the enemy, more like other human beings who, when they shut their eyes, thought about their wives and children and mothers. But if they found the four British soldiers, they would turn into the enemy again. They would be angry, barefoot insurgents who spoke a different language and lived their lives to different rules and to a different rhythm. And, without humanity or mercy, they would destroy the four Britons, delighting in their pain.

Dave remembered his face and found it had stopped itching.

Gradually, all the insurgents fell asleep.

Dave considered the possibility of killing every last one. He knew Angus would be thinking the same thing. He was a loose cannon and he would be suffering agony now because the possibility of slaughtering twelve Taliban was too exciting to miss, even if it meant sacrificing his own life. Dave was glad Finn was also here, a more sensible, tactical soldier with a strong survival instinct.

Now it was the turn of his foot. It began to tingle and then sting. It was insistent. It sent messages up his nerves to the control centre in his head that it wanted to move. Permission refused. But the foot was under attack, it stung so badly it ached, it tortured him with tiny weaponry. There was a battle, a blue on blue, going on in his left foot and he could stop the pain just by moving it. He remained motionless. But he was tempted. The ragheads were all asleep; would they wake if he just moved his foot one centimetre? The pain was blotting out rational thought. He knew the only way to make it go away was to move his mind some-where else.

What was the time? He could not look at his watch

but Dave was sure it was past 0400, the time they had hoped to depart. The fire was still burning but it was low. Its light did not flicker on the cave walls but glowed softly.

Dave wondered if maybe the ragheads intended to stay here all day. All fucking day. Christ. Every single body part would be screaming its objections by then. And even if he could stay still that long, what about the younger soldiers? Angus's frustration would surely get the better of him. Doc's knee would be agony. Maybe it was impossible for four men to lie here for a whole day, silent and undetected.

Just as despair began to draw his attention again like an itch or an ache or a chill, but from deep inside, he heard a distant call. It sounded like a sad lament. Dave took a few seconds to remember what that strange, haunting voice was saying. Filtered by the valley, the rocks, the cave walls, it was the Muslim call to prayer. Now, at least, he knew the time: 0515. His plan to skirt the valley and get to the relief by dawn was fucked.

Get up, you lazy bastards, and go down to the mosque to pray!

The men slept on and Dave's despair engulfed him. Then, suddenly and simultaneously, they all woke. It was not a gradual process, or a slow one. They opened their eyes and sat up. Some of them rubbed their hands in the dirt as though washing them in water; others went straight into a kneeling position. Instinctively, although dawn was still far off, they knew which way was west. The cave was dotted with praying bodies, all kneeling, all facing Mecca. A few mumbled, others prayed silently, all assumed the position of humble supplicant to Allah.

Like this they were terrifying. You could see they

499

were an army. You could see them bound together by something stronger than a tough sergeant and scary officers. You could see that they believed everything they did was infused by the will of a higher power.

And now it began to seem that the higher power was looking after Dave. Because the men got up, stretched, rolled up their mats if they had one – some had just slept on the dirt floor – and scratched at the fire to put it out. There was no eating and no drinking. They picked up their weapons and walked out of the cave. Outside men called the dogs. A few talked, most remained silent. A couple were gripping the young lad again, poor bastard. Dave made a mental note to be nicer to Slindon. Then he remembered it was thanks to Blue Balls Slindon that they'd lost comms and decided to punch him instead.

As suddenly as they had appeared, the men evaporated. Dave was used to them disappearing from the battlefield; now he understood that evaporation was how they usually moved off. No preparation, no food, no water, no pissing about on radios or waiting for orders or sergeants doing kit inspection. In fact, hardly any fucking kit. It was just up, pray, grab a weapon and out.

Their footsteps, their snapping dogs and their occasional voices all said that they had headed off down the ridge.

No one dared to move. The soldiers continued to lie on their stomachs in the cave's dark silence. Then, slowly, very slowly, Dave reached for the night-vision goggles, switched them back on and pulled them down over his eyes. Which meant moving his arm, his hand, his fingers. His body was so surprised that it resisted. His fingers felt strangely far away, as if they belonged to someone else and he was borrowing them. It took a few moments to reacquaint himself with them and a few more to secure their co-operation. And then the NVGs were on and glowing green and he could see.

An empty cave. Nothing. No one.

Cautiously he began to reinhabit his own body, moving first his angry left foot. It had given up being angry and fallen asleep. Now it didn't want to wake up. He stretched his left arm, then his right leg. His body felt naked now it was no longer attached to the cave wall, as if he had grown into it during the night and put down roots in the rock.

'Wait,' he breathed to the others. Using his voice, even this ghost of a voice, felt like starting a rusty motor. They had been motionless for only about four hours. Was it fear which had made his body disintegrate in that time?

The men remained face down and silent and they did not change position but Dave saw that they had all begun to make tiny stretching movements.

He climbed down from the ledge slowly. He had to jump the last section. When his feet felt the impact of the ground beneath them after the long night without movement, pain shot through them. He staggered. Iron bars were pushing up through his heels, sending shock waves through his legs.

But he could not afford to falter now. He forced his feet to walk round the tiny glow from the hot twigs the insurgents had left in the fire. He walked out of the cave's stale, smoky, icy atmosphere. His body moved slowly, like an old man's. Would he one day be chivvying his body back into movement like this every morning? He hoped he died first. But not yet.

Outside the air was night cool but it lacked the cave's

cruel chill, and it was fresh. He breathed deeply. Had he been holding his breath for the last few hours? The cave air had been lifeless; now he was breathing in a growing, living world. A careful look around through the goggles told him that the men had gone. He glimpsed green movement two canals away across the valley and heard a dog bark. Where were the insurgents going? PB Red Sox? Or were they looking for four British soldiers on the run?

He focused on his goal. They had to reach the relief party, with its injured man and its fallen Mastiff. But the fresh air brought a new, stark, frightening possibility into his mind. Maybe the relief had already been rescued. As he returned to the cave to rally the others it occurred to him that when they finally arrived at the dead zone, aka the Bronx, they would find the exploded Mastiff, the other wagon, the men, the weapons and the casualty all gone.

39

The four soldiers took a lot longer to move than the
Taliban and they were already running late enough to
jeopardize the mission. After the call to prayer, the
populace would be up and moving, although there was
still an hour before dawn.

The lads wanted to whisper together about the night.

'Shit! I felt the fucking bat's wings almost touch my
face,' Angus was saying. 'I moved, I couldn't help it!'

'What were they putting on that fire? Smoke nearly
choked me,' said Finn.

'Yeah! The smoke! Shit!'

Doc was noticeably silent.

'How's the knee?' Dave asked him. 'Want me to bind
it before we go?'

'I told you, binding won't help. At least it's had a
good rest.'

'I wish I could've watched those blokes. Were they
animal-herders or something?' Angus said.

'They were Taliban,' said Dave.

All the men stared at him.

'*What?*'

'Insurgents. All fully armed.'

Angus turned bright red. 'We could have shot the fucking lot of them when they went to sleep!'

'There were twelve men there. They're still alive but so are we. Now let's get moving; it'll soon be light.'

They swung their day sacks on to their backs. Dave sent Finny ahead and he and Angus helped Doc down the steep slope. Dave heard rocks slide and fall beneath their feet. But he had already decided. With the dawn coming, silence was less of a priority now than speed.

At the bottom of the slope they swung left. Counting on his belief that the dogs hunting them had already left the area, he told Finn to cross the first canal so that they were inside the worked fields where there were no landmines. Then, instead of wading through deep water, they could move fast along the bank towards the relief. It was high-risk because they passed near clusters of compounds.

As they crossed the water they found its temperature had dropped further since last night. Or maybe they were all still bone cold from the cave. The canal's freezing fingers grasped them around the knees, thighs, groins and chests and then they were out, shaking it off like dogs.

Finny set a fast pace, Dave behind him, then Doc and finally Angus, carrying Doc's day sack. Doc kept up by doing a small skip on his twisted knee. It was just a matter of time before he slowed down. Dave knew it was ridiculous to rush Doc to get as far as possible before he tired. He would just tire earlier. It was like driving faster to the petrol station when you were running out of fuel. He tried twice to get Finny to walk at a slower pace but Finny seemed unable to make any more concessions to the medic's knee.

When he looked back Dave could see something

which worried him. Boot prints. The locals would not need dogs to scent them out. They would simply have to look at the ground to know that soldiers had passed this way recently.

It wasn't dawn but the possibility of dawn was present. You could feel the air beginning to reorganize itself to make room for the sunlight which would soon flood the place and heat the world rapidly through twenty degrees. They passed two compounds at such speed that by the time the dogs detected them and began to bark, they were gone. Dave hoped the dogs were chained up.

He had decided they must remove their boots when they rounded a corner and Finny stopped. Mid-pace. Dave nearly plunged past him into the body of a skinny Afghan boy who was staring in alarm at Finn. At the appearance of a second soldier his eyes widened still further.

Behind him was a herd of goats. Now there were four soldiers and the goats were staring at them all with as much disbelief as the boy.

With immense effort, Dave smiled. He knew it was a crooked and insincere grin and he did not blame the boy for looking terrified instead of smiling back. Even the goats looked terrified. Maybe they guessed that Dave was calculating the consequences of killing their herder.

Finn smiled too, equally ghoulishly. The boy stared from one face to the next. Dave reached into his webbing and managed to fish out a brightly wrapped candy. The boy looked at it. Dave tried to make his smile less like a dog baring its teeth and more like a warm, fatherly hello. He stretched out his hand with the sweet but, when the boy reached for it, at the last minute Dave pulled it back and pointed to his own face. He held a finger up to his lips. He shook his head and put his hand over his mouth. He whispered: 'No talk!'

The boy nodded as if he understood.

'No talk!' he echoed obediently. Was this one of the children who learned English in school? Or was he just a good parrot?

Dave gave the boy the sweet and Finn found more candy and did the same. The boy was smiling now. He was a scrawny lad of maybe ten or twelve years old, so small that when he smiled his teeth wiped out the rest of his face.

'No talk!' he said every time Finn gave him a sweet, putting his finger to his lips.

'OK, we've bought him off for now. Let's go. By the time he tells his mates, we'll be away from here,' said Dave. But the boy did not want to let them pass.

'Greedy little bastard wants more sweets, fuck him!' said Finn.

'I've got a few,' Doc volunteered.

The goats had lost interest now but the boy's eyes were bright. And he didn't want sweets. He had been staring at the men, their uniforms and their weapons, but his eyes always returned to one place. Their boots.

He put his finger to his lips. 'No tell!' he said, pointing at Doc's feet, which were the smallest.

Dave said: 'He's after your boots, Doc.'

Angus said: 'What is it about greedy little kids which makes me want to slot them?'

'They remind you too much of you,' suggested Finn.

Doc said: 'This little guy's got a great future in the fucking souk. He wants my boots and he's bargaining for them.'

'Bargaining? More like ransoming,' muttered Dave.

But the medic was already unlacing the boots. Since it was hard for him to bend over, Angus helped him, murmuring murderously under his breath about Afghans and their children.

'We should all take our boots off anyway,' said Dave.

Finny and Angry stared at him.

'What? Our boots? Take them off?'

'We're leaving prints.'

Doc Holliday stepped out of his boots and placed them on the ground in front of the delighted goatherd.

'No tell,' said Dave. And he tried to demonstrate 'No show' too. Smiling, the boy kicked off his plastic sandals and stepped into them. They were far too big and the laces hung from them but he could not contain his delight. He laughed with excitement.

'Glad you like them, mate,' said Doc, taking off his socks and stuffing them into his webbing. Angus watched, grimacing with disgust.

'Stink bombs,' explained the medic. 'Very useful weapon.'

Grinning broadly, his pockets stuffed with sweets, the boy swaggered off in his too-big boots. He looked ridiculous. He could only walk by turning his toes out at a ludicrous angle. He attempted to march like a soldier, laughing with delight, his goats maaing and following him. All that was left of him was his plastic flip-flops and one empty sweet wrapper. Dave swooped on the wrapper and stuffed it in his webbing.

'How long before he forgets "No show" and "No tell" when someone sees him, finds out where he got the boots, phones our friends from the cave last night and they get on to our trail?' asked Doc.

'Not long, so we have to get moving. Doc, can you wear his flip-flops?'

'No fucking way.'

'OK, lads, boots off now. If you can't carry them or they get in the way of your weapon, they go in the canal. Finny, you get the kid's flip-flops on. At least they won't be able to follow our trail by sight.'

'You don't think four blokes with helmets, camouflage and weapons is a bit of a giveaway?' asked Doc. No one replied. They were all taking off their boots miserably.

'I can't be arsed to carry them. I'll never get my rifle out if I do,' said Finny. He held them over the canal. 'I'm going to miss you, my friends.' He shut his eyes as he dropped them into the water.

They set off again, but more slowly.

'I hate these fucking sandals,' Finn told Dave.

'Yeah, but they're leaving great flip-flop prints,' Dave whispered back.

Daylight was arriving too quickly. At first the dawn had been just a finger of light in the east but now rays and heat were spreading out across the landscape as if the sun was hurrying the soldiers along.

They were about to reach a more populated area when Finny stopped and gestured for Dave to join him before they stepped out of the leafy woods. Ahead lay a jigsaw of compounds. The nearest had been bombed out, so that only part of two walls still stood. Within its empty shell was a woman with her back to them. Her head was covered, but carelessly, as if she didn't really expect to encounter anyone. She was stretching up to throw clothes across a washing line. She seemed to be alone, an impression reinforced by the way she was humming tunelessly to herself.

Finn looked at Dave. Neither man needed to say a word.

Dave turned to Angus and Doc and whispered: 'This only takes two. Cover us.'

Dave grabbed his plasticuffs and a trusty First Field Dressing. If he was trapped on a desert island with only one thing, he hoped it would be a British First Field Dressing. It had a thousand uses and right now it was going to stop a woman humming.

They ran from the woods to the woman, their bare feet soundless. She did not turn around. In fact, she was such an easy target that Dave felt guilty, as if he was stealing a baby. Finn grabbed her from behind, holding his hand over her mouth. She jumped spectacularly but Finn held her fast while Dave bound her. For a moment he saw her eyes, huge, terrified, violated.

'Sorry,' he said gently. But now two men had touched her body. Would she be regarded as unclean by her family, by the locals? She put up no resistance and he took her headscarf and covered her eyes with it and then slipped the plasticuffs on her wrists and ankles. She was so small and thin that he could carry her single-handedly to the woods. He could feel her heart thumping, as if it was a fish which had leaped out of her body and into his hands.

Finn stayed behind briefly to strip the clothes off the line and the bushes where the woman had laid them to dry. Then he followed Dave back to the others, stooping once to pick up the sandal which had fallen off the woman's foot.

Dave placed the woman carefully in the shrubs where she would be found but not too soon. She did not struggle or move. He wished she had. Her complete submission made him feel uncomfortable. Maybe she thought they would shoot her.

'Each of you, get a dishdash on!' he ordered the lads.

The men pulled the damp, flowing garments on over their Osprey. Finn silently passed Angus the woman's sandals and Angus put them on and minced a few paces in them, pulling a face.

'Too fucking small! The dishdash's too fucking small as well, I can't breathe.'

'You won't be breathing ever again unless you wear it.'

Dave wound a garment around his head into a loose approximation of an Afghan hat and Doc did the same. The other two went bareheaded. Their rifles inside their clothes, they proceeded. The whole operation had taken less than ten minutes, perhaps only five, but in that time the sun had taken control of the sky. It was spilling light everywhere, not the grey light of dawn but the cauldron of light which was heating the world.

'How much further, Sarge?' whispered Angus. He was throwing anxious glances at Doc's knee. The medic's limp was more pronounced. He was slowing down. His face was growing white with pain and he was starting to sweat.

Dave wasn't sure of the answer. He just knew they were going in the right direction, his navigation from the canals confirmed by the direction of the sun. As they progressed they saw men in the fields or sighted a distant group of women with washing or an old man crouched by a sluice gate.

'I feel like a girly in this dishdash,' moaned Angus. 'And the sandals are, like, made for an elf.'

'They're a right pain,' agreed Finny.

'Yeah, but you're leaving good footprints,' Doc reminded them.

'Don't walk army style now there are people around,'

Dave told them quietly. 'We're blokes on our way somewhere and we're laughing and joking. They need to hear our voices but not what we're saying.'

They fell into pairs. Finny and Angus joined the other two but said nothing. Doc and Dave tried to look as though they were chatting. Dave put an arm around Doc in a friendly Afghan male sort of a way, only this friendly Afghan male was easing the weight of his friend's knee.

'You had that knee problem long, Doc?' asked Dave, for want of something to say.

'Yeah, I snapped a ligament when I was operational in Sierra Leone with Special Forces,' replied the medic nonchalantly. Finn and Angus stared at him. No one had ever heard him refer to his SAS days and some people said that Doc's past was a myth. 'Had a load of operations but it never righted itself. I have to say that it didn't even hurt this much when I first did it. Come on, laugh, someone, there are washerwomen over there.'

'Ha ha ha ha,' said Dave obligingly, but not, he feared, convincingly.

'Good,' said the medic. 'Good enough to pass selection. That's one of the things they test: your laugh. I mean, after you've been holed up on a river bank with nothing to eat for three days.'

'Ha ha ha ha,' said Dave.

'Better!' said Doc. 'Ever thought of applying for Special Forces?'

'No.'

'Angus wants to. His old man was in SF,' said Finny. Angus's dad had pretended to be in the SAS but he had been an army cook, and Finny knew it.

'Fuck off,' said Angry.

'You'd get through selection,' said Doc.

'Who?' asked Dave.

'You. Especially you, but actually all three of you could be Special Forces if you wanted. Even a troop from Hereford couldn't have done a better job here than you guys have. And I just want to say thanks to you all.'

There was an embarrassed silence. No one ever talked this way, especially not Doc. Not ever. Dave began to wonder if he had some kind of a fever. But when Doc continued he could tell the medic was speaking from the heart. The way, thought Dave, only really brave men can.

'I would have died last night if it hadn't been for you. And a lot of blokes would have killed me when I asked because I was jeopardizing your lives, no question. But you carried me instead. Thanks, boys. Thanks to all of you. Now laugh, someone, quick.'

They were very close to a small group of old men squatting near the canal, talking and chewing.

'Ha ha ha ha,' Dave tried.

'Talk!' Doc said.

They chatted about nothing, their voices low. They were acting for their lives. Dave, feeling his heart thud, tried to emulate the relaxed, unhurried gait of the Afghan men he had seen wandering in the Green Zone. Finny and Angry had got the idea and were having a conversation which was punctuated with loud laughter.

One of the old men called something out and Dave gave him a half-wave but did not break his stride or interrupt Doc, who was talking manically about his life in Hereford. Dave did allow himself a glance at the men. They looked very old. Too old, he hoped, to carry mobile phones they could use to ring their Taliban grandsons.

'I hate walking in these stupid little sandals,' said Angus. 'I'm going to be fucking miserable if I don't get a pair of boots on these feet soon.'

'Not much further,' Dave assured him. He could not resist glancing back at the old men. Shit! One was holding a phone to his ear and hollering into it, the way old codgers always did. The others were not watching the soldiers with any interest, so maybe the old man was just phoning his wife to tell her to get the coffee on.

'This is the back of fucking beyond and everyone's going to know everyone else. Four blokes no one recognizes are like the news headlines around here,' said Finny.

'There are often blokes around no one recognizes. The Taliban billet foreign fighters on the locals all the time,' Dave told him.

And then they rounded a woody corner and a new vista opened out: the usual medieval jumble of mud compounds, goats, the odd camel, greenery. About six hundred metres away, the desert began. And on the lip of the Green Zone, between the green world and the bleak desert, was a track. On the track was a huge, incongruous monster of a twenty-first-century machine. It was lying crooked like a great, injured metal animal. A short way behind it was another Mastiff. A helmeted British soldier was visible up in its turret behind an HMG. Still further behind, distantly emerging from around the long ridge, was yet another Mastiff, with perhaps another behind that. It was a rescue party from the FOB.

'Yes, yes, oh fucking yes!' said Doc.

'Thank Christ,' said Finny.

Angus looked with his lips parted, as though witnessing a miracle.

Dave just continued walking grimly. Six hundred metres more. And as Jamie Dermott said, it's not over till it's over.

'Serendipity,' commented Doc. 'We arrive to help them at the same time as the rescue party.'

'Yeah,' agreed Finn. 'Might as well turn round and go back, eh?'

'We could stroll on over to Red Sox,' suggested Doc lazily.

'Yeah, I enjoy stretching my legs,' said Finn.

Doc was gazing at the arriving Mastiff. 'The rescue'll have a medic on board,' he said. 'But I'm fucked if anyone else is going to treat McKinley's leg after I came all this way to do it.'

Dave said: 'Lads, as we cross the last field, get out your First Field Dressing. Get it out and wave it. Just in case any moron takes us for Taliban.'

'They won't do that if they see our SA80s,' said Angus.

'We'll play it safe,' Dave insisted. 'Just get your field dressings ready.'

'Let's hope we don't need to get our SA80s out. Let's hope we have a pleasant stroll all the way there,' said Doc.

A second later, gunfire cracked the air around them.

It came from behind. Dave had a sensation, or more of an instinct, that a round had passed very close by. It was followed by a spray of further rounds. The men threw themselves on to their belt buckles, disentangled their rifles from their clothes and began to fire back.

'And I thought we were home and dry!' shouted Finny, firing back angrily.

The battle was desultory. These were not the hardened insurgents Dave had watched in the cave last night, not unless the Taliban Slindon had broken away with a few mates.

Dave rapidly narrowed the enemy firing position to a couple of compounds. A muzzle flash on the roof of one of them gave him their exact location. It was less than three hundred metres away. Walking along by the canal, the three of them had been an open target but the enemy had put their weapons on fully automatic and fired indiscriminately and missed, when a bit of quiet concentration and aim would have killed at least one of them. If Dave were sergeant of the Taliban platoon, he'd be gripping his boys for that. But he was sure there was no sergeant out there and not much of a platoon. Someone had alerted local lads to their presence and they had come running with their AKs. They were untrained and inexperienced.

The firing continued and then began to peter out. They were probably so unprepared that they'd used up their magazines. Or they had paused to greet reinforcements.

With six hundred metres to go, Dave did not want a battle here and he did not want the enemy closing in on them. He wanted to keep moving forward to safety. They could jump in the canal and try to proceed, heads down. But they would make slow progress with Doc wading through water. A longer, but faster, route was a little to the north: an almost empty drainage ditch that led to a wooded area. Ironically, he was sure that this wood was visible through binoculars from PB Red Sox. It would give them good cover and after that they would have only a couple of hundred metres of open ground to run across to the relief, covered by British soldiers with HMGs. They just had to run fast enough. With a shoulder to lean on, Dave thought Doc could do it.

He told the lads the plan and they ran, heads down, to the drainage channel. Even Doc managed a passable run.

'So we didn't fool them,' said the medic breathlessly as Dave linked shoulders to help him down into the channel. 'And I thought I was a master of disguise.'

'Maybe we did too much laughing,' Dave said. 'Oh, fucking hell!'

A round had come so close that he felt as though it had nudged him. He ducked right down into the ditch mud and pulled off his day sack. Sure enough, a round had whistled clean through it.

Doc looked at the hole.

'Must have been a lucky hit. Because they're all over the place with their weapons,' he said.

'Unless some more experienced reinforcements have got there,' said Dave. 'Did you hear it? Sounded like a Dragunov.'

'Fuck, let's get moving,' said Doc. 'Mmmm, mud between the toes feels so good.' Another round whistled too close to their heads.

'My wife paid a lot for a mud treatment once,' Dave told him, stumbling behind. 'You've got yourself a bargain there, Doc.'

Now he had mentioned Jenny he had to make a mental effort to wheel her out of his mind again, as if she was a very heavy weight on a barrow.

Up ahead, Finny shouted: 'Now they're fucking sharpshooting! That's a Dragunov!'

'Keep down and keep going!' roared Dave. He remembered the motorcyclist in a long turban and glasses who had eyed him and perhaps targeted him. But that was in another part of the province, miles away near FOB Carlsbad. This could not be the same sniper.

'Sarge, I want to stop right here and slot them!' Angus pleaded.

'No! Move!'

As they reached the woods, firing from the enemy stopped. Dave guessed it wasn't because the insurgents were having a brew. It was because they knew four men were fleeing and they wanted to catch up with them, or at least get close enough for some clear shots. He turned back briefly and saw the landscape was empty now. No old men, no goats, no camels, no women, no children, just muzzle flashes. Even the civilians could do that Afghan evaporation act.

He was running hard, an arm under Doc's arm, half supporting him, half pulling him along.

He turned back once more. Through the trees he glimpsed about five figures, their robes streaming behind them, weapons waving. They were running out of the compound and across the field towards the soldiers, trampling crops underfoot, kicking aside foliage. Dave was in time to see the first soar over a drainage channel like a steeplechaser.

The woods ended suddenly and the four soldiers catapulted out of them. From PB Red Sox this had looked like a deep, shady forest but once they were inside it had turned out to be no more than a thin line of trees. The shadow had been welcome but they were almost instantly out of it and running for their lives across a flat field of growing cotton, the ground still soggy from the night's irrigation.

'They're closing on us!' Dave yelled at Angry and Finny. 'Get your dressings out, wave them, and go! Go, go, go, you two!'

They were at the end of a long night's epic journey. The two younger soldiers had earned the right to run forward to the safety of the Mastiffs and save themselves, at least.

But they disobeyed orders. Without speaking, or even looking at each other, Finny fell back until he was behind Dave and Doc. He ran backwards, scanning the treeline, covering the others, waiting to return the enemy's first shot.

Angus drew alongside Doc and took his other arm. Doc had been doing a strange, balletic hop and jump but now Dave and Angry were able to lift the medic and keep running. Between them, Doc mimed running. But his feet were not touching the ground.

Dave was the only one who had managed to get out his field dressing. He waved it now with the same hand which held his rifle. He hoped that would be enough to tell any soldier stupid enough not to have identified their SA80s that they were British. Breathless, their mouths coated, their nostrils full of fine soil, their feet bare, they ran towards the British soldiers.

'We're nearly there!'

Into Dave's head, unbidden again, came Jamie Dermott's words. And with a heavy heart he knew it wasn't over yet.

40

Danny Jones was on the mastiff's HMG watching the strange antics of the Taliban.

It had been a long, lonely night for the relief party. They had a T3 casualty hovering between life and death. They had to guard the exploded Mastiff and keep themselves safe too. A rescue party had set out from a nearby patrol base but there had been an explosion and they had not arrived and were feared dead. The rescue party had included their sergeant. They had been attacked twice, but they knew that the Taliban were busy elsewhere and they had been able to deal with the ambushes. But all the same, there had been enough attacks to stop them exploding or moving the Mastiff which blocked their path. Contact with PB Red Sox had been lost. Bastion was pinned down in a dust storm and could not help them. The FOB had been pinned down by the enemy. What a fucking night. The boss was in a foul temper. And now, weirdest of all, just as a rescue party from the FOB was arriving, the Taliban appeared to be fighting among themselves.

O'Sullivan the sharpshooter had been the first to notice the four men in dishdash strolling along by the side of the canal towards them, chatting and laughing. They looked like insurgents to O'Sullivan. Jonas had agreed that there was something very soldierly in the way they walked. They both would have liked to open fire but the insurgents were six hundred metres away and they were not visibly carrying weapons.

Then the men had started firing behind them. It wasn't clear who had opened fire but the four insurgents got down in a drainage channel. They were having some sort of skirmish with a compound they had just passed.

'I reckon our boys are inside that compound. I reckon we've taken it,' said Jonas.

'We'd know if ISAF had men out there,' said O'Sullivan.

'Not if they were the Jedi. On an operation.'

'Special Forces? You reckon they're after those four blokes?'

'I reckon they're not asking them in for a brew.'

'Maybe it's a sort of gang thing. Taliban on Taliban?'

'Nah . . . not right in front of us.'

The four insurgents had disappeared from view in some trees now. No one else was watching them because attention had turned towards the rescue party, thundering up the track. At last. The boss was busy on the radio. Everyone was looking relieved.

Then the four men broke cover. They were running directly at the relief party across a field, all of them armed.

'Fucking cheeky bastards!' said Jonas. 'Barefoot ragheads! Let's get them!'

He didn't even bother with the machine gun. Sledgehammer to crack a nut. He reached for his SA80 as O'Sullivan raised the sniper rifle and caught the men in his sights.

'They're not carrying AKs!' he exclaimed. 'They've got SA80s.'

'Stolen weapons!' yelled Jonas, taking aim. 'Get them!'

'And one's waving a First Field Dressing! Stoooooooooop!' shouted O'Sullivan at the top of his voice. 'Stooooooop! It's Sarge! Look, he's got a First Field Dressing!'

Everyone in the relief party, hot, dirty, sweating and exhausted, turned to stare at the sight of the four men in dishdash running across the field towards them.

O'Sullivan leaped down and into the blue lane which had been mine-cleared. He ran to the end of it by the exploded Mastiff, gesturing for the men to enter this way.

'Here, here, Sarge, the blue lane's here!' he roared at the top of his voice.

Rifleman Colin Grove had only been in Afghanistan a week. Two weeks ago he was still at Catterick. The course had ended with a big bash for his eighteenth birthday and then he was off to Bastion. Before you could say rifle, he had met his new platoon and was being shipped off to FOB Nevada with them.

'It's not like this all the time,' the lads in his platoon had assured him during last night's firefight. 'In fact, it's never been like this before.'

During the night Grove had been through all the emotions a new soldier in the heat of battle experienced: fear, horror, delight, exhaustion. It had taken a while to understand that they really were fighting to save the FOB and themselves. No one could help them by air because of a dust storm. They were fighting for their lives.

The battle had gone on and on. It was like the whole of training at Catterick in one night. And then, when dawn came and the fighting had finally eased, no one had said: Have a brew and get yourself to bed. They had been ordered out of the gate towards the furthest patrol bases where two Mastiffs were stuck in the desert with a T3 casualty after an explosion.

They had driven through the gates and found themselves under fire again.

'We have to keep fucking going!' the platoon commander had said. 'We've got to get to a casualty and then we've got to get to Patrol Base Boston Red Sox. Stupid fucking name.'

Colin Grove experienced Afghanistan from the ground for the first time in the back of a Mastiff through a thick fog of exhaustion. His sergeant sent him up on top to feed the belt through for the gimpy man and to get some fresh air since the lad looked white enough to puke. From up here, Grove saw the desert sizzle, watched the indifferent faces of the women working in the Green Zone and heard the call to prayer.

They went up a steep incline, rounded a corner and the party they had come to help was suddenly right in front of them. There were two Mastiffs and the furthest was wrecked and standing in water. There were blue lines sprayed all around the scene. Grove knew what that meant.

The gunner was looking the other way when Grove saw the insurgents. Everyone was looking the other way: staring at the men around the fallen Mastiff who were looking with relief at the rescue party. Nobody seemed to have noticed that four ragheads were attempting to ambush them. And they were probably just the advance. God only knew how many were behind them; you could see them swarming back there in the trees.

The insurgents must be either very brave or very stupid. They risked annihilation by running across an open field but they had rightly calculated that, at the arrival of the rescue, everyone's attention would be elsewhere.

Colin Grove raised his rifle and took aim. He had been playing Call of Duty 4 a lot but he had never expected to have a battle experience exactly like it. And now it was actually happening. Four ragheads lining up in front of him. He could shoot them all. He decided to start with the biggest one, a brute of a man, barefoot and running with one arm around a comrade like a nancy boy coward. Another bloke was waving something green, probably some kind of Muslim attack emblem. After the big guy, that one would be next.

Grove took aim and fired and saw, with satisfaction, the big man run for one more pace, stumble and then slump towards the ground. He heard: 'Stoooooooooop!' He didn't want to, but he lowered his rifle.

Doc Holliday knew Angus had been hit. He heard the noise of the round entering his body, a sound he had never heard before, a small thud and a hiss, as if someone had opened a valve. He felt Angus's hold on him loosen and then, instead of supporting him, Angus suddenly became a weight. He was dragging on Doc's shoulder. Doc felt him go and feared he would go down with him. He tried to put his arm under Angus's and pull him back but he wasn't strong enough. Angus flopped to the ground.

It was Finny, behind, who guessed what had happened. Because he could see that their pursuers had halted at the edge of the woods rather than expose themselves to the heavy weapons on the Mastiffs. Finny had opened fire before they could. He was even sure he had slotted one. He had kept on throwing a continual stream of rounds at them and they had backed off a bit, enough for Finny to be sure that the round which hit Angus had not come from behind. Which meant Angus had been shot from in front by one of their own men.

Finny remembered Dave's instructions and pulled out a First Field Dressing. He waved it above his head shouting: 'Wankers! Blue on blue! Don't fire!'

He looked across to the Mastiff and saw Patrick O'Sullivan and some of the other lads from 2 and 3 Sections wading across the canal towards them, shouting over their shoulders. And there was Danny Jones on the HMG screaming at the wagons which had just arrived, waving his hands. And there was another bloke standing on top of the next Mastiff with his hands on his head in horror.

Dave and Doc stumbled to a halt and knelt by Angus, who had fallen forward, face down into the cotton crop. The back of his neck, above his Osprey, was hanging open like a shirt, revealing a tangle of blood and bone and tubes.

'Shit!' said Dave. He supported the lolling head and gently pulled the body over. At the front of Angus's neck was a small wound, like a tiny red flower, although it was growing in size as they looked at it.

There was no doubt in Dave's mind that Angus was dead. He knew it was true. But he didn't want to believe it.

'Angry! Speak!' he shouted. But Angry did not move.

The Taliban fighters in the trees behind them opened fire again and this time were hit by a return volley not just from Finny but from the soldiers beyond the canal.

Doc leaned over to examine the body. Dave could hear a lot of shouting. He could hear the words *blue on blue*, over and over again as if people were yelling them from up and down the convoy and the words were echoing around the Green Zone.

'Shit,' said Doc. 'Shit. His spinal cord's completely banjoed . . .'

He put his fingers on Angus's pulse.

'Can't you do something?' Dave heard his own voice; it was shocked, furious.

'There's no pulse. How could there be a fucking pulse when his neck's been pulverized?'

Dave wanted to shake Angus. He wanted to shake him alive again.

'Let's try to resuscitate!' Finny shouted. 'Fuck it, we must be able to do something.'

Doc's voice was calm and quiet. 'No point, mate.'

'They'll have called MERT!' yelled Finny. 'When MERT get here they'll sort him out.'

Other men from their platoon were clustering around them now. Gayle and Fife were covering while the others loaded Angus on to a stretcher, shouting, jostling, gabbling into radios. Doc, Dave and Finny stood up, dazed.

'You fucking wankers!' Finny roared at the men buzzing around the Mastiffs. 'You opened fire on us! You could see we were running away from the Taliban, we had SA80s, Dave was waving a British First Field Dressing, and you fucking, fucking idiots shot Angus McCall! You killed him! You killed Angry!'

Dave and Finny, on either side of Doc, followed Angus's body as it was carried across the cotton towards the track.

'Stupid, stupid tossers! Who don't use their brains before they fire. You fucking killed my mate.'

Finny's voice was cracking he was throwing it so hard across the cotton, across the desert, across the world to a small newsagent's in Kent where Angus's father would soon be up, counting newspapers, laying them out for his customers, his hands grubby with newsprint, unaware that tomorrow his own son would feature in those newspapers.

'You stupid, stupid fucking bastards!' roared Finny.

'That's enough,' Dave told him.

'They shot Angus. They shot Angus McCall.'

The big man was dead. It was unthinkable. It was impossible that someone whose voice could fill whole NAAFIs, who occupied so much space in this world, could just disappear from it.

They walked up the blue lane as MERT arrived. The helicopter landed on the track behind the line of Mastiffs.

Finny ran up to the stretcher before the lads carried it away. He was crying.

'Fuck it, Angry McCall,' he shouted at Angus's body, tears streaming down his face. 'You were big and often stupid but you were so fucking brave and a fucking good mate and you were always doing the wrong thing for the right reason. I was lying in a cave worrying about what you were going to do to someone all fucking night and now I don't have to worry any more and I wish I did! How could you get yourself shot now after all we went through? I know what you want me to do.

You want me to kill the geezer who did it? Don't you? Don't you, Angry?'

Dave and Doc joined him by the body. Dave, for reasons he didn't understand, took Angus's hand. Another dead hand. It felt like the last one. Rubbery, inhuman.

'Angus. You were a good soldier, the best. Goodbye, mate.'

He would have said more but he felt his throat constrict. It was the wrong ending to one helluva night's soldiering.

He looked up and saw Aaron Baker standing right by him, his face twisted in pain.

'Shit, Sarge, shit,' was all he said.

'Who shot him?' roared Finny, looking around him. 'Who killed my mate?'

Jason Swift was there, his face tired and pale. 'Stop, Billy Finn, or I'll have to take that rifle off you.'

Finny stared at him. 'Take my rifle? Off *me*? There's some bugger around here should have the rifle taken off *him*. Because he killed my mate . . .'

'Stop, Finny,' said Dave, finding his voice again. 'That won't do any good. Angus is dead. We've got to deal with the living now.'

'We're not going to let someone get away with this?'

'We've got RMP to fill in forms and ask questions.'

They were forced to stand aside for a stretcher. On it was Gerry McKinley.

'Oh shiiiiit,' said Finn.

'There goes my patient,' murmured Doc. He signalled for the stretcher-bearers to pause. He pulled back the bloodstained sheet which was covering McKinley's lower leg, looked at the mess, and pulled it back again, rolling his eyes.

'Tell me this man's still alive,' said Dave faintly.

'Yeah. Well, he was a few minutes ago,' said one of the bearers. On another corner of the stretcher was Andy Kirk, McKinley's best mate, his face hollow.

'We've just about kept him alive. He's had so much fucking morphine that . . .' They did not hear the end of his sentence. The bearers were already running towards the Chinook.

'Finny, I want you on that helicopter, too,' said Dave.

'Good idea,' agreed Doc.

'No, Sarge!' yelled Finny.

'Please. Go with Angus's body. He'd appreciate that.'

Finny considered for a moment and then ran after the stretcher.

'We came a fucking long way to help McKinley,' said Doc, 'and MERT gets here first.'

Danny Jones shrugged. 'Well, it's only two kilometres,' he said. 'I don't know why it took you so long.'

Dave and Doc looked at each other.

'Oh. Yeah. It's only two kilometres,' said Doc. 'What took us so long?'

Dave said: 'You should get on the Chinook, too, Doc.'

'I'm not going on any fucking Chinook,' growled Doc. 'I want to get back to Red Sox and make sure the boys are OK.'

Dave said: 'I didn't get you through last night alive to have you arguing with me now.'

Doc threw him a filthy look and then, to Dave's surprise, gave him a bear hug.

'You are the best, Dave Henley,' he said. 'If anyone tries to give you shit over what happened out there, they'll have me to answer to.'

He turned and limped towards the Chinook.

Dave looked around for Chalfont-Prick. But the idiot

was busy talking to another officer in the rescue party. Dave turned to the nearest platoon commander, someone else's commander. 'Sir, as soon as we can move forward, we should urgently head towards PB Red Sox. They've got few men and they've been under very heavy fire. Just outside the PB there's a wrecked Mastiff with a T4 in it.'

The commander looked at him uneasily. Dave realized that with the Afghan cloth still wound around his head, dishdash stretched over Osprey, no boots on his feet and a hellish night behind him, he might not look like an army recruitment ad.

'Are you all right?' the commander asked. 'Are you sure you shouldn't go to Bastion too?'

A man approached with a small golden cross on his uniform.

'Can I help anyone?' he asked, looking directly at Dave.

Dave recognized him. Here was a man he always ignored but who had his uses. 'I'm OK, thanks, padre,' he said. 'But I may need your help when we get to PB Red Sox. I have to see how my men did last night. Then I've got to break some very bad news to them.'

When the gates opened at PB Boston Red Sox and the convoy rolled into the courtyard, Dave had a strange feeling that he'd come home, even though he had actually spent less than twelve hours in the fucking shithole.

His heart thumped as he counted men. Lancer Reed sat on the ground by the compound door, his back against the wall, smoking. He would already know about the death of Lancer Dawson. And, thank God, there were the lads standing near him. Sol, Mal, Binns and Bacon. They were holding their weapons in a way that suggested they had abandoned their firing positions for the arrival of the convoy.

When they saw him, smiles split their faces. Dave could not smile yet. Because he could see only five men. Then he looked over to the tower and there was Tiny Hemmings. Good. Six men, thank God, but there should be seven. Who was missing? Shit. Someone dead. Someone injured. Who was left after Reed, Sol, Mal, Binman, Bacon and Tiny? Dave's brain was too tired to work that one out.

He leaped out of the Mastiff the moment it stopped, the padre right behind him. He went straight to Sol.

'Any down?' he said.

'No, Sarge.'

Relief. It started in your head but worked its way through your body, softening your blood vessels, weakening your skeleton so that sometimes it was hard to stand up. At that moment, he saw Slindon firing from the compound wall. The seventh man.

'Oh Sarge, we had one fucking awful night!' said Streaky. 'First your crash and we knew Dawson was dead and then we nearly ran out of ammo and we had them swarming all over the Mastiff out there like a bunch of flies and we was so short that we couldn't do much about it except I did a bit of sharpshooting and got two of them and Binman got one and we was scared, so scared, man, that they was going to come swarming all over this compound next and Tiny got shot in the arm but Mal bandaged it and it's only on the edge, like, the very edge of his arm and—'

Sol was still grinning from ear to ear.

'Enough, Streaky,' he said. 'We're all here. That's the main thing. And Dave and the boys made it . . .'

Sol Kasanita. The optimist. The believer in a merciful, bountiful God, whom he worshipped daily and especially on Sundays. He stopped speaking suddenly when he saw Dave's face. Instantly Dave's expression was mirrored by Sol. Eyes sad. Mouth drooping.

'Oh shit, Sarge. Where're the others? I thought maybe they'd gone to the FOB or Bastion or . . .'

His voice trailed away. The men's eyes slipped from Dave for the first time to the man who stood behind him. Sober-faced, quiet. The padre. Bearer of bad news; bringer of comfort. Their faces dropped. Dave swallowed.

'Lads. I'm really sorry. Prepare yourselves. I have to tell you that . . .' His throat closed and wouldn't release the words. He had to fight with all the fibres and muscle and flesh there for his voice to escape. The words finally came out strangled. But they were clear enough for the boys to understand.

'I'm sorry that I have to tell you Angus McCall is dead.'

He looked from eye to eye, face to face, as the men received the news. Over the last twelve hours each of them had certainly become acquainted with both terror and hopelessness. But each remained young, strong, bright-eyed. The death of Angus was another blow and it would cut some of them deeply. But they would weather it and recover. Their lives would continue, gathering years, passing milestones. And as the years went by they would have reunions, noticing the small changes in each other, the extra kilos, the grey hairs, the joys and disappointments etched on one another's faces. Jamie Dermott and Angus McCall would not be at the reunions. Their faces in fading photos would start to look young and empty of the many experiences life

531

would bring those who were left. They would always remain the Jamie and the Angus whom 1 Section had known here in Afghanistan.

There was a moment of disbelief. Then Mal's face became a mask, a caricature of horror. He swayed and leaned on Sol, who stared back at Dave. Slindon's mouth hung open. Binns put his hands to his head as if warding off a blow. Bacon looked at the ground, chewing his lip.

Quietly, like a voice speaking from far away across the desert, haunting as the call to prayer, the padre recited the old words they knew so well:

'They shall grow not old, as we that are left grow old:
Age shall not weary them, nor the years condemn.
At the going down of the sun and in the morning
We will remember them.'

41

The plane with 1 Platoon on board left Camp Bastion three days later. Dave's hands had been full those three days, answering questions, making statements, speaking to the bereaved men, visiting the wounded, talking to Rose McKinley on the phone.

Kila had told him about Jenny. There had been no details until he made a call home and found his mother and mother-in-law caring for the kids because Jenny was in hospital having surgery to her jaw. She was not expected to be discharged for a few more days. She found speech difficult.

He rang Leanne.

'Shit, Dave. Shit. I don't know what to say. Steve just went AWOL. Shit. See, the psychiatrist gave him this medication and I checked that he'd taken it every morning but it turned out he was flushing it away . . .'

'Why? Why?' asked Dave. 'Why would he hurt my Jenny?'

Leanne spoke carefully. 'Well . . . he thought he was helping you. See, everyone was so pissed off with Jenny because they thought she was . . . you know. Having it away with the general. I mean, it was just gossip. Harmless gossip.'

'And you thought that too?'

'I did think it. But I don't now. See, Eugene's been really helpful. Really kind. And he's . . . not . . . not that sort of bloke.'

'But you think Jenny's that sort of woman?'

Leanne floundered. 'Well. No.'

'Then why the fuck did you and everyone else spread rumours and gossip and shit about my wife?' shouted Dave. 'Look where it's ended. Someone mentally ill picks up the fucking baton and runs with it and all the so-called harmless gossip ends with Jenny in hospital having plates put in her jaw!'

'I'm sorry, Dave. I'm really sorry about what Steve did.'

'If you were part of the gossip machine, you should accept a bit of responsibility for this yourself!' yelled Dave. Then he regretted it. 'Oh, I'm sorry, Leanne. Things are tense enough here. We've lost a man and you'll have heard about Gerry McKinley.'

'Yeah. Seems Rose and me've got a lot to talk about.'

'Look, I'll come and see you as soon as I'm home and I'll visit Steve too.'

When the plane touched down at RAF Brize Norton, there was a car waiting for Dave.

'It was my idea. Thought you'd like to get straight over to see Jenny,' said Iain Kila gruffly. 'Just leave your platoon to me.'

The men were still boarding the bus. Some of the lads came over to say goodbye as Dave climbed into the car.

'Good luck, Sarge.'

'Hope she's all right, Sarge.'

'Give her a big hug from me.'

'Yeah, right, like she wants a hug from a big, ugly, smelly shit like you . . .'

'Get back to the fucking bus!' roared Kila. 'And give her my best, Dave.'

The car set off. Jenny was in a specialist unit for facial injuries about thirty miles from home and Dave had been told to prepare himself, both for her appearance and for the fact that she couldn't talk much. He already knew it must be fucking awful if the army had sent him a car.

He would not relax until he had seen her but it was good to be home. And to know that he would be seeing Jenny at last and that she was going to be all right. The English countryside passed his window. Gentle green hills. Shining grass. Trees laden with their new summer leaves. Afghanistan was a bleak, hostile place: no one coming from this benign country could ever belong there.

It took Dave a while to discover which ward Jenny was in and when he found it a sign on the door said that he was here outside visiting hours. He ignored it. Another sign told him to use the hand disinfectant on entering the ward. He complied. He walked to the nurse's station, ready to apologize for arriving at the wrong time, ready to explain, ready to insist.

But the woman took one look at his uniform and smiled.

'Sergeant Henley? Your wife's been waiting for you. She's been told you're on your way.'

Dave followed her down a long corridor. He felt stupid in camouflage. It was not fucking effective in a hospital where everything was white.

The nurse said: 'Mrs Henley's just had an operation and she's still bandaged. Don't be alarmed. Very soon the bandages will be off, the swelling will go down and the surgeon has assured her that she will be just as she was before.'

Dave said, unsteadily: 'Very beautiful then. Very.'

The nurse turned back to him and smiled. They had reached a door at the end of the corridor now and she opened it quietly and peered around it.

'He's here!' she said cheerfully. Then she disappeared and Dave was left standing in the doorway.

Her face wrapped in white bandages, under white sheets, surrounded by white walls, was a woman. His Jenny. He walked towards her very slowly. She watched him. Tears were welling up in her eyes. They were starting to stream down her bandaged face.

'Oh Jenn,' he said. They had both travelled long, hard roads and they had endured them apart and not together. 'I'm here now. I'm back.'

She reached out for him as he crossed the room, with its drip and patient notes and clipboard and array of buttons and equipment over the bed. He sat down and folded her in his arms. She was crying and she was thin and she was scarcely recognizable but she had that sweet smell of Jenny.

He said: 'I don't ever want to leave you again.'

He felt her body sobbing against his.

'You've been through too much,' he said. 'And I wasn't here to help you.'

She pulled back and looked into his eyes.

He said: 'Your bandages are all wet.'

She sort of smiled.

'Can you speak?'

The jaw might have been broken, the face might have been bruised, but the strength he loved her for was still there. He watched her steel herself against pain. With determination, her mouth half-closed, she said: 'I love you, Dave. And there's never been anyone else.'

He put his arms around her again.

'I know, Jenn. I've always known that. I couldn't believe all the crap people were telling me. But they just kept on saying it and when you're so far away things get distorted by the distance . . .'

He looked into her clear blue eyes. Her real face was discernible under this mask of yellow bruises and bandages but he saw sadness. It had settled on her eyes, as if her tears had deposited it there.

'Jenn, I want to punch out Steve Buckle.'

Her eyes opened wide.

'I know I'm supposed to be understanding about how ill he is and I'm trying to say all the right things about how he's been traumatized. But deep down I just want to punch him out. When I look at your face and think of him hitting you . . .' Steve. Too big, too loud, too angry, standing over Dave's Jenny, fists flying. Dave reddened at the thought. His hands became knuckles. One day he would ask Jenny to tell him exactly what had happened. One day, when he could trust himself not to retaliate.

He looked back at Jenny's face and saw that she was watching him and had become even sadder. He took her hand and held it firmly in his own.

'No more punching,' she said slowly.

'OK, love. No more punching. I'll have a cup of tea with Leanne when I get back to camp and then I'll go up to Headley Court to see Steve and I won't punch him or put rat poison in his beer, I promise.'

She smiled. That sad, bruised smile.

'Is Steve going to get better?' he asked.

'Eugene visits. Says he's improving.'

Eugene. A name Dave had hated for months. 'I'll

537

have to thank Eugene,' he said carefully. 'For dealing with Steve. When I wasn't there to take care of you.'

Jenny nodded.

He said: 'I'll have to visit Rose McKinley, too. Gerry McKinley's lost a foot. He's in Selly Oak. We thought he was going to die but he'll be OK. I'm not sure whether to tell her what I know about it.'

She waited. The way she always waited for him to tell her things, knowing he would, knowing he trusted her.

'I was at the PB with an advance party. Gerry was following on with the others and the Bergens got blown off the top of the Mastiff into a field. Chalfont-Prick sent Gerry out to get his Bergen because he said it had secret mapping in it but, guess what, when they investigated, it turned out to be a load of crap. No secret mapping. Just a mobile phone he shouldn't have had.'

Jenny stared at him.

'One of my men got blown up for the boss's fucking BlackBerry,' said Dave, his voice getting louder. 'And two men died trying to get to him. It wasn't some new sprog on top cover who shot Angry McCall out of ignorance; it was Chalfont-Prick out of selfishness. When I found out, I went to the NAAFI. Chalfont-Prick was sitting there with all his officer mates. I walked right up to him. And punched him. On the nose. And no one stopped me because they all knew I was right.'

It had felt good. The surprise and then shock on the priggish face of the platoon commander had been even more satisfying than knuckle on jaw.

But Jenny was looking aghast at the thought of knuckle on jaw. Maybe he shouldn't have told her.

'They'll court-martial you,' she said at last.

'Oh no they won't. He's going. They could throw the book at him and his uncle's defence review's all finished so there's nothing to stop them. But they're quietly letting him out of the back door.'

Jenny continued to stare at Dave. Searching his face. As if she was looking for something.

Finally she said: 'Afghanistan.' Dave knew what she meant. For some people it was a country. For others it was a war zone. For Jenny it was an intruder. Afghanistan had forced its way into her life and her marriage, stealing things which were precious, violating her peace, leaving her life in disarray. And all because she loved a soldier.

He dropped his voice and spoke quickly and urgently. 'Jenny, this tour . . . I spent some of it on the edge. On the edge of endurance. Or maybe on the edge of despair. There was one night, at the end, when I was in a cave. I was lying on this wall in the dark. It was really cold and I couldn't move. Because I was just a couple of metres away from about twelve Taliban fighters.'

She looked horrified. He continued rapidly.

'Jenn, I lay there sure I was going to die. And I thought about you. How much you mean to me. How badly I've treated you. I thought about dying and leaving you alone with the girls, how you'd have to cope and how unhappy you'd be. That was when I was on the edge, knowing our lives together could be finished when we're still at the beginning. That was when I hit rock bottom. And then . . . I know this sounds crazy . . . I saw Jamie Dermott. He just came into my head. And he told me it wasn't all over yet. And I knew I shouldn't give up. Shit, Jenn, he was right. Jamie was right. I came through it alive, we're here together again, the girls are safe at home, you're going to recover. Jenny, everything's going to be OK.'

She was crying again. Women.

Epilogue

Lance Corporal William Finn, Sergeant S. Holliday of the Royal Army Medical Corps and Angus McCall's parents waited nervously in the ante-room at Buckingham Palace.

'We deserve another Military Cross for going through this,' muttered Finny to Doc.

'Just because I can do the Heimlich Manoeuvre doesn't mean I can bow without tripping over my feet,' said Doc dismally.

Angus's mother was large-boned and large-faced like Angus. 'If Angus was here, he wouldn't be nervous. Getting a medal wouldn't bother him one way or the other,' she said. Angus's dad had been divorced from her for years and now he ignored her. He had the furtive look of a man who needed a cigarette and was prepared to sneak behind a potted plant if necessary.

'Nah, nothing bothered Angus,' Finny agreed generously. 'He was the best, Mrs McCall. All the boys in the platoon miss him a lot.'

Sergeant Dave Henley found the prospect of meeting the Queen more daunting than an encounter with the Taliban. For your average skirmish in Helmand

Province there was no strict protocol to observe and the enemy didn't seem to care much if your uniform was a bit ally. Here at Buckingham Palace that sort of thing was considered important.

But when he heard his name and walked in for the Queen to award him the Conspicuous Gallantry Cross, he immediately located Jenny across the room, saw her great happiness and found himself grinning from ear to ear.

Evidently the Queen knew the whole story. 'Your bravery is exceptional, Sergeant. Tell me, how did you manage to stay so still and so quiet for so long with the enemy just a few feet away?'

'Well, ma'am, I thought about my wife and my two little girls. And I decided I couldn't let death separate me from them,' Dave heard himself say.

'Is your wife here today?' asked the Queen.

Dave glanced across at his Jenny, smiling happily.

'Yes, ma'am. And sometimes I feel that she should be the one awarded a medal.'

The Queen gave him a regal but conspiratorial grin. 'Actually, you aren't the first soldier to say that to me,' she told him. 'Just make sure you say it to her sometimes.'

Smiling warmly, she pinned on his medal. 'Well done, Sergeant Henley.'

Glowing, Dave walked to the back of the room. Later they would go out with the boys. Leanne and Steve would join them. They would put everything that had happened on this tour behind them and start to look forward again.

Jenny turned to him and they smiled at each other. She had emerged from her bandages and bruises and the day-to-day chores of motherhood as though from a chrysalis. Her face was healed; her smile was even; her dress made her look like a bright blue butterfly. And, looking around this most exclusive of rooms, Dave was sure of one thing. His wife was the most beautiful person here.

War Torn

Andy McNab & Kym Jordan

WITH TWO TOURS of Iraq under his belt, Sergeant Dave Henley knows what modern war looks like. But nothing can prepare him for the posting to Forward Operating Base Senzhiri, Helmand Province, Afghanistan. This is a battlezone like he's never seen before.

He's in charge of 1 Platoon, a ragbag collection of rookies who he must make into a fighting force – and fast. But this is a brutal, unforgiving conflict which takes no prisoners. Their convoy is ambushed on the way to the FOB, leaving two men grievously wounded – before they've fired a shot.

Back at home, Dave's wife, Jenny, seven months pregnant, must try to hold together the fragile lives of the families left behind, who all wait for the knock on the door and the arrival of bad news . . .

'Excellent . . . This book will ring true to soldiers who have worked in Helmand province and, uniquely, their families'
SOLDIER

Red Notice

Andy McNab

DEEP BENEATH THE English Channel, a small army of Russian terrorists has seized control of the Eurostar to Paris, taken four hundred hostages at gunpoint – and declared war on a government that has more than its own fair share of secrets to keep.

One man stands in their way. An off-duty SAS soldier is hiding somewhere inside the train. Alone and injured, he's the only chance the passengers and crew have of getting out alive. Meet Andy McNab's explosive new creation, Sergeant Tom Buckingham, as he unleashes a whirlwind of intrigue and retribution in his attempt to stop the terrorists and save everyone on board – including Delphine, the beautiful woman he loves.

Hurtling us at breakneck speed between the Regiment's crack assault teams, Whitehall's corridors of power and the heart of the Eurotunnel action, *Red Notice* is McNab at his devastatingly authentic, pulse pounding best.

RED NOTICE: *You have been warned . . .*